FOR THE SAKE OF SEX

No matter how she tried, the delicious daze wouldn't lift. Not as long as he was touching her, she realized. At first she had submitted to the caress of his fingers to prove it didn't affect her. Now that she knew better, she had to bring this sudden intimacy to a close.

Fighting the threatening sensation of weakness, Mara took a step away and turned her back to him, looking for a distraction.

"What's the matter?" Sin asked in a voice that said he knew.

"Nothing's the matter." Mara seemed to lack coordination. Her movements were jerky and out of synch. "Don't paw me like that, please. I'm not interested in sex for the sake of sex at this point in my life."

"Oh?" There was a lot of curiosity in the one-word question. "When do you think you will be?"

from "The Thawing of Mara"

<u>BOOK YOUR PLACE ON OUR WEBSITE</u>
<u>AND MAKE THE</u>
<u>READING CONNECTION!</u>

We've created a customized website just for our very special readers, where you can get the inside scoop on everything that's going on with Zebra, Pinnacle and Kensington books.

When you come online, you'll have the exciting opportunity to:

- View covers of upcoming books
- Read sample chapters
- Learn about our future publishing schedule (listed by publication month *and author*)
- Find out when your favorite authors will be visiting a city near you
- Search for and order backlist books from our online catalog
- Check out author bios and background information
- Send e-mail to your favorite authors
- Meet the Kensington staff online
- Join us in weekly chats with authors, readers and other guests
- Get writing guidelines
- AND MUCH MORE!

Visit our website at
http://www.kensingtonbooks.com

JANET DAILEY

Try to Resist Me

ZEBRA BOOKS
KENSINGTON PUBLISHING CORP.
http://www.kensingtonbooks.com

ZEBRA BOOKS are published by

Kensington Publishing Corp.
850 Third Avenue
New York, NY 10022

All Kensington titles, imprints and distributed lines are available at special quantity discounts for bulk purchases for sales promotion, premiums, fund-raising, educational or institutional use.

Special book excerpts or customized printings can also be created to fit specific needs. For details, write or phone the office of the Kensington Special Sales Manager: Kensington Publishing Corp., 850 Third Avenue, New York, NY 10022. Attn. Special Sales Department. Phone: 1-800-221-2647.

First Printing: July 2006
10 9 8 7 6 5 4 3 2 1

Printed in the United States of America

CONTENTS

GIANT OF
MESABI

Chapter One

The plane's shadow skimmed across the treetops. Within the pine forest, the blue of a Minnesota lake winked briefly in the sunlight and a ribbon of concrete lengthened through the trees.

Inside, Alanna Powell gazed eagerly out the window, her heart quickening as the airport came into view. Tawny blond hair framed the fresh-scrubbed beauty of her face. Her pointed chin had a willful thrust, and the look in her violet eyes, her most outstanding feature, revealed a flashing spirit. Yet her finely shaped lips displayed a hint of vulnerability.

She braced herself against the seat when the plane's wheels touched and rolled on the tarmac, relaxing gradually as they negotiated the runways to the terminal. Alanna searched the long windows for a glimpse of Kurt through the dark glass, knowing it would be pure luck if she saw him from here.

A tightness gripped her throat. What if Kurt wasn't there to meet her? With an almost imperceptible movement of her head, Alanna shook away the thought. When she'd called him yesterday to say she'd be on this flight from Minneapolis, he had agreed to meet the plane without hesitation. He hadn't even waited for her explanation that she wanted to surprise her parents.

It was crazy to be so apprehensive, she told herself. But that was what love did to a person. She hadn't seen Kurt since the Easter break almost two months ago. He'd made it plain that he was attracted to her then, but so much could have happened since then.

The plane rolled to a full stop at last and the captain announced their arrival at the Chisholm-Hibbing airport. Unclipping her seat belt, Alanna rose to join the file of passengers disembarking. Her hand moved down from the waistband of her wheat tan skirt, checking to make sure the buttons down the front were securely fastened, except for the last two above the knee that let the hem flap to reveal her legs and show some thigh.

She went through the jetway in single file, more or less, with the other people on the flight, dodging a few enormous garment bags, carried, as usual, by the slow-pokes who hung up everyone else during departures so they could save themselves a few minutes at baggage claim.

There was no sign of Kurt in the group of people gathered to meet the arriving passengers at the end of the jetway. She knew the plane was on time; the captain had said so. Maybe Kurt had been delayed. Her steps slowed as she scanned the area.

Then she saw a familiar-looking man bent over a drinking fountain, and Alanna's heart leaped in joyous relief. All her fears vanished in that instant of recognition.

"Kurt!" She laughed his name, her heels barely touching the floor as she ran to him. "I thought you'd forgotten about me!" As he straightened and turned, she started to fling herself into his arms with uninhibited happiness. A half step away from the broad chest, she realized her mistake. "You!" Anger and astonishment mingled in the accusing pronoun.

Her retreat was cut off by his strong arm curving around her waist.

"Don't stop now," he said, giving her a sensual smile. "If I'm going to stand in for my brother, I might as well get his kiss, too."

"No!" The vehement denial was a waste of breath.

A large hand moved up her back and he twined his fingers in her tawny hair. She pushed her hands against his muscular chest but she might as well have been pushing against a granite wall. He had her exactly where he wanted her.

Alanna couldn't escape the descending mouth or the steel band of his embrace. She didn't even have time to stiffen in resistance as he kissed her with hard, slow pleasure, taking advantage of her fractional moment of hesitation. His lips were cool from the icy water but the kiss was hot. Really hot.

In the next second, she was released. A pair of blue eyes, a deep shade of indigo, glittered down at her. He had to see the vivid flush in her cheeks. A rush of anger flamed within her, the exhilaration of battle flashing through her nerve ends.

"How dare you!" she said tightly.

His half-closed eyes surveyed her from head to toe, and he seemed to note her indignant stance. It was hard for Alanna to tell—his lashes were thick and dark, the expression in his eyes unreadable. A smile without humor curved the mouth that had just possessed hers.

"Give me your claim tickets and I'll get your luggage. I suggest you wait until we're in the car to unleash your temper and wounded outrage." His gaze flicked around them to indicate a more than mildly interested audience.

Nothing like a passionate kiss in public to get attention, Alanna thought with barely controlled fury. She half expected to hear someone tell them to get a room. Her poise was already shaken, and the trace of mockery in his tone didn't do anything to restore it.

Seething inwardly, Alanna fumbled through her purse for her ticket folder and the baggage checks attached to it. With rigid control, she thrust the papers into his outstretched hand.

How could she have been so stupid? She just hadn't seen that it wasn't Kurt but his brother, Rolt Matthews. The two men weren't all that different, she told herself silently. Both were tall and dark with leanly muscled physiques. And Rolt's face had been turned away as he took a drink from the water fountain. Still and all . . .

The arrogant set of Rolt's shoulders was enough to make her glare at him as he walked away from her. He was taller than Kurt by an inch or two, with a catlike fluidity to his easy strides. His dark brown hair was the shade of coffee, shot with a golden hue in the sunlight, not bordering on brown-black as Kurt's was. It grew long and thick about his collar, brushed carelessly away from his face, which didn't look much like his brother's.

The sun-bronzed planes of Rolt's face held a certain ruthlessness; the carved lines around his mouth etched with cynicism. And he had a rakish air of virility, blatant and overpowering, a dominant force that demanded to be reckoned with.

Rolt Matthews could be defined as dark, while Kurt was of the day. Handsome and charming, Kurt was the antithesis of his older brother. Alanna had been drawn to him since their first meeting some years ago. Yet it was only this Easter that Kurt had taken any notice of her and the attraction she'd always felt was able to blossom.

Her lips trembled, tender from the hard mastery of Rolt's kiss. She'd kept her distance from him—as surely as she'd been drawn to Kurt, she'd been repelled by Rolt. Whenever his gaze rested on her, so startlingly blue with its enigmatic glitter, she was uncomfortable. His hooded looks with their trace of mockery disconcerted Alanna more than she cared to admit. Yet Rolt seemed to know it and, worse yet, he seemed to think that her uneasiness was funny.

That was why he had kissed her, she guessed. He'd disappeared into the crowd around the baggage carousel, giving her a few minutes to recoup—and to think. Her fingers clenched the clasp of her purse, the metal as hard and unyielding as his chest had been beneath her hands. Her flesh burned where it had been in contact with the male length of him.

During Easter, she'd made no secret of her attraction to Kurt. There had been no need, since he returned it. Always when Rolt had been around—fortunately, not often—he'd watched them with aloof interest, leaving Alanna with the impression that he found their relationship kind of juvenile.

Juvenile. Alanna breathed in sharply at the word. As if. Kurt was twenty-nine, she was twenty-one. They were adults, not a pair of infatuated teenagers as Rolt seemed to think. No doubt his five-year advantage caused him to look down on his brother.

And rumor was that Rolt had more women than he knew what to do with. Guess that was enough to make him regard a budding romance with a cynical eye—oh, hell. He was coming back. Alanna heard his purposeful strides approach before she saw him effortlessly carrying her heavy luggage. Rolt paused for an instant beside her, his alert gaze sweeping over her.

"Car's outside," he stated. "Let's go."

"The sooner the better," Alanna agreed briskly. He favored her with a nod to indicate that she should go first and open the door for him. The glint in his eyes told her that he knew how much she disliked him and that he didn't care. With a haughty tilt of her chin, Alanna walked out of the building and surveyed the line of waiting taxis. She felt like telling him in no uncertain terms that she would find her own way to her parents.

Coward, she told herself. She wasn't going to give him any indication that she was even slightly intimidated by his presence. He took the lead, saving her the trouble of pointing out that she couldn't find his car telepathically, and they walked through the rows of vehicles until he stopped, set down her luggage, and pulled out a keytag that he pressed with one thumb.

The locks of a late-model, black SUV chirped open. Swinging up the back door and stacking her luggage in a few swift moves, Rolt moved to the passenger door and opened it. There was no way Alanna could avoid the hand that helped her into the leather bucket seat, but the instant the door was closed, she rubbed away the sensation of his touch. Rolt walked around, opened his door, and slid behind the wheel.

Even though she hated to break the silence, Alanna knew she wouldn't be able to sit quietly until she learned why Kurt hadn't met her. Something told her that Rolt was not going to volunteer the information.

Glancing at his aloof profile out of the corner of her eye, she felt a surge of irritation rise inside. He was so self-assured, annoyingly so. And indifferent to convention and other people's feelings—the kiss had been proof of that.

"Why wasn't Kurt able to meet me?" she demanded finally.

His gaze flicked to her, masked and unrevealing. He started the motor and reversed the car out of the parking lot. "He was, uh, unavoidably detained. Some equipment at the plant broke down. An emergency."

The answer was too glib. Alanna guessed it was meant to be, but she couldn't keep from rising to the bait. "Couldn't have been that much of an emergency if you're here. I mean, the world revolves around you, right?"

There was a movement of his mouth in what should have been a smile, but other than that, Rolt didn't acknowledge her comment. His attention remained focused on the road as he pulled into the traffic.

"I don't suppose it occurred to you to handle the emergency in Kurt's place and leave him free to meet me." She compressed her lips tightly, anticipating the answer before he gave it.

"It occurred to me." Again his gaze swung to her for fleeting seconds, lingering suggestively on her lips before returning to the highway. "But I wouldn't have missed picking you up for anything."

"Why?" Her temper flared at his unnecessary reminder of the kiss he had taken. "It wasn't a pleasant meeting."

"Oh, yeah?" His wide shoulders lifted in gesture of unconcern for her reaction. "But not easily forgotten all the same."

"Or forgiven," Alanna added darkly.

"Do you expect me to apologize?" It was obvious by his tone that he found the idea ludicrous.

Her fingers curved over the leather armrest, golden tan like the seats. She wished it was his hard flesh her nails were digging into instead of the supple leather.

"Not you," she declared in a contemptuous breath. "I don't think you know the difference between right and wrong."

"Maybe I do and maybe I don't."

"You just don't care."

"Think so?" A dark eyebrow arched. "Could be I'm just not up for an ethical discussion. Hell, it was only a kiss. No big whoop. What do ethics have to do with it?"

Alanna sputtered for a few seconds, too incensed by his apparent disregard for the fact that she was his brother's friend and, she hoped, more than that.

"I'm dating your brother," she pointed out tightly. "And I don't think it's appropriate for you to go around kissing his girl."

"Are you his girl?" His narrowed gaze pinned her. Knowing she couldn't answer, he negated the need to with a cool smile. "Not that it matters whether you are or not."

"It should," Alanna retorted. "Believe me, I have no interest in—"

"—making love to you," Rolt finished for her, the wolfish slash deepening near his mouth.

"I was about to say 'you paying attention to me,'" she snapped, reddening at his bluntness. "But if you want to be more explicit, I'll agree with that, too."

Her sideways look of reproach was wasted on his profile as he stared at the road ahead. Alanna found herself looking at the strong hands gripping the wheel of the powerful car. They controlled it with such ease, guiding the car into curves and around corners. She knew these same hands would guide a female body just as expertly, taking his partner into the intricacies of love. Their touch would be firm and authoritative, yet teasing and arousing as they caressed her—*gulp*.

With a guilty start, she stared straight ahead. Her cheeks flamed at the direction her thoughts had taken. She despised Rolt. How could she possibly even imagine such things?

"Why are you so upset because of one kiss?" His gaze flicked to her heightened color.

Self-consciously she flipped a thick strand of tawny hair away from her face, smoothing it down to conceal her embarrassment and appear nonchalant.

"Or do I just rub your fur the wrong way?" His low drawling voice seemed to reach out to stroke it right. "Does it bother you that I find you—"

"Easy to tease?" Alanna finished his sentence for him.

"Is that what you think?" Rolt said smoothly.

Her chin lifted a little. "It's true. And I know you think I'm naïve. Whatever. I really don't like your tone of voice."

"Gee whiz. The wrong tone of voice, huh? Guilty as charged, I guess. I apologize."

Even his apology sounded like bait. Alanna stared out the window to avoid his mocking, pretending to be extremely interested in the commercial district of Hibbing. "Don't play dumb games with me, Rolt," she said tautly. "I'm not interested."

"But maybe I'm interested in you." He said it quietly and so seriously that Alanna's curiosity forced her to glance at him. The bronze mask of his features told her nothing, but the lazy glint in his eyes seemed to make light of his statement. "I'd have to plead guilty on that charge, too."

His gaze swept over her in disturbing assessment, taking in her legs last. Alanna drew the buttoned front of her skirt together at the hem. His mouth quirked at her prim demeanor.

She *hated* being teased. Of course, he'd done it on purpose, instinctively knowing it would unnerve her. And she hadn't disappointed him.

"It's impossible," she insisted, more because she thought there was a chance it could be true and doubted her own ability to fence with a master of the game.

"Tell me, Alanna"—he slowed the black SUV at a stoplight and gave her his undivided attention—"do you really like my brother?"

She drew in a sharp breath. "That's none of your business!"

"You're going out with him," Rolt pointed out.

She wanted to smack him. But he probably would have liked that. Anything to get a rise out of her. She noticed he was watching the uneven rise and fall of her breasts.

"Just curious," he added idly.

"You can keep on being curious!"

The light changed to green and he shifted the car into drive, laughing softly. "I don't have to. You've already answered my question." His sliding look went right through her. "Are you, uh, saving yourself for Kurt?"

"Well, not for you," Alanna hissed. "Never for you."

"Careful," he warned with laughter in his voice. "Never is a long time."

Alanna was about to argue that it wasn't long enough as far as Rolt was concerned, but at that moment she realized that, instead of turning at the road that would take her to her parents' house, he had stayed on the highway.

"You missed the turn," she pointed out.

"No, I didn't."

He sounded so certain that Alanna glanced back over her shoulder to the crossroads, nearly convinced that she was mistaken. "My parents live down that road."

"I'm not taking you home."

He couldn't be serious. But one look at his face told her he was. "Where—"

"Kurt's at the mine. You did want to see him, didn't you?"

"Is that where we're going?" Alanna demanded, tired of his macho manipulativeness.

"Of course"—he took his foot off the accelerator—"unless you want to go directly home."

"I would like to see Kurt," she said, annoyed all over

again at his deliberate failure to tell her. Sarcasm laced her voice as she added, "It never occurred to me that you would take me there. After all, Kurt does have an emergency on his hands."

Her jab seemed to have missed its mark. "I think he can be spared for a few minutes to see you. I can take over for him."

"Uh-huh. And you could have let him come to the airport to meet me." Alanna rubbed the throbbing ache in her temple. "You know, the way you're acting right now is a lot like the way you acted toward my father," she murmured bitterly. "He never should've sold controlling interest to your company."

"The iron vein had played out. Your father didn't have the financial ability or the knowledge to switch the operation to processing taconite. If he hadn't sold out to us when he did, in another year he would have been bankrupt. That's the truth, whether he or you will ever admit it," Rolt stated in a cold, unemotional tone. "Besides, you wouldn't have met Kurt—or me."

Alanna didn't comment on his observation. The buildings of the city were no longer rolling past her window. The landscape was mostly rural now, studded with dark green pines. They were on the Taconite Trail Road in the middle of the Mesabi Iron Range.

In this arrowhead area of Northern Minnesota, much of the nation's iron ore had once been mined. The veins in the Vermilion, Mesabi, and other ranges had been so rich, it was thought in the beginning that they would last forever, but progress and war had revealed a lack of foresight. Now the abundant taconite was being processed into iron in the enormous foundries and factories rising above the trees.

Concealed by the green landscape, the large iron mines were vanishing. Abandoned open pits were being fast reclaimed by nature, trees and brush taking over the empty land. Hardy plants, some in flower, covered heaps of old tailings and other detritus from the old mines.

Alanna had spent her childhood here. The twisting, winding canyons and ridges had been gouged out of the earth by heavy machinery to expose the iron veins. Plundered of its valuable ore, the land was healing but slowly.

Mesabi was an Ojibwa Indian word, meaning Land of the Sleeping Giant, a name given to this range of mountains because of its resemblance to the sleeping figure of a man. Virgin forests had once covered its slopes, first exploited by fur trappers, then felled by lumbermen's axes or uprooted by iron-seeking excavation equipment. The towering pines the Ojibwa had known, ten feet in diameter and more, were gone, and young trees grew in their place.

While the sleeping giant rested, other giants walked the land. Shimmering with resentment, Alanna's gaze slid to the impassive man behind the wheel. A giant, that was how her father had once described Rolt Matthews, referring to his stature as a man, not to his physical size. He was tall and muscular and a compelling figure, but that wasn't what set him apart from others. Or so her father had told her.

Dorian Powell, her father, was a sensitive, erudite man. Despite his earnest attempts, he had never been a successful businessman. The iron mine—the family wealth—had been inherited from his father and grandfather. When the vein played out, so did the family resources.

In her heart, Alanna knew that Rolt's statement was accurate—her father would most definitely have gone bankrupt if Rolt's firm hadn't purchased controlling interest. But she also knew her father's reasons for selling weren't purely about monetary gain. His main concern had been the economy of the area and the people who worked for him. After the sale, he had stepped aside, relegating himself to the role of a mere stockholder.

When she'd protested and insisted that he should have a more active part in the transition and future operation, her dad had smiled and shook his head. "It's a job for only one man—someone who'll drive himself as hard as he does those around him. These are hard times for heavy industry, Alanna. They don't call this the Rust Belt for nothing."

She hadn't wanted to hear, but she'd listened to her father's musings anyway.

"There were times when I was more concerned about an illness in some employee's family than I was in the day's production. You can't let things like that bother you. You've got to stand apart from the workers, immune to their problems. You can't let personal feelings, yours or anyone else's, interfere with business. It can't matter whether an employee likes you or not. The man in charge has to be above that—a giant. You can't let anything stand in your way if you want to be successful. Rolt Matthews won't."

"What you mean is that he's cold and ruthless," Alanna had retorted.

"I suppose you could describe him that way," Dorian Powell had agreed, "but he'll make the company profitable and everyone will benefit, including us."

Cold and ruthless. The adjectives described him perfectly. He kept to himself, above it all. To Alanna's knowledge, since Rolt had taken over control of the company, he had never associated with anyone from the company outside of business hours. Kurt was the only exception. Even then the occasions they were together were rare.

Her gaze shifted for the second time to the strong, tanned hands on the wheel. She wondered briefly about the women he had known. Alanna didn't doubt that his touch could evoke powerful sensations, but she doubted whether Rolt ever felt anything himself.

The SUV slowed and turned off the highway, and Alanna glanced up to see the entrance gate to the plant. The security guard posted at the closed gate bent slightly to view the car's occupants. With a respectful nod to Rolt, he swung the gate open and let them through. As they drove by, Alanna thought she recognized the guard. His hair had grayed and his shoulders were stooping with advanced years, but he still looked familiar.

"Isn't that Bob Schmidt?" She had only been out to the plant once in the last five years, then just to pick up her father. "I went to school with his daughter, Justine."

"Could be. I don't know his name."

Rolt's lack of interest in the man's identity was another clue to his character. Or lack of character, she silently corrected herself. Her father would have known. He prided himself on knowing the name of every man who worked for the company. But Alanna didn't bring that up.

It wasn't important that Rolt know the guard's name. As long as the payroll clerk and the computer got it right, that was all that mattered to him. His attitude chilled Alanna regardless of its business merits. She admired her father, the sensitive failure, much more than she did Rolt, the lean and mean CEO. Talk about controlling personalities. Thank God Kurt didn't take after his hard-hearted brother.

Inside the gates, the plant bustled with activity. Smoke billowed from pollution-controlled stacks atop the large buildings. Heavy trucks rolled to and from the large pits, kicking up dust clouds that choked the air and left a film on everything in sight. The din was unceasing, yet within the luxury vehicle, only a low drone could be heard.

Nothing was as Alanna remembered it. There were no cheerful waves from the employees who'd once come to meet her father in the yard. No one talked much. Work was all and efficiency reigned. There wasn't time for anything else.

"You haven't been here since your father sold, have you?" Rolt asked as he parked the black SUV in a reserved space.

"Only once, briefly," Alanna admitted coolly.

He switched off the motor but made no move to get out. "A lot has changed since your father's time." He watched her, a considering look in his eyes. "I don't think you like that, do you?"

Her violet eyes swept over the scene again. Guessing that he had somehow already read her thoughts or that she had betrayed them in her expression, Alanna gave a short negative shake of her head.

"We're making a profit, which is more than your father ever did," Rolt stated.

"You know, a man's worth isn't measured only by how much money he makes," she retorted.

The expectant gleam in his eyes indicated that he had anticipated her response. She was left with the feeling that he had almost invited her remark.

"It's the challenge. Turning around a business that's dying and putting it back in the black is incredibly satisfying," he told her quietly. "I fought and I won. Money isn't the goal, it's the scoreboard. A man works to obtain his goal whether there's money at the end or not. It all comes back to the challenge."

"You sound like an authority on the subject," Alanna said frostily.

"Let's say that I always get what I want."

There was something about his statement that put Alanna instantly on guard. Suddenly the quiet elegance of the luxury SUV seemed to close in around her. There were people everywhere around them, yet she didn't feel safe next to Rolt. Her pulse raced in silent alarm.

"Thank you for the motivational speech—I needed that," she said. He didn't miss the jab this time.

"Alanna . . ." Rolt sighed and stopped, thinking through what he wanted to say. "You can't argue with making a profit. Not when heavy industry is shutting down factories all over the USA and moving operations abroad. We're going strong right here."

He had a point—a good one—but Alanna wasn't in the mood to give him a gold star for it. "Spare me the Economics 101 prep course. I came here to see Kurt." Her tart tone was a cover for her sudden attack of nervousness.

Her fingers closed over the door handle. She didn't want to wait in the car until Rolt walked around to open her door. Before she could release the latch, his hand had circled her wrist to hold her in the seat.

"Wait," he told her.

Alanna turned, apprehension rounding her eyes although she tried to conceal it. "Why?" She breathed the wary question.

Amusement glittered briefly in his eyes. She nearly flinched when his other hand moved, but its target was the sun visor above her head. Rolt flipped it down, revealing a lighted makeup mirror.

"You might want to do some repairs before you see Kurt." The smile lines around his mouth deepened. "Unless you don't think he'll notice that your lipstick is smeared."

A scarlet blush heated her cheeks as Alanna saw the

smear of gloss around her lips. He had deliberately waited until the last minute to point it out to her—oh, come on, she told herself exasperatedly. You could have thought of it. Yes, Rolt's move had totally confused her, but that didn't let her off the hook completely. Either way, that oh-so-hot kiss was going to be on her mind when she was saying hello to Kurt.

Quickly she wiped away the smear with a tissue from her purse. His silent observation of her was unnerving, and her fingers began to tremble as she added fresh glossy color to her mouth.

"Don't forget to blot it," Rolt mocked.

She shot him an icy look that said more than she did. "Where'd you learn so much about putting on lipstick?"

"I'd rather not say." He grinned at her wolfishly.

With hurried movements, she pressed the clean side of the tissue against her lips. "There," she said, indicating that she was finished and ready to leave the car.

"One more thing," he said. "Undo that top button. Give Kurt a good look at what he's been missing."

She stared at him, speechless for a moment. But only a moment. Two could play at being outrageous. She undid the first button. Nice and slow.

His eyes flickered down, then back to her face.

She undid the next two, popping them out of the buttonholes one by one. "How's that?"

He looked down again for a fraction of a second into the shadowed valley between her breasts. The lace edge of her bra was barely visible. She noted with some satisfaction the way his eyes widened. An involuntary wave of sensual heat flamed through her body.

"A little cleavage always arouses a man's interest," Alanna said sweetly.

"Yes, it does."

His tone was bland but she saw the wicked glint in his eyes. She buttoned her blouse back up. "Game over."

"Is it?" Rolt turned to open his door and step out. A rush of noise and dust raced in.

Chapter Two

The sparkle of temper was in her eyes, heightened color in her complexion. The tawny gold of her hair swung in soft curls about her neck, silken and shimmering. Rolt's hand rested proprietarily on the back of her waist as he guided her through a warren of cubicles to his private office.

Alanna was aware of the interested and speculative glances they received from the employees, male and female. A few faces were familiar, but she doubted that they recognized her. They were mainly interested in the fact that their boss was escorting a young woman to his office.

She wondered what they would think when they saw her with Kurt. They would probably conclude that she was playing one brother off against the other. If they only knew how uncomfortable the possessive hand on her back made her feel, they would appreciate the control she was exercising to keep from pushing it away.

A woman looked up from the computer screen in front of her as they walked through an office door. She was attractive in a plain sort of way, probably in her middle thirties. Alanna glanced at the wedding band—a single woman's reflex but she couldn't help it—on the employee's left hand before meeting her curious gaze.

Rolt's hand shifted to her elbow, keeping Alanna at his side as he paused at the cubicle. "Are there any messages, Mrs. Blake?"

"They're on your desk. Only one was urgent and it's on top," the woman answered in a crisp, professional tone.

He turned away, drawing Alanna awkwardly along toward a second door that obviously led to his inner sanctum. Over his shoulder, he tossed out an order to his executive assistant. "Find Kurt and have him sent to my office right away."

The assistant didn't have a chance to acknowledge his request as Rolt guided Alanna through the door and closed it behind him. His grip lessened and she immediately slipped free of the dreaded contact.

"Make yourself at home." His mouth quirked slightly as he moved farther into the room. "It'll be a few minutes before Kurt arrives."

His strides took him away from her. Alanna breathed easier and glanced around. It was hardly a typical office and not at all homey. The desk his secretary had referred to was more like a table, topped with a thick slab of Lucite that held a state-of-the-art flatscreen LCD monitor and an expensive laptop as well. That Rolt Matthews was a master multitasker did not surprise her. His workspace gave the impression of openness, without even a drawer under the clear tabletop. But then everything that mattered was stored on the huge computer beneath, she thought. No doubt only he had the password.

A straight-backed chair and not an overstuffed leather chair was behind the Lucite table. It was modern and looked amazingly uncomfortable. Definitely not something that a person would relax in and contemplate his successes. There were two or three other chairs just like it situated near the table. Dark oak shelves covered one wall and part of a second. Books and papers were stacked on the shelves somewhat haphazardly, but there were no filing cabinets.

The rest of the room was furnished with an enormous three-piece sectional sofa and a retro-style low table that followed its curving arc. The sofa was covered in a knobby material in variegated stripes of blue.

The drapes, covering nearly the length of one entire wall, were of the same material as the sofa. Beneath her feet, the carpet was a long shaggy blue, plush and thick. Charcoal sketches of black and white adorned the remaining walls.

If she had to name the style, Bachelor Bold would do. With just a touch of Seventies Shine. The only thing lacking was a chrome martini shaker. The decor was decidedly masculine and completely informal. It was so at odds with the other office areas Alanna had passed that she was a little nonplussed and it must have showed in her expression.

"Is something the matter?" Rolt sounded amused.

He was standing beside the desk, or table, looking through the pink slips of telephone messages—now that was a real retro touch, she thought approvingly, but computers had never supplanted the good old While You Were Out pads. He glanced up at her.

"You have to admit this is not your typical office," Alanna said. "Whoever heard of an executive without a massive walnut desk?"

He laughed softly and tossed the telephone messages on the table top.

"I don't need drawers and compartments, but I do like a lot of clear space to work. As for the rest of this"— Rolt scanned the large room impassively, dwelling briefly on the oversized sofa that would have dwarfed any average living room—"it has a practical purpose, too. I hold department meetings in here. We spread the papers and reports on the coffee table and get through everything in record time."

"Oh. How innovative."

"There's something about a conference room that makes people pompous and long-winded. I don't have the patience for PowerPoint memos and long presentations."

Alanna stiffened. The conference room, with its massive, traditional table and matching chairs, had been her father's favorite place. "Is that right. Well, you're in charge."

"Yeah. Just thought you'd like to see how I do things."

"Thanks so much. You never do anything without a reason, do you?" she declared, and immediately wondered what his true reason had been for meeting her at the airport.

"I wouldn't say 'never,'" mocked Rolt, subtly reminding her of the last time he had remarked on her use of the word. "It is convenient, though, when the desire for creature comforts also fulfills a practical purpose."

"My, my. I never would have guessed that you were vulnerable to human needs," Alanna replied tartly.

His gaze raked her with slow thoroughness from head to toe. "Do you really doubt it?" he asked in a low voice.

Nearly fifteen feet separated them, yet the caress of his enigmatic blue eyes had been almost a physical touch. It was as if he had personally explored every intimate detail of her body. Tension stretched between them, taut and vibrating, tingling down Alanna's nerve ends.

A slow warmth crept up her neck, and she turned away before it reached her cheeks and he saw it. Rolt was just too perceptive. She refused to make any reply to his suggestive question.

She moved away, putting a safe distance between herself and Rolt. The closed drapes offered her a destination and she took it. Before her hand could lift the knobby material aside, the roll of a cord opened them.

Her startled look sought the reason and found Rolt, the thick carpet muffling his footsteps as he had joined her at the window. Quickly Alanna looked back to the window, her heart beating rapidly in alarm.

"Quite a view of the countryside when the weather cooperates." His voice came from just over her right shoulder. Alanna stiffened, trying to judge how close he was to her without glancing around. Too close, her radar told her. "Unfortunately the dust usually leaves a film an inch thick on the glass. That's why I generally leave the drapes closed unless there's been a hard rain. It's a waste of time to have the windows washed."

Today the industrial haze obscured the landscape, turning it into indefinable shapes and silhouettes. Yet Alanna's gaze remained steadfastly fixed on the dust-covered panes. The musky scent of Rolt's aftershave drifted in the air, tantalizing her. She longed to move away, but to turn in any direction ultimately meant facing Rolt.

And Alanna felt uncomfortably vulnerable. It was as if he knew the havoc he was wreaking on her senses and delighted in shattering her poise. The knowledge added fuel to her fire of dislike.

"How much longer will Kurt be?" she demanded tersely.

"Does it matter?"

His hand touched her forearm. His intention was obviously to turn her around, probably into his arms. But Alanna didn't want that. Pivoting away from his touch, she pushed his outstretched hand away from her, eyes flashing her fury.

"Yes, it matters," she hissed. "If it will be very much longer, I prefer to wait for him outside."

Rolt towered above her, strangely remote as he looked down at her, his gaze narrowed. Though she was intimidated by his poised attitude of retaliation, Alanna didn't back down under his piercing look. A flicker of a smile touched the corners of his mouth.

"That won't be necessary," he replied smoothly. "He's cooled his heels long enough in the outer office."

"He's here?" she breathed in frowning disbelief.

"Mrs. Blake notified me of his arrival a few minutes ago." There was a complacent gleam in his eyes.

That was impossible. She had been with him every minute. "How?"

Briefly inclining his head, he indicated the table behind them. The movement highlighted the golden cast to his coffee-brown hair. "E-mail. Works great."

"So it does," she said calmly, feeling like an absolute idiot.

He didn't seem to notice that. "I hate buzzers," he said by way of explanation.

Her fingernails dug into the palms of her hands. "Do you mean Kurt has been out there all this time I've been waiting for him?"

"Not quite all of the time," Rolt qualified, and turned away to walk to the phone. Picking up the receiver, he punched a button and spoke into the mouthpiece. "You can send Kurt in now, Mrs. Blake."

His audacity infuriated Alanna beyond measure. Stymied by her inability to express it, she could only glare at him. There was no time for any joyous anticipation of Kurt's arrival. The interconnecting office door opened and he walked in.

"You wanted to see me." Kurt's attention on entering was naturally focused first on Rolt. He was several feet inside the room before he noticed her standing at the window. His handsome face was immediately wreathed in a big smile. "Alanna!"

This was not the way she had visualized their meeting with her totally ticked off at his brother and unable to respond with the same degree of gladness in Kurt's voice.

"Hello, Kurt." Her answering smile was stiff and insincere.

He walked toward her, the light in his eyes warmly admiring. She sort of wanted to rush into his arms, knowing she would be welcomed, but she was too aware of the silent and mockingly observant Rolt. She didn't move, awkwardly waiting for Kurt to come to her.

"Sorry I wasn't able to meet you at the airport." He seemed to pick up the annoyance hidden in the shadows of her eyes, but he didn't say anything about it.

"It's all right." Alanna shook her head, trying to relax. "Ro—your brother explained the problem." Unwillingly her gaze slid to Rolt. There was something arrogant about his stance and the way he kept his jacket open with his hand in the pocket.

"I think she's waiting to be kissed, Kurt." His low voice traveled across the room to taunt Alanna.

"I don't need a hint," Kurt laughed softly, apparently finding nothing offensive in his older brother's remark, but then he wasn't aware of what had happened at the airport.

Kurt's sunny blue gaze hadn't strayed from her face. It continued to beam on her as his hands closed over her shoulders and drew her toward him. He would never understand her desire to avoid the kiss and she was, to say the least, reluctant to explain. Under the cir-

cumstances, there seemed little else she could do but
lift her head to him.

The pressure of his mouth warmly covering her own
would have been something she normally would have
cherished and returned. As it was, with Rolt noncha-
lantly watching them, it was impossible for Alanna to respond except in the most halfhearted manner.

When Kurt lifted his head, there was a perplexed
light in his gaze as he searched her face. Knowing he
hadn't failed to notice her lack of response to his kiss,
she tried to sidetrack his attention from the fact.

A fingertip lightly touched a corner of his mouth.
"I'm afraid you have lipstick all over you," Alanna said
kittenishly. Whatever would work to distract Kurt was
okay, but she winced inside at her own duplicity.

"I don't mind," he smiled.

"Here." Rolt's voice broke into their private conversation. He moved to within a few feet of them, offering
his linen handkerchief to Kurt. "Use mine."

Alanna threw him a look of pure panic. Had he gotten her lipstick on his mouth and then wiped it off? He
couldn't—he wouldn't be so cold and cruel to his own
brother.

She searched his eyes. Rolt's expression was bland.

"No thanks, bro," Kurt said calmly. "That thing is
pure white."

Alanna looked at the proffered handkerchief. It was.
Thank God. The square of linen was perfectly laun-
dered, lightly starched, and impeccably white. Her secret—and how the hell did he get to make it my secret,
she thought with a flash of anger—was safe.

"Take it, Kurt. I wouldn't mind having Alanna's lipstick on it."

"Yeah, right." Kurt gave him a level look. "I'll get a
tissue from Mrs. Blake." He banged the door on his way

out and came back, rubbing his mouth with a tissue. "Let's go, Alanna."

"Um—okay. Sure." She looked from one man to the other, aware that she was between two brothers who'd probably been at war one way or another since the younger son's birth

"What? Was I out of line?" Rolt slapped his brother on the back. "Sorry," he said—with glaring insincerity, Alanna thought. He wasn't sorry at all. He was winking at her. She snapped out of her surprise when he continued. "But you better treat her right, Kurt. That's all I can say."

"I intend to, Rolt," Kurt said with an air of resignation.

"Here's the car keys. Alanna's luggage is already in the back, so you might as well use it." Rolt tossed the keys to Kurt, who made a fumbling catch. "Go ahead and take her home."

"Okay." Kurt's fingers closed over the keys, concealing them in his fist. He put an arm around Alanna's shoulders and she felt instantly sorry for him and—even though she felt horribly guilty for admitting it, even silently—she also wished that he wasn't such a wuss. Next to Rolt, he seemed very much the younger brother and not exactly grown up.

Rolt moved toward his Lucite desk as they turned to leave. "Hey, bro, before you go . . . fair warning."

"Huh?" Kurt just looked at him.

Rolt picked up the telephone and punched out a series of numbers, not even bothering to glance at his brother as he spoke, or at Alanna. "I just changed my mind."

"About what?" Kurt said.

"Alanna. What else? Now I'm joining the competition."

Gasping, she couldn't believe that she had heard right. His boldness was unbelievable—he was talking about her as if she wasn't even in the room, then referring to her as if she was some prize to be won and not a human being capable of deciding for herself which man she preferred.

Hadn't she made it clear that she wasn't exactly dazzled by him or impressed by his brand of corporate bull snot? Well, uh . . . no. She hadn't. He really had kissed her at the airport and she hadn't struggled enough. She should've kicked him in the shin or higher. And then that scene in the car. Alanna reminded herself nervously that she'd unbuttoned her blouse just to show him who was boss, even though she'd buttoned it right up again.

But she had never expected Rolt to flat out tell his own brother that he was going after his girl. Alanna didn't know whether to unleash her temper or laugh at Rolt's limitless ego.

Kurt, who had stiffened at the announcement, was evidently torn by conflicting reactions, too. He glared silently at his brother, but the moment passed when either of them had an opportunity to respond. Rolt had reached the party he had dialed. "Hey, Sam. Got a message here that you called . . ."

Kurt's hand tightened on her shoulder. "Come on, let's go," he said gruffly.

The firm pressure of his hand guided Alanna out of the office. She was as eager to leave as Kurt was. Neither spoke as they left the building. In the car, Kurt jammed the key in the ignition, then leaned back in the bucket seat without starting the motor.

"About what happened in there—" He broke off and sighed heavily.

"I know Rolt is your brother," Alanna interrupted,

"but he's the most overbearing, arrogant man I've ever met. Do you realize the way he maneuvered both of us?"

"I'm beginning to get a fairly good idea." His dark brows drew together in a scowl and his hands clenched the steering wheel, knuckles turning white with the fierceness of his grip. He gave her a sideways glance. "He meant what he said, Alanna. I know him too well to doubt that."

"You mean about me?" At Kurt's nod, she exhaled a contemptuous breath. "I can't stop him from trying, but he isn't going to get anywhere."

"Rolt attracts women the way flypaper attracts flies."

Alanna frowned. "Nice metaphor."

"First one that came to mind. But you do have to admit that he—"

She interrupted him with a wave of her hand. "This is one woman who's completely immune to his brand of primitive charm," Alanna declared emphatically.

"Everyone has strong feelings toward him one way or another," Kurt insisted, "sometimes feeling both ways at the same time, including myself. But I don't think anyone can remain immune."

Alanna knew which category she fell in—the one violently against Rolt. He had made a fiasco of her homecoming. Nothing had gone as she had planned. He had dominated nearly every second of it. Even now, she was sitting here alone in the car with Kurt and what were they talking about? Rolt.

Gazing at Kurt, so dark and so handsome, Alanna knew he was everything she had ever dreamed about. Rolt would never change that. He would never be able to come between them no matter how hard he tried. She was foolish to even get upset or angry at him.

"I've missed you," she murmured. The shimmery fire

of frustration became a glow of loving adoration as she gazed at Kurt.

A crooked smile slowly moved across his mouth. "Have you?" The troubled light was slow to leave the eyes that searched her face. Then one hand reached out to clasp hers. "I wanted to meet you at the airport," he declared huskily. "If only that damned equipment hadn't broken down, I would have."

"Well, we can't change that." Alanna wanted him to know that it wasn't important any more. "Let's start from scratch."

"Okay," Kurt agreed, "starting now."

He curved his other hand around the back of her neck and gently drew her halfway to meet him. He claimed her lips with a long, satisfying kiss and this time, without the disconcerting presence of his brother, she responded to it. When it was over, he remained close to nuzzle her cheek and tease the corners of her mouth.

"I could do this all night," he murmured, his warm breath caressing her skin. "But bucket seats aren't designed for serious fooling around." Lightly he kissed her lips once more and moved away. There was a wry twist of his mouth as he started the engine. "I wonder if Rolt ever made love in this car."

"Not competitive or anything, are you?"

"No, not at all," Kurt said ruefully.

Alanna felt a flash of guilt at the way she had teased the older Matthews brother while sitting in this very seat. It zapped her good and hard. She sighed inwardly as she leaned back in her seat. Rolt was not going to be an easy man to forget or ignore. Irritatedly, she brushed a silky curl away from her cheek.

"Let's celebrate your homecoming tonight," Kurt said as he drove out the gate. "I'll pick you up at six and we can get an early start. How's that?"

Alanna glanced at her watch, readjusting the direction of her thoughts. "It's my first night home. Mom and dad will expect me to spend some time with them."

"Make it seven, then," he compromised, sliding her a fond look. "You'll be home all summer. They can see you every day and I'll see you every night."

"Every night?" she teased.

"Well, I can't leave any free time open for Rolt to make a move," he stated. "He'll come around, you know."

"He's going to be in for a very rude surprise if he does." There was a defiant tilt of her chin. "I'll show him the door so fast that he won't realize what's happened until it's over."

"I'd like to be there," Kurt laughed. "That would have to be a first for him."

Alanna joined his laughter, suddenly relaxing, no longer ticked off by Rolt's assertion that he would win her, only amused. She felt a vengeful pleasure at the thought of the moment when she would tell him to get lost. She would enjoy dealing that blow to his male ego. It really needed deflating.

After their laughter had erased the subtle tension, it was easy to change the subject. Alanna chattered happily away about the university, her exams, and her plan for the summer vacation, not mentioning all the things she'd planned to do just with Kurt.

Her high spirits at returning home were in full bloom when the car pulled into the driveway of her home. With a suitcase in her hand and Kurt following with the rest, Alanna walked eagerly to the front door. It was opened before she had a chance to reach for the doorknob. A tall, spare woman stood within the white frame, her angular face brightened by a smile of astonished delight.

"We didn't expect you until tomorrow!" she exclaimed.

"Hi, Ruth! I finished my exams a day early and caught the first flight out of Minneapolis," explained Alanna.

"You should have let us know," the woman remonstrated, giving her a quick hug before ushering her into the house and holding the door open for Kurt, laden with the rest of Alanna's suitcases.

"I wanted to surprise mom and dad." She glanced around the empty living room. "Where are they?"

"Your father's out playing golf and Elinore is upstairs, resting before dinner." The housekeeper motioned for Kurt to set the bags inside the door.

"How is she?" Alanna's smile became slightly serious as she gazed earnestly at Ruth Ewell. Their housekeeper was really part of the family. She had been hired first as daily help when Alanna's mother had been expecting her. On doctor's orders, Elinore Powell had stayed in bed for most of nine long months, hoping to avoid the miscarriages that had ended her other three pregnancies.

During the months before and after Alanna's birth, her mother and Ruth Ewell had become friends. She had continued working for them on a daily basis until her husband passed away four years ago. Elinore had insisted that Ruth move in and live with them after that.

Because of the close, almost sisterlike relationship between her mother and Ruth, Alanna had never looked on her as a domestic employee. She had become more of an adopted aunt than a paid housekeeper. Since her mother's stroke two years ago, Ruth had been the rock that the household stood on.

"Her left arm is still a bit numb, but the doctor says she's doing nicely. Of course, Elly insists that she's as fit as a fiddle," Ruth confided in a skeptical tone, using her pet name for Alanna's mother. "But I notice she always lies down for a couple of hours in the afternoon, so she isn't as strong as she pretends." She waved a hand, slightly gnarled with arthritis, toward the living room. "You two make yourselves comfortable and I'll make coffee."

"Thanks anyway," Kurt shook his dark head regretfully, "but I'm afraid I'll have to pass. I'd better get back to work."

"Surely you can spare time for one cup," Ruth cajoled.

"No, I—"

"Ruth?" Elinore Powell's questioning voice came from the stairwell to the second floor. "Who's there?"

"It's Alanna and her young man." The answer was shouted back with a beaming smile on the couple. "She's come home a day early."

Alanna slid a sideways glance at Kurt, wondering if he minded being referred to as her young man. He caught the look and smiled at her gently, slipping an arm around her waist as if to reinforce the claim that they belonged together. A warm, pleasant feeling of being cared for stole over her. Soft contentment was etched in her expression as she turned to meet the petite woman gliding gracefully down the stairs.

Always fragile in appearance, Elinore now looked even more delicate. Her heart had never been strong, yet there was an aura of resiliency about her that made it seem she could overcome anything, even ill health. There was a translucent quality to her complexion and an undiminished sparkle in her eyes. Streaks of silver gilt in her once blond hair only added to her ethereal loveliness.

"Oh, honey. It's so good to have you home." Her mother's voice trembled with emotion as she embraced

Alanna, a shimmer of happy tears in her ageless eyes. With innate grace, Elinore turned to Kurt. "Were you an accomplice in Alanna's plot to surprise us?" she smiled.

"Yes," he nodded. "She phoned me."

"So you could meet her at the airport," Elinore concluded astutely. "I know it probably isn't necessary, but I want to thank you for meeting her and bringing her safely home."

Alanna hesitated for an instant, feeling the flick of Kurt's gaze on her, but she didn't bother to correct her mother's impression that Kurt had met her at the airport as planned.

"I heard Ruth mention coffee," her mother continued. "You will stay for a few minutes, won't you, Kurt?"

"I really have to get back to the plant," he refused a second time. "We had equipment problems this afternoon. It was good seeing you again, Mrs. Powell, and you, too, Mrs. Ewell. Good-bye, Alanna." He bent his head and unselfconsciously brushed a light kiss across her lips. "Seven?"

"I'll be ready," she promised.

With a polite nod at the two older women, he left. Alanna didn't try to conceal the glow of pride in her eyes. The housekeeper and her mother exchanged knowing glances.

"Why don't you bring that coffee into the living room, Ruth," Elinore suggested. "I'm sure Alanna would like a cup. There's plenty of time to unpack later."

Alanna had no objections to a caffeine break. In truth, she suddenly felt very much in need of coffee, hot and sweet with a sinful touch of real cream.

"Come on." Elinore linked her arm with her daughter's and led her toward the living room. "You still haven't told me how you managed to leave a day early."

Settled on the traditionally styled sofa of yellow and green print, Alanna explained about the last-minute rescheduling of her final exams and discussed how she felt she had done in the various classes, laughing with her mother and Ruth over some of the peculiarities of her professors. Then she plied them with questions about what had been happening at home and for news of some of her friends from school, especially Jessie, Ruth's daughter.

Alanna and Jessie had been close friends, but Jessie had married almost immediately after high school graduation and moved out of state. Through letters and Ruth, they still kept in touch.

Jessie had recently sent snapshots of her and her family, and Ruth quite proudly showed them to Alanna. "Here's Jessie with little Amy. She's three months old there. Isn't she a little doll, with that button nose and dark hair?" Alanna agreed and was handed another photograph. "That's Mikey. He's growing so fast. Jessie said in her letter that he's a typical terrible two-year-old."

Gazing at the photographs, Alanna couldn't help thinking how very happy Jessie looked. There was a positive bloom in her cheeks, especially in the photograph where she was holding the baby and looking at her husband, John. Alanna didn't know him very well, but he was a good-looking man in a solid sort of way.

Theirs had been a whirlwind courtship and radiant was the only way to describe Jessie after three years of marriage. Alanna hoped that was the way it would be for her, too. She tried to visualize a picture of herself and Kurt. But before the image could form, Ruth was speaking again.

"Now that they have a healthy boy and girl, Jessie thinks the family is officially complete. Sam and Andrew each have four, but she has no intention of trying to keep up with her brothers."

Ruth was referring to her sons, Alanna knew. She looked up when the mantel clock in the dining room chimed. "Heavens!" Ruth exclaimed. "If we're going to eat dinner at a decent hour, I'd better get started."

"I'll help," Elinore offered, starting to rise from the sofa as Ruth straightened.

"You stay here and talk to Alanna," the woman said firmly. "You haven't seen her since Easter."

"If you need me, just call." Her mother didn't pursue her offer and Alanna was reminded of her shaky health.

As Ruth left the room, she turned her attention back to the photographs, but her thoughts were on her mother. It was still difficult to accept after all this time that her mother's activities were limited. She still exuded a vitality that belied her weakness. A sigh came from her mother, wistfully sad, drawing Alanna's gaze. "Is something wrong, Mom?"

"Not really," she smiled. "I was just wondering how long it would be before I'll be able to show off pictures of my grandchildren. Or even if I'll be around to see them born."

"Oh, Mom, don't talk that way," Alanna murmured with a catch in her voice.

"I didn't mean to scare you," Elinore laughed, a bright melodious sound. "Honey, once you turned sixteen, the boys started knocking at our door. Not that you took any of them seriously."

"Did you want me to? You kept telling me to do my homework. Which didn't keep me from climbing out my bedroom window more than once."

Her mother patted her shoulder. "Oh, we knew that. Your father would lie awake and tell me exactly how he was going to murder the boy, and I always pointed out that he would have to catch him first. Your grades were excellent, and we didn't worry about the occasional, um, episode."

Alanna shook her head. She saw no reason to share the details of some of those "episodes," now or ever.

"I'm not expecting you to settle down just yet. You have to finish college, and commence a fabulous career and all that." Her mother snapped her fingers. "Easy as pie. I just want you to have a husband and family in your life, too."

"I'm twenty-one. That practically makes me an old maid, doesn't it?" Alanna teased, relief flowing through her that her mother had an optimistic outlook on the future.

"Seriously, Alanna," her mother smiled, "what about Kurt Matthews? Is he the one? Are you in love with him?"

A momentary stillness swept over her but she nodded. "I think so."

"Think so?" Disappointment and affection ran through the responding voice. "My dear, I doubt if it's love if you only think so. When you're in love with a man, he either makes you so impossibly angry that you can't think straight or he transports you to some heavenly plateau."

"Is that right?" There was an impish light in her eyes as she glanced at her mother. "Is that the way Dad makes you feel?"

"After thirty years, he still has the power to exasperate me beyond endurance," Elinore admitted laughingly. "But the heavenly plateau part—well, you have to come down to earth. That's something that exists only in the sweet romance of courtship. Which is just as well, because you can't go through life with your head in the clouds. But it's fun while it lasts."

Alanna smiled and nodded. Secretly she thought her

mother's notions about love were a bit old-fashioned and sentimental. Love wasn't like that today. And it probably never had been except in romantic dreams and movies and silly songs. Love wasn't something that happened. It was something that grew out of genuine affection and admiration into something more solid. But she didn't voice her opinion. There was no reason to debate the point.

Chapter Three

During dinner, Alanna kept wondering why her father was so preoccupied. His eyes, faintly troubled, kept straying to his wife, and there was a noticeable tension about his finely chiseled mouth. It seemed to accent the aging lines in his handsome, sensitive face. His hair was iron-gray, receding at the temples, yet still giving the impression of being thick and full.

They were such a perfect couple, Alanna thought, not for the first time. Devoted to each other, more concerned about each other's wants and needs than their own. Perhaps that was what was bothering her father now. She knew her mother's health was poor, but maybe he had detected something new tonight, something that gave him cause to worry. He would be more apt to pick up on things like that than Alanna, who'd been away for too long. She studied her mother circumspectly, trying to see her through her father's eyes, but she noticed nothing.

"Oh, Dorian"—Elinore looked up from her plate—"I called the plumber. He'll be over tomorrow morning to see what's the matter with the pipes in the laundry room. I meant to tell you earlier and forgot."

Her father sighed heavily. "I'm beginning to think we should have all new plumbing installed. First it was the upstairs bathroom; then it was the kitchen. Now the laundry room." He shook his head. "There's only the downstairs bathroom left."

"The house is old," her mother pointed out. "You can't expect it to last forever."

"I'm beginning to think it's become a white elephant." He made a studious job out of slicing a mouth-size portion of roast beef on his plate. "I was golfing today with Bob Jackson—he's gotten into real estate lately," he added in explanation. "He told me that the market's hot these days for homes in our area. He said our house would be worth plenty if we put it on the market."

"You aren't thinking of selling, are you, Dorian?" Her mother set her silverware on the table and stared at him in disbelief.

"We aren't getting any younger, Elinore," he said, not meeting her gaze. "With Alanna away at college most of the year, this house is really too big for our needs. The upkeep is getting out of hand and not just the plumbing. We're going to need a new roof before winter."

"Even so . . ."

"We could sell it and buy a nice condo, and invest the rest. No more paying to heat empty rooms or shoveling snow, raking leaves, or mowing lawns. Let's be honest. This house is beginning to be a burden."

"Dorian Maxwell Powell, I don't want to hear another word!" her mother exclaimed.

"Would you sell it?" Alanna breathed, her throat constricting at the idea of strangers living in her home.

"He is not going to sell it," Elinore stated emphatically.

"I never said I was." His tone was placating. "I was only pointing out that it would be the practical thing to do."

"I don't care if it's practical or not," her mother retorted. She picked up her knife and fork again. "I don't see how you could even suggest such a thing. You were born in this house. It was built to your father's specifications down to the last detail. It would be like selling your heritage. How could you even consider such a thing?"

"Now, now, Elinore, don't get so upset," he soothed with an apologetic smile. "I just thought that this big old house might be getting too much for you and Ruth to take care of and I didn't want . . ." He faltered, choosing his next words with care. "If you wanted something smaller, I thought you might not say so because of the very reasons you mentioned."

"Oh, honey." Elinore seemed touched by his thoughtfulness. "This is our home. It always has been and it always will be if I have any say in it."

"Of course you do," he smiled. "I guess it was foolish of me to bring it up."

"It certainly was," Elinore sniffed.

Alanna smiled, marveling again at the selfless consideration her parents showed for each other. She glanced at her watch. It was after six. She wouldn't have much time to get ready before Kurt arrived.

"I'm going to have to skip dessert if I want to be ready when Kurt gets here," she declared.

"But I made your favorite," Ruth protested. "Strawberry shortcake with fresh cream from the Johanson farm."

Alanna looked regretful. "Save me some. I'll have it for breakfast in the morning."

"You shouldn't be eating dessert for breakfast," Ruth said in a disapproving tone.

"Why not? It isn't any different from having fresh fruit and toast," she teased.

Cleaning her plate, she asked to be excused and hurried to her room. By the time she had showered, applied fresh makeup, and changed, Kurt was already there. She could hear him in the living room talking to her mother as she came down the stairs. Her father stepped out of the library and paused, his serious expression softening at the sight of her.

"You look lovely, Alanna." Dorian walked to the foot of the stairs to meet her. His gaze ran over her, admiring the amethyst sparkle the lavender dress gave to her eyes. "Even if I am biased, it's still the truth."

"Thank you, Daddy." She kissed him lightly on the cheek and glanced toward the living room. "Has Kurt been waiting long?"

"No more than five minutes, but once he sees you he won't mind," he answered, smiling. "Tell me, are you serious about him? Should I be in there interrogating him like a future father-in-law?"

Twice in one day—first her mother and now her father. Alanna couldn't believe it. She laughed with a trace of bewilderment,

"You're as bad as Mom," she declared. "You both seem intent on marching me down the aisle. I have a year of college to finish yet."

Pain flickered briefly in his eyes. "Of course you do," he repeated, a chagrined smile touching his mouth. "Your mother and I are just naturally anxious to know that there's someone who'll love you and look after you the way we do."

"I'm capable of looking after myself," Alanna reminded him gently.

"I know that, honey," her father nodded. "But I guess parents always think about their daughter getting married to a nice guy who works hard. I know that sounds old-fashioned but so be it. Rolt's brother seems like an up-and-comer. He's pleasant and intelligent and I know Rolt will always look out for his interests."

Not exactly, Alanna thought. She debated whether to tell her father exactly what kind of brother Kurt had. Her father wouldn't admire Rolt if he found out that the guy was planning to try to steal her away from his brother.

She swallowed back the words. It would only upset her father to have his confidence in Rolt shaken. He would start worrying about the plant and all the employees and their families who depended on it. "I think Kurt can take care of himself without any help from his brother," she said instead,

"I guess so," her father said, but in a doubtful tone that irritated Alanna. "But Kurt just doesn't have the drive that Rolt does. After all, Rolt is—"

"A giant. I know, Daddy." She sighed. "Next you'll be wondering if I shouldn't marry him instead."

"Well . . ." A fatherly twinkle danced in his eyes. But Alanna seemed so serious that the light faded from his eyes. "When you do marry, it has to be to the man you want," he added.

"I know." A rueful smile curved the vulnerable line of her mouth. No matter what he said, she knew he simply wanted her to be happy. Parents just had odd ideas sometimes about what would make their children happy. "I'd better not keep Kurt waiting any longer," she declared, and gave her father a quick hug because she loved him. "Don't wait up for me."

He smiled as she moved toward the living room, but Alanna thought his sensitive face looked sad and troubled behind the cheerful smile. She didn't have time to wonder why when she saw Kurt rise to meet her.

* * *

Several times during the rest of the week the impression returned. There wasn't any specific reason why, but Alanna couldn't shake the sensation that something was wrong. It was like a dark cloud lurking near the sun, casting a shadow without dimming the light.

Once, when her mother was napping and they were alone, Alanna voiced her concern. They were sitting in the living room, her father staring off into space.

"What's wrong, Dad?" she asked.

"Hmm? What?" He looked at her blankly, not catching the question.

"Is something wrong? You look as if you have some deep, dark problem weighing you down," Alanna teased, making light of her serious question.

"Old age," he sighed, his mouth quirking.

"Oh, you're not old," she protested, but a quick mental calculation reminded her that he was nearly sixty.

"Sometimes I feel very old—and tired."

But he still hadn't answered her question. "Are you worried about Mom?"

His light brows drew together in a line of hurt. "I can't help worrying about her, Alanna." He reached out and clasped her hand. "I love her."

"I know, Daddy." She squeezed his hand affectionately. "So do I."

"It's hard to accept that life doesn't go the way we hope or even plan that it will."

He stared again into space. "Your mother and I had great plans for our retirement. There was so much I wanted to do for her and show her."

His voice trailed off, but Alanna finished the unspoken thought. Her mother's weak heart had changed everything. Disappointment and regret were getting the better of him.

"But she has you, Daddy," Alanna pointed out. "And that's what she wants most of all."

"Yes," he nodded absently. But the look in his eyes said that he'd wanted to give his wife much more.

Of course it would bother him that she couldn't enjoy the traveling and activities they'd once planned. And Alanna guessed that he regretted not doing much of it earlier when her mother's health was not a concern.

"Well, there's no sense letting it upset you," she murmured. He hadn't replied and Alanna had let the subject drop.

She watched them now, her father hovering, her mother protesting, and couldn't help smiling. "I think you should wear a hat," her father was saying. "The sun can be pretty hot."

"I'm not made of ice cream. I won't melt in the sun," Elinore insisted in exasperation. "I'll sit in the shade if it gets too warm."

"I think I'll put a hat in the car just in case," he decided.

Elinore glanced at Alanna and smiled, shaking her head at the hopelessness of arguing with her husband. "Are you sure you don't want to join us for Sunday dinner? Ruth fixed a picnic lunch."

"Sounds great but no thanks," Alanna said. "Kurt's coming over at four o'clock. You and Dad would have to cut your afternoon short just to bring me back here."

"It doesn't seem right to leave you here alone on your first Sunday home," her mother sighed.

"Don't worry about it," she insisted. "I'm looking forward to a relaxing afternoon. I have a good book to read and I'm going to lie in the sun and read it."

"Well, if you're sure," her mother said grudgingly.

"Mom, if you're not careful, you're going to turn into a bigger mother hen than Dad!" Alanna laughed.

"Heaven forbid!" The answering response joined her laughter.

A few moments later, her parents were gone. With her book in one hand and her iPod in the other, Alanna wandered out onto the patio at the back of the house. The concrete area was almost the only section of the vast lawn that got the afternoon sun. Large pine trees and one maple tree shaded the rest.

Redwood lawn furniture was scattered in casual order about the patio. Setting the iPod and its headset on a circular redwood table, Alanna slipped out of her cotton beach jacket and tossed it on a nearby chair. Her brief bikini matched the jacket, a bold print of crimson and gold. She hit shuffle, then put in the earbuds and settled on to the redwood chaise lounge.

Reaching behind her neck, she undid the halter straps of her bikini top and the side ties on the bottom as well. She let them fall to her side to avoid getting white stripes, even though she didn't plan to get too toasty brown. With sunglasses protecting her eyes from the glare of the sun, she opened her book and began reading, quickly becoming engrossed in the historical saga.

"Beautiful." A male voice murmured the compliment.

Alanna glanced up, startled. Between the music in her ears and her own absorption in the novel, she hadn't heard anyone approach. But there, a few feet from her chair, towered Rolt Matthews. Someone she hadn't seen or heard from since the day she'd arrived in Hibbing, which had lulled her into a false sense of security.

Stunned, her mouth refused to function. She stared at him, momentarily unable to speak. He was dressed casually, in a plain white linen shirt and jeans. The breadth of his chest was clear under the lightweight shirt, accenting the tapering length of his waist. The first few buttons were undone, and she could see just a little golden-brown chest hair. Nice. Very nice. A gentle breeze rippled through his thick brown hair, gilded by the sunlight. There was a sensual twist to his mouth. He took a step forward, and the spell was broken.

"How did you get here?" she asked him angrily.

"No one answered the door. I came around to investigate."

The intensity of his hooded gaze made Alanna suddenly aware of the bikini strings hanging freely at her sides, and of how much the loosened top exposed the full curves of her breasts. She set the book over her thighs and quickly tied her bikini back up again. He looked away, managing to be a gentleman for once in his life, she thought crossly.

Swinging her feet to the sun-warmed concrete of the patio, she stood up. The brief bikini made her feel practically naked, but her beach jacket was lying on the chair Rolt was standing beside.

"Um, I think you should leave. I really don't want to see you." Sounding composed and controlled was difficult.

Rolt ignored the taut request. "I noticed your parents' car is gone. Your housekeeper's off for the day, too, isn't she?" He reached down and picked up her beach jacket, holding it in his hand. His gaze raked her soft curves.

"You sound like a stalker."

"Well, I'm not." He grinned but it didn't put her at ease.

Alanna's skin burned. A slow warmth began to rise in her neck. She wanted the jacket desperately, to conceal her figure from his insolent blue eyes, but she wasn't about to ask him to give it to her, not for anything.

"Go away, Rolt." She tossed her head back in proud defiance.

"And leave you here alone to entertain yourself? I couldn't do that," he mocked.

"If you don't leave, I'll call the police," Alanna threatened. "Or scream for help."

"Calling them would probably be faster. The neighbors' houses are too far—they won't hear you. The chief is a friend of mine, so tell him I said hi."

Alanna inhaled sharply, trembling with rage. "What does that mean? You prowl around whenever you want to and he doesn't care?"

"Nah. He'd throw me in jail if I tried anything. But I wasn't going to. Just came by to see how you were doing."

"And now you can go."

"Do I have to?"

"You know I don't like you, Rolt."

"That does make it difficult," he said. "But not impossible."

"What's not impossible? Just keep in mind that I'm going out with your brother. You don't feel guilty about that at all, do you?"

"I've decided that I don't want you for a future sister-in-law. I want you for myself."

"Okay. You've made yourself aggressively clear on that point. But I don't want you," Alanna said emphatically. Suddenly she was still as a thought occurred to her. She tipped her head to one side and gazed at him. "Wait a minute. You know I don't like you but you find that a challenge. Is that it?"

The indigo shade of his eyes deepened. "Maybe." His aloof voice made it neither a yes nor a no.

She felt certain she was right. "Tough luck. I most definitely prefer your brother to a cold fish like you."

"Cold?"

"Yes, cold," Alanna repeated forcefully. "Cold and insensitive. You have no feelings, no compassion for anyone but yourself. Not even your brother."

His mouth thinned. "Then how do you explain the way I feel toward you?"

"I'm out of reach, that's all. Emotions don't enter into it, otherwise you wouldn't be here when you know I don't like you at all."

"Maybe I want to change your mind," Rolt suggested.

"You'll never do that!"

"My brother's not the right guy for you." There was a gleam of fierce possession in his eyes. "He would never make you happy."

"And you would, I suppose," she jeered.

"Let me try."

"You're out of your mind." Alanna turned her head away, fuming at his unbelievable conceit. A thousand angry words ran through her mind, yet they would not be enough to serve her purpose. There was another way, however, that she might accomplish it. She glanced at him over her shoulder, her gaze wary and skeptical. "Forgive me if I find that hard to believe, but you hardly know me."

His gaze was measuring. "I think I know you better than you do."

"Really?" Alanna moved deliberately toward him, coming nearer to stand in front of him, tilting her head back to meet the full force of his gaze. Her heart beat faster. Her plan was daring and dangerous. "Then why don't I like you?"

"Because you're afraid," Rolt answered easily. "You're afraid of me and of yourself."

For a moment his reply disconcerted her. Bewilderment glittered briefly in her violet eyes. She quickly concealed it, but not before Rolt noticed.

"Oh, please," she said. "You're not one of those guys who watches soap operas, are you? You talk like one."

He smiled, giving her a faintly superior look. "No."

The gleam in his eye plainly laughed at her answer.
Alanna breathed in, controlling her anger. Gathering
her courage, she reached out, letting her fingers touch
the front of his shirt. She felt him stiffen and a tingle of
approaching victory ran through her nerve ends.

"I'm not afraid of you," she repeated, slowly letting
her fingers travel up his shirt to the collar.

Standing on tiptoe, she lifted her head toward his
mouth. Rolt waited, not moving even when her lips
lightly touched his. Alanna swayed closer, her hands
clasping behind the strong column of his neck. His own
hands settled on the bare curve of her waist, resting
there without actually holding her.

As the kiss lengthened, Alanna felt his mouth moving sensually in response, deepening with desire. Feigning
reluctance, she took her suddenly trembling lips away
from his, but she made no attempt to move away from
him. She let his hands remain on her waist while her
head rested on the granite solidness of his chest. A seductive light blazed darkly in his eyes when she looked
up at him.

His head dipped slowly toward her. Alanna checked
the movement with fingertips pressed against his mouth
and a small negative shake of her head. Rolt didn't
argue or force the issue, waiting, the seductive look not
leaving his gaze.

"You see, I'm not afraid of you," she murmured. For
a few seconds more, she kept her face expressionless.
"Do you know why I kissed you?" Her fingers drifted
back to his chest.

"Why?" His voice was even, faintly amused, not revealing any of the passion blazing so vividly in his eyes.
His control was amazing.

"Because"—her gaze fell from his as she took a deep
breath—"I wanted you to know what I feel for your
brother is something I could never feel for you. I don't

want your kisses or anything else you're offering. I want him. For one very good reason—you're disgusting."

On the concluding word, she started to wrench free from his unresisting touch, but her scathing comments didn't seem to impress him. His hands left her waist, but only to grip the soft flesh of her upper arms and pull her against him. Immediately his arms encircled her.

She tossed her head back to glare at him coldly. His eyes were hard, the line of his mouth compressed with silent fury. Alanna was immediately angry with herself for letting him intimidate her.

"Never?" Rolt asked in a low voice.

Before she could dodge him, her mouth was taken by his. Sensual and masterful in a way that was new to her—dangerously new—he shattered her illusion that a kiss was an act of love and affection. What he was doing was all about possession, dominating her, making her his.

Her bare legs carried the imprint of the denim he wore. Muscular thighs, like solid rock columns, pressed hotly against her flesh. His hold made her arch; her senses already swamped by his heady, musky scent.

He released her, brushing a fingertip over her swollen lips. Alanna breathed in shuddering gasps. Her sense of defeat made her cheeks burn—or was it the desire she knew she felt?

"Get out of here!" Her words were choked by the bitter sob that rose in her throat.

"Whatever you say," he said calmly. "But you look like you enjoyed that."

She had. But she was damned if she was going to tell him so. Kurt didn't kiss that way, Kurt kissed like a nice guy.

"No. Not really." She had nearly said she never would, but caught herself in time, not wanting to give Rolt the slightest reason to try again. She doubted she could withstand him a second time.

"Okay, Alanna." The self-assured note in his voice made her tremble. Rolt laughed softly when he saw her uncontrollable shiver. "Remember that when Kurt kisses you. I won't tell him what we did."

Her heart leapt in fear. The low, mesmerizing voice wasn't threatening, but Rolt wasn't a man she could trust. It was as if she were looking into the future and seeing her fate written in the indigo glitter of his gaze.

Her head made a tiny movement of protest. Then his hand traveled down the slender curve of her neck to cover her breast, her heart hammering madly against it.

"Such soft skin, Alanna," Rolt continued huskily, "I can't resist touching you." An inarticulate sound came from her throat, almost a surrender.

Alanna swayed unsteadily. She felt hot and cold at the same time, numb with shock yet every nerve alive. The ambivalence of her reaction was frightening. She couldn't understand how she could feel so many things at the same time.

Something was wrapped around her shoulders, and she glanced up, dazed. The beach jacket covered her bikini, providing her protection too late. Rolt was standing beside her, watching her. Blankly she met his enigmatic look.

"I want you to have dinner with me tomorrow night," he said.

For a moment she could only stare at him, still lost in her split world. But her sense of self-preservation finally surfaced.

"No," she refused flatly.

Rolt shrugged, as if to say it was only a matter of time, and accepted her decision. When he spoke, his voice was soft yet very clear, quietly unrelenting.

"I'm not going to forget that kiss. You won't forget it either."

Alanna turned her back on him. "Just get out of here," she whispered.

Her eyes were tightly closed as she heard Rolt leave as quietly as he had come. Alanna's position didn't vary, not until the distant sound of a car engine turning over reached her. Another minute more and he was gone. Alanna dropped down onto the chaise lounge with a sharp sigh, but she didn't cry. There was too much anger, frustration, and confusion for tears.

Chapter Four

The porch light dimly illuminated the front door. The night air was scented by the ever-present perfume of pines, and crickets and cicadas droned endlessly. There was little traffic on the street at that late hour, and it was far away.

She and Kurt stood in the shadows. He held her lightly, his kiss giving the impression of tentative ardor. Unwanted, unbidden, the mastery of Rolt's kiss came back to her and rocked her senses. The memory returned so suddenly, so unexpectedly, that she wrenched away from Kurt's embrace. When she saw the puzzled look in his eyes, she realized that the brothers were very different men—and that she wasn't at all sure which one she wanted now.

"What's the matter? What have I done?" Bewildered laughter laced his voice.

Alanna turned away, taut, unable to meet his searching gaze. "It's . . . it's nothing." A trace of irritation at her own behavior accompanied her faltering denial of any wrongdoing on Kurt's part.

"Something is wrong," he insisted, his hands turning

her tense shoulders around so she faced him. "Tell me what it is," he coaxed gently. She looked into his handsome features, and a wave of hopelessness washed over her. There wasn't any way she could tell Kurt about Rolt's visit this afternoon or explain the way it had affected her.

She shook her head a little wearily. "I—I have a slight headache." That had to be the oldest excuse on record, but Kurt had no reason to question her statement. He accepted it at face value and smiled ruefully. "You should have said something earlier," he told her.

"I thought it would go away," Alanna said.

"You probably got too much sun this afternoon," Kurt suggested.

Too much Rolt, she thought grimly. "Yeah, that could be it," she said politely.

"I don't want to let you go in, but I guess I'd better. I'll call you tomorrow, okay?" His dark head was tipped to one side.

"Yes," Alanna agreed, and lifted her mouth for his good night kiss.

He brushed her lips lightly, but they remained cool and untouched by his gentleness. The memory of Rolt overshadowed the reality of the moment, dissolving any pleasure she might have found with Kurt.

Inside the house, she leaned against the closed front door, shutting her eyes for a brief instant. *You won't forget,* Rolt had said. She hadn't. The memory had come between her and Kurt tonight, and she had the uneasy feeling it wasn't going to be the last time that it would happen.

Around ten the next morning, the phone rang. Alanna was closest, so she answered it. "Hello?"

"How's your headache?"

Her first thought was that it was Kurt phoning as promised. "All gone," she replied with forced lightness.

The low mocking laughter that followed her words made her realize her mistake. It was Rolt. "How did you know about that?" she breathed angrily.

"When I saw Kurt this morning, I said something about how rested he looked. He explained that he'd come home early last night because you pleaded a headache." His taunting voice laughed at her excuse.

"Why did you call, Rolt?" she demanded.

"Do I have to have a reason?"

"No, but I'm sure you do." And it was probably to gloat.

"Maybe I wanted to hear your voice."

"Well, I hope you enjoy hearing this." Alanna slammed the receiver down, wishing she had broken his eardrums and doubting if she could be that lucky.

She glowered for a second longer at the telephone, then pivoted away. Her mother was watching her curiously. "Was that Rolt Matthews on the phone?"

"Yes." Alanna's answer was abrupt, a leftover piece of her temper.

"I was wondering when he would get around to calling," Elinore said with a knowing lilt in her voice.

"What made you think Rolt would call?" She was wary and on edge.

"Remember when he and Kurt were over here during Easter? Well, I could tell by the way Rolt kept watching you that he was interested. You were probably too wrapped up in Kurt to notice, but I did," her mother declared.

"Well, I can't stand him!" Alanna snapped.

"He makes you angry, does he?"

"Yes! He's—" She stopped short, suddenly recognizing the sparkle in her mother's eye, and guessing its cause. "Don't look at me that way, Mom," she declared impatiently. "It's not what you're thinking. He may enrage me, but he will never raise me to some heavenly plateau!"

She contented herself with an indignant glare that would have done a teenager proud and left the room. Even her own mother was going over to the enemy camp.

She railed against the unfairness of it. Rolt cast a long shadow, a giant's shadow, and it seemed to be looming over more and more of her life.

During the rest of the week, Rolt didn't attempt to make any further direct contact with Alanna. He didn't have to, since he had managed to interfere quite successfully in one way or another. Twice she had seen him briefly when she was with Kurt, and her parents had invited him over for dinner one evening. Luckily it had been an evening she had already planned to spend with Kurt.

Most of the time it was simply the thought of him that disturbed her. Each time she was with Kurt, Alanna would remember that afternoon and the things that Rolt had said and done. She couldn't forget then. She couldn't relax with Kurt. When he touched her or held her, she kept measuring her reaction, wanting to avoid a repetition of that night on the porch.

As a consequence, she was tense and unnatural. To cover it, she became overly friendly and affectionate to prove to herself as well as to Kurt how much she cared for him.

With her fingers twined in his, she led Kurt from the dance floor to their small table in the crowded bar, laughing over her shoulder into his handsome face. Saturday night had filled the bar with people, and their voices and laughter made it difficult to hear the music of a local band. Not that it really mattered. Everyone was there to have fun. Music was the background.

White jeans and a gauzy white embroidered tunic weren't the perfect choice of clothes to wear in these crowded circumstances, but Alanna knew it set off her slimness and the light golden tan she had allowed herself. A little more eyeliner highlighted the unusual violet shade of her eyes. In this carefree atmosphere she felt quite bewitching.

To her annoyance Kurt was acting like he was under her spell. He didn't release her hand as they reclaimed their chairs after a dance. The chairs were drawn close together so that their shoulders touched.

Kurt leaned over and nuzzled the tawny curls near her earlobe. "I love you, Alanna," he murmured huskily. He drew back a few inches, a faint look of wonder in his eyes as if he was surprised by the words he had spoken. "I love you, Alanna," he repeated with conviction.

She had been waiting for these words since Easter. Now, more than ever before, they made her feel safe. Rolt's sexual magnetism paled beside those three little words that every woman longed to hear, and her spirits soared.

"I love you, too, Kurt," she said with genuine warmth.

"This is a crazy place to tell you." His gaze swept the noisy room briefly before returning to her face.

"It's a wonderful place," she protested softly.

"We've known each other for—how long? A month?"

"Something like that. Maybe a little longer."

"Well, some people fall in love in hardly any time, right?" Kurt reasoned.

"Occasionally," Alanna said.

"We should be in some luxurious restaurant, drinking champagne." He shook his dark head.

"In Minnesota?" Alanna teased.

"Yes, in Minnesota," Kurt grinned. "That's where I

should have taken you tonight instead of here. Or I should have waited to tell you until we were alone."

"Does it matter?" She tipped her head to one side, lips parting in an invitation. "I mean, does it really matter where we are?"

"Not if you say you love me again."

"I love you."

"Alanna!" He breathed her name in a caress as his mouth descended toward the promise of hers.

"Hey, Kurt. Alanna—what a surprise to find you here." Rolt's dryly mocking voice separated them instantly. "I would have thought you'd take Alanna to someplace less public."

Her head came up, as if scenting danger. That moment of feeling secure and safe was gone. She no longer was sure that Kurt's love would be able to protect her. Not from Rolt.

"Seemed like a good idea at the time. It's only now that I'm beginning to see its disadvantages," Kurt conceded. Alanna felt his smiling look turn sad and briefly returned a strained imitation of it.

"What are you doing here, Rolt?" The flash of her eyes accused him of spying.

"I stopped by for a quiet drink, forgetting it was Saturday night," he returned evenly. "I was on my way out when I happened to see the two of you."

"Don't let us stop you," she said sweetly.

Rolt laughed and pulled up an empty chair to sit down at their table, uninvited. "Sometimes I think you don't like me, Alanna."

"I was just wondering how a detail-oriented control freak like you could forget it was Saturday night." She gave him a humorless smile. "What happened? Didn't your state-of-the-art computer go beepity-boop and remind you?"

"I shut it off," he said lazily. "I don't work all the time, you know." His gaze drifted suggestively to her mouth, almost physically touching it to remind her of the kisses he had stolen.

Alanna crimsoned. Somehow he made her feel as if her resistance had only been a token thing. Added to that was the sensation of guilt for failing to tell Kurt of that one visit. An arm circled her shoulders and for an instant she tensed, recalling another strong arm that had captured her. She had to force herself to relax against Kurt's reassuring hold.

"Maybe you've noticed that I've been monopolizing Alanna's time lately," Kurt said. "Doesn't give you much of a chance to compete for her, does it? I hate to tell you this, bro, but you're too late now." His arm tightened around her shoulder, drawing her closer. Then he pressed a kiss on her temple. "In the not too distant future, Alanna is going to be a member of the family, all legal and binding."

His statement brought a brief surge of confidence. Alanna glanced swiftly at Rolt to see his reaction to Kurt's announcement. The long look he gave her was hooded and unreadable. He seemed neither surprised nor upset by the news.

He nodded in a way that seemed to indicate resignation. "That's something I can drink to." Rolt smiled crookedly. "Waitress?" he turned, signaling to the girl passing their table with a tray of drinks. "Scotch and water for me, please, and two more of the same for them."

"There's one thing about my big brother," Kurt told Alanna. "Once he knows he's beaten, he admits it. Of course, he hardly ever loses. So he can afford to be gracious in defeat."

Yet Alanna didn't trust Rolt. She hoped that what Kurt said was true, but she couldn't forget the way Rolt seemed to assume that she could belong to him. When the drinks arrived, she fingered her cold glass and eyed Rolt warily.

He lifted his glass and touched it first to Kurt's, then held it against Alanna's. His enigmatic gaze held hers, not allowing her to look away. "To the day—" his voice was firm and strong "—when Alanna becomes Mrs. Matthews."

In that frozen moment, she knew that he meant Mrs. Rolt Matthews. He had not acknowledged defeat. What's more, Rolt was aware that she knew it even if his brother didn't. It was there in the glint of his eye.

"Drink up, Alanna," Kurt prompted. His hand covered her motionless fingers and carried the glass she was holding to her lips. She spluttered a little, irritated at being forced to drink, even if it was only a sip.

"Now that I've toasted the future bride, do you object if I dance with her?" Rolt asked.

"Not at all." Kurt removed his arm from around her shoulders, magnanimously releasing her into his brother's custody.

Don't you see what he's doing? Alanna screamed silently at Kurt. But he merely smiled into her pale face and prodded her in the direction of his older brother, now standing expectantly beside her chair. Feeling abandoned, she rose, frozenly accepting the guiding hand on her back.

The small dance floor was crowded, as was the entire bar. Yet Alanna managed to hold herself stiffly away when Rolt turned her into his arms to begin the slow steps to the music. Her fingers were rigid in his hand and her other hand rested on only a small square of his muscular shoulder. She looked sideways at the other couples rather than at her partner.

"All your maneuvering won't work, you know," she murmured beneath her breath. "I do love Kurt and I'm going to marry him."

"Are you?" he countered smoothly.

Alanna flashed him a seething look and clamped her lips tightly shut. It would be a waste of breath to try to convince him—he was too arrogant and conceited to listen. She lapsed into silence.

"How are your parents?" Rolt asked.

"Fine," she answered icily.

"Are they?" His murmuring voice was filled with knowing doubt.

Alanna missed a step and his arm immediately tightened around her waist. It wasn't a desire for small talk that had prompted his inquiry about her parents. She knew it as surely as she knew her name.

"Why do you say that?" she asked warily.

"I thought your father seemed upset about something when I was there for dinner the other evening." Rolt shrugged in seeming indifference. "I got the feeling he doesn't think much of Kurt."

The statement was self-serving, to say the least. "You're wrong," she said flatly, needing to lie. Her father thought well of Kurt mostly because Kurt was Rolt's brother, but Alanna wouldn't admit that to Rolt even on pain of death.

"Do you know what's bothering him?"

"He's concerned about my mom," she said briskly, having no desire to discuss it with him.

"Did he tell you that?"

"Yes, he did."

The crowded dance floor meant that elbows and shoulders were constantly pushing against her, diminishing the precious inches that kept her apart from Rolt. With the loss of each inch, his arm tightened to keep her from regaining it. His muscular thighs were now brushing against her, but her mind was too occupied with the puzzling reasons for his questions to dwell on that.

"Why are you asking all these questions about my parents?" she challenged him.

"I was just curious about why your father seemed upset. Of course, if he told you that he was concerned about your mother, then I'm sure that that must be the reason." His answer was too smooth.

A tightness gripped her throat. "What do you know that I don't?" she demanded.

Rolt looked down at her. "What makes you think I do?"

"You do know something," she declared with angry certainty. "What is it? I have a right to know."

"I'm sure you do," he agreed.

"Then tell me."

"This isn't the place for a private discussion." His gaze arced around them.

"I want to know," repeated Alanna.

Rolt stopped and she realized the music had ended. "All right," he conceded, "I'll tell you." He paused, his gaze running over her upturned face, his expression masked and unreadable. "Come to my office on Tuesday evening at six. I'll tell the guard at the gate to expect you."

"Tuesday?" She frowned in protest.

"I'm leaving in the morning. I'll be out of town until then."

Her hands clenched with frustration. "This is all a trick, isn't it?" she accused. "You're making all this up just to get me to meet you."

"The only way you can be positive of that is to meet me Tuesday and find out." He gave her a very polite, very annoying smile. "Shall we go back to the table before Kurt gets impatient?"

Alanna pivoted sharply on her heel. He was deliberately being mysterious. She knew that no amount of anger or pleading would make Rolt tell her anything now, if there was even anything to tell. She wasn't convinced there was, but by the same token, she wasn't convinced there wasn't.

Although Rolt left almost as soon as they returned to the table, his brief appearance ruined the rest of Alanna's evening. She couldn't recapture that mood of contentment and happiness from Kurt's avowal of love. She tried to respond with the same degree of sincerity, but she knew she was faking it, although she didn't think Kurt noticed.

Her concern for her parents didn't keep her from wondering what Rolt knew that she didn't. She had no way of knowing until Tuesday. Having to wait only added to her conflict. She had no idea if Rolt really did know something about her parents or if he was only pretending that he did in order to get her to agree to meet him.

Either way, she thought, what difference would it make? Just because they'd be in the same room—okay, alone in the same room—didn't mean she was suddenly going to change her mind about him. So she had to concede that there was a very real possibility that Rolt did know something.

Twice during the intervening days she cornered her father and asked questions that she hoped sounded casual. They weren't and his answers weren't any help. About all he would say was that he was tired, had a sore shoulder from playing golf, and was concerned about her mother.

Tuesday found her with nothing to do but get into the garden, which had become somewhat overgrown during the long, hot days of midsummer. Alanna frowned and tugged impatiently at the stubborn weed growing in the iris bed. She didn't want to meet Rolt tonight, but it seemed the only way to put an end to all her doubts and questions. The June sun made her sweat and it trickled between her shoulder blades before being absorbed by the back strap of her halter.

A car pulled into the driveway. Alanna paused to glance over her shoulder, rubbing the back of her gloved hand across her forehead. A sigh broke unexpectedly from her lips at the sight of Kurt stepping out of the car. Not the reaction she should have to a surprise visit from her prospective fiancé. Immediately she curved her lips into a warm smile of greeting as she straightened.

"Kurt, this is a surprise!" she declared.

"Talk about surprises," he laughed, his gaze running admiringly over her. "Somehow when I pictured Mistress Mary working in her garden, I never saw her in sexy shorts and top. I should visit her garden more often." His hands circled her waist and he kissed her soundly.

"Mmm," she sighed when he finally let her breathe again. "Now I understand why she was so contrary. She was constantly being accosted by handsome men." His hands were still locked behind her back, holding her close to him. Alanna tipped her head back to gaze into his face. "Seriously, Kurt, how did you manage to get away from the plant in the middle of the day?"

"I had an errand to run, so I took a late lunch hour," he explained.

"And you just happened to be in the area and thought you would stop, is that it?" she asked, smiling.

The teasing laughter left his eyes as he unlocked his hands. "I had one last thing to do," Kurt told her. "I stopped by the jeweler's and picked this up."

He took a ring box from his pocket and opened it. "It's beautiful!" breathed Alanna. She gazed at the ring, one large diamond surrounded by a circlet of smaller ones in the shape of petals.

"To make it official, Alanna, will you marry me?" he asked softly.

"Yes." Her answer was almost inaudible. The ring somehow made it all seem so much more real and unchangeable.

"Let me have your hand," said Kurt, removing the ring from its velvet holder.

Alanna raised her left hand, hastily peeling the cotton glove off, and held it out to him. Reverently he slipped it on to her finger.

"I'm afraid it's too loose," he said with a sigh.

"It doesn't matter," she protested, not wanting to lose her talisman. She felt it would protect her and she didn't want to think about from what.

"Yes, it does. I want it to be perfect—as perfect as you are, Alanna," he declared huskily.

"I'm not perfect."

"To me, you are." He slipped the ring from her finger, replacing it in the box. "The jeweler said he could easily size it. I'll take it back to him this afternoon and pick it up after work tonight. And the next time I put it on your finger, it won't come off."

"No." Alanna shook her head, gazing forlornly at the box but it was out of sight in his pocket.

He crooked his forefinger under her chin and raised it. "We'll do it up right tonight. Champagne, candlelight, the works," he promised. "A real celebration."

Her teeth nibbled nervously at her lower lip. "I can't, not tonight, Kurt," she murmured.

"Why not?" He tipped his head to the side, trying to read the expression she veiled with her lashes.

Alanna couldn't find the words to tell him she was meeting Rolf or the explanation such an announcement would require. "It's a family thing." She seized on a half-truth since the only reason she was meeting Rolt was because of his insinuations that he knew something about her parents. "If I could, I'd break it, but—"

"That's okay," he interrupted. "We'll celebrate tomorrow night."

"Yes," she agreed, relieved that he didn't press her for a more definite explanation.

"I suppose I'd better get back to work before brother Rolt sends out a search party," Kurt said reluctantly.

"So he's back from out of town," Alanna commented.

"He got back just before noon, which is part of the reason for my late lunch break." He bent his head and kissed her. "Till tomorrow night."

Alanna waved to him as he reversed his car out of the driveway. Her interest in the garden had vanished, and her spirits were ridiculously low as she turned toward the house. She blamed it on Rolt. Just the mention of his name succeeded in spoiling her pleasure.

As she entered the house, her mother was just going up the stairs. She paused. "Was that Kurt I saw drive in?"

"Yes, it was." Alanna ran a nervous hand through her tawny hair.

"Isn't he working today?" Elinore asked curiously.

"He was on his lunch break."

"Was it important? I mean, he usually doesn't come by during the day," her mother said.

Alanna walked toward the living room. "He had an errand to run and stopped to say hello."

"I see. I'm going upstairs now to lie down for a little while, dear."

"Okay, Mom."

As her mother disappeared up the staircase, Alanna suddenly felt slightly sick. Why hadn't she told her mother about the engagement ring? For that matter, why hadn't she mentioned the engagement before now? It wasn't as if she was afraid her parents wouldn't approve of her choice. They liked Kurt. She had known since Saturday night that he wanted to marry her. Why hadn't she told them, or at least hinted about it? She should be deliriously happy at this moment instead of fighting waves of nausea. Why wasn't she?

It would be all right, she assured herself. Everything would be as it should be just as soon as she had that dreaded meeting with Rolt tonight. She was letting it worry her unnecessarily.

Chapter Five

Slowing the car, Alanna turned it into the plant entrance, which was blocked by steel gates. A security guard stepped forward as she stopped. There were nervous tremors in her hands, and she clutched the steering wheel to hide them.

The guard bent down to peer through the opened car window. "Can I help you, miss?"

"Yes, I'm Alanna Powell. I have an appointment with Mr. Matthews," she answered with a stiff smile.

The man paused to check his clipboard and nodded confirmation. "Mr. Rolt Matthews is expecting you." After specifying to his satisfaction which Matthews she was seeing, he signaled a second guard to open the gate and waved Alanna through.

Her face was warm as she drove in. She guessed that there were a more than a few employees, in high and low positions, who were familiar with the fact that she was dating Kurt steadily. Her appointment to see his brother was something that wouldn't go unnoticed. She wished she had mentioned it to Kurt. She made a promise to herself to do it tomorrow evening before the gossip reached him and made her meeting with Rolt sound like something more than it was.

Parking her car in the empty space beside the black SUV, Alanna picked up her bag from the seat and stepped out.

She hesitated outside the car, staring at the building door. Her fears that she had come on a fool's errand returned. The impulse was there to leave without seeing Rolt, but she would never be certain whether he knew anything if she did.

Her legs felt weak as she walked to the door. Fleetingly she regretted not eating dinner with her parents before coming, but it would have made her late. Considering the state of her nerves, the food would have probably been an uncomfortable ball in her stomach instead of providing her the strength she felt had deserted her at this moment.

Inside the building, her footsteps echoed hollowly in the empty hall leading to Rolt's office. She caught a glimpse of her reflection in a glass partition, noting automatically that she looked good, but she wished she hadn't bothered changing into much nicer clothes. She didn't want to appear attractive for Rolt; she would rather have looked like some nonentity.

It was too late to think of that now. She walked through his secretary's office to the interconnecting door. Her hand clenched once, nervously, then she knocked.

"Come in," was the muffled response.

Her stomach fluttered as she opened the door. Rolt was sitting at his desk, his head bent in an attitude of concentration over the papers spread before him. Alanna closed the door and waited just inside the room for him to acknowledge her presence.

At the click of the door, he glanced up absently, then almost immediately the indigo darkness of his eyes narrowed for a piercing second. Her heartbeat quickened under the penetrating look. Then his gaze moved to the gold watch on his wrist, as if confirming the time.

"Take a seat." He was already bending over the papers again as he spoke. "I'll be through here in a few minutes."

Alanna hesitated, fighting a white-hot urge to walk over to his table and scatter his precious papers to the floor and demand that he tell her whatever it was that he was supposed to know. She had waited three days and that was long enough.

No, her common sense told her. Losing her temper would only give Rolt an added advantage. This meeting was going to be strictly formal and polite. They would discuss the subject and not go into the personalities involved, his or hers. Cooling the brief surge of anger, she walked toward the half-circle of the sofa.

"There's a bar on the far wall. Ice is in the refrigerator below. Help yourself," Rolt told her.

Alanna glanced at the bar briefly and sat down on the sofa. "No, thank you." The last thing she needed was to have her thinking muddled with alcohol. Besides, she would be driving home from here.

Leaning against the sofa back, she opened a magazine on the technical aspects of mining she found on the coffee table, leafed through it, and quickly set it aside. The silence in the room was unnerving, broken only by the rustle of papers from the desk and the occasional scratch of a pen on paper. Rolt worked on, comparing his figures to a spreadsheet on the monitor in front of him, completely ignoring her presence in the room—something Alanna couldn't do as she openly gazed at him.

His expression was closed, uncompromising. He concentrated on his task and let nothing interfere. The blue drapes at the window were not completely closed. The shaft of sunlight from the window streamed over the desk, casting him in a golden light suitable for a saint. Not that he was one, she thought wryly.

The sunlight wavered as if a filmy cloud was drifting in the way of its source. It intensified the tan of his skin until it appeared bronze, a marked contrast to the white of his shirt. The uncertain light highlighted the craggy planes and angles of his masculine features. The impression Alanna had now was of something savage and noble, inherently male and proud. The cloud passed and the light was steadily bright. His features again became uncompromising and closed.

She looked anywhere but at him, wishing she'd thought to bring a book. When she looked back, Rolt was watching her, his gaze alert and inspecting. He laid the pen down with an air of finality and rose from the straight-backed chair.

"Sorry to have kept you waiting." His words were routine, said out of politeness and sounding insincere.

"Of course," Alanna answered coolly.

Strong fingers closed around the knot of his tie, loosening it and starting to pull it free. "Do you mind?" Rolt paused.

She doubted that it really mattered to him whether she gave her permission, but she did. "Not at all."

The tie was removed and stuffed in his jacket pocket. He shrugged off the camel tan jacket and draped it over the chair he had vacated. Alanna was gripped by the sensation that she was watching him shed the trappings of civilization. He became even more male and somehow dangerous.

When the top three buttons of his white shirt were unfastened, he stopped. Alanna felt faintly surprised. She had almost expected him to strip away the shirt as well. Her senses had stirred alarmingly during these electric seconds and she looked away to bring them under control.

Instead of walking to the sofa, Rolt moved to the window, stopping in the slit of sunlight. He gazed out the dusty panes, his feet slightly apart, a stance that suggested arrogance and power. A giant looking over his domain, Alanna thought. Her impatience grew as he remained silent.

"What is it you claim to know about my parents?" she asked at last.

Rolt gave her a long, measuring look over his shoulder, then turned around. "I'm going to have a drink. Sure you don't want one?" he asked, calmly ignoring her question.

"I'm positive." Alanna found it difficult to keep the irritation she felt out of her voice. The bar was on the wall behind her. She listened to the opening of the refrigerator door, the clink of ice in a glass, and the closing of the door. Then there was only silence. She clasped her hands tightly together in her lap, refusing to glance around at him.

"My parents," she prompted icily.

Liquor splashed over ice. "What about them?"

"That's what I want to know." Alanna turned on the sofa cushion, glaring at Rolt. "You used that as an excuse to lure me here, didn't you?" she accused.

He met her look with bland unconcern. "Yes."

"Why was I so stupid?" she muttered. With jerky, angry movements, she grasped her bag and rose from the sofa. "You don't know anything about my parents."

A half step toward the door and his quiet voice stopped her. "I didn't say that." Alanna turned to eye him warily. "I only admitted that I used them to get you here. Which is not the same as admitting that I know nothing."

"Well, do you?" she challenged, tired of the cat-and-mouse game.

"Sit down, Alanna." Rolt walked from the bar, a stubby glass in his hand.

"No," she said unequivocally. "I want to know about my parents and I want to know now." There was an unmistakable threat in her voice.

His mouth twitched as though he found her barely suppressed anger amusing, but it was a fleeting movement. He walked away from the sofa, and sauntered back to his desk.

"You said your father told you that he was concerned about your mother. She has a bad heart, I believe." He paused in front of the table to glance at Alanna.

"Yes." She volunteered no more than that.

"Indirectly it's the reason why he's worried."

Alanna tipped her head to one side, definitely skeptical. "What is the direct cause?" she asked.

"How familiar are you with your father's financial situation?" countered Rolt.

"I know they're set for life," she said with a haughty coolness. "Between the sale of his stock to your company and the remainder he kept, they don't have to worry."

"That was true at the time of the sale."

That statement drifted in the air before its impact finally settled on Alanna. The haughtiness left as she searched the bronze mask. She was motionless as she tried to read between the lines. His implication sent shivers of apprehension down her spine. Slowly she began walking toward him.

"What are you saying?" The demand was breathy, lacking in strength.

"Your father never was a very good businessman or manager. He invested part of the money in blue chips

and high-yield bonds, safe stuff. The rest went into speculative tech stocks. Unfortunately, they tanked. Trying
to recoup his losses, he cashed in the others and invested the proceeds in more risky ventures. Including a
hedge fund currently under investigation by the SEC.
To put it simply, Alanna," Rolt paused for effect, "he's
close to broke."

That just couldn't be true. Lifting her gaze, she said,
"He still has the income from his stock here in the
taconite plant."

"Yes, he has that, but it isn't large enough to maintain his present standard of living. If your mother had
another heart attack, it would probably wipe him out
completely. The house is already mortgaged. And he
was at the bank this past week to apply for a loan, using
his stock here as collateral."

The color drained from her face. The whole dismal
picture, and its repercussions, began to take shape. If
her father received the loan and was unable to make
the payments, the stock would forfeit and his only
source of income as well.

"He wanted to sell the house," Alanna said in a
frozen voice. "That's why he was saying all these things
to my mother. And she wouldn't even consider it."

"At this point, selling the house would only buy him
a little time. He should have done it a year ago," Rolt
stated matter-of-factly, "before he mortgaged it."

"I don't understand." Alanna brushed a bewildered
hand across her forehead and eyes. "How could it have
happened? Without any warning?"

"Your father had plenty of warning," he pointed out
dryly.

"There must be something we can do," she said desperately. "I guess we'll have to sell the house. Mom
won't object once she understands the situation. We'll

move somewhere smaller, cheaper. I can get a job. For that matter, Daddy can probably find something. He's intelligent. He still has his health."

"He's already tried to find work, but it's next to impossible for a man over fifty-five to get hired for an upper-tier management position. Face it, Alanna, he's only been at the top thanks to his father. Even if you leave out the age factor, he simply doesn't have the experience."

"It isn't Dad's fault that he inherited the company," Alanna protested.

"And as for you working," Rolt continued, "are you suggesting that you'll support them for the rest of your life?"

She didn't hesitate. "I don't see why not. They supported me."

"What about marriage?"

"I don't see that that's any of your business."

Rolt shrugged. "It's another factor that you have to consider, that's all. I'm trying to give you the complete picture. Your, ah, future husband might not be so understanding if you decided to take on the responsibility of your parents' debts. Your father owes a lot of money."

"He'll understand." She was thinking of Kurt— strong, wonderful Kurt.

"Do you think so?"

She noticed the ironic tone of his words but didn't let it get to her. "Yes," was all she said.

"Your plans are well meaning, but totally unworkable. You're asking your father to sell his home. He wouldn't make much of a profit and that money has to last. He's in good health but your mother isn't—and it also has to cover medical care."

"I'm aware of that." Her voice was thin and strained.

"They won't be able to afford frills. No country club membership. No traveling. The chances of his being able to find a decent job are virtually nil. He's over-qualified and he's over fifty. Therefore, he would have to sit at home, with nothing to do but wait for you to give him a handout. What about his pride, Alanna? It would break him and in turn it would break your mother."

Her eyes shone with unshed tears. She knew what Rolt said was true but she was reluctant to admit it. Proud, sensitive Dorian Powell, bred to be a gentleman and the provider for his family. It would kill him to take money from her.

Alanna turned away to hide her trembling. "What's your brilliant alternative?"

"I could help."

"He wouldn't accept charity from you," she said tightly.

"There is a way it could be done without him ever being aware of that," Rolt said softly.

"How?" Her breath caught.

"I could arrange an increase in his investment income. And if necessary, I can put him in a public relations position, so he can keep his health insurance. That's going to be their single biggest expense."

"Could you?" Alanna turned around, her hope rising.

His gaze was level and unwavering, indigo dark and hooded. "Yes, I could, I will help him . . . if you're willing to work with me."

Alanna stiffened, motionless for a minute. "And what exactly does that entail?"

"Find out what running a business really means," Rolt said.

"Why would I want to do that? I'm a liberal arts major."

He nodded. "So I heard. But take a guess at your starting salary when you graduate, if you can even find a job."

Alanna gave him a level look. "About twenty-five to
thirty thousand. Just because I'm interested in litera-
ture and the fine arts doesn't mean I can't get a job."

"True enough. You're a good-looking woman and
that doesn't hurt."

She folded her arms across her chest. "Thank you for
that sexist comment. Apparently nothing has changed
in the last thirty years."

He only shrugged. "The salary range you mentioned—well that's before taxes. You won't be able to
help your parents."

"We'll get by," she insisted.

"You could do better than get by someday. Why not
spend the rest of the summer in a management training program? Maybe think about going for an MBA
when you're done. I don't know why more women
don't go into business programs. You strike me as someone who's got what it takes."

"It's impossible," she declared with a violent shake of
her head. "According to you, we're not going to have
enough money to live on. So how can we afford the tu-
ition? And where is this management program being offered? I probably won't be able to finish my last year of
college as it is."

"You don't have to go to college. I'll teach you what
you need to know. Then you can take the real-world experience, plus the credits you already have, and get
your MBA anywhere you like."

"Are you talking about me becoming your assistant?"

"Something like that, yeah."

Alanna got up and paced around the room. She
could feel his intent gaze following her but she avoided
eye contact. "Nice offer, but no thanks. Did I mention
that I'm engaged to your brother? That's going to make
working with you a little . . . difficult."

"When did that happen?"

"Kurt bought me a ring today."

He looked at her left hand. "Where is it?"

"It didn't fit. He's having it resized."

Rolt lifted his glass and downed the rest of his drink. "Engagements are no big deal. That's hardly an obstacle."

She held up both hands. "Back up. I happen to love Kurt. Isn't that an obstacle?"

"Only in your mind," he dismissed it aloofly. "Depends on whether you want to make something of yourself or stay with being daddy's little girl."

"Insulting me doesn't seem like the best negotiating tactic, Rolt."

He grinned. "You get right to the point and you stand your ground. That's part of what makes a good executive."

"You're serious, aren't you?" Alanna asked incredulously.

"I don't think you have a choice, not if you really care about your parents as much as you claim," Rolt said.

"There's always more than one way around a problem." She moved to the huge window, not really noticing the view from it, agitated and uncertain. "Kurt will help me. We can come up with some plan where Father won't guess where the money is coming from."

"Kurt doesn't have that kind of money. He works for a salary and he can't hang onto it. I don't even want to know how much that ring cost."

"Since he didn't tell me, I can honestly say I don't know." She doubted that Rolt's dismissive words about the ring had much to do with its price. No, he was ticked off because Kurt had bought it for her. Had claimed her. *Tough luck, Rolt.*

"In our family, you work your way to the top or you don't make it. It isn't handed to you on a silver platter."

He set the glass on the table, the ice clinking against the sides. "No, Alanna, Kurt can't help you. I can, but he can't."

"I just don't think that getting involved with you in any way is a good idea."

"Got an alternative?"

"I don't like feeling like I have a gun to my head!"

He went back to his spreadsheets but didn't sit down, just rifled through the pages as if he needed something to do. "You don't. Your parents have enough to get by, to use your phrase, for at least a year or two. What I'm talking about is a long-term investment in your future that will benefit you and them. And I can help you with that."

"I don't know." A frustrated sigh broke from her lips. She whirled to face him, her expression angry and resentful. "Isn't there a way you could do it with no strings attached?"

"Did I mention any conditions? I don't think I did," he said blandly.

"No, you didn't. But I can't help thinking that you stand to gain and I stand to lose."

"Good call. You're right on that score, except that you have nothing to lose. I would expect you to work hard. That's all. Sure, I would benefit. I don't generally do things simply out of the goodness of my heart," Rolt murmured wryly. "I want to see you succeed, Alanna."

She knew the appeal was wasted even when she said it. "Did it ever occur to you that if you helped my father without any conditions, I might be so grateful that I would change my opinion of you?"

"It occurred to me," he acknowledged. "But being grateful is for wimps. Being successful is about getting ahead and getting to the point where you don't have to rely on anybody."

She was silent, noticing the coldness in his tone

when he said those last few words and wondering about the emotional pain it hid.

"And that's what I want. That concludes today's lesson in Real Life 101, Ms. Powell. Class dismissed. So are you willing to try?"

Alanna thought she saw a small opening. She looked away so he couldn't see what she was thinking. "But if I agree to be your assistant, will you help my father right now?"

"If you mean offer him a public relations job, the answer is yes." Rolt, closed the opening with mocking emphasis.

"That is what I mean. He has his pride—and he can't know that you gave him a busywork job. But he is good with people, Rolt, and he always has been. This company and the mine could use some positive publicity."

That zinger hit home. She could see it on his face as he struggled to reply calmly. "Just so long as it improves the bottom line. That's what I care about."

His arrogance filled her with rage. She crossed to stand close to him in a few swift steps and he looked up, surprised. He didn't have time to dodge the open palm of her hand when she struck at his complacent face. The needle-sharp sting of contact had barely occurred when he caught her hand in the steel vise of his fingers. The line of his jaw was tight and ominous.

"You still haven't answered me, Alanna. Yes or no?" His voice was deadly quiet.

"Let go of me!"

He did and she stopped struggling, her breathing deep and agitated from anger and frustration. With a defiant toss of her head, she tried to stare him down.

It was a losing battle. His roughly hewn features were very close as his enigmatic gaze studied her. The harsh line of his mouth thinned into a smile. "We're evenly matched. This is going to be interesting."

With lightning speed, she thought over his unexpected proposal once more before she replied. She could make his life so interesting he would beg for mercy. And learn all about corporate strategy while she was at it. The thrill of battle fired up her courage. "I think we are, Rolt. And my answer is yes."

He drew back a little, as if he hadn't expected her to agree. And Alanna advanced.

"Shall we shake on it?" She extended her hand.

He took it—and drew her to him. An embrace was inescapable—and she felt no inclination to slap him this time. Just looking up into his eyes made her resistance dissolve.

His mouth came down on hers. Her willing submission to his kiss evoked a lethal tenderness that destroyed her defenses. Rolt took advantage of the lowered barrier, expertly parting her lips and tasting the full sweetness of her mouth. She melted in his arms, responding to his seductive mastery. His hand had drifted downward to caress her shoulder.

Long and deep, he kissed her, and a languor stole through her body. His mouth explored her eyelids, the sweeping curve of her lashes at the corners, burning her cheek as it moved to her earlobe, and blazed an evocative trail down the soft curve of her neck. An uncontrollable shudder quivered through her—born of desire, she discovered, instead of protest, and the realization rang a bell of alarm.

With a quick wrench, she twisted herself away from the undermining caress of his lips. She stood before him, her hands pushing against his chest to an arm's length away. He held her, not attempting to eliminate the distance between them, nor allowing her to completely break away. Alanna stared into the smoldering blue of his eyes, bewildered by the response a man she disliked had aroused, and angered that it should be so.

"Confused?" Rolt questioned in soft amusement. "Didn't you think this could happen?"

"No," she protested, thinking that she might as well play the innocent. If that was what made him lower his guard, then it was a tactic worth using.

Quiet laughter sounded in his throat. Before she could think of anything to deny the accuracy of his taunting questions, he had closed the distance and was effortlessly sweeping her off her feet and into his arms.

"Put me down!" Alanna gasped in breathless indignation.

Rolt smiled lazily. "You aren't fully convinced yet."

Oblivious to her ineffectual attempts to wriggle free, he carried her to the sofa. Alanna found herself sitting on his lap—and she liked being there. His sensual kisses once again staked ownership of her lips. Her hands stroked his chest. One slipped inside his shirt, encountering the burning heat of his skin. Fire seared through her veins at the disturbing contact, and whatever resistance she had left melted. Her will seemed to have no control over the responses of her flesh.

His fingers closed around the knot of the scarf around her throat, tugged it loose and stripped it away, exposing the full length of her slender neck for his exploration. His weight pressed her backward as he investigated the ridge of her collarbone and the hollow of her throat.

The sensuous storming of her body and mind seemed without end and a traitorous part of her didn't want it to stop. A hand moved over her waist and hip in a stimulating caress. Unfastening her blouse, he slid a hand beneath the silky material.

Through the haze of erotic sensations came a thought of another man: Kurt. The man she was going to marry. She realized with a flash of pain how afraid she was—not of Kurt or of Rolt but of her own uncertain future and that of her parents. Why else would she let his brother make love to her this way? It was not only her own pride and self-respect she was betraying, but Kurt as well.

As the warm touch of Rolt's mouth moved over the rounded swell of her breast, Alanna nearly lost her newly regained sense of self in the overwhelming fire of his embrace. With a last, determined effort, she rolled free of his arms and stood beside the sofa. Her shaking legs couldn't get her any farther.

Rolt held her gaze with mesmerizing ease. He sat there, his legs stretched over the cushions, his back resting against an arm of the sofa. Alanna stood above him, yet he was in command. Leisurely his hand reached out, curving around the back of her knee, stroking the sensitive skin absently. A jolting quiver of awareness trembled through her.

"Please don't do this, Rolt," Alanna whispered, completely unnerved by the overpowering physical attraction he held for her.

Putting his feet on the floor, Rolt straightened, his hand gliding upward, briefly catching the hem of her skirt to reveal the initial curve of her thigh before the material folds hung straight once more. When he towered above her, his hand rested on her waist. Her nerve ends throbbed at his closeness. She pivoted sharply, knowing she had to get away.

But his hands gripped her waist, drawing her shoulders against his chest. He buried his face in the soft tawny curls about her neck. Alanna closed her eyes against a heady sensation of desire. His hands slid across her stomach, molding her against the hardness of his frame. Her fingers pushed weakly at his hands.

"No," she protested huskily. "This is crazy. It's only a physical . . . an animal attraction."

"What's wrong with that, Alanna?" he murmured against the sensitive cord in her neck, "I'm looking forward to our first all-nighter."

"Nothing doing. We can't fool around. Everyone in the company will talk," she breathed.

"Let them."

"No, Rolt." But she knew he'd found her weakness— his brand of sensuality was well nigh irresistible to her. Strong. Masterful. No holds barred.

No matter how much she wanted him, she hated the idea of surrendering so soon. The arrangement he'd proposed would never work if they were going to jump into bed. Love had nothing to do with it. She couldn't name the feelings he evoked in her but they were intense, she knew that much.

"Okay, maybe we shouldn't be doing this." Rolt nibbled at her ear when she twisted her neck away from the disturbing exploration of his mouth. "We'll go over the spreadsheets and you can see what I'm up against."

"No, no, no. Business and pleasure don't go together." Alanna sighed in confusion. She couldn't think straight, not when he was holding and caressing her the way he was.

"You're right. I'd much rather be doing this." Exerting the slightest pressure, he turned her into his arms. Like a feather caught in a whirling wind, Alanna had no ability to dictate her own direction. She let herself be drawn into the vortex of his deepening kiss, her hands clinging to his hard shoulders to keep some measure of equilibrium.

When he finally lifted his head, she could see the light of victory glittering in his eyes. Not by word but by deed, she had involuntarily given him the upper hand.

But she intended to get it back. She intended to follow his so-called management training course to the letter and beat him at his own damn game.

If only she could control her responses to Rolt's kisses. Just being in the same room with him did something dangerous to her thought processes. She didn't want to choose between Kurt and Rolt, especially when she was going to get in major trouble no matter which brother she chose. She didn't want them both—that just wasn't possible. Good brother, bad brother. And one very confused woman. Tune in at four. Her life was turning into an afternoon talk show.

Wrenching her gaze away from his, she broke free of his loose hold and stepped past him. She squared her shoulders, preparing to take back her agreement. She couldn't possibly be his assistant—Rolt Matthews was pure temptation and she didn't have what it took to resist him.

As she lifted her head, she stared directly into Kurt's face, cold with contempt. Paralyzed by the sight of him standing in the opened doorway, she was barely aware of Rolt coming to her side and sliding a supporting arm around her waist.

Kurt's gaze raked her from head to foot, lingering on the gaping front of her blouse. Instinctively her hand reached up to cover it, a fiery warmth of shame burning her cheeks. It wasn't the only part of her disheveled appearance that bore signs of Rolt's lovemaking. She wanted to curl up in a little ball and die.

"Oh, hell, Kurt," Rolt said quietly. "Don't you ever knock?"

"No. Didn't know I had to, but I guess that's changed." Kurt's condemning gaze moved to Alanna's face. "A family thing, you said." He bitterly reminded her of the reason she had given for being unable to see him tonight. "I never guessed you meant my own brother."

"Kurt, please." Alanna swallowed back a sob. "I—"

He broke in, not allowing her to finish. "Why didn't you just tell me you were attracted to Rolt? I would have been jealous as hell, but I would have understood."

"No, you don't," she protested. "He said—things happened a little too fast—look, this is as much my fault as it is his. There are a lot of things you don't know, Kurt."

"Spare me the details," he said. "Is that little speech supposed to make me feel better? At least it doesn't sound like you rehearsed it. You're spontaneous, I'll give you that. But not sincere. Not by a long shot."

"Stop it!" she cried. His barbs had enough truth to them to hurt.

Kurt's gaze slashed to Rolt. "Tell me, older brother— are congratulations in order, or should I say condolences?"

"Couldn't say. You wouldn't believe a word anyway," Rolt said.

Alanna breathed in sharply. "Would it make any difference if I said I was sorry?" She didn't dare tell Kurt that she had been about to tell Rolt that she couldn't be his assistant, not when he had nearly seen them in a passionate clinch. True though it was, it didn't sound true. It sounded self-serving and bitchy and faithless. Guilty on all counts, she thought miserably.

"Sorry for what? That I found out? Don't say that the devil made you do it. You didn't seem exactly unwilling, Alanna, not when I opened the door. I doubt if you ever were," he accused tightly. "And to think I trusted you."

"I really am sorry!" Her voice lacked conviction. Kurt wasn't stupid and they had been almost caught in the act.

"If you haven't gotten around to buying the lady"— sarcasm underlined the word—"a ring, I have one for sale cheap. It's been tried on once and guaranteed to fit. There's no sense both of us wasting our money on her."

Alanna flinched visibly at the bitter scorn in his voice. Acid tears burned her eyes, but she had no right to cry. She knew that she deserved part of Kurt's obvious disgust. "Don't, Kurt, please," she murmured in a trembling voice.

"I'll leave." His mouth twisted sardonically, his handsome features suddenly bearing a stronger resemblance to his older brother's. "I can guess how anxious you must be to go back into his arms."

His gaze slid pointedly to the masculine hand resting possessively on the curve of her waist. Alanna hadn't been conscious of its silent support until that moment. As she moved forward to elude it, Kurt turned to leave.

"No, Kurt, wait!" She hurried after him. "Let me explain, please!"

He stopped, turning slightly. The icy disdain in his blue eyes checked the hand she held extended to touch him, freezing it in midair.

"Explain what?" he demanded coldly. "That you're a liar and a cheat? I know that already. You and my brother deserve each other."

Alanna recoiled as if he had slapped her. The words died in her throat. She stared at the floor, listening to Kurt's footsteps as he walked away. When not even their echo could be heard, she turned. She felt frozen and knew it was shock that numbed her.

Rolt was still standing beside the sofa. His alert gaze was watching her, yet not betraying a flicker of his thoughts. She lifted her chin a fraction, wide, pain-filled eyes meeting his look.

"You didn't ask him to come here tonight, did you?" By this point she was ready to believe the worst.

"What do you take me for? No, I didn't."

"Good." There was a slight break in her bland voice.

"How is it good? I feel like hell, Alanna. I want you so much that I hurt my brother. He's not a bad guy—I mean, he's not the right guy for you, but I never intended him to walk in on us like that."

"Guess what," she said lightly. "You get to explain our arrangement to him."

Rolt gave her a cynical smile. "Right. That I selected you to be my assistant. I can just hear what Kurt's going to say: Donald Trump, move over."

"I think that . . ." She let the sentence trail off, unwilling to admit what should have been obvious to her from the start. She didn't want to marry Kurt—she knew he wasn't the one, though she felt awful about what he'd seen. She would never have willingly hurt him so. But the fact remained that her impulsivity—and her sexual attraction to his brother—had made her act like someone who didn't know what the hell she wanted.

And she'd just figured that out, in a big, blinding flash: she wanted security. Her parents weren't going to be able to provide it, and her peaceful little world had just been blown wide open. As Rolt had said, that meant getting to the point where she didn't have to rely on anybody but herself.

"I still want to go through with—" she hesitated "—our arrangement. Obviously there are going to have to be some ground rules. Like we are not, repeat not, going to fool around."

"Anything else?"

"Give me time to think." She walked to him, standing motionless as he gazed down at her. "I've got a lot on my mind all of a sudden."

Rolt merely nodded. "I'll keep my word about helping your father."

"You don't have a choice about that," Alanna warned him coldly. "And you also get to tell him that he's going to head up the public relations department."

Rolt looked at her for a long moment, then turned away. He didn't seem at all concerned about her emotional withdrawal. "Okay. Button up. Let's go tell your mom and dad the big news."

Chapter Six

The black SUV followed Alanna's car like an ominous dark shadow. Alanna wouldn't let herself think about what she'd done. There would be time enough for regrets and self-recrimination later. With her mind blank, mechanical reflexes guided her car into the driveway. Rolt was only seconds behind her.

Alanna stood beside her car, waiting for him to join her before entering the house. As he walked toward her with effortless, long strides, his strong features were thrown into sharp relief by the angle of light from the setting sun.

Suddenly she could feel the hard length of his body molded against hers and the betraying arousal of her senses in response. With a brief shake of her head, she chased the unnerving sensation away. This physical attraction was the one thing she had to guard against at all costs.

"Shall we go in?" She anticipated his yes, and turned toward the house.

"In a minute." His hand gripped her elbow to detain her, but immediately she jerked it free. "You're right. I can't do that when we're inside, Alanna," Rolt reminded her mockingly. "This relationship is all about business. Isn't that what you want your parents to believe?"

"Yes," she said icily. "And I don't think Kurt will tell them anything different. He's going to be too humiliated to show his face for a while."

"You and I are both to blame for that," Rolt said flatly. Alanna only nodded and started again toward the house.

This time he followed a step behind. When his arm reached around her for the doorknob, Alanna paused, waiting for him to open the door. Instead she found herself suddenly trapped between Rolt and the door. She looked up to remind him scathingly to behave, but the words never had a chance to leave her lips.

With the graceful and deadly accurate swoop of an eagle, his mouth closed over hers. For a fleeting second Alanna was immobilized by searing surprise. When she would have twisted away from his hard kiss, he was already releasing her. It was a good thing the door was made of solid wood, with no windows for her parents to see what he'd done.

But she was so angry at herself for being caught unaware—and at him for taking advantage of it—that she couldn't speak.

The door opened under his hand. "We can go in now." He smiled arrogantly down at her and added, "Now that there's a sparkle in your eye and a really nice blush on your cheeks. We can't meet your parents with you looking like you're about to face a firing squad."

"Why does working for you suddenly seem like the worst idea I ever had?" she hissed.

His muted laughter heightened the pink in her cheeks as he followed her into the house. For all intents and purposes, he was in charge and that didn't ease her anger. She had to put on an act for her parents. She didn't want them suspecting that she had any motive other than her own future if she went to work for Rolt.

As they entered the living room, her father folded up the newspaper and rose to meet them, slipping his reading glasses into his shirt pocket.

"Hello, Rolt. Elinore said she thought it was your car that drove in behind Alanna," her father said with a smile of welcome. "Is it business or pleasure, I hope, that brings you here tonight?"

"Both," Rolt replied.

Watch it, Alanna thought. She couldn't help worrying that he would do something he shouldn't. She looked his way, silently telling him to mind his Ps and Qs. Her heart turned over at the unbelievable warmth shining in his eyes. She simply couldn't look away.

Careful, that inner voice warned, *don't be taken in by his charm. Remember why you agreed to work for him. Think of yourself first. And your parents.* Rolt Matthews came in a distant third, Alanna thought.

It was with an effort that she tore her gaze away from Rolt. A self-conscious feeling made her avoid her father's puzzled look at her and glance swiftly at her mother sitting on the couch. Elinore was eyeing the two of them with an expectant gleam.

"We came by to tell you that Alanna's decided to take me up on my offer."

"What offer?" Her mother looked from him to her daughter. "Is there something I don't know?"

That innocent remark made Alanna wince. Rolt saw it and covered for both of them.

"I think she's got what it takes to succeed in business," Rolt said simply. "She's highly intelligent, thinks quickly, and I have a feeling she can run circles around me or any other executive in the mining industry. So I asked her if she wanted to be my assistant," Rolt said. "I assume that's all right with you."

He got right to the point, Alanna thought miserably. Then again, he'd complimented her on that very quality.

"Oh," her mother said with some surprise. "I was wondering why she was with you and not Kurt."

Rolt's smile looked a little forced. "Well, the decision didn't really have anything to do with Kurt."

"I see. You mean it's Alanna's decision, of course. If that's what she wants to do, it's all right with us, isn't it, Dorian?" the older woman said. "But please sit down, you two, and tell us more."

Her mother was unfailingly polite, but Alanna knew Rolt didn't care whether her parents approved of their arrangement or not. And she knew she was going to work for him with or without their permission.

Dorian was momentarily stunned by the news, but not her mother. "If you won't sit down, then I'll have to drag you over here. I want details." She rose from the couch, her face wreathed in a smile as she took Alanna by the hand and they sat down together.

"Is this just a summer thing?" Elinore asked.

"For now. We might extend our, ah, arrangement into the fall."

Her mother looked alarmed. "You are going to finish college, I hope."

"Yes, of course, Mom. But Rolt and I were discussing other options, including my getting an MBA."

"Really?" Elinore glanced up at Rolt, who remained standing, as did Dorian.

"The idea intrigued me. I don't think I could get very far in today's job market with just a liberal arts degree."

Her father scowled and Alanna regretted her comment. He had a liberal arts degree. From an Ivy League college, of course.

"How exciting, honey. Learning by doing is really the

best way to master anything. I think that's a great idea," Elinore exclaimed. "And you know something, it doesn't really surprise me."

"Oh?" Alanna wondered if her father was going to say anything. He might not like the idea of her outranking or outearning him someday, but that was just too bad. She wouldn't have taken Rolt Matthews up on what was essentially a dare if she hadn't intended to succeed.

"What with the mine and the affiliated company being the biggest employer in town, I thought you might work there someday," her mother said.

"Good guess, Mrs. Powell," Rolt said, smiling. "Alanna isn't the only female in the family with a knack for business."

Alanna cringed, noticing the unhappy look in her father's eyes. She hoped her ambition didn't make him feel over the hill or not up to the mark or whatever it was he was feeling. Rolt would have to tell him about the public relations position, but Alanna wasn't sure how much that would cheer him up.

"Oh, now . . ." Her mother stepped back, holding on to Alanna's hands as she smiled happily from one to the other. "Call it a mother's instinct or female intuition, but I just knew all along that Alanna was going places."

"Of course she is," Dorian spoke at last. Then he laughed, still with a trace of bewilderment, at the unexpected turn of events. "She's my daughter, too, you know."

The thoughtful look in Rolt's eyes kept Alanna from saying anything more for another moment. When her father turned to speak to her mother, Alanna mouthed a question at Rolt. *Are you going to tell him about the PR job?*

He replied with a single unspoken word. *Later.*

"You know, Elinore," her father chuckled, "for such a

petite thing, you have a very strong personality. Always have had it. But I didn't mind being bossed around by you. Alanna is like her mother in many ways," he said to Rolt.

"Daddy, you're going to have Rolt thinking he's made a mistake," she said with a forced laugh.

"You mean I haven't?" Rolt's voice was a stage whisper that everyone could hear.

She would have loved to scratch his eyes out at that moment. He was enjoying this situation tremendously and all at her expense.

"Of course not," her father rejoined with a loving smile at his daughter. "Now, Elinore, this means we're going to be seeing a lot of the Matthews boys. Better find out what they like to eat."

"Well, no," Alanna said, throwing a save-me look at Rolt. He smiled at her serenely. She was on her own. "Actually, Kurt and I decided to—we decided to just chill out for a while. You know, see other people."

"Oh!" Her mother seemed quite startled by that announcement and Alanna couldn't blame her. She braced herself for the inevitable question. "What other people, honey?"

"No one in particular," Alanna mumbled, not looking directly at Rolt.

"Well, I shouldn't ask nosy questions," her mother murmured in sudden remorse. "But I did think that Kurt was very fond of you, Alanna."

"Yes, Mom, I know." The pain in her voice was genuine.

"I saw him tonight," Rolt said, not explaining the circumstances. "He was doing okay. It'll work out for the best."

"Yes," her mother agreed. "But I tell you, that's one reason I wouldn't want to be young again. All that breaking up and making up. Life is a lot easier when you settle down."

Her father nodded. "It happens. Best to realize that things aren't working and be honest about it. A little pain now is better than a lot of pain later." Sensitive as he always was, he recognized that the conversation made Alanna uncomfortable without knowing the true reason. "But there isn't any need to discuss that. Elinore, maybe you could check to see if there's any coffee left and some of that delicious cake Ruth made. And tell Ruth the news, too."

"I certainly will," Elinore agreed enthusiastically. "When Alanna is ready to rule the world, I'll pass my scepter on to her."

"In due course, my dear," Dorian laughed. "In due course."

She shifted way over on the sofa when Rolt sat down beside her. He didn't exactly sit close, but his arm was draped along the back to let his hand rest near her shoulder. A small liberty, but she slid him a resentful glance from beneath her lashes just the same.

Her father turned to them as her mother left the room. "Elinore has her heart set on Alanna getting her degree, you two," he said affectionately and with a hint of apology. "Graduation—and then grandchildren."

"One thing at a time, Dad," Alanna said tightly.

He didn't seem to hear. "She always wanted a houseful of children, but unfortunately she wasn't able to have them. We consider ourselves blessed that we have you, Alanna. So don't you be worried about disappointing your mother because you want to jumpstart your career."

"Actually, Dad, I haven't thought about that too much," she said nervously. "No plans for marriage at the moment, no plans for children."

"Hey, kids are great," Rolt said affably. "I plan on having several someday."

Alanna wanted desperately to change the subject. And she wanted his hand off the back of the sofa, as far away as possible from her shoulder. Something about his nearness made her feel weak and vulnerable, especially combined with the topic of conversation, and she steeled herself to ignore it.

The tall, spare housekeeper swept into the room, her angular face looking happy. Alanna could have cried with relief. Amidst the hugs, congratulations, and explanations, the subject of children was lost.

"I hear we're going to have you around through the summer and then some," Ruth declared. "That's good news right there. And she'll do you proud, Mr. Matthews. I've known Alanna since she was a baby."

Her mother entered the room with a tray of coffee and cakes, and Ruth rushed quickly to take it from her. "I told you to leave that, Elly. It's too heavy for you."

"Nonsense," her mother said. "I only have a few feet to go anyway. You just sit back down."

Ruth did, insisting she would pour. The spout of the pot was poised above the first cup when she put it back on the tray. "Just think, Elly, you get to take her shopping." She glanced at Alanna. "When is your first day? You can't be a corporate cutie without the right clothes."

Alanna was about to say that she had no intention of being a corporate cutie, but she never had a chance to speak.

"Right away," Rolt answered. "Smart as she is, she's got a lot to learn."

She turned to glare at him and deny his statement. His fingers dug into her shoulder in warning. They hadn't discussed her first day but she hadn't dreamed it would be that soon. Of course, what difference did it really make?

"June!" Elinore exclaimed. "But there's less than ten days left of this month. Summer goes by so fast. Just promise me, honey, that you'll stay through the fall. We can arrange for you to withdraw without losing credit and you can plan to enter an MBA program when you're ready to do that. I guess Rolt will be advising you on that."

"I think Alanna would rather make up her own mind, Mrs. Powell," Rolt said gently.

Alanna couldn't agree more.

"Of course, she'll be working with other executives as well," he added.

She managed a wan smile. It actually was a relief to learn that she wouldn't be forced to spend an extended length of time exclusively in his company.

"Isn't that nice," Ruth said somewhat absent-mindedly, picking up the coffeepot. "My, this feels empty." She lifted the lid and peered inside. "Yep. Not a drop left. I'll go and make another pot."

"Please, none for me," Rolt said, removing his arm from the back of the sofa. "It's time I was leaving."

"Not so soon," her mother protested,

"Yes," he insisted, straightening to his feet.

He said good-bye to each of them in turn and started from the room. Alanna remained seated until she felt the expectant looks from her parents and realized they thought she would want to accompany him to the door. With gritted teeth, she rose quickly.

"I'll see you to the door, Rolt," she called after him.

He halted in the doorway to the hall and waited until she had joined him, out of sight and out of earshot of her parents and Ruth. "Hey, there," he said. His hand cupped the side of her face. "It's been a hectic evening, all things considered. Have an early night and I'll see you tomorrow."

"Tomorrow?"

"Yeah. You don't need to wear a cute little suit. Just something conservative."

"We wouldn't want to give anyone the wrong idea, now would we?"

"Of course not," he grinned. She knew he intended to kiss her. There was nothing she could do to stop him. No one could see. That was the way Rolt had planned it—the glint in his eyes told her so.

His mouth closed warmly over hers. She kept her lips cool and unresponsive. She would show him that just because she had been a fool for him once—no, twice if she counted the time on the patio—it wasn't going to always be true. In fact, she was determined it would never happen again.

When he lifted his head, her eyes glittered triumphantly. *How do you like kissing an ice cube, Rolt?* His mouth twisted in dry amusement.

"You can do better than that," he murmured. "But I'll wait for another time to prove it to you."

She smiled sweetly. "You're in for a long wait."

His thumb rubbed the corner of her mouth for a second, then he released her. "You have to get up bright and early. Sleep well."

She knew she wouldn't.

Chapter Seven

Two months of following Rolt Matthews around, learning everything there was to know about mining, about metals, and about running a multimillion-dollar business had made Alanna thoroughly sick of it. Being an assistant to a hard-driving CEO had its perks: an expense account, flying on a share-time corporate jet wherever and whenever Rolt wanted to go, and box seats for the NHL playoffs. She'd given those to Rolt's secretary, not caring to watch hockey players high-stick each other in the teeth.

But when all was said and done, she was basically too tired to enjoy the rest of her life. Flying in a private jet was a thrill the first time, even the second, but not the third. Rolt concentrated on his endless paperwork and she had quite frankly lost interest in the idea of getting an MBA. Alanna was a whiz at getting through the spreadsheets and filling him in on the information he needed, but it was definitely not what she wanted to do for the rest of her life.

There was some good news on the home front—her mother's new medication seemed to be really helping her heart and Elinore was even thinking of returning to work. Over Dorian protests, of course. But her mom was quick to point to Alanna as her inspiration and he couldn't very well argue with his daughter's success.

Her dad was actually enjoying his move into public relations, something Alanna had hoped would happen. Her parents weren't out of the woods, financially speaking, but the immediate crisis had passed, and her worries about them were no longer at the forefront of her mind.

She longed for the good old days of studying Victorian novelists and English poets. That time of her life seemed impossibly leisurely to her now, a golden idyll that had ended too soon. Alanna knew she was romanticizing her college experience, but there had to be more to the life than the bottom line and a passion for profit.

In fact, if she had to name one thing she was really missing, it was passion. Rebuffed more than once by her, Rolt kept his distance and their relationship was coolly professional. Yet he claimed most of her time. The constant contact kept her in a state of unsatisfied frustration. The fact that she didn't want to become involved with him didn't make him any less sexually attractive.

But Alanna had insisted on her first day of work that he leave her strictly alone. Being male—no, being Rolt, she silently corrected herself—he had tried to get close to her a few more times. Then he'd obeyed her order. She hadn't even had to mention newsworthy cases of sexual harassment, because he no longer seemed interested.

She was sitting next to him in the SUV, looking over a report from a subsidiary on her laptop and updating him on its principal points. He drove into the night, listening intently as he always did. Rolt was all business. All the time. They were going to spend the weekend at

one of his houses, breaking down profit and loss state-
ments and figuring out where money could be saved.

Had he suggested spending the weekend at a hotel,
Alanna would have refused. A hotel room was dominated by the bed. In a house, there were other rooms.
Of course, she would have been assigned to her own
room, but even a corporate suite would have seemed
too intimate a place to work with him.

Tall pines overshadowed the lane leading to his
house. They grew so close to the road that it was nearly
like driving through a tunnel. She glimpsed the roof
first, in a lit-up clearing just below the crest of a hill. No
doubt the caretaker had left everything in readiness for
Rolt's arrival.

The house was built of unfinished cedar, rustic and
rambling, blending naturally with its forest surroundings. Homey, Alanna admitted, in spite of the fact that it
belonged to Rolt, who never stayed anywhere long
enough to call one place home.

He pulled into the driveway, stopped the car, and
walked around to open her door.

"My suitcases," she reminded him as he walked toward the wooden steps leading to the front door. She
got an odd thrill out of ordering him around sometimes, half-wishing he would fire her for insubordina-
tion. He seemed not to notice.

"I'll bring them in later." He unlocked the door and
waited on the wide, rustic porch for her to join him.
When she would have walked past him, his hand stopped
her. "There is an old custom about carrying your personal assistant across the threshold, you know."

"Very funny. I believe that only applies to personal as-
sistants who sleep with their bosses."

"Let's pretend." He swept her up in his arms and she
gasped, too surprised to say anything.

Her first impulse was to object, but she stifled it and

let his strong arms cradle her against his chest. Her pulse stirred for an instant at the hard contact with his muscular flesh, but she kept her grip on her icy composure. Rolt nudged the door open with his foot and carried her into the house.

"The custom has been observed. You may put me down now," Alanna said with chilling calmness.

His face was very close to hers, his gaze steady and unreadable. She could make out every detail from the faint, sun-weathered lines at the corners of his eyes to the harsh grooves carved near his mouth. For several long seconds, he held her. A peculiar tension vibrated along her taut nerves.

The arm under her knees relaxed, letting her legs slide to the carpeted floor. The other arm tightened its hold, flattening her breasts against the granite wall of his chest. She held herself rigid, neither struggling nor submitting.

Rolt tipped her chin upward. "Mind if I—"

She amazed herself by not saying no, or pushing him away. His mouth descended on hers with slow insistence. Controlled passion edged the possession. Alanna blocked out the hard strength of his arms and concentrated her thoughts on Kurt, the man she should have married, the man she would have married. It helped her ignore the persuasive pressure of his kiss.

There was a tightness to the line of his jaw when he raised his head. "Do you want me to kiss you or not?" For all the coolness of his voice, his eyes were chips of fiery blue.

"I don't know," she replied. Resisting his charm probably annoyed him more than anything she could say. And in truth, she didn't know. But the long weeks of punishing work had gotten to her. Alanna was feeling almost irrational.

His arm tightened for a second, then let her go. She

stepped away from him, aware of a faint quiver in her knees, but she had successfully repelled his kiss. So much for keeping her sanity and her distance. Coming here with him was probably the quickest way to lose both.

Ignoring Rolt, she glanced about the room. Smooth cedar paneled the walls, punctuated by large windows with a fireplace of large sand-colored stone. The carpet of cream beige was luxuriously thick, its rough texture in keeping with the style of the home. A long sofa was in front of the fireplace, covered in a rich brown velvet, and flanking the sofa were matching loveseats in a cream and brown plaid. The beamed ceiling concealed indirect lighting, left on, she was sure, by the caretaker.

A wide hallway allowed her a glimpse of the dining room with windows running the length of one wall. The planks and railings of a sun deck were visible through the panes. Rolt, who had been standing some distance behind her, moved a little closer. Alanna turned, as if she had forgotten his presence, which was an impossibility. The look in his eyes invited a comment about the house.

"It's very nice," she said indifferently.

"I'll show you around."

Without waiting to see if she wanted to, Rolt walked past her into the wide hallway. Faking a lack of interest, Alanna followed. He gestured toward an open door leading off the hall, one she hadn't noticed.

"The study, where I sometimes work in the evenings," he said, and continued into the dining room.

Alanna looked in briefly, and had the impression of a warm, dark cave, lined with books and dark leather furniture and the same pale beige carpet.

"The dining room, and beyond it the sun deck." Ochres and bronzed golds brightened the room and she could just see a breathtaking view of the lake at the bottom of the hill, sparkling in the moonlight. "The kitchen is through there." His hand waved toward a wide arch and the natural wood of the cupboards that could partially be seen. Alanna glanced around at the kitchen filled with expensive, state-of-the-art appliances in a setting that was decidedly homespun. She followed when Rolt returned to the hall and the open L-shaped staircase leading to the second floor.

At the top of the stairs, another wide hall encircled the open stairwell, protected by a smoothly finished cedar railing to match the paneled walls. Three doors branched off from the hall, two on the front side of the house and one on the lake side.

"The bedrooms," Rolt said.

She shrugged. "Obviously."

"The two on the other side are the guest rooms and this is the main bedroom." He opened the door to the main bedroom as she had expected he would.

A king-size bed dominated the spacious room, a spread of shimmering brown velvet covering it. Windows flanked the bed, parted squares running nearly floor to ceiling. Again there was a panoramic view of the tree-lined lake, glittering mirror-smooth in the distance.

"Very nice."

"There's a walk-in closet behind that door." Rolt gestured toward the left. "And the private bathroom is on the right side. You can look around while I bring your suitcases up."

Alanna looked at the doors he had indicated, but didn't investigate. Nor did she make any remark about the suitcases. She didn't move until she heard Rolt at the bottom of the stairs. Then she walked into the hallway and around the stairwell to the other bedrooms. Both were small, at least by the standard of the master bedroom, and tastefully furnished.

When she heard Rolt reenter the house, she walked

quickly back to the master bedroom. Setting her two suitcases near the bed, he straightened, giving her a long, level look as if trying to measure her mood.

Alanna turned around to face the window, wanting to take no chances that he might read what was on her mind.

"If you'll excuse me"—his voice had an edge to it—"I'm going to change."

"Into something more comfortable?" she inquired acidly.

"Exactly." His mouth quirked. "I don't generally sit around the house in a suit and tie. And I'm tired. You probably are too. We've been going all day."

Alanna didn't move from the window as he entered the walk-in closet. Minutes later he emerged. Her heartbeat quickened in alarm.

"Don't worry," his voice laughed silently at her frozen position. "It's safe to turn around. Even if I am a handsome devil."

"Oh, please." With a defiant toss of her head, Alanna glanced over her shoulder, bracing herself only to find there was no need. Rolt was wearing a pair of beat-up jeans and an old blue shirt. Amusement glittered in his eyes as he noted the relief that flashed across her face.

"While you unpack, I'm going to wash the wedding decorations off the car. Just kidding."

She didn't laugh. Being here with him, alone in one of several houses he owned, did feel a little like what she thought being on a honeymoon would be like.

With a brief nod, he left again. For the second time, Alanna waited until he was at the bottom of the stairs. Then she picked up both suitcases and carried them across the hall to one of the spare bedrooms. Opening the suitcases, she began unpacking her clothes and putting them away.

The first suitcase was empty and the second one had

only a few items left in it when she heard the front door open and close. She paused for several seconds, straining to hear the sounds of Rolt's footsteps on the thick carpet. She heard him on the stairs and stiffened for an instant, nibbling apprehensively at her lower lip as he reached the top.

The door to the spare room where Alanna stood was ajar. She knew that when Rolt didn't find her in the master bedroom, he would notice it. A second later he was in the hall. Quickly she got busy buttoning a blouse on a padded hanger. Although her back was to the door, and the carpet muffled his footsteps, she knew the very instant he entered the room as prickles ran along the back of her neck.

"What are you doing in here?" As if he hadn't already guessed.

"Unpacking," Alanna made a show of making certain the blouse hung straight, the collar smooth.

"The master bedroom is across the hall," Rolt said very calmly, making it sound as if he thought she wasn't already acquainted with the fact.

"I prefer this one," she responded airily, and walked to the closet to hang the blouse with the other clothes she had put there.

"Is that right?" he asked, his voice dry and low.

Returning to the suitcase, Alanna was forced to let her gaze at least ricochet off his. His expression was grim, making her think for a second that he would pull her clothes out of the closet and carry them into the master bedroom. But she couldn't back down and she wouldn't.

"Do you have any objections?" She kept the air of unconcern in her voice as she took another blouse from the case and began draping it around a hanger. The tension in the air was now electrically charged.

"Yes," he responded. Then his tone visibly relaxed. "But we'll discuss them in detail later."

He left the room. She noticed, chalking it up to her odd mood, that his absence made her almost as nervous as his presence. She sat weakly on the bed, the blouse rumpled in her lap. It hadn't been exactly a battle, just another small skirmish. She could only cross her fingers and hope that her luck would hold.

Just keep telling yourself that you don't want him.

Half an hour later, her clothes were all put away and she had changed out of the navy-blue suit she usually wore when they traveled into a scarlet pantsuit. The wide flared legs swirled about her ankles and the draping neckline of the tunic top accented her slender throat.

Alanna stood in front of the mirror, idly flipping the ends of her hair with a brush. She couldn't spend the rest of the evening in the bedroom, and there was no longer any reason to stay. With a sigh, she placed the hairbrush on the dresser top and walked into the hall. There hadn't been a sound from downstairs. She had no idea if Rolt was in the house.

At the bottom of the stairs, she saw him out on the deck. One foot was on the lower railing running around the edge. An elbow rested on the upper railing as he gazed down the hill at the lake. Alanna debated whether to join him or to wait in the living room for him to come in search of her.

She was about to decide on the living room, feeling it might not be wise to take the battle to the enemy. She still had to shore up her defenses. If ever they were going to connect, she had an uncanny feeling that tonight was the night.

At that moment, Rolt straightened and turned, looking directly at her, evidently able to see through the window as clearly as she could. "The view of the lake is excellent from here," he said.

Startled at the clearness of his voice when he was outside and she was in, it took Alanna a full second to realize that the door to the deck was open. She hesitated another second before walking his way.

Rolt leaned against the railing and waited. The disturbing intensity of his gaze nearly made her turn around and go back into the house. She wasn't afraid, she reminded herself, and kept walking steadily to the rail stopping two feet to his left.

The lake was what he had invited her to see, so that was what she looked at. The deck was elevated above the slope of the hill. The trees at the top of the hill had been trimmed to keep the view from being obstructed and still leave foliage on the hillside.

"All settled in?" His voice was pleasantly low. She liked him a lot better when he wasn't being a corporate commando, she realized.

"Yup," she said, adding coolly, "that is quite a view."

"Glad you like it," Rolt answered.

"Isn't it inconvenient to have a country house, though, especially in winter when the roads are bad and blocked with snow?" Alanna needed to keep the conversation going. For some reason, she couldn't tolerate silence between them, not while they were contemplating this serenely beautiful view. She seized on the first thought that came to mind.

"Sometimes," Rolt acknowledged. "But after the noise of the plant, and just living in the fast lane in general, I like the peace and quiet here. No neighbors to trouble you—human neighbors, that is. Just coyotes and squirrels and loons."

No neighbors, Alanna thought, none that she could run to, whatever the reason. The thought made an odd sensation run up her spine. She was all alone out here with Rolt. She couldn't help wondering how long the sleeping giant of Mesabi would continue to sleep.

"Alanna."

She jumped at the sound of her name. She tried to conceal it by turning to face him, but she saw the flick of his eyebrow that said he had seen.

"There was something I wanted to ask you," Rolt said.

"What's that?" She brushed a stray curl from her cheek, searching her mind for any question he might want to ask and coming up blank.

"Were you planning to cook tonight's dinner or should I?"

She was tempted to say that she wasn't very hungry. The fact was her stomach felt suddenly very empty at the mention of dinner.

"I will," she said, glad to have something to do that would take her out of Rolt's company.

Chapter Eight

After that first night had passed without incident, they'd gotten up early to work straight through until six in the evening. The sun lingered with infuriating stubbornness before finally sinking behind the western horizon to end the long Indian summer day. Twilight challenged the encroaching darkness for a brief time, then fled after the sun.

Its departure was Alanna's signal to exit. With a pretense at casualness, she closed the uninteresting magazine and tossed it on the seat cushion beside her. The action attracted Rolt's gaze. They had barely exchanged a word for at least an hour.

The threatened discussion of his objections to the sleeping arrangements hadn't taken place. Alanna guessed that he'd skipped it last night out of consideration for her tiredness. Even now it seemed that he didn't intend the discussion to take place in the living room. She was certain he had another room in mind. Rising from the sofa, she flicked him a deliberately cool glance.

"Good night, Rolt," she said in an offhand way, and walked toward the staircase in the hall.

"Turning in so early?" His response was dry with mockery.

Alanna paused on the first step, her hand resting on the newel post.

"It's been a long day," she answered diffidently.

He didn't wish her a good night, an omission that she thought about as she went up the stairs. It served to stiffen her resolve. Inside her room, she locked the door. Then, to be on the safe side, she walked over to the long dresser and noted that it had wheels on the bottom. She rolled it around a little to make sure she could move it unaided. Just in case she needed to push it in front of the door, she thought, telling herself that she wasn't paranoid, only practical.

Feeling a little more secure, she glanced around the room, her gaze stopping on the bathroom door. The two guests shared the same bath. Alanna rushed to lock that door and dragged a chair in front of it. There, she thought with satisfaction, the entrances were blocked. She could sleep.

Stripping, she changed into her nightgown and robe. The set, a gift from her mother, was made of a clinging silky material, ivory with an abundance of lace decorating the nightgown's bodice. Alanna would have preferred her shapeless cotton gown, but wasn't about to go look for it now.

Sleep was far from her thoughts. Alanna didn't even go near the bed. She wondered why she felt the need to put up defenses and lock doors. He wasn't going to rape her. Nothing at all was going to happen. Unless she wanted it to.

Pacing restlessly, she considered her situation from several different aspects, knowing that she wanted him, believing that she shouldn't—and getting stuck on the one inescapable fact: they were out here in the woods alone.

He wouldn't come near her, he wouldn't dare. That sweeping-her-up-in-his-arms had been no more than manly bravado—although she suspected he would have taken the stairs two at a time if it meant getting her into his bed.

Nothing doing, she thought. Not tonight, and not any night in the future. She wanted the pleasure of telling him off for trying, though.

Alanna waited and waited and waited. Ten-thirty, eleven o'clock, eleven-thirty, and still there was no siege at her door. From her window, she could see the square of light shining out from the living room below. Weariness was invading her muscles. The bed looked more and more inviting, but she forced herself to stay awake by pacing some more. The mounting tension scraped at her already raw nerves.

Walking to the window for what seemed the hundredth time, she leaned against the frame. What was he doing down there? Why was he waiting? For her to grow tired and lower her defenses?

She stared into the darkness. Then, blinking in disbelief, she realized that the living room light was off. Rolt must be coming upstairs. Spinning, she faced the door.

Her fingers clutched the top of the robe together. She suddenly had visions of Rolt bursting through the door, laughing at the verbal abuse she hurled at him, stripping the gown from her and throwing her onto the bed. Her lips could almost feel the arousing warmth of his mouth.

She must have had one glass of wine too many. She thrust the image away. That would never happen. Rolt would not overwhelm her without first feeling the fury of her wrath. Quickly she turned off the light, throwing the room into darkness. Let him think she was in bed asleep. Holding her breath, she listened.

Rolt was at the top of the stairs and moving along the hall. A door opened and closed—it had to be the master bedroom. There was a series of indefinable sounds that might be made by someone getting ready for bed. Water ran briefly, then there was silence.

Minutes ticked by and Alanna watched the door. There was absolutely no movement from the master bedroom. Gradually she was forced to realize that Rolt had gone to bed. To bed! A silent scream of frustration exploded inside her.

You want him. The thought was so powerful that for a minute Alanna thought she had spoken aloud.

Nearly an hour later she accepted the fact that Rolt had indeed gone to bed and crawled beneath the covers of her own. She slept fitfully, waking at the slightest night sound, till finally, near dawn, exhaustion drugged her into a heavy sleep.

Slowly, reluctantly, she awakened to a midmorning sun, momentarily confused by the unfamiliar room. Remembering where she was, she tensed, listening. There was only silence. Where was Rolt? There was a noise outside her window. Slipping from under the covers, she went to investigate.

In the drive below she could see Rolt walking toward the corner of the house. He was carrying a rod and reel and tackle box. She watched him disappear around the house in the direction of the lake. She didn't question her good fortune at being left alone, but took advantage of it instead. She moved the chair away from the bathroom door. The porcelain tub was exactly where she wanted to be. A long soak would ease the aching tiredness of her muscles and help spark her senses back to life. She turned on the taps and added a generous amount of the bubble bath she found on the shelf.

Then, while the tub was filling with water, she brushed the woolly taste from her mouth and laid out the clothes she would wear on the bed. Later, immersed up to her neck, Alanna felt deliciously indulged and pampered. Frothy bubbles peaked and mounded around her. The comfortably hot water was soothing. She rested her head against the back of the tub and closed her eyes, enjoying the sensations.

The door to the second bedroom opened. Foolishly she had forgotten to lock it. She sat up with a start and just as quickly sank below the concealing bubbles. She had forgotten about Rolt. She couldn't do that any more. He was leaning against the door frame, staring at her.

"Get out of here!" she said indignantly.

"Sorry." The aroused look in his eyes betrayed his bland apology. He wasn't sorry at all.

"I'm taking a bath," Alanna retorted.

"I noticed that." The grooves near his mouth deepened slightly.

"I would like some privacy." She pressed her lips tightly together. It wouldn't do to lose her temper when she was in such a vulnerable position.

"You should have locked the door. You were so quiet I didn't know you were here."

"Want to hear me scream?"

"If it makes you happy. You know good and goddamn well I'm not going to lay a finger on you unless you want me to." Rolt folded his arms in front of him. There was an unmistakable challenge in his stance that dared her to try to throw him out. "Are you going to be in there much longer? I'm getting hungry for breakfast."

For the last two weeks, after the road trip before this one, making breakfast was a task that, to her everlasting dismay, seemed to have been automatically assigned. She'd made the mistake of fixing him a passable dish of bacon and eggs that he'd praised to the skies. Not something she could put on an application to business school, unless she was going for a Master's in Bacon Administration.

"Go and fix your own!" Alanna glared, hating him for putting her in such an awkward position.

"I couldn't deprive you of the privilege," he mocked.

That did it. "Privilege!" she exploded. "Let me tell you something, Rolt. Being a personal assistant is a thankless job. No matter how much overtime I make and how much you say what a good job I'm doing, I'm never going to like doing it."

"Does that have to do with the job or is it me you don't like?" he asked, unruffled.

"Like you would care either way."

"I do care. I really want to know what's on your mind."

She fumbled for a washcloth under all the bubbles and flung it at his middle, figuring she couldn't miss. He dodged left and it made a soggy noise as it hit the wall, then slid down to the floor.

"Fixing a meal for you is not a privilege!" She watched him pick up the wet washcloth and wished she had another one. Bent over like that, he was in the perfect position.

"I was kidding." He tossed it back into the water and she closed her eyes, but not quickly enough to keep the bubbles from splashing into one.

"Ow!" She rubbed her stinging eye, making it worse. "You were not! You love to be waited on!"

A slow, sensual smile lit up his face. "Depends on who's doing the waiting."

"Not me. Not no more. Not nohow. You have to be the most impossible being on earth! You're not even a being—you're a robot! An all-American corporate robot!"

His eyes grew cold and hard. "You've been rehearsing that little speech for quite a while, haven't you?" Rolt taunted her. "Do you have any more stored up?"

"Yeah!"

"Don't stop now." His lips curled in a jeer. "Let's hear it all. I have plenty of time."

Alanna couldn't decide whether the bathwater had suddenly cooled or her temperature had risen to boiling point, but her skin suddenly felt cold. She wanted to be out of the tub, with something more substantial covering her than the slowly dissipating bubbles.

"Will you get out of here?"

"Come now, motormouth," he taunted again. "You haven't even begun to insult me."

The submerged washcloth drifted close to her hand. Her fingers closed around it. This time she flung it at his head, a spray of water scattering over the tiled floor, and a few drops landed harmlessly on his bronzed features.

"I said get out of here!" Her voice trembled hoarsely.

"Discounting the fact that your aim was off, you should have thrown something more deadly than a washcloth," Rolt informed her, straightening away from the door frame and moving toward her.

Wildly Alanna reached for the rosettes of soap in the dish beside the bathtub. She pelted him with two of them, but the third didn't have a chance to leave her hand as he caught her wrist.

"Drop it," he ordered. She squeezed it harder, with predictable results: the pink rosette slipped out of her fingers.

She clawed at the hand that held her wrist. A twin grip closed around the other hand and Rolt dragged her out of the tub. Water and bubbles splashed everywhere as she tried to resist when he hauled her against his chest. The slippery tile floor offered little footing, hampering her efforts to kick at him.

Her whole body was tingling with rage. And—she had to admit it—sexual excitement. An answering fire smoldered in his.

"Let me go!" she snapped.

"With pleasure," Rolt snarled, and abruptly released her. He ripped a large, beach-size towel from the rack. "Here." He wrapped it around her, unconcerned by the rough way he handled her, his touch anything but tender as he tucked the ends of the towel above her breasts. The towel's fringe tickled the back of her legs. Alanna just gaped at him.

"Your virtue and modesty are still intact." Ridiculous patches of bubble bath dotted his shirt. His clothes were wet where her dripping body had been pressed against him. Beads of water glistened on his muscular arms, clinging to the dark hairs. With a last, insolently raking glance, he turned to leave.

Alanna couldn't let him have the last word. It wasn't enough that he was leaving. "Don't you ever come near me again!" Her foot stamped the wet floor in a childish display of temper.

Rolt stopped in the doorway, motionless for an instant. Then, like the gradual release of a tightly coiled spring, he turned, seeming more like the giant she had often likened him to as he loomed before her. Alanna backed toward the door to her bedroom. The small space of the bathroom became too confining, and Rolt followed.

"I won't. Because I try to do the right thing." His jaw was clenched, biting down on the anger that vibrated through his voice. "Not because I take orders from you."

"You'd better," Alanna said with bravado as she kept retreating in the face of his sure advance. "You're out of control."

"Really?" he said scornfully. "Did I do anything last night that made you feel unsafe?"

Did he know that she'd thought about pushing a dresser in front of the door? She'd put the propped chair back, hadn't she? Alanna clutched her towel and looked around to be sure.

"The living room is just below," Rolt reminded her cuttingly. "I heard you pushing furniture around last night and I doubted that you were simply rearranging it at that hour."

Too incensed to keep her mouth shut, Alanna tossed her head defiantly. "Crazy as it may sound, I actually half-wanted you to try. Can you believe that?"

"Is that an invitation? I accept."

"No! The other half didn't want you to come anywhere near me!" She struck at him. He dodged the blow and let it land harmlessly on his shoulder.

His hands grabbed her upper arms and she tried to prevent him from drawing her against him. Although failing in that, she did succeed in wedging an arm above his, loosening his grip, forcing him to circle her back to hold her.

But the blows she rained on his chest and shoulders didn't faze him. She aimed a fist at his mouth, the mocking curl of his lips. She felt it split, the bright red of blood showing against the white of his teeth. She had the sense to feel fear at what she had done.

Her eyes widened as he lifted her bodily off her feet and tossed her angrily backward. The bed broke her fall, and a gasp of surprise came from her throat. She stared at Rolt's glowering face, unable to move as he towered above the bed.

Recovering her wits, she started to roll to the opposite side of the bed away from him. But he was too quick for her, grabbing an arm and spinning her onto her back, pinning her to the mattress with his weight.

Her hands strained against him, trying to push him off, but Rolt caught them and stretched them above her head. She stared at him, knowing she was trapped. Her violet eyes were wild with despair as they met the hard glitter of his. He lowered his bloodstained mouth, covering hers in a long, fiery kiss, parting her lips until the taste of his blood was on her tongue.

Her head moved, trying to fight yet feeling the will to resist weaken. The heat of his body warmed her skin. The dampness of his clothes intensified his heady, masculine scent. The firm touch of his hand on her bare shoulder furthered the destruction of her defenses. Her physical ache for fulfillment was real and undeniable, adding to the overwhelming vulnerability that threatened her.

Somewhere Alanna found the ounce of reserve needed to keep her from responding with the fervor she felt. She couldn't give in to Rolt, no matter how much she desired him.

She drew in a shuddering breath when, with an expression of angry disgust, he moved away from her, standing up beside the bed. Her trembling hand clutched the loosened folds of her towel.

"So it comes down to this, huh?" he said grimly. "A battle of wills. We'll see who gives in first."

With an abrupt turn, he walked away from the bed toward the hall. Alanna stared, feeling a sudden overpowering need to have his arms around her and the warmth of his body next to hers.

"Rolt," she called softly after him.

He halted, turning at an angle. "What is it, Alanna?" His voice was curt and unyielding.

A bitterness rose in her throat. She'd almost let physical attraction override her self-respect and pride. She hated Rolt. "Go to hell!" she breathed with sobbing fury.

The line of his mouth curved in a cold smile. "I bet you could take me there. Might be fun."

As the door closed behind him, Alanna rolled onto her side. The bedcovers were damp where they had lain on top of them. She was filled with the humiliating sense of whose will was stronger. She would have surrendered just now if Rolt had persisted another few seconds.

Do not fall in love with him, she thought desperately. Fall in love? The phrase was a lightning bolt that jolted her upright. That was ridiculous! How could she even consider such a possibility? Just because funny things happened inside her whenever Rolt came near or touched her didn't mean she was falling in love with him. But doubt crept in. She wrapped herself up in the blankets and thought it over for a long time.

The aroma of frying bacon greeted her when she finally came down the stairs. The plague of doubts and fears had been pushed to the back of her mind. Yet, as she entered the kitchen, she eyed Rolt warily, half afraid he would guess the crazy ambivalence of her feelings toward him and take advantage of it.

He was standing in front of the stove, his back to her, tall and broad-shouldered, lean-hipped and muscled. Alanna's skin tingled with the memory of being molded against his hard frame. She trembled, not wanting to be aware of him. She wanted to flee the room, and would have if Rolt hadn't chosen that moment to glance over his shoulder.

"How do you like your eggs?" There was absolutely nothing in his expression to indicate that the tumultuous scene in her room had ever taken place. But his lip was still a little puffy.

"Over easy." Alanna tried to match his composure.

He cracked two eggs over the skillet and dropped the contents in the sizzling butter in the pan, discarding the shells. "Breakfast is about ready. There's orange juice in the refrigerator. The glasses are already on the table."

Taking the pitcher of juice from the refrigerator,

Alanna set it on the small breakfast table in the kitchen. The place settings were already there for two people. She had expected a cold war to spring up between them. If not that, then she had thought Rolt would content himself with verbal jabs.

But not this. He was almost companionable—aloof, yes, but still companionable. It made him more dangerous to her hastily reconstructed defenses than before.

Lying in the bed upstairs, rolled up in the blankets like a giant caterpillar, she'd decided that the best thing to do was to have him drive her home immediately. Now, with breakfast imminent, the mood was cozy. It was almost like they were . . . married. She pushed the thought away and decided to stay.

The rest of the weekend passed in that same vaguely congenial atmosphere. They swam, boated, lazed in the sun, and walked in the woods. Rolt's invitations were always accompanied by an opt-out clause. "You're welcome to come if you like or stay here if you don't."

When they were working, they didn't talk much or laugh. They were two strangers doing things together simply because there was no one else to do them with.

Yet Alanna found herself remembering and savoring the times Rolt had touched her. When they had gone boating, he had lifted her from the dock to the boat, and out again on their return. Swimming, he had helped her up the ladder. Walking through the woods, he had occasionally held her hand to steady her over rough ground. The times he had smoothed sunblock on her shoulders and back were the hardest to forget. The contact had never lasted long, but Alanna was aroused by his touch.

At any time, she knew that the slightest indication from her would have changed the impersonal contact to a caress. The knowledge pulsed below the surface each time they were together.

Early Monday morning, she was awakened by a knock on her door. Blinking the sleep from her eyes, she sat up, hugging the covers about her.

"Yes?" she said thickly.

The door opened and Rolt stood outside. He was impeccably dressed in one of his best suits, and Alanna thought fleetingly of how civilized he could seem when he wanted to. His indigo eyes examined the tangled curls of her tawny hair and her blurred, sleepy expression.

"I'm on my way to the office," Rolt told her impassively. "I'll be home around one o'clock for lunch. Order in from town. I don't care how much they charge to deliver way out here, and I don't care what you get. You're just not allowed to cook. I don't want another split lip."

She yawned. "Good. I hate cooking."

He grinned. "See you." He left. A few minutes later she heard the sound of the car pulling out of the drive.

Three times during that week he came home for lunch. Twice Alanna went into town to visit her parents, talking more about the work they were doing than she did about Rolt. The weekend was almost a repeat of the first, with the exception that on Saturday night they were invited to a dinner with a business associate and friend of Rolt's.

It wasn't difficult to pretend to be his adoring assistant, especially when Rolt was behaving himself. He was being a peach, in fact. Less of a workaholic and more of a—*did she dare to even think it?*—a lover. Not that anything had happened.

But it seemed to Alanna that admitting that she could fall in love with Rolt made it more likely that she would. She fought against the prospect, constantly reminding herself that she wanted to get out of the corporate culture before it ate her brain, which would mean getting away from him. Admitting to him and to her parents that she didn't want to be the first female director of a major mining company wasn't something she looked forward to. After more than eight weeks of nonstop work, about all she wanted to do was sit in the sun.

Which was what she was doing right now. Alanna sighed and poured more lotion into her palm, rubbing it into her thighs. It was becoming impossible to live under the same roof with a man as sexy and compelling as Rolt and ignore her own desire for him. It wasn't natural for a man and a woman to live together and separately. This relationship couldn't last. She had seen the look in his eyes sometimes when he watched her. He wanted her—that hadn't changed.

Initially her goal had been to make Rolt's life miserable. Now she was concentrating all her efforts on not being caught in her own trap. Her chances of succeeding were growing dismally smaller each day, and she felt frustrated and helpless.

Staring out over the landscape of Minnesota green, she tried to lose her thoughts in the beautiful view from the sundeck. She smoothed the lotion on her shoulders, stretching her arm to try to reach more of her back.

"I'll do that."

Alanna jumped at the sound of Rolt's voice. Her rounded eyes saw him standing behind the screened sliding door leading into the dining room. His suit jacket was off and hanging by the hook of his finger behind him.

She glanced quickly at her wristwatch lying on the table beside her lounge chair.

"I didn't expect you for another hour," she murmured self-consciously. "You did say one o'clock?"

He slid the screen open and stepped onto the

planked sundeck. "I got away earlier than I thought," he shrugged, and tossed his jacket over the back of a lawn chair, continuing his path to her.

Alanna set the bottle of lotion down, flustered by his early arrival. "I haven't even ordered lunch. I—" She started to rise, but the hand on her shoulders pushed her back down.

"It doesn't matter. I'm not particularly hungry . . . for lunch." The infinitesimal pause before he added the last word had Alanna's heart skipping beats.

Her lashes fluttered down in silent acceptance of the hunger of her senses for his touch. The lounge chair creaked once in protest when his weight settled in the cushion behind her. The coolness of the sun lotion was on her back, then firmly smoothed over her skin.

Not an inch of her back was ignored. His hands followed the curve of her spine to the small of her back, taking sensual pleasure in stroking her. Strong but sensitive fingers moved over her waist and rib cage, tantalizingly near the swelling of her breasts, then traveled on to the nape of her neck.

A fire was being kindled inside her, the warmth was building. She knew it would burst into flame at any moment. She moved her shoulders in an instinctive and unwilling signal of protest.

"That oughta do it," she said with a faint breathy catch to her voice.

Rolt didn't stop. "It's more effective against sunburn if it's rubbed in." The husky tone was nearly as seductive as his hands.

"Don't!" Alanna tried to conceal her uneven breathing. She slid forward on the chair's cushion to elude his hands.

With one she was successful, but the other hand curved around the front of her shoulder and half turned her to face him. She had difficulty meeting his gaze, so she looked at the opened front of his shirt, an equally evocative sight. His hand moved to the side of her neck, a thumb raising her chin. His eyes smoldered with the same desire that burned inside her.

"It's still no, is it?" Rolt asked.

"Yes," Alanna whispered, "it is."

She knew the pulse in her neck was hammering against his fingers, and she couldn't make her heart slow its rapid beat. Her lips had parted slightly, unconsciously inviting a kiss. His kiss.

Rolt's gaze slipped to them. For a taut second, she wished Rolt would ignore her answer, but it wasn't to be fulfilled as he released her and stood up. Right now she wished with all her heart that he had less self-control. A lot less.

Chapter Nine

"Your distributor cables are corroded," the mechanic said.

Alanna looked at him blankly. When it came to the inner workings of a car, she knew absolutely nothing. The only time she thought about it was when the car wouldn't run, as was the case now. "Can you fix them?" she asked anxiously.

"Yeah, sure," the man nodded, "but not tonight. I don't have replacements for your particular model on hand. And I don't have time to make it over to the parts store before it closes. I could have it ready for you first thing tomorrow morning."

Alanna sighed and handed the mechanic the keys. "Go ahead and tow it into your shop and fix it. I'll be by in the morning to pick it up."

"Between nine-thirty and ten o'clock, it should be ready," he agreed, and walked away.

"Daddy"—she turned to her father standing in the driveway with her—"can I borrow your car to get to Rolt's house? I'll bring it back in the morning when I pick mine up."

Dorian shook his head regretfully. "I'm sorry, honey, but I have a meeting tonight or I'd be glad to lend it to you. I'll give you a ride later, though."

"Oh, no, Dad, I can't let you drive all that way." Alanna felt awful for refusing him, but she knew what an acceptance of the offer would lead to. Her father would suggest that her mother accompany them, just for the drive. Once they arrived, she would be obligated to invite them to see Rolt's hideaway, as her mother kept referring to it. They had been hinting for an invitation for over a week now.

Alanna just didn't want to answer any questions, that was all there was to it. "You could drive me to the plant and I can ride home with Rolt. He'll be finished work soon."

Her father's disappointment was obvious, but he couldn't argue with the practical suggestion. "I'll let your mother know where I'm going and be right out."

"Tell her good-bye again for me," Alanna said, since her first attempt to leave her parents' home had been postponed when the car had refused to start.

Later, during the drive to the taconite plant, her father commented, "Rolt is really making a success out of this operation. You can be very proud of him, Alanna,"

"I am," she smiled briefly.

"Before you took off with him, he mentioned that there might be an increase in my stock earnings. It turned out to be a substantial one," he informed her. "Rolt's quite a businessman."

"Yes, he knows his stuff." Silently Alanna realized that he had kept his word about helping her father. Which meant a lot of pressure was off her. The panicky need to take care of everyone that had driven her to take Rolt up on his offer and become his assistant had subsided.

Her parents were doing all right. That helped, too. The lines of strain and tension had disappeared from around her father's mouth and eyes. The burden must have been heavy—she was glad that it had been lifted at last.

When they stopped at the entrance gate, the security guard smiled broadly in recognition. "Hello, Mr. Powell, Ms. Powell." And they were waved on through.

Her father dropped her off at the door near where the black SUV was parked, insisted that he couldn't come in with her if he wanted time for a leisurely meal before his meeting, and left.

Many of the office staff recognized Alanna when she entered the building. She hadn't been to Rolt's office for quite a while. The curious glances and occasional smiles of greeting from the staff made her wonder if they were remembering the numerous times she had dated Kurt before suddenly taking off, as her father had put it, with Rolt. She felt uncomfortable and a little defensive.

Rolt was in the outer office talking to a man in a dark suit when she walked in. The warmth of his gaze melted away the chill of apprehension that had hurried her through the halls. She moved eagerly toward him, going right past his secretary, Mrs. Blake, without seeing her.

"You wouldn't believe what's happened," Alanna smiled.

She would have stopped in front of him, but his arm encircled her waist and drew her against him to receive his kiss. Her lips automatically responded, bringing a dark glow to his eyes that didn't go away when he raised his head.

Turning to the bemused man watching their greeting, Rolt said, "This is Alanna. Tom Brooks, with the shipping firm out of Duluth."

She felt a flood of color warm her cheeks, brought on more by her unrestrained response than by the fact that it had been witnessed.

The man smiled briefly at Rolt. "I had heard you were with someone new. In fact, I was hoping this was your new bride you were kissing." He turned to Alanna. "Someday soon, huh?"

"Ah, no. Not as far as I know. Nice to meet you." She shook his hand, Rolt's arm slackening its hold around her waist only slightly.

"Now what brought you here?" Rolt prompted. "You said something had happened."

For a blank instant, Alanna met his gaze. "Oh geez," she breathed a shaky laugh. "My car broke down— something to do with the contributor cables."

"The what?" Tom Brooks said, laughing.

"I don't know the first thing about cars. But mine won't be fixed until the morning so I'm here to catch a lift."

"I think that can be arranged." Then Rolt frowned, a brow arching. "How did you get here?"

"Daddy brought me. I stopped by to see them today and the car wouldn't start when I went out," she explained.

"I have to go over a few things with Tom first." He glanced at his secretary over the top of Alanna's head. "There's nothing else after that, is there, Mrs. Blake?"

"No, sir."

Alanna blanched. She hadn't seen the secretary. But Mrs. Blake had to have seen Rolt's arm around her waist. And heard the other man ask Rolt if Alanna was his new bride.

"As soon as Tom and I are finished, we can leave," Rolt said.

"I promise I won't keep him long, Alanna," the man smiled.

Alanna glanced around the room, the vague feelings of discomfort returning at the thought of waiting in the office until Rolt was free to leave. She didn't want to be the recipient of any more speculating looks from the staff. Sitting in the office would be like being on display.

"I think I'll wait in the car, if that's all right," she told Rolt.

"Of course." He removed his arm from around her waist and reached into his pocket. "It's locked. You'll need the keys."

Taking them, Alanna smiled politely at the other man. "It was nice meeting you, Mr. Brooks." With a quick, faintly uncertain smile at Rolt, she walked from the room into the hall.

As she moved down the corridor, a familiar figure approached from the opposite direction. It was Kurt, but his ready smile wasn't there and his eyes were expressionless. He seemed so different from the man she had once loved. Almost a stranger.

Alanna's steps faltered as she realized she had referred to her love in the past tense. She hadn't seen Kurt since that night he had found her with Rolt. She'd been swept up into the whirlwind of Rolt's life, so much so that she'd given little thought to the way she'd hurt his brother. Awash in guilt, she watched him approach.

"Hello, Kurt," she greeted him quietly when he had nearly reached her.

He nodded briskly without speaking, his expression masked, his shoulders stiff. He would have walked on by, but Alanna stopped, partially blocking his path.

"Please don't walk away," she begged.

He halted, his abrupt manner indicating he was anxious to be on his way and didn't welcome her interruption.

"I can't think of anything we have to say to each other," Kurt responded coldly.

"Just listen for a minute," Alanna said pleadingly, keeping her voice low. "You never gave me a chance to explain my side of what happened."

"I don't see what there is to explain. It's all fairly obvious." His gaze was as bleak as an arctic sky.

"Things aren't the way they appear on the surface."

"Aren't they?" he mocked. "You did hook up with my brother."

"Do you know why?" Alanna gazed at him, hoping he would give her the benefit of the doubt. "The real reason?"

"Alanna," he sighed in irritation, "what's your point? What would it change?"

"Maybe it would change the way you think of me," she answered honestly. "It hurts to have you thinking I just ditched you."

"But you did." Kurt turned his head away, staring at the blank corridor wall. "Okay, so you want to talk, explain whatever it is. Go ahead, I'm listening."

"Not here." Alanna glanced around, conscious of the people in the offices along the hall and the nearby cubicles. "It's too public. Besides, Rolt will be coming out. He's in there talking to some guy from Duluth."

"You want to meet me somewhere, is that it?" he asked flatly.

"To talk, yes," Alanna said. "I'll meet you for lunch tomorrow at twelve-thirty."

Alanna didn't want to be seen with Kurt at a public restaurant. If anyone they knew saw them, the gossip would get back to Rolt way too fast.

"Could we meet at the Iron Range Interpretative Center?" she asked.

"You don't want Rolt finding out, is that it?"

"Yes," she admitted.

He shook his head as if questioning the wisdom of what he was agreeing to. "I'll meet you there tomorrow." Without another word, he walked past her.

* * *

The sky was overcast, a gloomy pearl gray with darker, threatening clouds on the horizon. The whispering wind carried the warning of an approaching storm, chilling Alanna to the bone.

She buried her hands deeper in the pockets of her yellow windbreaker and watched Kurt's car drive into the Center's parking lot. Behind her was the striking concrete and glass building of the Iron Range Interpretative Center.

The site, atop the crest of the old Glenn Iron Mine, held a commanding view of the inactive, open-pit mine with its man-made gorges and canyons. Nature trails wound around the base of the modern building. When Kurt got out of his car and walked to meet her, Alanna turned to stare at the impressive structure.

It didn't seem to matter that her relationship with Rolt had nothing to do with love. The sting of guilt was still there to make her feel uncomfortable about meeting Kurt.

She chided herself for it, feeling even more nervous when Kurt stopped beside her,

"It's beautiful, isn't it?" Her angle of view provided a glimpse of the bridge jutting out over the mine. "Have you been inside?"

"No."

"Neither have I recently. Not all the exhibits were there when I went through it. It's complete now, I understand. But what I saw was fascinating." Remembering the flag exhibit in a mirrored room, Alanna thought about the people who had immigrated to Minnesota from all over the world. "It doesn't deal with just the discovery of iron and its mining and development. It tells you about the people too, their life, working the mines, in the summer and in the logging camps in the winter." She was talking rapidly, avoiding the issue that had brought them here.

"The people were mainly immigrants from Rumania, Yugoslavia, Germany, Norway, Sweden, England, Ireland, and many other countries. It was a melting pot of cultures, religions, and languages. There's a film that tells some of the reasons why they came to America and their first impressions. Most of them couldn't speak English and were unaccustomed to the extremes of the Minnesota climate. Homesick—"

"Alanna," Kurt broke in impatiently, "it's all very interesting, I'm sure, but that isn't why I'm here."

"I know." She sighed reluctantly, turning to face him, then lowering her chin to stare at the ground. "I don't know where to begin."

"Try at the beginning," he suggested dryly. "Why did you get involved with Rolt if it wasn't for love or money?"

"That's hard to say." She paused for a moment but before Kurt could make a remark, she rushed on. "I know Rolt probably gave you the impression that I'd been seeing him while I was going with you, but it wasn't true. He came over to the house once on a Sunday afternoon and that was the only time I saw him except when I was with you."

The disbelief in Kurt's gaze made Alanna impatient. "I was with you practically every night. I didn't have time to meet Rolt—unless you think I slipped out to meet him after you'd brought me home."

"All right." Kurt conceded the possibility she was telling the truth. "If you hadn't been seeing him, why did you go to his office that night?"

"Because he said he knew something about my parents."

"Your parents?" Her answer startled him.

Alanna breathed in deeply and began to explain about the financial problems her father had incurred. "Rolt said he would help Dad without him ever learning about it if I would, um, work with him."

A spatter of raindrops fell. Kurt took hold of her arm. "We're going to get wet standing out here. Let's go to my car." With shoulders hunched against the scatter of fat drops, Alanna hurried toward Kurt's car. Neither spoke as Kurt opened the passenger door for her and walked around to the driver's side. Rain pattered on the roof, the only sound for several seconds once they were inside.

"How do you explain that love scene I walked in on?" Kurt asked finally, sliding her a challenging look. "You weren't by any stretch of the imagination resisting him."

"No, I wasn't." Alanna stared at her hands, twisting them in her lap. "I don't have any excuse for that, except that your brother is really good at physically arousing a woman. I think he was testing me."

"Obviously you passed," Kurt muttered, gazing straight ahead.

"That was the wrong thing to say—that he was testing me. I—I'm still sorry, Kurt. I never meant to hurt you." She shook her head, feeling the piercing swiftness of his gaze turning to her.

"Oh, come on, Alanna," he growled beneath his breath. "You've had enough time to make up your mind by now. It wasn't me you wanted."

She hesitated, pressing her lips together.

"Nothing's happened between me and Rolt."

"What are you trying to say?" He looked at her skeptically.

"I have stayed at one of his houses. We have separate rooms," Alanna murmured, lifting her chin with a trace of defiance. "Nothing's happened."

"Rolt? My brother? The king of casual sex?" Kurt frowned incredulously.

The unflattering description made her turn red. There wasn't anything she could say that wouldn't sound ridiculous. "He's waiting for me to come to him." She hooked a curl behind her ear.

"So far you haven't," he said, yet managing to put a question mark at the end.

"How could I—" The rest of the sentence remained in her throat. It should have finished with "when I love you," but Alanna couldn't get the words out.

Her gaze desperately sought Kurt's face, trying to find the attraction she had once felt. Now it was the faint resemblance to Rolt that stirred her senses. She looked quickly away, blinking at the tears burning her eyes.

Kurt's hand touched her shoulder, gripping it gently to turn her toward him. He leaned forward, his mouth descending on hers. The burning ardor of his kiss ignited only a gentle flame of emotion, not the powerful passion that Rolt's kisses sparked. Her lashes remained lowered when Kurt stopped and sat back in his seat a little.

She hoped she was hiding her disappointment. She sure as hell wished she hadn't kept this meeting with Kurt. It wasn't fair of her to hurt him more.

"It isn't there, is it?" he said quietly. "What we once had," he added.

Alanna shook her head, keeping her eyes lowered as she acknowledged that he was right. She heard the regret in his voice and shared it.

"To be honest, Alanna," Kurt continued quietly, "that last week I thought something was missing. I had the feeling you were withdrawing from me each time I held you in my arms. That's why I was so ready to believe that you had been seeing Rolt on the side. It was easier somehow to think of losing you to him than just losing you because you didn't love me. It doesn't make sense, I know, but—that's the way I felt."

"I'm sorry, Kurt," she murmured. "I wanted to love you. I really thought I did."

And it would have made it so much easier to protect herself from falling in love with Rolt. Seeing Kurt had opened her eyes to the truth. She already was in love with Rolt.

"Well, that clears up a lot of things. Guess we understand ourselves and each other better." He sighed as if he wasn't certain that was good.

"No hard feelings, Kurt?" She tipped her head to one side, her gaze sad and wistful.

"No." He smiled grimly. "I'm still sorry I lost you, but I'm not bitter any more. Eventually the hurt will leave, too."

There wasn't much left to say, and both of them knew it. Alanna reached for the door handle and released the latch. She smiled weakly over her shoulder at Kurt.

"Take care," she said in good-bye.

"You, too." But there was a tightness in his expression that said he still loved her, regardless of her change of feelings.

By the time Alanna had driven back to the house by the lake, the intermittent rain had stopped, but the sky remained threatening. The meeting with Kurt had left her feeling dispirited and restless, confused by a problem she didn't know how to solve. Loving Rolt should have made things simpler; instead they seemed complicated.

She wandered through the house, listening to the thunder rolling closer. Lightning flashed in crackling arcs and spikes. Dinner was in the oven when the wind came, whipping and bending the conical tops of the pines. The rain came with a rush, blinding sheets hammering at the windows. The fury of the storm grew steadily.

The table was set and dinner was warming in the oven, but Rolt wasn't home. At first Alanna didn't let herself become concerned. The storm had probably held him up. The roads would be slick and the visibility poor. When one hour stretched into two hours late, panic set in. Alanna dialed the number of his private line at the office, but there was no answer. She called the entrance gate, only to have the security guard on duty tell her that Rolt had left the plant almost two hours ago. She began imagining problems as trivial as a flat tire and soon progressed into accidents with Rolt lying injured in some ditch along the way.

When she picked up the telephone the third time to call the police, the line was dead, knocked out by the storm. Raking her fingers through her tawny hair, Alanna glanced at the rain-coated windows. A jab of lightning exploded somewhere close by and thunder shook the glass.

The front door burst open, and Alanna pivoted. Her first thought was that the howling wind had blown it open. A rush of moist, turbulent air swept into the living room, cooling her cheeks. A molten-silver flash of lightning illuminated the night, lingering for several seconds.

Outlined in the doorway was the dark silhouette of a man. His dark hair was wind-tossed and his stance, feet slightly apart, was intimidating. Rain glistened on the wooden planks outside the threshold. In that charged and lightning brilliant instant, the man didn't seem real—a mythical being, a giant.

The giant moved, and the breath that had been caught in Alanna's throat was released in a joyous sigh. She raced to the doorway as Rolt stepped in, dripping rain, his expensive suit plastered against his muscular frame. His face was dripping, lashes dark and spiky from the water.

"Rolt! Where have you been?" She ran into his arms. Her relief at seeing him safe and apparently unharmed was too great to be held in. She buried her face in the wet lapel of his jacket as he pushed the door closed, shutting out the wind-whipped rain. She could hear the solid, steady beat of his heart.

"What took you so long?" she breathed.

"There was a tree across the road, and I had to walk," Rolt answered, his breath warm against her hair although his voice was oddly aloof.

Alanna became aware of the way she was clinging to him. The wetness of his clothes was beginning to be absorbed by hers. Her hands slid from his shoulders to the hardness of his chest as she levered herself away. Thunder rumbled threateningly and she shivered at the violence of the storm he had walked through.

"Afraid of storms?" His indigo eyes watched her.

"Not usually," she laughed nervously. "But I was worried about you. I called the plant and the guard said you'd left two hours ago."

"Yes, I did. I'm sorry you were worried."

"I guess it couldn't be helped." His hands were resting lightly on her hips. Alanna edged a few more inches from his chest, nerves jumping, "Dinner is overcooked, but it's probably just as well. As soaked as you are, the best thing would be some hot soup. And a dry change of clothes."

When she would have moved away, his hands tightened on her hips. "Were you really worried, Alanna?" The hard brilliance of his eyes searched her face.

"Of course I was." A finely strung tension gripped her. She felt suddenly defensive. "I have feelings, Rolt."

"But you think I don't," he said in quiet accusation.

Alanna looked away. "Huh?" Her pulse was quickening under his disturbing regard. "I know I said that but I didn't mean it. Just sometimes you act like you don't, when you get all cold and corporate." She was stammering, faltering over words and explanations. "Rolt, there are times when you are ruthless—you have to admit that."

"It seems to be the only thing that works." His face was set in uncompromising lines.

"This isn't the time to be discussing it." Alanna pushed more firmly against his chest. "If you'll let me go, I'll fix your soup." She tried to sound firm and not affected by his touch. "And while it's heating, you can go upstairs and get out of these wet clothes before you catch pneumonia. A hot bath would do you good. I'll bring the soup up and you can have it in bed," she said, trying to treat him as a child in need of motherly attention.

"No." His tone was clipped and a muscle leaped in his jaw. "I'm not going to bed alone, Alanna, not any more."

She gasped in surprise when he swept her off her feet into the cradle of his arms, checking the sound. He held her there, staring enigmatically into her startled face. His drenched clothes chilled her skin, but Alanna didn't notice it. The fire burning inside distracted all her thoughts.

Slowly he walked to the stairs, carrying her effortlessly in his arms as he mounted the steps. At the head of the stairs, he turned to the master bedroom. The drumbeat of her heart seemed louder than the thunder to Alanna.

The phone rang and Alanna slowly opened her eyes, annoyance at being so rudely roused creeping slowly through her sleepiness. Sunlight flooded the room with blinding force. She was lying on her side, the coolness of a sheet against her naked skin. A sensual warmth burned her back, extending over her waist and stomach. Her hand slid down to investigate the heat and encountered a muscular, lightly furred arm.

She stiffened for an instant, then languidly relaxed under its pressing weight. Rolt's warm breath caressed her shoulder, stirring the tangle of hair at the nape of her neck. She snuggled closer to him in heady contentment.

A delicious thrill ran through her veins at the memory of his easy mastery of her responses. She hadn't known that sex could be that good.

A flush colored her cheeks as she remembered the way their insatiable hunger had turned them to each other a second time in the night. She savored the memory of being loved, and loved again, and falling asleep in Rolt's arms.

The discordant ring of the telephone interrupted her reverie. With a start, she realized it was the sound that had wakened her. Fortunately she was lying on the side of the king-size bed by the nightstand where the phone was.

As she started to move to answer it, the arm around her waist tightened instinctively. She glanced quickly at Rolt over her shoulder. He was still sleeping. The rough angles and planes of his face were gently strong in repose.

Not wanting to disturb him, she stretched an arm toward the receiver, lifting it off the hook before it could ring again. Absently, she realized the line downed by the storm must have been repaired.

"Matthews residence." She spoke softly into the mouthpiece, her voice still drowsy.

"Alanna, this is Kurt," came the reply. "'Did I wake you?"

"Not exactly." She was suddenly and embarrassingly conscious of Rolt lying beside her.

"I've been trying to call for over an hour, but the storm knocked your phone out last night."

"Yes, I know," she murmured.

"I was calling to find out if you know what time Rolt left for the plant this morning, I was supposed to meet him at nine and he isn't here yet," Kurt said.

Her gaze slid to the clock on the bedstand. It was a quarter past ten. She swallowed, unable to tell Kurt that Rolt was still sleeping. With her.

"No. No, I don't know. He might have overslept." Alanna allowed a little of the truth to slip out.

"There were quite a few trees downed by the storm. He might be waiting somewhere for a road to be cleared," Kurt suggested.

"Yes. If I hear from him before he sees you, Kurt, I'll have him call," she promised quietly.

"Thanks, I—"

Alanna never heard the rest of Kurt's sentence. Cool air tightened her stomach and waist as Rolt's arm moved. His fingers firmly took the receiver from her hand. Breathing in sharply, she turned partially on her back to meet the wicked light in the dancing dark blue of his eyes. His weight shifted so that he was pressing her shoulders on to the mattress.

"Kurt, this is Rolt." Even as he spoke into the telephone, his mouth was exploring the corner of her eyes, the curve of her cheek and jaw, mortifying Alanna beyond words. Kurt must have been as stunned as she was. "Are you there, Kurt?" Rolt asked, a note of sleepy triumph in his voice, the line of his mouth curving against her skin.

Teasingly he traced the outline of her lips. They parted tremulously under the tantalizing caress. Alanna moved away in protest, ashamed of letting Rolt make love to her while talking to Kurt. Rolt wouldn't release her. She twisted her face into the pillow and he shifted his attention to the vulnerable curve of her throat.

Distantly she heard the hollow sound of Kurt's voice coming through the wires, but she was too swamped by the dizzying sensations to hear his words above her quickened breathing. Gooseflesh shivered deliciously over her skin as Rolt found a particularly sensitive spot on her neck.

"Sorry about breaking our appointment. It was quite late before we got any sleep last night and Alanna was trying to be considerate by letting me sleep in this morning. Weren't you?" Rolt laughed softly against her throat, sending more shivers of irrational pleasure dancing down her spine.

"Rolt, don't," she whispered achingly.

"Let's change it to one-thirty. Does that work for you?" The fiery trail of his mouth continued its downward exploration, investigating the shadowy hollow between her breasts, then choosing the rounded curve of one for closer inspection. An uncontrollable shudder of desire quaked through her, and her fingers curled into the muscled bronze of his naked shoulders. "And you'd better tell Mrs. Blake I'll be unavoidably detained until noon."

He lifted his head and leaned across Alanna to replace the receiver on its cradle. When he moved back, his arms were on either side of her head, propping him above her. He lazily studied her flushed cheeks and the sparkling look in her violet eyes.

"Now where were we?" he murmured.

Much later, Alanna lay in the crook of his arm, her head resting against the solidity of his chest, rising and falling at last in even breathing. The dreamy afterglow of satisfaction softly curved her mouth. If she didn't move for a thousand years, it would still be too soon.

But the emptiness of her stomach was reminding her that she hadn't eaten since noon yesterday and she doubted that Rolt had either. Reluctantly she moved away from the warmth of his body, and slipped out of bed. Aware of the sunlight shining brightly on her naked curves and Rolt's eyes watching her, she walked self-consciously to the man-size robe lying over the back of a chair and put it on, tying a knot in the sash at the waist.

"Where are you going?" Rolt asked in a lazy, caressing voice.

"To fix breakfast." Alanna turned, brushing the hair away from one side of her face with a nervous hand.

He was propped on his side, an elbow beneath him, the bedcovers down around his waist. His bare chest and shoulders gleamed bronze in the sunlight, contrasted by the white of the sheets and pillows. The dark light in his eyes made her blood run swiftly.

"Come here."

Alanna walked to within a few inches of the bed and stood. His hand caught at the ends of the sash and drew her forward until her knee was bent on the mattress. Her senses threatened to whirl her into abandonment again.

"You didn't have dinner last night. You must be hungry," she murmured in protest.

"My appetite doesn't seem to be for food." He released one of the ends of the sash and pulled at the other to loosen the knot, watching the front of the robe open. "I think I'll burn all your clothes and make you wear only this," he said idly, then glanced at her reddened face. "Except that I'd probably never leave the house."

His gaze held hers for heart-stopping seconds. The

hungry rumbling of her stomach snapped the invisible thread that bound them. Rolt smiled suddenly.

"You'd better fix that breakfast. I don't want you fainting on me."

Alanna was at the bottom of the stairs before her legs finally stopped trembling. When Rolt came down, he had showered and shaved, and was dressed in a business suit. The smile he gave her when she set their plates on the table melted her like butter on a hot pancake. The silence during the meal was golden and wonderful.

"You're so domestic. Makes me nervous," Rolt said.

"Don't worry. It won't last."

"Believe me, what happens in the bedroom is a lot more important to me than what happens in the kitchen. Not like I can send out for an Alanna any time I want real loving."

"Aw, shucks."

Rolt finished his third cup of coffee and grinned at her. "It's time I left. Or I just might be tempted to jump you again."

Alanna nodded, rising from her chair. "I'll drive you to where you left your car."

They walked to the front door. There, Rolt halted and faced her. Alanna stopped, glancing uncertainly at him, meeting his probing look.

"Ready to move your things into my room?" His hand slipped inside her robe, cupping her bare breast. "Or shall I move my clothes into yours?" he asked quietly.

"I'll move mine," Alanna promised, a little breathlessly.

His exploring hand slid around her to the small of her back, drawing her against him to receive his hungry kiss. The clean scent of him was a heady fragrance. His mouth carried the taste of rich coffee. It remained on her lips when he lifted his head.

"We'd better leave now or I'll never go," he declared huskily.

The door was jerked open and Alanna walked through it, hiding a pleased smile. It was a wondrous discovery to learn that she could shatter his composure, that his control wasn't as iron-clad as she had believed. He was as open to her freely given passion as she was to his.

The rain-washed world outside looked beautiful and bright. Her heart sang joyously.

Chapter Ten

The silver gleamed against the white linen tablecloth. The crystal goblets sparkled with rainbow brilliance. The high polish of the china plates glistened richly. Alanna moved the small, pretty floral arrangement an inch, wondering if she should tell him that she wanted flowers like these for her wedding bouquet, when that day came.

Down, girl, she told herself. He hasn't proposed. Yet.

She stepped back and surveyed the table. Candles stood tall and straight in their silver holders; a bottle of champagne was chilling in its bucket of ice.

In the kitchen, the soup was warming on a burner. The salad was waiting in the refrigerator with the dessert. The steaks were marinating, ready to be put under the broiler. Everything was in readiness for Rolt's arrival.

Including herself. Alanna had been floating on a cloud all day. And tonight she wore a lavender cloud, a filmy dress of chiffon with a plunging neckline. It made her feet ethereal and feminine and excitingly alluring. Gliding at least an inch or two above the floor, she moved to the sliding glass door near the sundeck and frowned impatiently at the western sun.

"Oh, please go down early tonight," Alanna requested urgently. "We can't have a romantic candlelight dinner with you shining in."

A car stopped in front of the house. She pivoted toward the wide hall connecting the dining room to the living room, and waited breathlessly in anticipation. The front door opened.

"Alanna?" Rolt's voice demanded an answer.

"I—I'm in here." A bubble of happiness nearly cut off her voice. She didn't rush to meet him. She wanted him to come into the dining room and see her preparations for their evening.

Long strides quickly brought him into view, but her welcoming smile faded away at the coldness of his expression. His gaze swept over the table, stopping on her.

"What's this? A victory celebration?" he said.

Alanna shook her head in disbelief. This couldn't be the same man who had left the house this morning, or more accurately, at noon.

"I don't know what you're talking about," she answered uncertainly.

"Don't you?"

Alanna winced. Until now she'd thought she'd seen the last of his talent for putting people on the spot.

"Kurt didn't keep his appointment this afternoon."

She looked at him blankly. "I don't understand."

"Really?" he retorted, ignoring her confusion. "He left a message with my secretary saying he was unavoidably detained. That was his exact phrase—unavoidably detained." His repetition of it reminded Alanna that Rolt had used the same expression this morning; the implication jolted her. "Nice twist of the knife by my brother, don't you think?"

"What are you saying?"

"What's the matter?" He scowled, making no secret of his bad mood. "Didn't you know that my little brother had already let the secret out? Were you hoping to let it slip tonight?"

"You don't know what you're talking about!"

"Don't I?" Rolt pivoted sideways as if he couldn't stand to look at her. Just as abruptly, he glared at her. "You had me fooled completely. I never dreamed for an instant that you would leave me this morning and meet Kurt this afternoon. And you knew it, too."

"I didn't meet Kurt," Alanna protested.

His dark brows arched arrogantly. "Where were you this afternoon, Alanna? I phoned here and there wasn't any answer. Your cell phone put me straight into your voicemail. You weren't with your parents either."

"Oh, the cell phone—I left it in the glove compartment of the car. I couldn't find it, let alone hear it. All I did was go into town"—she gestured wildly toward the bottle of champagne—"to buy the champagne for our dinner tonight."

"By sheer coincidence, it happened to be that you were gone at the same time Kurt was unavoidably detained, is that right?" A muscle ticked in his jaw.

"It happens to be the truth. I went into town, bought the champagne, and came straight back, without meeting anybody!" Her eyes burned with unshed tears. He was being obnoxious. She wasn't going to give him the satisfaction of seeing her cry.

"Do you expect me to believe that?"

She sunk her teeth into her lip for a painful second. "I don't expect anything!"

Her voice was choked. She know she couldn't endure his suspicious questions without dissolving into tears. She started to hurry from the room, but Rolt intercepted her, grabbing her arm and spinning her around.

"Do you deny that this isn't the first time you've met Kurt recently?" he snarled.

She blanched. Her eyes widened in alarm. The line of his mouth tightened at her reaction.

"You thought I didn't know about your meeting with Kurt yesterday, didn't you?" He pulled her against his chest, looking into her stunned face.

Yesterday—it seemed much longer ago than yesterday that she had met Kurt in the parking lot of the Iron Range Interpretative Center. If Rolt knew about that, then it was no wonder he thought she had been with Kurt today. But after last night and this morning, how could he think that? "H—how did you find out?" she faltered.

"Office gossip. It has a way of traveling fast, especially if it has the potential of scandal. Someone overheard you arranging to meet Kurt when you talked to him in the hall."

"Yeah, I met him," she admitted. "I guess I should have told you but I didn't know I had to. It wasn't like you're trying to make it sound."

"You mean he didn't hold you in his arms or kiss you?" Rolt asked. "Not even for old times' sake?"

It didn't matter what she said, Rolt was going to believe the worst. Alanna gritted her teeth against the pain tearing at her heart.

"I am not going to discuss it with you," she declared tightly. "What's the use of defending myself when you've already tried and convicted me?"

"The facts speak for themselves," he retaliated.

"Don't be a pompous jerk, Rolt. You don't know what you're talking about!" Emotion laced her shaky voice. "You wouldn't know a fact if it bit your butt!"

"I know one thing for sure." Rolt let go of her arm and stepped back. Alanna had the impression that he had released her and put distance between them to keep from throttling her. "You aren't going to see Kurt again."

If he had phrased it in a less dictatorial way, Alanna would have admitted that she wasn't interested in Kurt, but his command was a red cape waving in front of her.

"Do you think you're going to stop me? How? By locking me in? Posting prison guards? I'm not going to put up with jealous crap, Rolt. Don't tell me what to do! You don't own me." Her temper flared up, blazing hot. "I will see who I want to, where I want to, and when I want to—and you won't stop me!"

"I underestimated you." The quietness of his voice was more menacing than if he had shouted in rage. "You can be sneaky when you want to."

"That makes two of us," Alanna snapped.

"Listen up. You try to see Kurt again and you'll lose me."

She shook her head. "Right now, I don't care. You don't have a God-given right to act like this."

He fell silent.

"I know what's happening here." Her mouth curved bitterly. "When you and I were making love last night, it was intense. We were as close as two people could be. I don't mean physically. Emotionally. And you got scared. And you picked a stupid fight and ruined a special celebration. Way to go, Rolt."

She started to walk past him, intent on leaving, but he stepped into her path. Her shimmering gaze lifted coolly to his face, surprised by the look of a wounded animal in intense pain that she saw in his dark blue eyes. Immediately his gaze hardened into blue steel.

"Where do you think you're going?" he challenged.

For an instant, Alanna thought she had seen in his eyes the same excruciating pain that she was feeling. But she realized it was damaged ego, disgusting male pride, too fragile to withstand any rejection.

"Isn't it obvious? I'm leaving," she stated forcefully. "Leaving this house. Leaving you."

"What do you want me to do?" His jaw worked convulsively. "Do you want me to get down on my knees and beg you to stay?"

"Quite an image. That would be something to see, the giant of Mesabi at my feet." Alanna laughed bitterly through her tears.

"Hell, yes, you can bring me to my knees. I want you that much," Rolt said harshly.

"I don't believe you."

"Nothing I can say or do will make any difference, is that it?"

"There is one thing I'd like to know." Her chin quivered, but pride kept her gaze level. "Before that seduction scene last night, did you know that I'd seen Kurt yesterday afternoon?"

"Yes."

Even though she had braced herself for the affirmative answer, Alanna still couldn't stop herself from recoiling as if struck by his hard, unapologetic voice. A hot tear burned down her cheek.

"Oh, I get it," she said softly, achingly. "You had sex with me just to be sure Kurt didn't beat you to it. Making love was the wrong phrase. I shouldn't have said it."

"Love!" Rolt took her by the shoulders. "You don't know anything about love!" Pulling her on her tiptoes, he drew her close to him. "Do you know what it was like to hold back for as long as I did, knowing you were dating Kurt, imagining you in his arms, kissing him? Do you have any idea how it felt to see that dislike in your eyes every time you looked at me? Love." He groaned the word huskily, anguished eyes sweeping over her face.

Alanna was stunned, not sure she was hearing this impassioned confession.

"The first time I saw you, you were only a teenager. When you grew up and went off to college, I couldn't stop myself from loving you. I still can't. Yes, I maneuvered you into being my assistant. I was crazy happy when you finally said yes. I think I would have done anything to have you next to me. Okay, so I didn't play fair, but whoever said life was fair? I thought I could make you love me in time. Last night—" He shook his head and let her go, not finishing the sentence. "And today you met Kurt."

From somewhere Alanna found her voice. "But I didn't meet Kurt."

"Alanna, don't lie to me," he sighed heavily.

"I'm not lying. Are you?" she whispered.

Rolt frowned, confused. "Lying about what?"

"Do you—love me?"

She had to pause to swallow the lump in her throat.

"Isn't that what I've been saying all along?" Pain furrowed his brow. "I love you, Alanna."

The statement was not accompanied by any flowery speeches or declarations, yet its stark simplicity conveyed the depth of his emotion.

"I love you, Rolt." At his worried look, Alanna hastened to explain. "I've been fighting against falling in love with you since we started working together—well, even before that. I was trying to make myself believe it was only physical attraction. The only reason I met Kurt yesterday was because I wanted to see for myself whether I still loved him. I'm not sure if I ever did. I only know that I don't love him now. He's nice and I'm fond of him, but it's you I love."

His gaze narrowed, thoughtful and wary. "Today—"

"Today I went into town, bought champagne, and came straight home." Alanna repeated her earlier explanation. "I didn't see Kurt, I was too anxious to come back to fix our dinner this evening. It was to be the first real dinner we'd shared, not as a CEO and his trusty assistant, but as lovers. In love. Complete with candlelight, champagne, and flowers."

She was caught in the crush of his arms, his face pressed against her lustrous hair. Her hands instinctively slid around him. Alanna felt him shudder.

"That's enough," he said softly. "Just give me a chance to make up for some of the stupid things I've done. Just don't leave me, Alanna. Don't leave me."

"I'll never leave you," she whispered the vow.

Rolt cupped her face in his hands, his compelling gaze holding the brilliance of hers.

"Never is a long time," he reminded her.

"Never," Alanna repeated the promise.

The muffled cry of a loon echoed over still lake waters. The sun smiled and winked at the empty place settings on the dining room table. It could take its time about sinking below the horizon. No one was going to be lighting the candles for a long, happy while.

THE THAWING OF MARA

Chapter One

"Mara?"

Over the whine of the electric mixer, Mara heard her name called, but she didn't bother to acknowledge it. Instead she added more sugar to the egg whites and continued to beat them until they formed stiff peaks. She was spooning the meringue onto the pie filling when she heard the hum of the wheelchair approaching the kitchen.

"Mara, the mailman just drove by." The man in the wheelchair rolled to a stop inside the room. "I'm expecting some correspondence from Fitzgerald. Would you see if it's come?"

Mara didn't turn around. "I'm busy right now, Adam." She continued to spread the meringue thickly over the pie, ignoring the instant of tense silence.

"Stop calling me that." The request was terse. "I am your father, in case you've forgotten."

Over her shoulder, Mara glanced at the man whose surname, Prentiss, she had rightfully carried since birth. Her heart turned to stone at the sight of the handsome man imprisoned in the wheelchair.

His hair was as black as her own, except at the temples, where wisps of silver gave him a distinguished air. Their eyes were the same deep color, and the similarity in their sculpted features made it clear that they were father and daughter.

"I'm not denying my parentage, Adam." Her voice was as cool as her attitude.

He turned pale, his fingers tightening on the armrests of his chair. Mara noted his reaction with indifferent satisfaction and let her attention return to the pie. After swirling the white top into decorative peaks, she opened the door to the preheated oven and set the pie inside to brown the meringue. All the while the man in the wheelchair remained silent.

"It looks good." Her father forced the words out, striving for lightness and a degree of familiarity. "What kind is it? Chocolate, I hope."

"It's lemon," Mara said, not changing the temperature of her voice.

"You should make chocolate cream pie sometime," he suggested.

"I hate chocolate pie." She set the beaters and bowl in the sink and ran the water from the tap.

"You didn't always hate it." It was almost a challenge. Then his voice became warm. "When you were growing up, we used to argue over who got the last slice of chocolate pie. We usually ended up splitting it."

"That was a long time ago." Her curtness dismissed the idea that the past had anything to do with today.

"Your mother made the best chocolate cream pies I've ever tasted," Adam Prentiss went on. "I don't know where Rosemary got the recipe, but—"

Mara turned. Anger blazed in her dark eyes, burning off the chilly aloofness that usually encased her. "Don't start. Don't even say my mother's name!"

"She was my wife," he stated, levelly meeting her glare.

"Was she?" The taunting challenge was drawn from years of bitterness. Even now just thinking about it made Mara tremble. "You conveniently forgot about that when you ran off with your bimbo, didn't you?"

"I didn't forget it," Adam Prentiss said.

"You had a wife and child." Her voice rose sharply higher. "You abandoned us and you didn't look back, not once!"

"You were only fifteen at the time, Mara," he said, attempting to reason with her. "You couldn't know—"

"I was there!" she flared up. "I know what happened. When you walked out on my mother for another woman, it killed her. It just took a few years before she literally died. She practically worshipped you. No matter what I said, you were the only person who mattered to her."

"Do you think I wasn't sorry?" her father asked. "Do you honestly believe I didn't wish there was another way? Do you think I didn't care?"

"All you cared about was that blonde," Mara retorted, and turned away in disgust. "And she was only a few years older than I was!"

"I was in love with Jocelyn and I won't apologize for that," he said quietly. "But as strange as it sounds, it is possible to care about two women at the same time. I did care about your mother."

"I don't believe you. I saw the callous way you treated her," she reminded him. "Even before you ditched us, you flirted with everything female."

"For God's sake, Mara, those incidents were perfectly harmless." His impatient reply was angry.

"Harmless?" A bitterly amused sound came from her throat. "Yes, Mom always used to laugh it all off, but I could see the hurt in her eyes. You must have seen it, too. But it never bothered you, did it?"

"I don't have to justify my behavior to you. I've never pretended to be perfect." He was coldly indignant.

"But you managed to convince Mom you were." Mara continued her attack with vindictive zeal. "She used to think she was the luckiest woman on earth because she was your wife. I hope I never act that stupid about a man."

"I was in love with someone else. Do you honestly believe I should have stayed married to your mother?" her father asked. "Both of us would have been miserable if I'd done that."

"So you walked out on her. That way she was the only one who was miserable," she pointed out spitefully.

"All right, I hurt your mother. I admit that," he declared in agitation. "But give me credit for providing for her financially. I turned everything over to her—the house, the land, money, everything I owned except my clothes. I had nothing. I still have nothing. You got it all when she died."

"Did you think she'd leave it to you?" was Mara's only reply.

"No." His sighing answer was a mixture of defeat and exasperation. "Haven't I paid enough, Mara? Jocelyn was killed in the crash that did this to me. I'm permanently crippled. The doctors have even warned that as I grow older, my condition may deteriorate to the point where I won't even be able to get around in a wheelchair."

As the fight went out of his voice, Mara's fiery anger left, too. An icy calm stole through her, freezing her emotions. Unmoved by a speech she'd heard too many times before, she walked to the oven where the curling peaks of the pie's meringue were the color of golden toast.

"If you're looking for pity from me"—with a pot holder, Mara took the pie from the oven and set it on a wire rack to cool—"you're wasting your time."

"I'm attempting to understand you," her father

replied wearily. "Why am I here? After my accident you went to the doctors and told them that you were bringing me here and you would take care of me. At the time I thought you'd finally forgiven me. But you haven't. So why am I here?"

"Unlike you, I felt a sense of family obligation." Mara returned the pot holder to its drawer. "Regardless of how I feel about you, you are my father. It's my duty to take care of you."

"Uh-huh." He studied her, brown eyes measuring brown eyes. "Are you sure I'm not a convenient excuse to shut yourself off from the rest of the world?"

A smile twisted her mouth. "It's all about responsibility. But I'm sure you don't understand that since you don't know the meaning of the word."

"Take off the halo, Mara. You're just too good to be true," Adam Prentiss said dryly. "Maybe that's why you don't have a whole hell of a lot of friends. Whenever people invite you somewhere, you always turn them down because you have to stay here to take care of me. Hardly anyone calls anymore."

"That doesn't bother me." Mara lifted her shoulders in an uncaring shrug.

"You rarely went out when your mother was alive, either, did you? You spent most of your time with her." There was a shrewd gleam in his look.

"Mom was very lonely after you deserted her." The flatness of her statement was calculated to lash at him. "She needed me."

"You used her as an excuse the same way that you're using me," her father said in a low, quiet voice. "You like to look down on the rest of us from the moral high ground. What are you afraid of, Mara? Finding out that you're as imperfect as the rest of us?"

"Believe whatever you want, Adam. I couldn't care less what you think." With a perfunctory smile, she turned from him and walked to the coatrack. Taking her wool plaid jacket from an iron hook, she put it on. "I'll go and see if the mailman left anything in our box."

"Go ahead and run from the conversation, Mara," he said. "It's just another way to shut people out."

At first she made no response as she paused at the back door. When she turned, her gaze sought the man in the wheelchair. "You're only trying to rationalize your own feelings of guilt, Adam," she said. "You know you need someone to take care of you, but you prefer to pretend that I'm doing it for some other reason because it makes you feel better."

"Oh, Mara!" He shook his head sadly.

Her gaze strayed from him to wander over the old, cozy kitchen. The oak cupboards and cabinets had been installed over a century ago, but time hadn't dulled the rich luster of the wood. The walls were papered in cheerful yellow and white checks that matched the tieback curtains at the windows.

An old oak table and spindle-backed chairs stood in the middle of the room. The tabletop was covered with a bright yellow cloth, a small wicker basket of red apples and oranges at its center. The floor was a continuous length of white linoleum that dated from the 1950s, speckled with red, yellow and green.

She had never had the kitchen redone, had never wanted to.

"I know it bothers you that this is my home," Mara said. "And being dependent on me isn't any fun. But you're really very lucky, Adam. Here you have a comfortable place to live and you can continue your work. For all intents and purposes, I'm a nurse and housekeeper—and even though you do your history research online, I end up typing it because you refuse to learn WordPerfect."

"I could hire an assistant. Stop playing the martyr."

Mara folded her arms across her chest, prepared to answer that argument for the hundredth time. "No one would come all this way to work with you. You're stuck with me. So why don't you think about that instead of seeking an ulterior motive for something that I'm only doing out of a sense of family duty?"

When she was answered with silence, Mara turned and opened the back door. "Don't let the wind blow your halo off," was her father's snide comment.

Her lips thinned as she pushed open the second door, its screen replaced with storm-glass panes. She closed the inner door while stepping outside. The second door swung shut on its own when she released it.

A brick path circled the house to the front entrance, then continued out to the gravel road. There was an autumn chill in the air, September's breath. A few leaves were scattered around on the green lawn even though there hadn't been a killing frost yet. The trees were still full and green, but soon they would be painted with autumn colors. Then the Pennsylvania countryside around Gettysburg would be arrayed in hues of gold and scarlet and rust.

With her hands in her pockets, Mara held her jacket front together and followed the brick walk out to the road. She usually held her head high, but after her father's biting rejoinder she held her head even higher. She despised him. The force of the emotion clenched her hands into fists in the pockets of her jacket.

How typical of him to try to make someone else feel guilty. Mara remembered how her mother had agonized over what she might've done wrong to make him run off with that other woman. Mara had insisted otherwise. The only thing she could blame her mother for was being such a fool over him.

A squirrel scurried around, busily stashing his winter supply of food. Overhead there was a flash of scarlet as a cardinal flitted among the tree branches. But the wildlife didn't draw even a passing interest from Mara.

At the mailbox, she pulled down the little hinged door and removed the letters inside. Pausing, she glanced through them. Most were addressed to her father, although there were a couple of bills for her. She never got letters and, unlike most people her age, avoided e-mail, instant messaging and blogging. All of it was a big, fat waste of time as far as she was concerned.

It was true that she had few friends, but she'd never felt any great sense of loss at her lack of companionship. In fact, Mara often felt sorry for those who had to constantly be with others. She was content to be alone, not depending on someone else to entertain her. She viewed it as a trait of strength.

Mara's independence was something that had developed over her twenty-two years. Part of it came from her environment—being raised in the country with none of the close neighbors having children her age, and with no brothers or sisters. Part came from the circumstances of her life. Her schoolmates had sympathized with her at her father's sudden departure, but they hadn't understood Mara's feelings of betrayal.

His desertion of her and her mother for another, younger woman wasn't something that could be kept quiet. Adam Prentiss was a noted Civil War historian, an authority on the Battle of Gettysburg. Everyone in the area knew what had happened and why.

Mara had just started college when her mother was diagnosed with late-stage breast cancer. She'd withdrawn without credit and cared for her mother until her death only weeks later; then Mara had handled the arrangements for the funeral and all the legal business of settling the estate by herself. Finally there had been her father's accident two years ago. All of it had contributed to an unconscious decision to rely on no one but herself.

She closed the mailbox and turned to retrace her steps to the two-story red brick farmhouse with its white windows and door. A car came down the country road. It slowed as it approached and honked its horn. She recognized Harve Bennett, the dark-haired driver.

"I have good news for you!" he shouted out of the open car window, and turned into the driveway that ran parallel with the brick walk.

Mara lifted an eyebrow in fleeting curiosity before she started toward the house. His message obviously had something to do with the cottage on the far corner of the property. Harve Bennett was young, but he had his realtor's license and had helped her with title questions during the process of settling of her mother's property and estate.

The cottage had once provided rental income. After her father had left, it had been neglected and gotten too run-down to be rented. A few months ago, Harve finally succeeded in persuading Mara to make the necessary repairs and fix it up. She'd agreed, partly because her father had advised against it, insisting that she wouldn't be able to recoup the cost from the low rent for a pokey one-bedroom cottage.

All the major work had been completed a week ago, and Mara had leisurely begun to furnish the cottage while Harve placed ads in the local papers and on Craigslist. There was no big rush to finish things, or so she'd thought. Judging by the wide smile on Harve's face as he waited for her at the front door, she was wrong about that.

"Hello, Harve." Her mouth curved in a polite reciprocation of his smile. "Good news, huh? Guess it's about the cottage."

She walked past him and opened the front door. Entering the house, she took it for granted that Harve would follow her—which he did.

"That's right," he answered. "I got a call today from a guy who's really interested in it."

The wide entry hall split the house's interior in two. At the end, an L-shaped staircase that had once been enclosed led to the second floor. The sliding oak doors to the study, formerly the parlor, were open, and polished hardwood floors gleamed underneath an area rug.

From inside that room on the left, Adam Prentiss called, "Was there any mail for me, Mara?"

"Yes." She paused and separated the envelopes addressed to her father from the others she had in her hand. "Give me a moment," she said to Harve and walked into the study. "Here you are." She placed the mail on the desk behind which her father's wheelchair was positioned.

He glanced beyond her to the man standing in the hallway. "Hello, Harve," he greeted him affably. "How's business?"

"We're selling a few houses," was the falsely modest response. "How are you, Mr. Prentiss?"

"Fine, fine," was Adam's dismissing reply, and he began looking through his mail.

As Mara turned to rejoin Harve, she looked him over. She'd bet that fresh-scrubbed, faintly freckled face had probably been responsible for selling quite a few houses. Although in his early thirties, Harve Bennett still had a wholesome innocence—a trick of nature, Mara was sure.

"Let's go into the kitchen," she suggested smoothly.

Whatever Harve had come to discuss, it was no business of her father's. And she didn't want Adam listening in on their conversation.

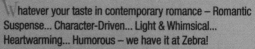

"Sounds great. I could use a cup of coffee if you have any made," he said unabashedly.

"I think so," she said, amused rather than irritated by his naturally pushy behavior.

Pushing open the swinging door to the kitchen, she walked to the coatrack. Harve was there to help her out of the wool jacket. She coolly smiled a thank-you before hanging the jacket on its hook.

"Okay, you said a guy called about the cottage." She walked to the counter where the coffeemaker was plugged in. "Someone local?"

"No, from Baltimore." Harve pulled one of the chairs away from the table and sat down, rocking it back on two legs and clasping his hands behind his head.

"From Baltimore? Why? Is he moving here?" Mara filled two coffee mugs and carried them to the table. "Cream or sugar?"

"Haven't you remembered by now that I take it straight?" he chided her, and let all four legs of the chair come down on the floor with a resounding thud. "It seems your prospective tenant is looking for a week-end retreat so he can get away from the hassle of the city and the pressure of work."

"I suppose he wants to see it," she concluded logically. Sitting in one of the other chairs, she mentally began to calculate how long it might take her to finish decorating the cottage if she devoted all of her spare time to it. "I have the bedroom furniture and the kitchen appliances in but—"

"He doesn't want to see it," Harve interrupted.

"You don't mean he's going to rent it sight unseen?" Mara looked at him in frowning surprise.

"I didn't mean exactly that he isn't going to see it," Harve replied, qualifying his previous statement. "He can't get away right now and I, er"—he grinned—"gave him the impression that you were already talking to other prospective tenants and wouldn't be inclined to let it sit vacant until he was free to come here to look at it."

"So how is he going to see it?"

"When I told him it was out in the country, secluded and quiet, he said it sounded like just what he was looking for. I almost got a commitment from him over the phone," said Harve, the pride in his salesmanship surfacing with the claim. "To make sure he wasn't renting a log cabin instead of a cottage, and to speed things up, he wants me to e-mail him some digital pictures of it. I told him I needed a new battery for my camera and promised I'd send them to him tomorrow."

"Tomorrow? That's worse than I thought," she muttered. "Why did you do that, Harve? You know it isn't completely furnished yet."

"I told him that. He said he was only interested in the bare necessities." Harve sipped his coffee, cradling the mug in his hands.

It was beginning to sound too good to be true. Mara felt a surge of skepticism that maybe everything wasn't as wonderful as Harve seemed to think.

"Who is this man? What do you know about him?" she demanded. "Is he young or old? After all the money I've spent fixing the cottage up, I'm not going to rent it to college kids so they can wreck it partying all weekend."

"It's difficult to judge people over the telephone," Harve began.

"So use Google. I assume he told you his name, where he works and all that."

"Yes, but there's nothing about him on Google, besides a few standard press releases."

"So you did get his name."

"Yeah, it's Sinclair Buchanan. I mean, he sounded

mature—"*How would you know?* Mara wanted to say but didn't.

Harve ignored her doubtful look and went right on talking. "I bumped the monthly rental five hundred dollars higher and he didn't even hesitate when I told him the price."

"That's a pretty big bump."

"I thought that would get your attention." A smug smile lit up his face.

"But why?" As far as Mara was concerned, the rent they'd planned to charge would've covered the repairs and then some.

"He sounded like he could afford it." Harve shrugged. "If he squawked at it, I could always say I'd read it wrong. As it is, you stand to make a healthy profit."

His reasoning was logical even if Mara found his ethics questionable. She lifted the coffee mug to her mouth, mentally refusing to be influenced by the *ka-ching* effect. She sipped at the coffee and set the mug down. "Still, Harve, I'm not going to rent it to just anybody, no matter how much money's involved."

"Don't worry, Mara. If, after he's seen the pictures of the cottage, he wants to sign a lease, I'm entitled to ask him for personal and credit references. I'll check Mr. Sinclair Buchanan out thoroughly," he promised.

"See that you do, because I'll want to see the results," Mara informed him, a note of warning in her tone.

"First things first." Harve wasn't concerned by her lack of total confidence in him; he had an extraordinary amount of confidence in himself. "I gotta take those pictures I promised him. To do that, I need the key to the cottage."

"I'll get it for you." Mara rose from her chair.

Harve was instantly on his feet. His hand was on her arm when she started to walk past him. "Better yet, why don't you come with me while I take those photos?" He was standing slightly behind her now, his low, coaxing voice coming from the general vicinity of her ear.

"I'm busy. Maybe another time." She brushed aside his invitation and would have walked out of his light hold, but he tightened it at the last minute.

"You're always telling me 'another time,'" he protested.

Mara felt the warmth of his breath against the bare skin of her neck, exposed by the short, smooth style of her sable-black hair. She felt a fleeting irritation. If Harve was aware of the number of times she'd put him off, why hadn't he gotten the message by now?

"Just can't. Not today." Her response was firm and unmoved by his veiled criticism.

An instant of silence followed, and Mara sensed that Harve was debating whether to push his luck. Finally his grip on her arm loosened and he stepped away, chuckling softly.

"Here we go again, Mara," he said. "You know, with most girls, I'd stop asking after the second no. But not you. Why is that?"

"I'll get the key to the cottage," was all she said.

"Cool, calm, collected." His exasperation was tinged with amusement. "As usual."

Her lips curved in a semblance of a smile, but she didn't respond to his question. She doubted that Harve had really expected a reply and anyway, she wasn't like most girls. Leaving the kitchen, she walked to the study where she kept the key to the cottage in the desk drawer.

"Are you going to the cottage?" her father asked when she removed the key.

"Nope. Harve has to go over to take pictures for some guy from Baltimore who's interested in it." She took secret delight in relating the news to her father, considering his doubts about the project.

"I thought it wasn't finished yet."

"The repairs are done. It just isn't all furnished yet, but this person doesn't seem to mind," Mara explained. But she didn't mention the high rent Harve had asked for. No, she would keep that to herself until the lease was actually signed.

"Just make sure you know something about your prospective tenant," her father cautioned. "There's more to being a landlord than just collecting rent. Some people tend to be destructive or careless with other people's property."

"I really don't need your advice, Adam," she retorted stiffly. "I've been handling my own affairs all by myself for quite some time. Virtually from the day you walked out."

He sighed. "I'm not trying to—"

"I know what you're trying to do," Mara interrupted with freezing contempt. "You may live in this house, but you won't control my life the way you controlled Mother's." She turned on her heel and swept out of the room.

Harve waited in the kitchen. His gaze moved over her as she entered. Mara's arctic indifference to his caressing look made him take a deep breath of confused frustration.

"Here's the key." She handed it to him.

He looked at it for a second before his fingers closed around it. "I'll bring it back when I'm finished. It shouldn't take too long."

"All right," said Mara, since some kind of answer seemed to be expected of her.

"Sure you won't change your mind and come with me?"

Harve looked resigned, as if he half expected the answer he was going to get, Mara thought. "No."

"That's what I thought." A wry smile crooked his mouth. "See you later."

"Yes. Good-bye, Harve."

"And don't worry about the cottage or Sinclair Buchanan. I'll make sure it's a clean, sweet deal," he assured her with a wink. "Or we'll pass on it."

When Harve had gone, Mara lingered in the kitchen. The decision would be hers. She was not going to be influenced by Harve or money, and especially not by her father.

Chapter Two

A week later Harve called to let Mara know that Sinclair Buchanan was definitely interested in leasing the cottage. A few days after that he came to the farmhouse with Buchanan's references, knowing that Mara almost never checked her e-mail.

"Hard copies, here you go. See, he checks out," Harve declared triumphantly as Mara went over the information. "Upstanding citizen with impeccable personal references, and a solid gold credit score."

Mara studied the papers for a moment longer, almost wishing she could find something to fault. There was nothing, but she couldn't shake off the feeling of unease. "Looks like you're right," she agreed, however reluctantly.

"Your enthusiasm is overwhelming," he grumbled. "This is a great deal, Mara. You're unbelievably lucky to get an offer like this for the cottage. Make my day, show a little excitement."

"Whoopee," Mara said in a flat voice and stacked the pieces of paper neatly to return them to the folder. "I'll wait until I see his signature on a lease agreement before I begin celebrating."

"His signature and a check for. the first and last months' rent, plus a security deposit. Don't forget that," Harve reminded her.

"I haven't forgotten," she assured him.

"In the meantime"—he removed a folded document from the inner pocket of his suit jacket—"let's get your signature on the lease so I can forward it to Buchanan for his."

He spread the printed form on the kitchen table and handed Mara a pen. She read it through before placing her signature of "M. Prentiss" on the line Harve indicated.

When it was done Mara felt better, as if she had made some important decision, even if it was really kind of ridiculous to feel that way. She'd signed a simple lease in legal boilerplate, hardly likely to change her life.

"Why so worried?" he chided. "From this point on it's merely a formality."

"I'm not worried, Harve."

As Harve had predicted, the final phase of the agreement proved to be a mere formality. The lease was mailed to Sinclair Buchanan. By return mail Harve received Mara's copy with the lessee's signature added and a check. When he brought the document to the house, Mara guessed the reason for his visit by the expression on his face.

"Here it is." He produced the envelope with an air of self-satisfaction. "All signed, sealed and delivered."

On the last word, he handed it to her with a slight flourish. Mara took it, removing the papers from the envelope and glancing at the signature scribbled across the line to be sure it was there. A cashier's check was clipped to the agreement. Mara glanced at the amount and raised a questioning eyebrow at Harve.

"This isn't the right amount. It's too much," she said.

"Yes, I know," he admitted, and gestured toward the papers she held. "There's a letter with it. Buchanan's driving up Friday evening. He sent a list of supplies he'd like stocked. That's why he sent the extra money—for supplies, any inconvenience and so on."

Mara found the letter and skimmed the list. It consisted mainly of staples and items—prepared hamburger patties, frozen pizza, beer—that she thought of as bachelor food, with a few basic housekeeping supplies thrown in as an afterthought. Her first impression was that his request was out of line, but she had to concede that at least he was willing to pay for this extra service.

"He's very generous," she observed, unable to keep the hint of asperity out of her voice.

"I thought it might be easier if you took care of the list," said Harve. "But I could arrange for one of the women at the office to handle it if you're too busy."

"I'll take care of it when I do my own shopping."

"That's what I thought." He smiled. "Another thing—I've made arrangements for him to come here to the house to get the key. He can't guarantee exactly when he'll be arriving, given the traffic on I-95 out of Baltimore. Our office closes at five o'clock, so it seemed best to have him pick it up here."

"That's fine," Mara agreed, and folded the papers to return them to their envelope. "He and I will have to meet sometime. It might as well be when he moves in."

She tried to ignore the nervous trembling in the region of her stomach, blaming it on the lunch she'd bolted in her hurry to meet with Harve.

"I almost wish I'd rented the cottage so I could have you for a landlady. The problem is I couldn't afford the price." Harve grinned lazily.

"I doubt very seriously that you're underpaid," Mara retorted, annoyed by his attempt to flirt and the way he turned on the boyish charm.

His grin widened. "As a matter of fact, I didn't do too badly this month. And with that check, neither did you." He pointed to the papers she held in her hand. "Why don't we celebrate? Have dinner with me Saturday night?"

Mara shook her head. "I'm afraid I can't, Harve. Mayb—"

"Don't. Just don't."

"Don't what?"

"If you say 'maybe another time' again, I'll do something drastic, Mara."

"Uh-huh," she said, not really paying attention.

"This time I'm not going to let you turn me down without a legitimate reason."

"Excuse me. Is there some law that I have to say yes, ever, just because you keep asking?" She took a deep breath, determined to keep her patience.

"Well, I mean it, Mara. Why can't you go out with me on Saturday night?" he demanded, the amusement leaving his expression.

"I can't leave Adam alone that long," she said.

"Your dad's perfectly capable of looking after himself for one evening. I asked you to have dinner with me, not spend the night," Harve pointed out.

"Like I would," she scoffed. "Anyway, I don't agree with you. Adam shouldn't be left alone."

"I won't accept that." He caught her by the shoulders and kept her facing him when she would have turned away. "C'mon, I've been asking you out for months. I can't get you out of my head."

"Oh, please, Harve"—her look was cool in its amusement—"spare me those awful lines! You can't really expect me to believe them."

"It's the truth," he declared, looking annoyed that she should doubt him.

"And I suppose you think of me while you date all those other women I've heard about. Let's see, your most recent conquests are an ICU nurse, an elementary-school teacher, a legal secretary—you do seem to like variety."

"For God's sake, Mara. What do you expect from me?" He let her go and turned away, running a manicured hand through his carefully groomed dark brown hair.

"I don't expect anything from you." Which was the truth in many ways.

"Okay, I see other women," Harve admitted a little defensively. "Why shouldn't I? Whenever I'm around you, all I get is the cold shoulder. I happen to be human—even if you're not."

"If that's your opinion of me, then why do you keep hanging around?" Mara challenged.

"Good question." Harve glared at her. "I don't know. So far it's been a waste of time."

Mara felt no emotion as he stalked out and slammed the door behind him. The gesture seemed so childish that she had to smile. But the whir of the approaching wheelchair wiped the smile from her face. She turned to face her father.

"Harve left in something of a rush, didn't he?" he commented.

"He suddenly remembered an important appointment somewhere else," Mara said.

"Really." His expression was skeptical. "I thought it was probably a severe case of frostbite."

"Do you think it's cold in here?" Mara wasn't going to take such obvious bait. "I don't feel it. Maybe you should put on a sweater."

"I don't need one," Adam retorted wryly. "I've become acclimatized to the chill." His gaze noted the papers she held. "I suppose that's the lease on the cottage."

"Yup. This Buchanan guy will be arriving Friday. Perhaps you'd like to look over the documents to make sure no one's taking advantage of me." She walked to his wheelchair and dropped the envelope in his lap.

Her attitude puzzled him until he looked at the lease and saw the monthly rental fee. Triumph glittered in her eyes when Adam looked up.

"What do you think?" Mara challenged.

"It's excellent." He handed the papers back to her. "I'm just wondering how you did it."

"Maybe it's one of the financial rewards of good, clean living," she suggested with a trace of sarcasm for the way he was always mocking her for being too righteous.

His dark head moved as he gave her a wryly amused look. "Were you properly grateful to Harve for doing this deal? Or did you show him the door because he'd served his purpose and you no longer had any use for him?"

Mara stiffened. "Harve knows he can take full credit for arranging the terms of the lease. Our relationship is strictly business. I'm not obligated to have dinner with him just because he got someone to agree to a much higher rent."

"Poor Harve," Adam mused. "I should have warned him that ice princesses don't mingle socially with mere peasants."

Mara was almost overwhelmed by an impulse to scream at her father to stop ridiculing her, but she fought it down. "I wouldn't worry about Harve. He already shares your opinion that I'm not human."

He held her gaze for a long moment. Some kind of silent appeal gleamed from the depths of his brown eyes, but Mara couldn't fathom it and didn't try.

Sighing, he turned his wheelchair and changed the subject. "So on Friday you officially assume the role of landlady."

"Yes." Mara automatically stepped forward to give him a little extra push over the doorsill, where the wheels sometimes caught. "I'll be going into town Friday afternoon to pick up a few things for Buchanan. If there's anything you need while I'm there, let me know."

"How about a loving daughter?" he asked in a low, weary voice.

"You had one once." She didn't elaborate further. He knew the rest.

Friday afternoon Mara separated the grocery bags, leaving the ones destined for the cottage in the back of the SUV, and carried the rest into the house. The grandfather clock in the entry hall chimed the half hour. It was after three, later than she had realized. Hurriedly she began taking out the perishables from the grocery bags and storing them in a refrigerator.

The door to the kitchen swung open to admit her father's wheelchair. "You're running late, aren't you?" he observed.

"Yes." Mara didn't pause in her task. "Did Sinclair Buchanan arrive while I was gone?"

"No."

"Do you have the key to the cottage?" She had left it with him before she'd gone to town.

"Right here." He produced it from the pocket of his cranberry sweater, a color that intensified his dark good looks.

Mara put the lettuce in the crisper and the cheese on a refrigerator shelf, the last of the items. Taking the key from her father, she walked to the back door.

"I'm going to the cottage. If Mr. Buchanan arrives

before I come back, send him down by the back trail," she instructed.

"Will do," he agreed as Mara went out the door.

The red brick farmhouse sat on one hundred acres of wooded land. The previous owner had cleared and farmed two hundred acres adjoining this property, intending someday to clear the rest of the woods.

When Mara's father had bought the place some twenty years ago, he'd sold off the farmland but kept the wooded land that surrounded the house. A neighboring farmer now leased the bulk of it to graze his cattle.

The cottage was located in the far corner of the property. There were two ways of reaching it. One was a gravel lane that led to the country road. The second was a dirt track that wound through the trees to the farmhouse. In bad weather, the latter was sometimes impassable, but that wasn't the case today.

The SUV thumped across the cattle guard, which, along with a fence, kept the neighbor's cattle from straying into the house's yard. The autumn scarlet of the sumac lined the way. A thin carpet of gold and brown fallen leaves covered the trail, rustling and whirling as Mara drove slowly along. Overhead the trees had exploded with color, most of the leaves still clinging tenaciously to the branches.

It was a gorgeous Indian summer afternoon with a cloudless blue sky and briskly invigorating air.

Her ribbed turtleneck sweater was all Mara needed in the mild temperature of this September day. The ivory color set off the silky black of her hair and complemented the forest green plaid of her pants.

Rounding a curve, she glimpsed the cottage through the trees. Where a second fence line intersected the trail was another cattle guard. Mara slowed the car as she crossed the iron grate and parked in front of the cottage.

The slanted roof of the low building was covered with shake shingles. The exterior siding was stained cedar and the windows and doors were trimmed with a burnt shade of rust. The cottage blended well with its woodsy setting.

Balancing a bag of groceries on her hip, Mara unlocked the front door and walked into the living room, dominated by a large, native-stone fireplace. The sparse furnishings didn't do justice to the potential of the room.

To the left was the kitchen, Mara's destination.

All the birch cabinets had been stripped and restained, and the countertops resurfaced. A small table and chairs occupied the breakfast nook and shiny copper pots hung above the stove. The atmosphere was distinctly warm and homey. Mara set the one bag down and went back for the others.

The third and last room of the cottage was the bedroom with a full bath off it. Mara didn't classify the small utility room as a room since it was little more than a large closet.

Given that it only had three rooms, the cottage gave the impression of spaciousness. But Mara didn't have time to admire its efficient design. All the supplies and food had to be put away.

The last bag was half-emptied when Mara thought she heard the sound of a car out front. She paused to listen and heard the slam of a car door. Leaving the can of coffee sitting on the counter, she made a detour on the way to the front door, stopping to glance out the kitchen window for an advance look at the cottage's new occupant. She had a brief glimpse of a tall, gray-haired gentleman approaching the front door before he disappeared out of her angle of sight.

Reassured somehow by the sight of that gray hair, Mara had barely straightened from the window when she heard a loud knock at the door. Unconsciously she squared her shoulders and lifted her chin to a lofty angle. The familiar aloofness settled over her as she went to answer the knock.

When she opened the door, her mouth automatically curved into a detached smile of greeting. Her gaze took in the towering bulk of the man outside, then met his smoky-blue eyes. Her expression froze in place. Like a movie special effect, tiny mental shock waves dissolved her previous image of the man.

Sinclair Buchanan wasn't old, although she could make a case for distinguished. Another word that fit him, she thought, was virile. The civilized impression given by the tweed jacket and dark trousers was banished by the unbuttoned shirt and the hard, browned flesh it revealed. The fact that his thick mane of hair happened to be iron gray was purely incidental.

All the while she was staring at him, he was studying her in an odd way, as if she wasn't what he had expected to see, either. Maybe there was some kind of mistake. Mara wanted to think so.

"Mr. Buchanan?" she asked.

He gave her a slight nod. "I stopped at the farmhouse and Mr. Prentiss sent me down here. Are you his daughter?"

The soothing pitch of his low voice was strangely unsettling, but Mara didn't want him to notice that it affected her. "Yes, I am. Mara Prentiss." The introduction seemed to demand a perfunctory handshake.

She offered him hers and found her slim fingers swallowed up by his. She didn't like the sensation of being engulfed by his sheer physical presence. It was somehow diminishing. Mara almost shivered as she withdrew her hand from his grasp.

He gave her a glance of detached amusement. "For

some reason, I expected to meet your father's wife or sister."

"My mother is dead." Mara didn't know why she offered the information.

"Mara Prentiss. M. Prentiss?" He referred to the signature on the lease.

"The same," she admitted, holding herself tall, as if she needed every inch of stature.

Behind the cloud blue of his eyes, there seemed to be a wicked light dancing. Mara thought she'd glimpsed it once or twice while they were talking. It gave her the impression of danger rather than mischief, something like the opaque gleam in the eyes of a cat playing with its prey.

"I assume you prepared for my arrival."

Mara realized suddenly she was still barring his entrance into the cottage. "Yes, I did." She stepped back to admit him. "I was just putting away the supplies you ordered."

One polished shoe had just crossed the threshold when a female voice halted him. "Sin, should I bring any of the luggage when I come?"

Mara's gaze jerked beyond him to the sleek gray car parked next to her SUV. A stunning redhead was just stepping out of the passenger side. Her white silk blouse was unbuttoned to show off her cleavage while a pair of midnight-blue jeans tightly hugged her hips. Despite the sexy clothes—*expensive* sexy clothes, Mara thought—the overall look was one of chic sophistication.

"Leave it," was his answer. "I'll carry it in later."

Tearing her gaze away from the red-haired beauty, Mara let it touch briefly on the man entering the cottage. Sinclair Buchanan. Sin for short. The nickname was apt, she concluded without being sure why.

Mara blamed her brief moment of surprise at the

presence of the woman on two things. All her attention had been focused on Sinclair Buchanan, so any distraction would have caught her off guard. The second was how long the woman had waited before making her presence known. It occurred to Mara that a wife probably would have accompanied him to the door. Even a mere Significant Other would have shown more curiosity or been more eager to see their newly leased cottage. Well, there was no telling what their relationship was until one of them explained. Mara wasn't going to ask.

Sinclair Buchanan was inside now and Mara redirected her attention to him. Aware that this was the first time he'd seen the cottage other than in downloaded photos, she felt she should make some attempt to familiarize him with the place.

"This is the living room." She stated the obvious, since Sinclair Buchanan was already making a slow, sweeping survey of the interior. Mara couldn't tell by his expression whether he was disappointed by what he saw or not, but she felt she should offer some excuse for the starkness of the room. "Harve probably told you that the cottage isn't completely furnished. If you want, I—"

"No, I'll see to the rest of it myself." He refused her offer to finish decorating the place before she had had a chance to complete it. "Is the fireplace usable?"

"Yes. The chimney's been cleaned and the flues checked," she assured him. "As a matter of fact, Harve and I got a fire going in it just a few weeks ago to be sure there was no problem."

Something in his gaze gave her the impression that he had put a romantic spin on her explanation. In fact, there'd been workers around finishing up the repairs, but she felt no need to add that.

"What about firewood?" he asked.

"There's part of a cord stacked behind the cottage

and plenty of kindling. You're welcome to gather the deadfall in the woods, but please don't cut down any trees," she told him.

Instantly she visualized him stripped to the waist and wielding an ax, splitting logs for the fireplace. She could even picture the sheen of perspiration glistening over the powerful muscles of his arms and chest. The image triggered a sudden surge of sexual feeling, which unnerved her because she couldn't control it.

In unconscious self-defense, she turned away from him to break the crazy spell. As she did, the redhead walked through the open door. Mara smiled as if it had been her intention all along to greet her as she entered the cottage, but the woman didn't even glance at her.

The redhead's brown eyes were alight with excitement as she made an inspection of the living room. When she came to a stop beside Sinclair Buchanan, her expression was alive with delight and anticipation. She circled one of his arms with both of hers and hugged him.

"Talk about rustic charm, Sin," she declared. "This is really quaint! Can't you picture an old sofa in front of the fireplace? We'll have so much fun decorating this place."

His look was indulgent, as if faintly amused, as he gazed at the upturned face of the woman. Fiery clouds of scarlet hair fell loosely around her shoulders. Mara was beginning to feel superfluous.

"Be honest, Celene. You're just looking forward to spending my money."

Not a very nice thing to say, Mara thought. His tone fell halfway between teasing and taunting, but his real feelings were anyone's guess.

With a put-upon pout, the woman named Celene seemed to choose the first interpretation. Mara wasn't in a position to argue with the decision. Celene was ob-

viously better acquainted with this man's moods and
meaning than she was.

"You know that isn't true, Sin," the redhead said. "I
enjoy spending anybody's money." She laughed. "I
pride myself on being totally impartial. Come on, let's
see the rest of the cottage."

Before he replied, his gaze swung to Mara. There was
something prompting in his look. Mara didn't know
what it was that he wanted, so she decided to leave it up
to him to explain.

"Shall I show you through the cottage or would you
prefer to explore on your own?" she asked.

"We'll find our way around. I don't think we'll get
lost," he assured her in a dry voice.

"I should hope not!" Celene's brittle laugh grated on
Mara.

"If you'll excuse me," Mara murmured coolly, "I'll
finish putting the groceries away." She paused to glance
at the redhead. "Unless you would prefer to do—"

"Please go ahead, Ms. Prentiss." Sinclair Buchanan
answered instead of Celene.

Mara couldn't help wondering if he made a habit of
interrupting. His gaze slid down to the woman on his
arm.

"Celene is helpless—or should I say hopeless?—in
the kitchen."

The woman smiled at the remark. "Sin knows me,"
she sighed, and turned her soft brown eyes on Mara.
"But then I've never claimed my talents were in that
area."

"I'm sure you're very good at whatever you do."
Mara's automatic response was meant to be polite, but
drew a low chuckle from Sinclair Buchanan.

The redhead gave him a playful slap of reprimand.
Celene's "talents" were obviously a private and intimate
joke between them.

Mara didn't want to find out more. Turning, she quietly walked into the kitchen.

The cottage was too small for her not to hear the murmuring of their voices as the couple wandered from the living room to the bedroom. To shut out the sound, she wiggled the rim of the coffee can under the wheel of the electric can opener and jammed down on the start lever, making it whir loudly.

Keeping busy seemed like a good idea. She pried off the lid and poured ground coffee into the canister for it, popped on its plastic lid, then set the half-full can inside the cupboard. She had just lifted a bag of flour out of the grocery bag when the two entered the kitchen.

"This is your territory, Sin. I'll leave you to inspect it," Celene declared. "There's something I want to get from the car. Back in a mo."

As the woman departed, Mara was all too aware of Sin Buchanan remaining in the kitchen. She opened the flap of the flour bag and reached for the canister. As she emptied the flour into it, she was aware of his movements, checking the appliances and the cupboards. His silver-streaked hair was like a beacon.

"I bought everything you had on the list," Mara informed him as she pushed the canister into its position with the rest of the set, "I hope you won't have difficulty finding anything."

"Don't think so," he replied. "Everything seems to be well organized." It was an observation rather than a compliment.

The dumping of the bag had left a fine film of flour dust on the counter, and Mara dampened a dishcloth to wipe it away. While she finished up in the kitchen, her new tenant wandered back into the living room. His return coincided with the entrance of Celene. There was nothing to keep their voices from carrying into the kitchen.

"I found the wineglasses, so I brought in the champagne to toast our little love nest." Celene's voice held a throaty note of seduction. "The cooler kept it chilled to perfection. Here, open it, Sin."

An assortment of spices and herbs remained at the bottom of the grocery bag. Mara tried to remain deaf to the conversation in the adjoining room as she began arranging the bottles on the spice rack.

"Don't you want to save the celebrating until later?" The pop of the champagne cork made his question meaningless.

But Celene answered it anyway. "No, I want to start now." Her voice was almost a purr. "This is the first weekend I've ever had you all to myself. No phone calls, no business, no interruptions." The last negative was emphatically stressed. Celene proposed the toast, "To our first weekend alone."

It was followed by the clinking of crystal and then silence. An inner voice seemed to order Mara to keep quiet and not betray her presence in the cottage, but she refused to obey it. The bottles thudded onto the spice shelf with the same regularity.

"Mmm, you know what we should do tonight, honey?" Celene answered her own question without giving Sin a chance to respond. "Build a roaring fire in the fireplace. Then we'll lie down in front of it and . . ." The rest of her suggestion was made in a whisper.

Mara's stomach knotted into a tight ball of nerves. The entire situation was making her irritated and on edge. A can of dried parsley flakes was the last item in the grocery bag. She shoved it quickly into place and folded up the paper bag, stowing it beneath the sink.

In the opening to the living room, Mara hesitated. The couple were in front of the fireplace, locked in a kiss. Celene's arms were wound around Sin's neck while she still managed to hold the champagne glass. One of his hands was on her rib cage, almost cupping her breast. His other arm was pressed against the small of her back, arching the redhead to his muscled body. That hand held his glass.

Moves they'd been practicing, Mara thought sourly. Neither had spilled any champagne in the process of getting up close and personal, since there was liquid in each of the glasses.

She started to retreat into the kitchen until their passionate embrace was over, but she stopped herself. Why should she scurry off as if their kissing made her uncomfortable? If anyone was going to feel awkward about her intrusion, let it be them, she decided. She took another step into the living room.

"Excuse me, I'm leaving now," she announced with composure, her voice cool.

Not ruffled in the least, they untangled themselves from each other without tipping their champagne glasses. Celene smoothed the fiery strands of hair from her cheek in a self-conscious gesture, but there was a pleasantly satisfied glow in her eyes, especially when they darted to Sin.

"Gee, I'm sorry," she apologized while he sipped at his champagne. "I'm afraid we got a bit carried away."

Secretly Mara thought that excuse might be true for Celene, but a glance at Buchanan made her doubt that it had been equally true of him. He looked fully in control of himself and his passions.

"No need to apologize." Her mouth curved, but it wasn't much of a smile.

Sinclair Buchanan moved, drawing Mara's gaze. His jacket was unbuttoned, the front held open by the hand thrust in the pocket of his slacks. That casual air was a pose; Mara realized that he was just as alert as she was.

"I haven't thanked you for making sure that we have something to eat this weekend," he said.

"It isn't necessary, Mr. Buchanan," Mara countered. "You paid for it, remember?"

He shot Celene a wry look that the redhead didn't see. As if he was used to paying for all kinds of things, Mara mused, and didn't necessarily like it. She put that thought aside and remembered to act like a landlady. "Well, I hope you like the cottage. If you or your wife have any questions, please contact me."

Celene broke into a laugh and immediately covered her mouth. "Oh, hell. She thinks we're married!"

"Yes." His amusement was more distant as he turned and lifted an inquiring eyebrow at the redhead. "I wonder where she got that idea . . ."

Mara's chin tipped to an angle a scant degree higher than before, the only outward sign of her recoiling shock. After the first confused moments of Celene's grand entrance, Mara had more or less assumed they were married but she had no way of knowing and really didn't care very much. All the same, she was reluctant to make another assumption in case it turned out to be wrong, too.

"It's my fault." Sin took the blame without exhibiting any remorse for his action. "I didn't introduce Celene when we arrived," he said, correcting the oversight. "Ms. Prentiss, this is Celene Taylor, a friend of mine. Celene, Mara Prentiss."

"Nice to meet you." Mara acknowledged the introduction stiffly and received a smiling nod in return.

"Celene is spending the weekend with me," he stated. "No restrictions in the lease against having friends visit, right?"

"No, of course not." Mara was piqued by his teasing tone and told herself that two could play at that game. "But you do realize there's only one bedroom," she reminded him coldly, and immediately wished she hadn't said it.

That devilish glint was back in his eyes. "Yes, I do know, Ms. Prentiss. You don't mind if I call you Mara, do you? First names are easier, now that we're all getting to know each other."

"Not at all." Wanting to give him a swift kick, Mara tried desperately not to snap out the answer. The only way out of this mess seemed to be a dignified retreat. "I know you'll want to bring your luggage in and get unpacked, so I won't keep you any longer. Bye, Celene. Bye, Sinclair."

Mara turned toward the door, only to be halted by a low male voice. "Aren't you forgetting something?"

She glanced over her shoulder, her look totally blank. "Huh? Forgetting what?"

"The key to the cottage," Sin replied. "I believe I need one."

Silently calling herself fifty kinds of a fool, Mara reached into her pocket and took out the key. Sin Buchanan walked over to take it from her. She practically dropped it in her haste to give it to him.

Her eyes blazed at the amused curl of his mouth. That opaque gleam was in his smoke-blue eyes playing over her face. Mara had never felt so powerless in her life. There was nothing she could do to change it.

"Thank you." His strong fingers closed around the key.

Mara nodded dumbly and pivoted toward the door. Somehow she managed to keep her steps unhurried as she left the cottage, but she was trembling by the time she reached the SUV.

Chapter Three

By the time Mara reached the house, her seething resentment was under control, turned down to a low simmer. Sinclair Buchanan had made her feel awfully foolish. She didn't like that or him.

And she should have followed her first instincts: her new tenant *had* sounded too good to be true. Why had she listened to Harve and rented the cottage without meeting Buchanan first?

Not that it would have made any difference, Mara concluded as she walked to the back door of the red brick house. "Sin" probably wouldn't have brought his girlfriend to that meeting. Not that she cared whether he had a girlfriend, she reminded herself. But the pair of them, mostly Sin, had made her look so damn prudish. And she wasn't. She didn't care how other people behaved.

Slamming the back door, she tossed the car keys on the kitchen counter. They slid against a grocery bag. Mara was reminded that none of this would have happened if it hadn't taken so long to buy the supplies in town. His groceries would have been put away in the cottage and she would have been safely here in her own house, ready to give him the key when he stopped by for it. Would've saved her a lot of embarrassment.

"Mara?" Her father entered the kitchen. Immediately she began unpacking the rest of their groceries. "That Buchanan guy stopped here. I sent him down to the cottage. Did you see him?"

"Yes," she answered without elaboration.

"How did they like the place?" he asked. "I caught a glimpse of his wife in the car. Striking woman. Beautiful, in fact. But not exactly the type who'd be happy in a cottage in the Pennsylvania woods."

"She loved it." Mara sarcastically stressed the verb, the woman's gushy "Sin, honey" echoing in her mind. "But she isn't his wife."

Her voice was hard and flat as she made the announcement. She continued to stack the canned goods in the cupboard without a break in her rhythm, but there was a hint of angry agitation in her movements.

"Not his wife?" Adam Prentiss said absentmindedly. "Oh . . . gotcha." He began chuckling as he realized what she meant. "My mistake."

Mara said nothing, not admitting it was a mistake she had made, too.

"There's nothing like bringing your own entertainment along with you to while away the hours."

"Don't be crude!" Mara slammed the cupboard door shut and it banged open again, almost hitting her. The world was conspiring against her, she was sure of it.

She closed it again, quietly, but an image of her new tenant and his mistress cuddling in front of the fireplace leaped into her mind. It grated at the edge of her raw nerves, inflaming them again.

Her outburst was greeted by a moment of silence.

When her father spoke, all trace of amusement was gone from his voice. His tone was serious and gently reprimanding.

"Sex isn't crude, Mara. It's a very beautiful thing."

"Oh, please. You are beyond disgusting. I don't want a lecture from you on that particular subject!" she snapped.

A long sigh came from behind her, followed by the turning of the wheelchair. When the swinging door had slowly stilled, Mara was alone in the kitchen. Her hands were gripping the edges of the counter, her knuckles white.

For the rest of that day and all of Saturday, she blocked out the cottage and its inhabitants from her mind.

On Sunday morning she rose early. While the coffee-maker got up to speed, she walked out to the mailbox for the Sunday newspaper.

Her father was awake when she returned. After helping him into his robe, she held the wheelchair steady as he levered himself out of the bed into it.

The whole routine seemed timed to coincide with the moment the coffee was ready. It emitted its last gurgling sound as Mara wheeled her father into the kitchen. In silence they shared a glass of orange juice and a cup of fresh coffee before she fixed their breakfast of ham and eggs and hot rolls.

With the morning meal over, she stacked the dishes in the sink and filled it with hot, sudsy water. Her father's wheelchair remained positioned at the table while he read the newspaper and sipped a cup of coffee.

Mechanically Mara began washing the dishes. One by one she rinsed them and stacked them on the drain-board to dry. Her mind seemed blank as she performed the task, her gaze straying out the window above the sink to the woods beyond.

A large patch of blue caught her eye, and focusing on it, she saw a figure coming up the rutted trail from the cottage. It was Sin Buchanan, dressed in a sky blue track suit. A black stripe ran down the long length of the legs. His muscled frame moved in effortless, athletic strides. The silver gray of his hair was at odds with the rest of him, a perfect male specimen in the prime of his manhood.

Mara watched him cross the cattle guard and approach the house at an easy, jogging pace. She expected him to turn up the driveway toward the gravel country road, and an alarm jangled through her nerves as she realized he was headed for the back door.

In a sudden spurt of activity she began working faster to finish the dishes, chipping one. A knock at the back door made her spine stiffen. The newspaper rustled as her father set it aside.

"I wonder who that could be," he murmured.

"I'll go see." Mara avoided his questioning gaze as she dried her hands with a terry towel.

She walked to the door, steeling her features to be expressionless. When she opened it, Sin Buchanan was standing outside, looking totally at ease. Mara felt a fluttering tension in her stomach.

The even rise and fall of his broad chest revealed that the long jog from the cottage to the house hadn't winded him. Her gaze lifted to his face and met his eyes. They seemed somehow shuttered, his inner thoughts hidden from her. If anything, his eyes only reflected the coolness of her attitude.

"Good morning, Mara." The sexiness of his low-pitched voice made her nervous tension worse.

"Was there something you needed, Mr. Buchanan?" Mara wasn't about to call him Sin.

"Yes, there is."

From behind her came Adam's voice. "Don't stand there with the door open, Mara—it's creating a draft. Invite him in."

A practical suggestion that couldn't be ignored, as much as Mara wanted to. Her fingers tightened around the doorknob. Her impulse was to step outside to speak to him privately, without her father listening, and not allow Sin Buchanan inside the house.

But there was a nip in the autumn morning. The warmth of Sin's breath was making a vaporous cloud in the outside air. Mara realized that if she attempted to conduct this conversation out of doors she would soon be shivering. The last thing she wanted to do was attempt to discuss business with her teeth chattering.

Reluctantly Mara swung the door wide to admit him. "Please come in." There was little welcome in her voice. The best she could do was tolerate his presence. She hoped her father wouldn't pick up on it.

"Thank you. I hope I'm not intruding." His response was just as polite, if not sincere.

As far as Mara was concerned, he was intruding and she had no intention of denying it. Unfortunately, her father thought otherwise.

"Of course not. We met when I gave you the key and now we're neighbors. You don't mind if I call you Sinclair, do you?"

The men shook hands.

"We've already had breakfast," Adam continued. "Mara was just washing the dishes while I finished reading the paper. But there's some coffee left. Mara, why don't you offer Sinclair a cup?"

She sent her father a silencing look. "Maybe he's had his morning coffee." Her glance challenged Sin to dispute her claim.

"As a matter of fact, I didn't take time for coffee before I left the cottage."

"Pour the gentleman a cup, Mara," her father instructed.

"We're down to the bottom of the pot," she pointed out, irritated that Sin Buchanan was taking advantage of the hospitality he had to guess she didn't want to extend.

"No problem. I like my coffee strong and black," he informed her, and glanced at her father. "Thanks for offering, Adam."

"Sit down." Her father waved a hand to indicate a chair at the table. "Make yourself at home."

Sinclair Buchanan did just that, choosing the chair that Mara had been sitting in, which was even more annoying of him.

Emptying the coffeepot into a mug, Mara carried it to the table and set it in front of him. "This is wicked strong. But you'll probably like it. Isn't Sin your nickname?" Her not-very-subtle joke was followed by an unbidden thought: *Sin by name, sinful by nature.*

His eyes glanced up at her, something she couldn't quite read in their steely depths. "That's correct," he said.

As Sin lifted the mug to sip the scalding-hot coffee, his gaze was directed at her father. "Adam Prentiss—I have the feeling I should know that name."

Adam had been studying his daughter, but he returned his attention to the man at the table. "I'm something of a local historian," he offered in explanation.

"Adam is being modest," Mara said. "He's a very well-known Civil War historian."

"That's where I've heard your name, then." Sin absorbed the information Mara supplied but didn't seem to hear the edge in her voice. "A close friend of mine is an avid Civil War buff, and your name probably came up in conversation."

Mara wondered who his close friend was and heard herself inquire skeptically, "Ms. Taylor?" The redhead didn't seem like the type to wear a long, frumpy dress made of itchy wool and stomp around the fields reenacting famous battles. Well, mostly it was men who did the reenacting, Mara silently corrected herself. Celene wouldn't do it. Too much mud and too much misery.

"No." Sardonic amusement danced in his eyes for a second but Sin's strong face quickly turned expressionless. "A close male friend of mine."

Mara had the distinct impression that she had walked into a trap he had neatly set for her, and she didn't like the feeling. Sin Buchanan was an irritating and offensive man. She wished she could stop rising to his bait and learn to ignore it.

He was speaking again, this time to Adam. "I believe John mentioned your name as the author of a book he'd recently read about the Battle of Gettysburg."

"That's possible," her father conceded with a faint smile. "I have written one on the subject. It's nice to know someone's read it. After the first flurry of reviews dies down, history books tend to gather dust on the library shelves."

"I confess that I know very little about the battle or the Civil War." But Sin Buchanan wasn't apologizing for his ignorance or previous lack of interest.

"When the South lost the Battle of Gettysburg, they virtually lost the war even though it dragged on for another two years—" Adam began to explain the significance of the battle in history.

"Could we skip the history lesson?" Mara asked before her father could warm to his favorite subject. She turned a challenging look toward Sinclair Buchanan. "You said there was something you wanted to speak to

me about?" No point in letting him forget the reason
for his visit.

He almost frowned, then seemed to relax. Behind
his lazy regard, Mara sensed he was silently laughing at
her. It heightened her feeling of antagonism toward
him.

"Yes, there is," Sin admitted. "I want to make arrangements to have someone to clean the cottage and get it
ready for my weekend visits."

"I see," she murmured, and waited for him to continue.

"Since I'm new to the area, I thought you might rec-
ommend a responsible person for the job," he explained.

She couldn't argue with his logical request, but she
couldn't help him either. Mara shrugged. "Offhand, I
can't think of anyone."

"Could I ask you to find someone? It's difficult to conduct interviews long-distance and it's time-consuming."

Silently Mara wished that he wasn't so damned logical. She wanted to disagree with him, but his proposal
made too much sense.

"I'm flattered that you trust my judgment."

He didn't seem to mind the frost in her tone. "We
both have a vested interest in keeping up the cottage.
Since you own it, you wouldn't want to see the property
neglected, while I want to enjoy it in comfort."

"That makes sense." Mara paused to control the sharpness of her tongue. "But you have to understand that
it's not easy to find a reliable person who'll be willing to
come so far out of the way. We're really out in the
boonies."

Her comment didn't elicit an immediate response.
Mara watched as Sin lifted the coffee mug to his firmly
defined mouth. His large hand encircled the mug, a
healthy tan coloring his skin. She felt her tension build-

ing from the volatile undercurrents rippling through the air. Her gaze strayed past Sin to her father, who was observing the subtly charged byplay between them with growing interest. Adam's presence aggravated the situation.

"I'm aware of that, Mara." Sin replaced the mug on the table, then slid his veiled gaze to her. "And I'm more than willing to compensate you for your services."

"Of course," she countered dryly. It seemed like money was never an object where he was concerned.

"In the meantime, I'll need someone to look after the place while I'm gone during the week. I don't know whether it's proper to ask my landlady to do it or not, but you're conveniently close to the cottage." His mouth quirked in a half-smile. "If you could spare the time to clean it after I leave and make sure it's aired and relatively well stocked with supplies before I arrive, I would greatly appreciate it."

Mara hesitated as she considered the alternatives. If she refused, there was the risk of dirt and dust collecting to the point where the cottage would need a major cleaning. Considering the time, money and effort she had put into the place so far, it would be crazy to neglect it.

"I can look after things temporarily while I look for someone reliable," she agreed without realizing that her tone of voice made it sound as if she was doing him an enormous favor.

"Thank you, Mara." Sin expressed his gratitude in a decidedly mocking way.

She stifled her surge of irritation with an effort. "Give me an idea of what you want in a housekeeper."

He shrugged. "You know more about that than I do."

"What are you willing to pay, then?"

"Whatever is fair. Perhaps you could make a suggestion on that." He put the question back to her.

"As long as the cottage isn't left in too much of a mess, it shouldn't take more than a couple of hours to clean and dust the rooms on a Monday, and about the same amount of time on Friday to air the place out and stock the pantry." Mara hoped he got the hint: no one would pick up after him if the cottage got too cluttered and dirty. "So that's twice, plus driving expenses to get the shopping done. A hundred dollars a week should cover it. Would you be willing to pay that?"

"I don't quibble over things like that," he informed her. "As long as I get what I want, I'm not concerned about the cost."

His supreme confidence grated on Mara. "Really," she said. "How lucky for you. Okay then, that's the salary I'll quote. Was there anything else?" Rising from her chair, she indicated by her action that if there was nothing, he should leave.

"No, that was all. Thanks for the coffee." Letting go of the mug, Sin stood up. She felt dominated by his height, although the indolent, sensual look in his eyes took the edge off that feeling.

"There's no need to rush off," her father protested amiably.

The dark fire in her eyes smoldered as Mara managed a fake smile. "I'm sure his, um, female friend is probably wondering where he disappeared to."

"Celene was sleeping when I left." Sin offered the information unasked. "She's not an early riser."

Probably touching up her roots and fluffing her eyelashes right now, Mara thought.

"She'll probably still be in bed when I get back and I'll have to wake her."

"How sweet." Mara had an immediate mental picture of just how Sin would go about it. "I'm sure she'll enjoy it." She moved toward the door to escort him out.

But Sin didn't immediately follow her as he paused

to say good-bye to her father. "Nice talking to you again, Adam."

"The pleasure was mine. As you can see, I don't get out much." Her father patted the armrest of his wheelchair, indicating his condition without asking for pity. "But I hope you find time to stop by for a visit again."

"Thank you. I'll try." His glance at Adam's daughter made it clear that he was aware she hadn't seconded the invitation. "See you, Mara."

There was controlled amusement in the warmth of his resonant voice. All she offered in return was a stilted good-bye as she opened the door for him.

His wide-shouldered bulk moved past her, his physical strength evident in the ease of his long strides. Mara caught a whiff of an expensive aftershave, no doubt purchased for him by the redhead. On his credit card—

She stopped the jealous thought, then realized he was out of the door. She shut it, but it wasn't so easy to shut out his existence from her mind. Turning, she walked back to the sink and the now lukewarm dishwater. Through the window she could see Sin effortlessly jogging back the way he'd come.

"Don't encourage him, Adam," she said, recalling her father's parting invitation. "I want the relationship to remain strictly landlord and tenant. Nothing personal, no complications."

"I'm sure Sin is aware of your views," he replied in an exasperated tone.

"All I'm saying is that you don't have to make friends with him."

"You never gave a hoot in hell about my friends, old or new. Why this sudden resistance to Sin Buchanan?" Adam was both puzzled and intensely curious.

"I told you." She didn't look up from the skillet she was scrubbing. "He's a tenant. Business and friendship don't mix."

"There's no business involved—at least, not between Sin and myself. He leases the cottage from you, not me," he reminded her. "So that argument doesn't stand up."

"Yes, I leased him the cottage," Mara snapped, "but I don't want him in this house!"

A slow half smile spread across her father's mouth. "He bothers you, doesn't he?" He tipped his head to one side, studying her for a long, unnerving moment.

"I don't know what you mean." She turned the tap on full force to rinse the detergent from the skillet.

"No," he replied and then paused. "Probably you don't."

Mara didn't want to explore the reasons behind that remark. "What are you going to do if Sinclair Buchanan comes here again?" she demanded.

"He's my neighbor. If he comes, I'll invite him in," Adam stated.

"You'd do that after what I've just asked you?" She turned on him roundly.

"I not only would, but given the chance, I will," he declared in open challenge.

"This happens to be my house," Mara reminded him in a cold voice.

"Sin Buchanan would be my guest. I've always invited whatever friends I pleased into this house in the past. You never objected before—why are you making an exception with Sin?" There was a shrewd gleam in his dark eyes that Mara didn't like.

But she couldn't very well keep her father from seeing people. They were isolated enough—she had no intention of turning into a character from a hokey old horror movie and denying her crippled father a chance to socialize.

"The circumstances are different," she said, feeling the need to say something in her own defense.

"No, they aren't," Adam said. "Besides, half the time when someone comes over to see me, you're off in some other room. If and when Sin ever comes here, you can go and hide in another part of the house until he leaves."

"Hide?" She checked herself in time to insist, "I'm not afraid of him."

"No?" A dark eyebrow lifted and leveled out in another second to its former line. "Well, he certainly does have the ability to upset you, doesn't he?" Reversing his wheelchair from the table, he swung it toward the hall door. "I'm going to finish reading the newspaper in the other room."

Mara stared after him. She hadn't lost an argument with her father since he had come to live with her after the accident. He always gave in to her—but not this time. And Mara was fully aware that he could be as stubborn as she was. For some reason, Sin Buchanan's presence on the property was changing everything.

Chapter Four

On Monday morning, Mara arrived at the cottage to find all three rooms neat and orderly. There were no dirty dishes in the sink or an unmade bed. No magazines or papers were scattered around the living room. A shopping list was taped to the refrigerator door for the upcoming weekend, and it took less than an hour for her to dust and sweep the cottage.

During the week, she interviewed three women who responded to the classified ad she'd placed in the paper. Two of them didn't have cars and the third simply hadn't impressed her. So on Friday she was the one who bought the groceries and aired the cottage in preparation for Sin's arrival, finishing well before noon to avoid accidentally meeting him.

On Saturday and Sunday mornings, Mara saw him out jogging. Both times she was washing the breakfast dishes. Each time he lifted a hand in a casual wave in the direction of the window above the sink, but he didn't approach the house. Mara didn't wave back, and she didn't care if he happened to think that was rude. She didn't mention to her father that she had seen him or that Sin had waved to her.

When she went to the cottage on Monday morning to clean, she discovered some changes had been made over the weekend. An old-fashioned davenport with upright armrests was positioned in front of the fireplace. It was upholstered in a plush fabric patterned with varying shades of green. An alpaca area rug in its natural cream color covered the square of floor between the davenport and fireplace.

An old easy chair, perfect for reading in, sat to one side. A tall floor lamp stood beside it along with a combination table and magazine rack of carved oak; and a handsome antique rolltop desk took pride of place with its matching straight-backed chair. The bare walls had been brightened by framed prints of countryside scenes done by local artists.

It needed a few more homey touches here and there, but this beginning was pleasing. Yet Mara found herself wondering somewhat critically how much of the decor was due to the redhead's influence rather than to Sin Buchanan's taste.

There was less cleaning to do than before, except for a basket of dirty sheets and towels in the utility room. Mara washed and dried them. As she started to put them away, she checked first to see if clean sheets had been put on the bed.

She flipped back the coverlet and blanket to see luxurious satin sheets in a deep chocolate color, and reached out a hand unthinkingly. The sheets were smooth and sexy to the touch, right out of a bachelor pad fantasy, Tacky but kinda wonderful, Mara thought.

Quickly she finished putting the clean laundry away and returned to her own home. She didn't mention the new furniture or satin sheets to her father. They'd both avoided anything having to do with Sin Buchanan since their discussion more than a week ago.

As she started to get lunch ready, the phone rang. Mara didn't pay any attention, knowing her father would answer it in the other room.

"It's for you, Mara," he called to her.

"I'm in the middle of getting lunch. Tell whoever it is I'll call back later." She continued peeling the shells off the hard-boiled eggs, thinking that it was high time she got a life. Making egg salad and picking bits of shell out of the sink did not count as a life.

"No," said Adam. "Lunch can wait."

She knew from experience that he would keep after her until she talked to whoever it was. Adam, who spent hours online tracking down odd information, thought phone calls were a wonderful way to be interrupted. She didn't agree, but she might as well get this one over with.

Mara rinsed her hands under the running tap. "I'll be right there!" She hurried toward the study while drying her hands on a towel. So who was it? Adam was behind the large desk when she entered, and he handed her the receiver. "This is Mara Prentiss."

"Hey, Mara. This is Sin Buchanan. Calling from Baltimore."

Big deal, she wanted to say. His familiar voice seemed so close that Mara wouldn't have been surprised to discover he was in the next room. Every cell in her body went on red alert.

"How are you?"

The polite phrase prompted a polite response. "Fine, thanks." Mara glanced at her father and realized he had known all along who was calling. She turned her back to him.

"Then your arm is all right?" It was a questioning statement.

"My arm?" Mara frowned at the telephone.

"Yes, I thought it might be broken. Usually when you wave at a person, they wave back unless there's something wrong." The comment was offered in a disinterested fashion as if Sin didn't really care to hear any explanation of why she hadn't returned his greeting.

"Oh." Mara didn't attempt one. "Was that why you called?"

"Not really. I wanted to find out if you'd hired a housekeeper," he told her.

Mara knew the previous remark had just been made to needle her. "I've interviewed three women so far."

"Any luck?" Sin asked.

"I wasn't impressed." She kept her voice coolly restrained and forced her fingers to relax around the receiver. "But the decision is yours to make, not mine. Want me to send their applications and references?"

"I trust your judgment. No need for that, is there?" There was an indulgent ring to his voice.

Mara gritted her teeth. If there was one thing she really hated, it was being patronized. "No, I suppose not."

"Okay. Well, please keep me informed." It was closer to an order than a request.

"I will," she promised with cool dignity, wondering if she should inform him that she'd discovered his swinging secret: satin sheets. His voice brought her out of her momentary reverie with a jolt. As far away as he was, he sounded like he was right next to her, his dark head resting on a chocolate satin pillow case and—

"See you, Mara."

"Good-bye," Mara responded, and replaced the receiver on its cradle without waiting to hear if he had anything further to add.

"That was Sin Buchanan, wasn't it?" her father asked.

"Oh, as if you didn't know," she said. "He just called

to see if I'd found someone to clean the cottage for him."

"What was that about your arm?" He eyed her thoughtfully.

Mara shrugged. "Somewhere he got the mistaken impression that I'd injured it."

"Where did he get that idea?"

"I really don't know," she lied. "You'll have to excuse me, there's soup on the stove that requires my undivided attention."

"It came from a can," Adam intoned.

"That doesn't mean you don't have to watch it," Mara said, and left the room.

That week Mara interviewed two more applicants for the position. Neither seemed right and she couldn't hire anyone she wasn't one hundred percent sure of. When the second had left, Adam rolled his wheelchair out of the study.

"That woman sounded capable. Why didn't you hire her?" he asked.

"She sounded capable," Mara agreed, stressing the verb as qualification. "But her hair wasn't combed right, her blouse needed ironing, and she had dirt under her fingernails."

"So?"

"If she's that careless with her appearance, what makes you think she'd keep the cottage neat and tidy?" she retorted.

"You could be right," Adam conceded. "But keep in mind, Mara, that no one's going to be as perfect as you are."

Mara rubbed her fingers against the throbbing in her temples and sighed. "Why don't you just be quiet,

Adam?" It was a toss-up as to which of them was ruder, but her remark held the faintest sound of a defeated plea for peace. She let her hand fall to her side and lifted her head, giving herself a mental shake. "Did you make notes on the Bull Run material you printed out? Is it edited and ready for me to type?"

"Yes. It's all on the desk," he replied, and watched her closely as she walked from the living room.

Another weekend came and went. The only glimpse Mara had of her tenant was when he went for his morning run. He always looked in the direction of the kitchen window, but he no longer waved.

On Monday morning Mara found a few more additions to the cottage. A wooden bookshelf stood against one wall of the living room, complete with a varied selection of books. An antique mantel clock caught her eye above the fireplace, flanked by a pair of hurricane lamps. Some clothes had been left in the bedroom closet and chest of drawers. Men's clothes. Mara couldn't help noticing that interesting fact. The expected list of supplies was taped to the refrigerator. Sin's careless and very masculine scrawl was becoming very familiar.

It rained most of the week and the weather stayed damp and cold. The trees lost their autumn hues, their leaves turning brown and carpeting the ground. So few remained on the branches that the trees looked motheaten and tattered.

When the sun burst through on Saturday morning, Mara took advantage of the break in the weather to rake the ankle-deep leaves from the yard. They were sodden and heavy, which made the chore a lot harder, but it felt good to be outside after so many days of being shut in by the rain.

This sentiment was shared by her father. His wheelchair was positioned on the patio where the sunlight made a golden square on the bricks. Even with the sunshine, there was the chill of coming winter in the air. A red plaid blanket was draped across Adam's paralyzed legs to provide the warmth his fleece-lined jacket couldn't.

Mara paused to catch her breath and glanced at him. All the raking had kept her warm, but after being outside for more than an hour, she guessed he was feeling the cold.

"Don't you think it's time you went inside, Adam?" She leaned the rake against the trunk of a tree.

"Not yet," Adam said. "This may be the last day of good weather before winter sets in. I want to enjoy every minute of it."

"Don't blame me if you freeze and catch pneumonia," Mara warned.

"You're very kind. I wouldn't dream of it." He smiled lazily, his handsome dark features looking years younger.

Mara shook out a large plastic garbage bag and began scooping up the leaves from the pile to stuff them inside it. The red knit of her cap made a vibrant contrast to the sable black of her hair. It provided the one spot of color in the drabness of her work clothes, the dark blue of her denims and khaki brown of her old jacket.

As she picked up the last armful of leaves, she heard her father say, "Hello, Sin. Beautiful day, isn't it?"

"It certainly is. How are you, Adam?"

In a swift glance over her shoulder she saw the tall, well-muscled man strolling toward her father. Instead of the jogging suit, he was dressed in dark blue cords and a down jacket that was unbuttoned to reveal a close-fitting ribbed turtleneck.

He seemed not to notice the chill in the air, but then he was dressed for it. Absently, he raked his fingers through the rumpled thickness of his iron-gray hair. As if feeling the quiet impact of her gaze, Sin glanced at her.

"You're working hard, I see," he commented.

"Yes, I am." Immediately she set to work jamming the leaves into a sack already more than half-full.

"Had any luck finding a housekeeper?" Sin inquired.

"Not yet." Her answer was needlessly clipped and abrupt. She tried to cover the effect of it by picking up the leaves that had scattered over the edge of the bag.

"Mara is something of a perfectionist," Adam explained in an uncomplimentary tone. "She keeps looking for the same quality in others and refuses to compromise."

Tight-lipped, Mara offered no defense since she felt she needed none. Gathering up the open end of the leaf bag, she attempted to carry it to the driveway, but the wet leaves made it too heavy for her to lift.

"Carry that for you?" Sin offered, and took a step toward her.

"I can handle it," she insisted with a stubborn flash of independence.

Sin hesitated, then lifted a shoulder in silent concession. Straining, Mara dragged the plastic bag across the ground. The muscles in her arms were trembling from the effort by the time she reached the driveway.

Determined not to show any sign of stress, she walked back to pick up the rake again and set to work on the leaves in the other quarter of the yard.

All the while, Sin stood near her father, talking to him—and watching her, a distinctly unsettling experience. The last pile of leaves didn't have to be bagged since she used them to cover the dormant flowerbed in front of the house.

"Why don't you rest for a while, Mara?" her father suggested when she had finished that. "You're making me tired just watching you work. You can rake the rest of the yard tomorrow."

"I think I will wait until tomorrow," she agreed, taking off her work gloves and flexing her fingers. "The forecast was for more sunshine." In truth, she was exhausted and needed a rest, if only until the afternoon. "It's getting too cold out here for you."

"You're probably right," he agreed, which told her he was getting chilled. She walked to the back of his wheelchair and turned it toward the house.

So far, she had pointedly ignored the man with her father, but Adam wasn't going to follow suit. "If you aren't doing anything special, Sin, why don't you come into the house?"

Mara froze in cold anger. "I doubt that Sin—I mean, Sinclair—would want to leave Celene alone for long, Adam. She's probably waiting for him at the cottage."

"No, she isn't," Sin said quietly. Unwillingly her dark gaze was drawn to him. "Celene didn't come up this weekend."

The information caught Mara by surprise. It unnerved her and she tried a smart-mouth remark to cover her confusion. "What do you do? Devote one weekend a month totally to rest?"

"Something like that," he agreed lazily.

"If no one's waiting for you, is there any reason you can't come in for a while?" Adam asked.

"None that I know of," Sin answered, his gaze flickering to Mara in silent challenge, but she refused to rise to the bait. It was one thing to argue with her father and another to argue with Sinclair Buchanan.

Without waiting for any more to be said, Mara began pushing her father's wheelchair toward the ramp leading to the front door of the house. The uneven brick walkway made the going difficult. Her arms were already tired from all the raking. When she reached the ramp, a hand came around her to grip the chair handles.

"I'll take it from here," Sin told her.

Mara didn't let go. "I can manage."

"Your father isn't a bag of leaves, and you had enough trouble with that." He firmly eased her out of the way and guided the wheelchair up the ramp with an ease that Mara knew she wouldn't have been able to fake.

At his backward glance to see if she was coming, Mara offered a barely audible, "Thank you," and walked up the ramp to open the door. Once inside, she immediately excused herself. "I have to clean up."

Her bedroom and bath were on the second floor. As she climbed the front stairs, Sin and her father went into the study.

After bathing, Mara put on a pair of tan chinos and a matching sweater with black and tan horizontal stripes. She used the rear staircase that opened into the kitchen. From the front of the house she could hear the muffled sound of male voices in conversation.

The coffeemaker was empty, so she prepped it for a fresh pot. While the coffee brewed, she put away the breakfast dishes she had left to dry on the drainboard. Then she poured herself a cup and sat down at the table. After the bath and change of clothes, a cup of coffee was all she needed to relax.

The door to the kitchen swung open before she had taken her first sip. The tension that she had fought so hard to remove threaded back through her nerves as Sin Buchanan walked into the room.

Minus the bulky jacket, his physique was still formidable. The thick ribknit of his sweater seemed in keeping with his raw vigor. He paused inside the doorway, his gaze sweeping slowly over her. Mara felt his inspection as surely as if he had touched her.

"Was there something you wanted?" She was sitting rigidly in her chair, a charged alertness in her senses.

"Your father sent me in to ask if there was any coffee," Sin said, explaining his presence in the kitchen, and moved forward with a quietness that was surprising in a man his size.

The steaming cup of coffee on the table couldn't be overlooked any more than the aroma of fresh-brewed coffee in the air. Mara found his level gaze difficult to meet. To avoid it, she rose from the table.

"I just made some. I'll fix a tray and bring it in to you," she said. Her voice was as cool as the coffee was hot.

"There's no need for you to bring it in. I'll wait and carry it in myself." He came to the counter where Mara had placed a serving tray.

"It isn't necessary." She didn't want him waiting. She wanted him gone.

"Why should I walk back empty-handed?" Sin countered with infuriating logic.

Mara didn't pursue the argument as she began arranging the mugs on the tray. "I hope Adam hasn't bored you with a lot of talk about the Civil War."

She made the barbed comment for want of something to fill the silence. Her father rarely bored anyone; he had been born with the gift of charm. Even her mother had gone on loving him after he had deserted her for another woman. Mara suspected the only reason she was immune to him was that she was his daughter.

"He didn't say anything about the Civil War." Sin watched her set the sugar bowl and spoon on the tray, then reminded her, "I don't need any cream or sugar for my coffee, thank you."

"Then what did you talk about?" Mara reached into the cupboard for the insulated coffee server.

"Many things," was his ambiguous answer.

"Including me, I suppose."

Sin watched silently for a moment as she poured the hot coffee from the pot into the server. "What makes you think we would have discussed you?"

"Nothing. Forget I said it." Mara didn't want to pursue the subject. She set the server on the tray. When Sin would have picked it up, she stopped him. "Just a minute. I'll put some cookies on a plate." Her father knew she had baked oatmeal raisin cookies yesterday and she suspected he would send Sin back to the kitchen if she didn't include some on the tray. As if in defense of her action, she explained, "Adam has a sweet tooth."

"Why do you call your father by his first name?" Sin's smoke-blue eyes studied her with disconcerting directness. "In almost every other respect, you seem typically old-fashioned."

"It's what I prefer to call him," was as much as Mara would say.

"And your reasons are private," he concluded.

"My reasons are my reasons. And family matters don't include outsiders." Her measuring glance let him know exactly to which category he belonged.

"But it has something to do with the estrangement between the two of you." He watched her arrange the cookies on a plate. "Adam mentioned he was crippled in a car accident."

"Yes, that's right." Mara replaced the lid on the cookie jar.

"Too bad that had to happen to such a vital man," Sin commented.

"You know, it's possible that he got what he deserved," she suggested, knowing how cold her comment sounded and not caring. And she didn't particularly care what Sin thought of her for saying it.

His gaze narrowed slightly. "Do you resent having to take care of him that much?"

"I don't have to take care of him. I choose to take care of him because he's the man who fathered me." There was a haughty air to the tilt of her chin.

"That doesn't mean you have to sacrifice all your free time," he commented. "He would be happy to hire an assistant, I understand. And you need to get out."

"And why do you think so?"

"Because you're young. It's a big, interesting world and you haven't seen much of it. Or maybe I should say that you haven't seen the best of it."

"My, my," Mara murmured, "I guess you and Adam did talk about me."

"What?"

"Nothing."

"Mara, you're a beautiful woman," he began.

"You can skip the compliments. They don't mean anything." She added the plate of cookies to the tray. "I've been around Adam too long not to have learned that."

"You don't care much for your father, do you?" It was a quiet accusation.

"Do you?" she retorted.

"I haven't known him very long, but he strikes me as a likable, intelligent man."

"But you don't know him as well as I do." That was the only explanation Mara felt she needed to give. Determined not to let the discussion continue, she picked up the coffee tray and turned to him. "I believe you said you would carry this into the study."

The full force of his gaze was directed at her. "Is the conversation becoming too much for you?" Sin guessed accurately.

"I'm tired of being a source of amusement for you." She didn't mince words in her answer.

"You take yourself and life too seriously," he chided. "You have to learn to laugh at things."

"Guess what. There are a lot of things that I don't find very funny." Again, she offered him the tray. "If you aren't going to carry this in, I will."

Sin held her steady gaze an instant longer before reaching for the tray. His strong fingers encountered hers as he took the tray handles from her grip. Their contact was hard and warm and brief. It seemed to leave an invisible imprint on her skin, because the sensation remained long after the contact was broken.

Alone again in the kitchen, Mara discovered her cup of coffee had become cold. She emptied it in the sink and refilled it from the pot. But she couldn't get back to the state of contentment that had soothed her soul before Sin had entered the kitchen.

The house was too confining, made smaller by the voices of the two men in the study. The bright sunlight shining outside became more inviting. Mara would have preferred slipping out the back door, but her strong sense of duty wouldn't allow her to go for a walk without first telling her father.

Taking her heavy plaid jacket from its hook, she put it on and walked through the house to the parlor-turned-study. Sin was the first to see her when she appeared in the double doorway, but she avoided looking at him and directed her attention to Adam.

"Just letting you know I'm going for a walk. I'll be back in an hour," she told him. "Would you like anything before I leave? More coffee?"

"Maybe some more cookies?" Adam suggested with a bright gleam in his eye. "Sin sampled them. They're really very good."

"The word is excellent," Sin said.

Was he trying to get on her good side? Mara wasn't

sure she had a good side these days. "I'll bring more, but you shouldn't spoil your lunch, Adam."

"No, you're right. If I fill up on cookies, I won't want lunch," he agreed, and glanced at Sin. "Mara's specialty is really lemon pie. It's always as cool and tart as its maker."

Mara turned away. "I'll be back in an hour." She walked to the front door, never hearing Sin's response to her father's lame joke.

Chapter Five

The middle of November arrived with blustering winds and cold temperatures. The ground was hard beneath Mara's feet as she trudged along the rutted track to the cottage, a small bag of groceries under her arm. It would have been faster and easier to take the car to deliver the supplies, but the bag wasn't very heavy and she'd chosen to walk.

The air was sharp and clear, an invigorating morning punctuated by the puffy clouds of her breath. A swirling wind rustled the thick carpet of leaves in the woods, the dark, skeletal outlines of the tree limbs etched against the blue of the sky.

This last week Mara had rarely ventured out of the house. Adam had caught a cold and she spent most of her time looking after him, and not doing much of anything else. This brisk walk felt good.

Adam's fever had broken in the night. His temperature had dropped to near normal that morning. When she had left the house, he'd been resting comfortably, assuring her that he would probably sleep for an hour or so.

Glancing ahead, Mara saw the cedar shakes of the cottage roof through the dark columns of tree trunks. She wondered which day Sin would be coming to the house to visit her father. Since that first time, Sin had regularly called at the house once a weekend to see Adam. Mara had no idea what the two men talked about, and she never asked.

She didn't repeat her objections to having Sin Buchanan in the house, not wanting to attach any importance to his visits with her father. So Mara spent most of her time when he happened to stop by just ignoring him.

As she approached the front door of the cottage, she reached into her jacket pocket for the key. She'd continued to run the ad in the paper for a housekeeper, but there hadn't been any more replies. Spending a couple of hours here Monday and Friday mornings had become part of her routine, another one of the chores she did on a regular basis.

Knowing it would take both hands to unlock and open the door, she set the grocery bag on the stoop. She inserted the key in the lock and turned the doorknob at the same time as the key; then pushed the door open, slipped the key back in her pocket and picked up the groceries.

Entering the cottage, she walked across the living room to turn up the thermostat, only to discover it hadn't been turned down. She stared at it for a puzzled second, then shrugged. Monday morning was when Adam had woken up with the chill and a fever. In her haste to get back to him, she'd probably forgotten to turn the heat down in the cottage after cleaning it.

Mara carried the grocery bag into the small kitchen and set it on the counter. Unbuttoning the cumbersome jacket, she slipped it off and draped it on the back of a kitchen chair. The nippy walk to the cottage had numbed her senses. She took the first item out of the bag and suddenly noticed a familiar aroma in the air.

In disbelief, she glanced at the coffeemaker on the counter. The fragrant smell of fresh coffee was coming from it. At almost the same instant she heard footsteps somewhere near the bedroom, and pivoted toward the sound.

There was Sin, larger than life, filling the archway to the bedroom. Clad only in a pair of ripped denims, he walked into the kitchen. The hard, muscled chest looked deceptively lean—and she felt a flash of delight at seeing his bare skin, nice and brown, broken only by the V-shaped pattern of dark chest hairs.

His steel-and-silver hair was uncombed, its thickness in sexy disarray. A deep sleep had softened the rugged cut of his features, but his eyes were alert as he took in the look of shock on Mara's face.

"Good morning." His greeting sounded so natural that it made her wonder if she had her days mixed up. Was it Saturday? No, it definitely was Friday.

"What are you doing here?" she recovered enough to demand, then said, "I didn't see your car outside."

"You didn't look. My car is there, parked alongside of the cottage," Sin informed her, regarding her with lazy interest.

That explained it, Mara realized. Since she'd walked instead of driving, her angle of approach to the cottage hadn't given her a glimpse of the far side where his car was.

"Then you're the one who turned the thermostat up and made coffee," she concluded, relieved that it hadn't been an oversight on her part.

"I must be," he agreed, "unless there's a ghost haunting the cottage that you didn't tell me about." His mouth curved into a half grin. "Did you think you'd lost it?"

"I . . . I had a lot of things on my mind," Mara faltered in her own defense. "Adam's been sick with a cold all week. He's better now. So it was possible I might have overlooked a few things Monday."

"Not you," he said lightly. "You're Miss Perfect."

"Why are you here?" His comment annoyed her. "It isn't Saturday."

"I decided at the last minute to come up a day early. Is that all right?" Sin asked, knowing that he didn't have to ask her permission. "I don't recall reading any restriction in the lease that said I couldn't use the cottage seven days a week."

"Of course there wasn't," Mara retorted impatiently. "But you could have let me know you were changing your routine."

"I told you it was a last-minute decision. I didn't think you'd appreciate a phone call in the wee hours of the morning."

"Um, no." He had a point there, Mara thought.

"And it was well after midnight when I decided to drive up here a day early," Sin continued.

Mara doubted that he'd been alone at that hour of the night. That thought prompted another: maybe he hadn't made the journey alone either. She looked beyond Sin to the bedroom and glimpsed the sleep-rumpled brown satin sheets.

Sin followed the direction of her look and her thoughts. "There's no one with me, if that's what you're wondering." Amusement edged the hard corners of his mouth when her dark gaze flew back to him.

"You've been spending more and more of your weekends alone lately," Mara said. "Don't you get bored without anyone to entertain you?"

"Not yet but that's possible," he conceded dryly. "But if it gets too dull around here, I can always argue with you."

This conversation was going nowhere. Mara wondered why she hadn't just walked out the second she'd seen him bare to the waist, lounging in the doorway wearing only ripped jeans.

Scratch that thought. His physical charm was just about irresistible. But he took obvious delight in laughing at her, no matter what she said or did. She turned away and took out her annoyance on the items in the grocery bag, not caring if she crushed the bread or dented a can or two.

"I've had a long week, you know. Taking care of Adam isn't easy work. And I don't feel like arguing with you. Now or ever," she added tightly.

He studied her profile, noticing the strain etched in her features but unable to guess that he was the cause of most of it. Her eyes were large black smudges against the ivory cream of her complexion. The line of her finely drawn mouth was tense, her emotions rigidly contained.

Sin walked to where the coffeemaker was plugged in only a few feet from her. Opening the cupboard door above it, he took out two cups and set them on the counter.

"Why don't you take a break for a few minutes, Mara, and have a cup of coffee with me?" he suggested. "It's fresh and hot. The groceries can wait until later."

Oh, how sweet. Well, he didn't have to pretend a solicitous concern for her well-being, because she wasn't impressed. She flashed him an icy look as he filled the first cup.

"Forget it. I don't want coffee." The sharpness of her retort made his eyes widen.

He set the carafe back in the coffeemaker as a heavy silence filled the air, charging the atmosphere. His steady blue gaze stayed on her.

"No problem." His voice was low. "But I could use the

caffeine. Gotta wake up, right?" He took a long sip from the cup he'd just filled.

Mara hesitated only an instant before answering coldly, "Go ahead." She continued unpacking the bag, her movements as brisk and rapid as she could make them without throwing things around. "But I don't need stimulating." The second the words were out of her mouth, she wished she hadn't said them.

"You sure about that?" Sin's voice changed subtly, a sensual quality entering it. "Makes a man want to prove you're a liar."

"Which says something about male arrogance, doesn't it?" Mara countered.

"Or female talent for provocative behavior," he said smoothly.

"I didn't mean it to sound so suggestive. I wasn't thinking—and, like I said, I'm tired." She clutched the loaf of bread in her hand, and she paused to pat it back to plumpness before realizing how silly she must look. She put the bread down and turned to confront him. "And I wasn't trying to be provocative."

"Whatever you say." Sin was closer to her than she had realized. She started to take a breath to make some reply when his hand touched her neck. His fingers began tracing the base of her throat, exploring its hollow, and all her muscles constricted. Mara's heartbeat was erratic, speeding up, then slowing down as his fingertips lingered or moved over her sensitive skin. Her gaze was locked with his and she had the sensation of being drawn into the blue depths of his eyes.

"I'll bet ice cream doesn't melt in your mouth," Sin declared in a soft, but very masculine voice that felt like a caress.

The straight line of his mouth never varied. There wasn't a hint of a smile. He seemed oddly detached, as if conducting some simple exercise that didn't require his concentration. His fingers began outlining the neck-line of her blouse. At the point, they brushed the top of her breasts before encountering a button. Then they started their upward slant to the base of her throat.

"What do you . . . No, it doesn't melt." Her voice was soft, too, thanks to the state of sensual confusion she was in. "I eat it too fast."

No matter how she tried, the delicious daze wouldn't lift. Not as long as he was touching her, she realized. At first she had submitted to the caress of his fingers to prove it didn't affect her. Now that she knew better, she had to bring this sudden intimacy to a close.

Fighting the threatening sensation of weakness, Mara reached up and pushed his hand from her neck. Then she took a step away and turned her back to him, looking for a distraction. The loaf of bread was on the table where she'd left it. She grabbed it just for something to do.

"What's the matter?" Sin asked in a voice that said he knew.

"Nothing's the matter." Mara opened a cupboard door to put the bread away. She seemed to lack coordination. Her movements were jerky and out of synch. "Don't paw me like that, please. I'm not interested in sex for the sake of sex at this point in my life."

"Oh?" There was a lot of curiosity in the one-word question. "When do you think you will be?"

Instead of putting him on the spot, she'd tripped herself up. It was a question she couldn't answer and she knew she didn't dare try.

"Like I'm going to answer that," she told him. "If you're lonely, call Celene and have her take care of you."

He only laughed. "Been there, done that, and it's no big thrill. But there's never a dull moment with you. Each time I think I have you trapped in a corner, you come charging at me from another direction."

"I don't happen to be doing it for your amusement," she snapped.

"I'm aware of that." A trace of a smile lingered, but his look was totally serious. "It's all about self-preservation, isn't it? You don't want anybody getting too close."

"If you've got the message, why don't you leave me alone?"

Sin completely ignored that. "You don't want anyone to be even physically close to you. You're a young, beautiful woman. That's a statement, not a compliment," he added. "And made for love."

"Oh, please!"

"Sorry. Let me rephrase that. Your body was designed for making love."

Mara shook her head. "Could we change the subject?"

"You brought it up," Sin pointed out.

"So I did," Mara sighed. "But that doesn't mean—"

"So how do you suppress your biological urges?"

"You are totally out of line. I don't see that it's any of your business." Mara closed the cupboard door on the bread and reached into the bag for a new can of coffee. But when she lifted it out, Sin took it from her hand and set it on the counter, shoving it out of her reach.

"But I want to know," he persisted.

His arm, braced against the counter, prevented her from reaching the coffee can. When she attempted to ignore him and deal with the rest of the groceries in the bag, his other arm blocked her way.

"Do you have a guy in your life right now?" he asked. Sin leaned in fractionally nearer, bringing his gaze level with hers.

There was almost a foot of space between them, but he seemed way too close. Mara pressed herself more closely against the counter until its edge was digging into the small of her back. "You mean you haven't asked my father about that yet? You two are such good friends—"

"No, I haven't. But I am asking you. And you haven't answered." His low murmur was seducing her, awakening needs and longings that she usually kept smothered. They were all surfacing with a new intensity. She hoped desperately that her customary poise wouldn't fail her and that this wonderful bewilderment was well hidden from him.

He looked at her lips. "Guess you're not going to."

"Ah . . . The answer is no," Mara whispered almost desperately.

"Good." Sin leaned closer, his head tipping to one side as his mouth sought the curve of her lips. Her lashes swept closed, but they didn't shut out the image of him from her mind.

The kiss began as a slow yet bold exploration of new territory. Gradually Mara responded. After a tentative beginning she began to warm to the role. No longer was she pressing herself against the counter. All that space between them seemed unnecessary.

Her fingers trembled uncertainly against his bare chest until they began to enjoy the feel of his smooth, muscled flesh. The pressure of his mouth increased. The exploration was over and Sin was claiming the territory. His hand curved across her back to draw her inside the circle of his arms. Mara felt the hard outline of his body pressed against hers, the heat from it burning through her clothes to her skin. Sin was no longer leaning forward but standing at his full height. Her head was forced to tilt backward to receive his kiss.

She had the dizzying sensation that she was teetering on the brink of a discovery. She only had to let go to find out what it was. But she couldn't. With a soft moan, she broke off the kiss and strained to be free of his embrace. Sin resisted her attempts for a fleeting second, then let her go. Stepping away from him, she covered her mouth with her hand as if she could rub away the sensual feeling of his lips on hers. Her breathing was rapid and shallow. She struggled to make it normal and quiet her pounding heart.

Chin up. Back straight. And keep away from him, she told herself. Mara began unpacking the groceries again and putting them away. Sin watched her but she pretended she wasn't aware of it.

"What happened, Mara?" Sin asked quietly.

She assumed he was referring to the kiss and the suddenness with which she ended it. "Nothing happened," she said.

"I don't buy that," he replied in a hard, decisive voice. "It had to take years to get all your feelings and emotions frozen that solidly. So what happened? Did you get dumped by someone you really cared about? Stood up on the church steps?"

"No to both questions." The coffee was put away and Mara began transferring the dozen eggs into the egg rack in the refrigerator.

"Okay, a married guy broke your heart," he persisted.

"No." Her control was fraying. "And if any of the answers were yes, I still would tell you no because it's none of your business!"

A muscle worked along his jaw as they confronted each other. "Is your father well enough to have visitors?"

The unexpected change of subject startled Mara and it took her a moment to make the adjustment before she could answer. "Yes, I think so."

"Okay," he nodded, and raked his fingers through his tousled hair as if realizing for the first time it wasn't combed. "I'll finish getting dressed and walk back with you."

Mara surprised herself by suddenly saying, "What

about your coffee?" She had wanted him to shut up and now she was stalling for time. Being this close to Sin was definitely affecting her brain.

"Nah. It's stone cold. And I've had all the excitement I can handle for one morning without adding caffeine." His mouth quirked in a smile that made her long for another kiss.

"It's cold outside. You'd be better off driving," Mara tried another tactic.

"I'm getting used to the chill in the air up here." He turned and disappeared into the bedroom.

She wasn't going to follow him. And if that remark had a double meaning, she wasn't going to comment on it. Mara called after him, "If you aren't ready by the time I'm finished here, I'm leaving without you."

There was no response to her warning and she hurried to make it come true. She had her coat on and was halfway to the front door when Sin joined her.

"Let's go," she said, a little huffily. Before he could accuse her of fleeing, she added in defense, "I left Adam alone in the house. I don't want to be away any longer than necessary."

"That's understandable." His hooded look seemed willing to give her the benefit of the doubt.

When Sin opened the front door, Mara was careful not to accidentally brush against him as she went by. He stopped to lock the door behind them and Mara started toward the back trail.

"Not so fast!" Sin called, a note of impatience in his voice.

"I told you I wasn't going to wait." She didn't check her stride. After she had taken two more steps, a hand grabbed her elbow, the thick padding of her sleeve softening its tight grip. He turned her around to face him. Mara wasn't going to stoop to the indignity of struggling against his superior strength. She stood silently in his hold, glaring up at him.

Her heavy jacket didn't lessen the impression the unyielding muscles of his thighs were making against hers, nor insulate her from the warmth of his body heat.

"What's the matter with you, Mara?" Sin demanded, his tone impatient. "Can't you wait a few seconds without storming off?"

"I have work to do. And my world doesn't revolve around you."

"Okay, okay." He seemed to release his obvious annoyance in a sighed breath. "Sorry. I just got the feeling that you were running from me. And . . ."

"And what?"

He released her elbow and started to slide his fingers through her sleek black hair. "I don't want you to, Mara."

Mara was still feeling the very pleasurable echoes of his previous caresses. She twisted her head away from his hand in rejection of his touch.

"Let me go and leave me alone!" The instant the demand was out, she was angry. "Damn," she swore softly. "I sound like some Victorian virgin." Resentment flashed in the look she sent him.

Sin did as he was asked and took a step away from her, a certain grimness to his mouth. "I wouldn't worry. You're neither meek nor mild, two essential qualities of a Victorian female."

Hiding her clenched fists in her jacket pockets, Mara started again toward the trail. "You can add not subservient to that little list. I don't know where my place is, but it isn't under any man," she declared, fighting the shaky feeling inside her.

"Literally or figuratively, is that it?" Sin taunted.

"That's it."

Mara set a brisk pace, as if trying to escape whatever was pursuing her. Sin easily kept stride with her, his long legs capable of outdistancing her if he chose. But they walked without talking.

Entering the brick house through the rear door, Mara paused to hang up her coat on the empty hook by the door. She flicked a glance in Sin's direction that didn't quite reach his face. It stopped somewhere between the second and third button of his jacket.

"Why don't you take off your coat and hang it on the rack while I see if Adam is awake?" Her voice had a brittle ring after the long, silent walk in the cold.

"Thank you, I will."

Her peripheral vision caught his movement as he started to unbutton his coat, but she was already walking toward the swinging door that led to the rest of the house. Her father's bedroom was on the ground floor. When she entered his room, his eyes were closed. She was half-afraid he was asleep. Uncertain whether to wake him or let him rest, she walked to his bed.

Adam opened his eyes and smiled wanly. "You're back."

"Yes. How are you feeling?" She looked at his face, thinking that his color had improved considerably.

"Hungry," Adam said.

"I'll fix you some broth. By the way, you have a visitor," she added, managing a stiff smile.

"A visitor?" he frowned. "Who—hello, Sin." He was looking beyond her to the door. "What are you doing here? Or have I lost a day?"

"You didn't lose a day. I decided at the last minute to come up early," Sin explained.

"I'm glad you did. Come in and sit down—not too close, though. I don't want you catching this cold," Adam laughed in warning. He glanced at his daughter as Sin sat in a straight-backed chair near the foot of the bed. "Mara was just going to bring me a cup of broth. Would like something? Coffee? Tea?"

"No, thank you," Sin refused, and didn't even glance toward Mara as she left the room.

It was a relief to have her hands and mind occupied with fixing the broth, even if it was a simple task. One of these days she was going to have to deal with the fact that she seemed to be living in the kitchen and not the real world, but not right now. Preoccupied and rather tense, she watched the blue flames flutter under the pan until the liquid in it simmered, then turned off the heat and poured the broth into a mug.

Her reappearance in the bedroom brought a momentary lull in the men's conversation. She cranked Adam's bed up and positioned the lap table in front of him.

As she walked over to get the cup of broth from where she had left it, Sin began speaking to her father. "Some day soon, I'd like to enlist your expert services to take me on a tour of the battlefield."

"Now, I would enjoy that," Adam replied. "How about this weekend?"

"No way." Mara set his broth on the table in front of him. "It's freezing out, and it's muddy."

"Not a problem." He dismissed her assertion with a lordly wave of his hand. "I feel fine."

"Mara's right." The agreement came unexpectedly from Sin. "November in Pennsylvania being what it is, going out isn't a great idea. You don't want that cold to hang around or turn into something else."

"You're outnumbered two to one, Adam." Mara adjusted the pillow behind his head to give him more support.

"I may be," Adam conceded, "but I hate to think that Sin is going to miss out on the tour. He's in the mood now. Who knows when he will be again?" he joked.

Mara didn't want to answer, and Sin said nothing.

"I've got the solution!" Adam declared, glancing from Sin to Mara with a bright gleam in his eyes. "Mara knows almost as much as I do about the Gettysburg battle. She can take you this weekend."

Holding her breath, Mara shot a quick look at Sin. Adam had to know that it was the last thing in the world she would want to do.

"Maybe not," Sin said pleasantly. "I don't think Mara wants to volunteer."

"Why?" There was too much innocence in her father's dark eyes when he looked at her. "You showed our cousin from California around the park and that friend of mine from Atlanta."

Mara was about to say that the circumstances were different. Those other people were virtually strangers to her, whereas Sin . . . No, she wasn't going to explain to her father.

"The complete tour takes a while," she lied bravely. "And I have a lot to do this weekend—you know, baking for the holidays, stuff like that. Whiskey cake is better when it's made weeks ahead. I won't have any free time until Monday."

"Are you doing the whiskey cakes this year? Everybody we know is eating low carb," Adam argued.

"Not for Thanksgiving and Christmas. I postponed too many things while you were sick." Mara stood firm.

"That's all right," Sin said. "Monday is fine with me. What time?"

"What time?" Mara repeated, feeling that she had just been caught in a trap. She glanced at her father, certain he had been part of the conspiracy, but he looked just as surprised as she was.

"Will you be here on Monday?" he asked.

"Yes. As a matter of fact, I won't be driving back to

Baltimore until the weekend after Thanksgiving," Sin told them.

"You didn't tell me anything about that at the cottage," Mara said.

"You didn't ask," he countered. "I intended to mention to you over coffee that you wouldn't need to come Monday to clean, but we got sidetracked with other issues. I would have remembered to tell you sooner or later."

Mara couldn't help wishing it had been sooner.

"So, what time on Monday?" he asked, repeating his earlier question.

"I don't know." Agitated, Mara couldn't find any way out of the mess. "After lunch, I suppose. That's when Adam usually rests."

"Works for me. I'm looking forward to the tour." His smile said just how much.

Chapter Six

A few minutes after one o'clock on Monday, Sin's silver gray car turned into the driveway. Mara had just finished drying the last of the lunch dishes. She folded the damp towel neatly and hung it on the rack to dry. The routine task was something she found soothing, like most housework. Almost meditative. But she had to admit, if only to herself, that housework wasn't ever going to get her out of the house—something that had begun to bother her.

A knock on the door interrupted her thoughts. She ran a smoothing hand over her black hair and went to open it. Sin was standing outside and he didn't immediately enter. His gaze raked her, lingering briefly on her legs. She wished she hadn't worn a skirt and black tights.

"Aren't you going to back out?" he asked.

Not exactly the way to get off to a good start, Mara thought. "No." Mostly because she wouldn't give him the satisfaction. "Excuse me." She turned away from the open door, not caring if he came in or stayed outside in the cold. "I'll tell Adam I'm leaving."

As she left the kitchen, Mara heard the door close and guessed that Sin was waiting inside. At her father's bedroom door, she knocked once and went in.

Adam spoke before she did. "I heard the car drive up. Was it Sin?"

"Yes. I wanted to let you know I was leaving and double-check to see if there was anything you needed," Mara told him.

"Not a thing," he assured her. "The phone's by the bed. So are my notes and books, and a pitcher of water."

"Are you positive you're feeling all right?" But he looked so disgustingly healthy that Mara knew there wasn't much hope.

"I'm fine." He gave her a knowing smile. "Sin is waiting for you. Don't you think you should be going?"

"Yes." Her hands felt moist from the nervousness she was trying so hard to conceal. "If you need anything—"

"You have a cell phone," he interrupted. "And I have half a dozen numbers to cover every kind of an emergency. Have a good time, Mara."

Sheer stubbornness made her say, "I sincerely doubt it." She left the bedroom and retraced her steps to the kitchen. Sin was waiting near the back door for her. "Ready to leave if you are," she said briskly. She bent down to slip on low-heeled, fur-lined boots.

"You mean your father hasn't suffered an unexpected relapse?" He reached forward to open the door for her.

"Adam feels fine." Taking her full-length winter coat, Mara draped it over her shoulders and walked past him.

"We'll take my car." Sin followed her outdoors.

"Since I'll be doing the driving, I would prefer mine," Mara insisted.

"Mine is warmed up," he said. "Besides, it's more comfortable than yours. But you can drive. No moving violations, no speeding tickets, right? I bet you're a perfect driver no matter what car you're in."

Mara didn't want to waste her energy arguing over which car they were going to take; she would rather conserve it in case it was needed later. And she didn't want to admit she was nervous at the prospect of driving Sin's luxury model.

As he'd said, the car's interior was comfortably warm. Not needing the coat, Mara stowed it in the back-seat before sliding onto the plush upholstered seat behind the wheel. She quickly studied the dashboard while Sin walked around the car to sit on the passenger side. When he was safely in and the door was shut, she backed out of the driveway onto the road. The car handled beautifully—in fact, it seemed to practically drive itself.

"I owe you an apology," he said after they had gone almost a mile.

"An apology?" she repeated coolly. "What for?"

"I honestly expected you to come up with an excuse not to take me on this tour," he admitted, sliding her a curious glance.

"Hoping I'd back out, huh? Maybe you're already bored with the idea of touring the battlefield?" Mara spared him a glance from the road. "Because if you've changed your mind—"

"Nope."

"I was thinking that maybe you only wanted to go to impress Adam," Mara said.

Sin shook his head. "I was curious about Gettysburg. Like the song says, I don't know much about history. Seeing it with someone who'd researched the history in-depth seemed like a good idea. Of course, at the time I expected that person to be Adam. It never occurred to me that you'd be my guide," he told her.

Mara flexed her fingers around the steering wheel. "Right. Sure. Why am I getting the feeling that you tricked me into this?"

"You volunteered," Sin reminded her.

"Not quite," she snapped.

"How was I to know it would matter?" His voice was smooth. "You sounded so sincere when you said you would be willing to show me around today." Sin fell silent for a moment. "Do you want to call off the tour and go back?"

"Oh, no," she said. "You're going to have a full and complete tour of the battlefield. Highly educational." She was going to see that that was all the satisfaction he got out of this untenable situation. "How much do you know about the events leading up to the Battle of Gettysburg?"

"Some, but why don't you refresh my memory?" he suggested dryly.

"The war between the states was in its third year. The North had yet to win a majority victory although General Grant had Vicksburg surrounded and under siege," Mara began. "Morale in the North was very low. People were weary of war and some even thought that the South should be allowed to secede from the Union—they wanted to end the war and all the bloody fighting and killing. Aware that the other side was losing heart, General Robert E. Lee turned his war-hardened veterans north."

"Spoken like a professor."

"I did go to college, you know," Mara said. "And I intend to go back."

He nodded. Adam must have told him that she hadn't gotten her degree, but the last thing Mara wanted Sin to think was that she had no ambition in life besides picking up after him or anybody else. She took a deep breath before continuing, hoping she didn't sound too pompous or lecturey.

"Lee felt a victory on northern soil would win the Confederacy the needed support of the European countries, and perhaps even force a peace with the North, so he directed his army of seventy-five thousand here to southern Pennsylvania."

"And no one opposed him along the way?" Sin questioned.

Mara slowed the car as they entered the town of Gettysburg. "No one. The Union knew Lee was moving, but their patrols couldn't locate his army, which sounds unbelievable when you realize his supply train of wagons was forty-two miles long. Both armies knew they would have to meet, but they didn't know where. They first encountered each other west of Gettysburg, so that's where we'll start our tour."

Turning west on Chambersburg Pike, Mara stole a glance at Sin's profile. It seemed sculpted in bronze, the strong, male lines emphasized. The skies outside were overcast, a gray background for the dark silver of his hair. He was distant, his thoughts elsewhere. Yet his vitality was a forceful thing. Even now it permeated the air surrounding her to the point where she felt it entering her with each breath she took.

At Stone Avenue she turned and slowed the car to a crawl. "Here on McPherson's Ridge is where it all started. There's a story that a group of rebel soldiers intended to make a foray into Gettysburg because they'd heard there was a shoe factory here, and after three years of war many of the Confederate soldiers were without shoes or decent clothes. They encountered a Union patrol before they entered the town, and the alarm was sounded. The location of Lee's army was discovered and the battle began."

"For want of a shoe," Sin absently quoted from an old verse, "a horse was lost."

As he gazed at the monuments and statues within the fenced enclosure, Mara collected her thoughts and struggled to keep her nervousness under control.

"There are hundreds of plaques and monuments scattered over the park," she said. "Whenever you see a statue of a general mounted on a horse, look at the horse's hooves. If all four are on the ground, the general survived the battle unharmed. If one is raised, that general was wounded. He was killed in battle if the horse is rearing. It's a convention of equestrian monuments, but I'm not sure when or how it started. In Europe, I guess," she concluded.

"Interesting," was his murmured comment. "I didn't know that.

With a turn of his head, Sin was looking directly at her. His gaze seemed to lock with hers. Despite the spaciousness of the luxury car, Mara was all too aware of his closeness. His arm was stretched along the back of the seat, his fingers inches from her shoulder. The broad expanse of his chest seemed to offer its use as a hard pillow for her head. A feeling of intimacy threatened to swamp her.

She wrenched her gaze from his to stare at the road. "Stop looking at me that way," she demanded.

"What way?" Sin asked blandly.

She couldn't answer that, so she changed the subject. History was safer. "In the afternoon, the rebels attacked the right flank of the Union army north of Gettysburg. They succeeded in routing the North and driving them through the streets of Gettysburg. But instead of keeping the Union soldiers on the run or taking the high ground of Cemetery Ridge, the Confederates withdrew and regrouped to wait for Lee, who was several miles away when the battle started."

Following the route of the Union's retreat, Mara drove back through town, pointing out the buildings that still showed the battle scars from that time. She told Sin of how General Hancock had rallied the Northern troops and of the arrival of General Meade and his army after a record-breaking forced march.

From Culp's Hill to Little Round Top, she explained that the uncoordinated attacks by the South the following day on the firmly entrenched Union forces on the high ground. "Possession of strategic locations seesawed, changing hands several times. The failure of the Confederate battle plan to encircle the Union army ended the day in a stalemate."

As she drove slowly along Confederate Avenue, it seemed fitting that the trees were stark and bare of leaves and the grass a withered brown. A wide, open field stretched before them to Seminary Ridge.

"Since Lee's plan to outflank the Union army failed the day before, he decided to send his army straight up the middle of their defenses, split them in two," Mara recounted. "That is the field Pickett's men had to cross—no trees, no cover. The rebel soldiers were lined up in rows, shoulder to shoulder, for a mile and a half, facing Seminary Ridge. You've heard the story of the Charge of the Light Brigade? It couldn't match Pickett's charge. They marched across this field with Northern soldiers blowing holes in them, but they didn't stop. The creeks around Gettysburg ran red with blood. Less than an hour later, ten thousand of Pickett's fifteen thousand men were casualties and they'd failed to take the ridge."

"Stop here," Sin ordered, and Mara turned off the highway to park alongside the road. "Let's get out and walk."

A cold wind whipped at her as she stepped from the car. She reached into the back for her coat and slipped it on. She didn't bother to button it, holding the front closed with her hands thrust into the pockets. Sin was standing a short distance from the car, overlooking the field Pickett's men had crossed. Mara walked forward to join him.

"Lee was here waiting when the survivors came back,"

Mara said, continuing her narrative in a low voice. "Some said there were tears in his eyes when he met them. He didn't blame them for falling. He told them it was his fault because he had believed they were 'invincible.' The next day, Lee led the remnants of his Confederate army and retreated south. It was July 4, 1863."

A brief shiver quaked her shoulders, but it wasn't caused by the cold wind blowing around her ears. It was a sober understanding of why the Union soldiers felt no glory in their victory that long-ago day. It had cost too many lives on both sides. Gettysburg seemed to still hold their ghosts.

Her sideways glance encountered Sin's. The look in his eyes hinted at a half-formed question, and she was curious to find out what it was.

"Was there something you wanted to ask?" She kept her tone impersonal.

Sin glanced toward the battlefield as if he wasn't going to answer. He stood quietly, the collar of his coat turned up against the wind.

"No," he said at last.

"From here we'll drive to the national cemetery where Lincoln made his address," she told him.

The restraining touch of his hand on her arm halted Mara and her gaze lifted from his hand on her arm to his face. Sin eyed her steadily and something flickered in his look that tripped up the even rhythm of her heartbeat. He was close enough for her to sense his warmth on this cold day—and she realized with a start that she needed it, even craved it. His strength and vitality seemed to dispel the ghosts of her own past that this sorrowful place evoked.

Momentarily caught, she wasn't aware of his hand moving to slide inside her coat and across her stomach. She drew a sharp breath of unwilling enjoyment as his other hand pushed its way inside her coat to spread his fingers over her skin.

Before the cold air could penetrate the open front of her coat she was drawn against the heat of his solid body. Her hands came out of her pockets to grip the bulging muscles of his arms in a halfhearted attempt at resistance. His mouth covered hers with sensual perfection.

The subtle pressure of his kiss sent all thought fleeing. At his invitation Mara responded freely, her lips parting under the provocative insistence of his.

An exploding desire flamed through her nerves, her body quivering in the pleasurable aftershock. The intimate caress of his hands over her soft flesh was igniting new sensations as powerful as life itself.

When his mouth moved slowly across her cheek, his breath fanned her already hot skin. Sin paused near her ear to nip sensually at the lobe, then explored the pulsing vein in her neck all the way to the sensitive hollow of her throat. The quivering weakness he evoked made their surroundings seem to disappear.

A car went by. Had there been more? In her shattered condition, Mara wasn't sure. She came back gradually to reality: they were standing out in the open, in plain view of anyone who drove past.

Her sense of what was right struggled with her new, wildly sweet emotions—and propriety won. Twisting her head toward her shoulder, she blocked his sensual, tender exploration of her neck and throat. She didn't have the strength or the will to slip out of his arms, but she was able to elude the attempt of his compelling mouth to retake possession of her lips.

"Stop." Her husky voice betrayed her emotions, impossible to control, especially when she felt his lips moving against her hair. "Sin, please stop! People can see us . . ."

After an instant's hesitation he slowly lifted his head, his hands sliding to her waist. Mara felt the tenseness of his muscles, his reluctance communicated to her along with the power of his control. She kept her face averted from his observant eyes, not wanting him to see how thoroughly he had conquered her.

The awareness of his gaze and the touch of his hands were too unnerving. She pushed at his arms, wanting to be released but lacking the will to achieve freedom on her own. As his hold loosened, she turned away and put distance between them with hurried steps. She pulled the front of her coat together for protection, drawing back into her shell, wanting only to erase the feeling of his hands moving over her bare skin.

But nothing could erase the way he had aroused emotions she had shut away for far too long. And Sin seemed aware of it: she could read the knowledge in the depths of his eyes. Never had she felt so transparent and never had she hated the sensation more.

As she walked swiftly to the car, she stared in front of her and refused to look at Sin. She was inside the car before she realized she had climbed in on the passenger side. Rather than admit she had been too shaken by his embrace and its aftermath to know what she was doing, she stayed where she was.

When she reached out to pull the passenger door shut, Sin's hand was there to temporarily halt hers. "Aren't you driving?"

Mara wouldn't look at him. "You drive." A tug of the door pulled it out of his yielding grasp.

Her hands were clenched tightly in her lap as Sin walked around the car to the driver's side. After starting the car, he paused to look at her. "You'll have to give me directions to the cemetery. I don't know how to get there from here," he said.

Mara still wouldn't meet his gaze as she stiffly faced

the front of the car. "We aren't going to the cemetery. The tour is over, so you can drive me home."

She half-expected an argument or at the very least some edgy comment, but there was none. Sin shifted the car out of park and turned it onto the road. As they drove away, Mara turned her head to look out the side window at the field of Pickett's charge. She knew what it was like to believe yourself invincible, only to be defeated by a superior force.

The drive back seemed extraordinarily long. With each passing mile the silence grew more oppressive and the atmosphere more charged. The dry winter air seemed to crackle.

The wooded landscape became more familiar as they approached the red brick farmhouse. When it came into sight, Mara's nerves seemed to scream with relief. But Sin didn't slow the car at the driveway. Instead he continued along the gravel road.

"You missed the driveway." Mara turned in her seat to look back at it. "Where are you going?" Her tone hovered between an accusation and a desperate demand.

His gaze left the road long enough to slide over her face in quick assessment. "You seem . . . a little shaky." He didn't bother to ask why but chose the wrong reason to prove he knew the true one. "I thought we'd have some coffee at the cottage so you could have time to recover."

Mara could predict what would happen at the cottage. His seduction of her would continue, this time in total privacy and before she had a chance to recover her equilibrium. Conscious as she was of her physical response to him, there was no way she was going to accompany him to the cottage.

"No thanks. No coffee. Not with you. Turn the car around and take me home," she ordered in a voice iced by an admitted fear of what might happen.

"All right." With an expressive shrug of his shoulder, Sin turned into the lane to the cottage but only to reverse the car. "If you want to have coffee at your house, that's all right with me. I only thought you wouldn't want Adam to see you in your present state."

"Adam has nothing to do with this. And I'm not inviting you in. Why should I?" she challenged. "I don't even like you!"

He stopped the car beside her house. As Mara moved to open her door, Sin's hand captured her chin and turned her face to his.

"At the moment, it's yourself that you're not liking very much, not me," Sin informed her. Before she could jerk away, he was planting a kiss on her lips without her having an opportunity to resist it.

She broke away and wiped her mouth with the back of her hand, hoping he would be insulted. He didn't seem to be. That goaded her into responding, "Don't ever come up to the house again unless you're invited . . . or it's in connection with some business about the cottage."

Mara climbed out of the car, her shoulders rigidly squared and her spine ramrod straight as she walked to the house. She didn't glance back when she heard Sin backing out of the driveway. She knew he'd only look amused.

Inside the house, she barely had time to take off her coat before her father was calling, "Mara, is that you?"

If it wasn't one man, it was another. She didn't even have a moment to gather her composure. Smothering a sigh, she draped her coat over a hanger and hung it up. Adam was bound to ask about the tour and Sin, and attempting to postpone his questions would only heighten his curiosity.

"Yes, it's me," she answered, her voice raised to make

herself heard. Knowing he expected her to come to his room, she started in that direction. In front of a mirror, she paused to glance at herself. The roses in her cheeks could be blamed on the cool temperature outside, but she could think of no excuse for the troubled darkness of her brown eyes or her still unsteady pulse. Not that the eternally self-absorbed Adam was likely to notice anything.

"Back early, aren't you?" He frowned curiously when she appeared in the doorway to his bedroom.

"It was too cold to spend much time walking around. A driving tour of the battlefield doesn't take very long."

"Even driving you made record time," Adam went on. "You couldn't have taken Sin on a comprehensive tour."

"I skipped a few places," admitted Mara, trying not to be defensive. "He wasn't all that interested in the tour to begin with."

"Where is Sin?" Adam glanced behind her as if expecting to see him. "Didn't you invite him in for coffee?"

"No."

"That wasn't very considerate." The sharpness of reprimand was in his voice.

"Why? He had his tour." And more, she could have added, because he'd had more than she had intended him to receive.

"It's just polite, that's all."

"Well, I'm sick of making coffee. And broth. And sandwiches. And—"

"What?" He stared at her curiously.

"Never mind."

"Mara, no one's chaining you to the stove except yourself. You don't have to turn into a domestic martyr. Even Martha Stewart got over that."

"Yeah. In prison."

Adam thought that over. "If you feel like a prisoner, I hope you don't think that's my fault."

An unexpected flash of understanding reminded her that he really was a prisoner, unable to walk or even leave the house without assistance. When it came right down to it, she could do whatever she wanted to do. And if that meant avoiding Sin from now on, she didn't have to explain that to Adam. But she was still rattled by what had happened less than an hour before—and she still had a feeling that the two men were in cahoots.

"Mara, I'm sorry," he said mildly. "I didn't mean to put you on the spot about something as trivial as inviting a guest in for coffee. For someone my age, it's an obligation—" Adam began.

Provided with the opening, Mara attacked in order to divert the conversation. "You know nothing about obligation, Adam. That and duty and loyalty are three words that aren't in your vocabulary."

His handsome face grew hard. "No? I think I have a better understanding of their meaning than you do."

"Ha!" It was a contemptuous sound. "I suppose the way you were able to twist their meaning is what enabled you to desert mother and me."

"I never deserted either of you," he retorted. "My sense of duty and obligation is what prompted me to make your future and your mother's secure from financial worries. Rosemary always came first in my loyalty and devotion because she was the mother of my child—you."

"You can't expect me to believe that," Mara said. "Your attempts to justify the way you behaved are just plain sickening."

"Is there a statute of limitations on the past, Mara? You can't change it, you know."

"That doesn't mean I have to like it."

"Listen to yourself. You sound so childish—and so cold."

"You're not entitled to criticize me," Mara said with haughty disdain.

"Apparently nobody is. You've put yourself up on a pedestal and encased yourself in marble." His brown eyes regarded her with intelligent dismay. "You have no feelings, no emotions, no heart. If you weren't my daughter, I would dislike you. As it is, I can't make up my mind whether I pity you or myself."

Mara paled under his stinging attack. "I don't need your pity," she countered.

"No, you don't need anything," Adam agreed in a colder tone than he had ever used. "And I thank God I'm not you. Because I need, and I feel, and I'm alive. But you—"

"Don't even try to finish that sentence." Tears burned the back of her eyes, but she refused to let them escape.

"It hurts to be honest with you, Mara. Believe me, it hurts." There was pain in his face. "And I have a lot to answer for. Maybe it's not realistic to expect you to ever forgive me, but I'd give anything if I had a daughter who would run to this bed and fling herself in my arms, a daughter who would cry and ask, 'Daddy, why did you leave me when I loved you so?'"

A tightness gripped her throat. "How would you answer that?"

"I don't know." Adam gave her a level look. "I've never had a daughter who came to me and asked that question. Only a daughter who's capable of love and emotion could ask it. If she were capable of feeling, she would probably understand my answer."

"What you mean is she'd be a sucker for your emotional games. Let's not even get into the lies." Despite the bitterness of her answer, Mara was being torn in two. His heartfelt words were appealing to the emotions Sin had aroused. She felt herself weakening. "I didn't mean that, Adam." Turning away from him, she managed a confused, "I don't know what to think anymore."

As she blindly fled his bedroom, she heard his murmured, "That's a beginning."

Chapter Seven

The confrontation had left an unexpected state of neutrality in its wake. Mara couldn't explain it. She only knew she couldn't summon her previous aloofness when she was around her father. An emotional barrier had fallen down, but she hadn't figured out which one it was.

Opening the oven door, she pulled out the shelf holding the roasting pan and basted the turkey it contained. Its succulent flesh was a rich golden brown. An aromatic blend of sage and giblet stuffing filled the kitchen.

Beside the roasting pan was a pan of candied sweet potatoes; and, cooling on the kitchen counter, a pumpkin pie. On top of a burner on the stove, peas simmered in a pan. The refrigerator held a relish tray and cranberry salad, along with way too much other food. She had everything and then some for a traditional Thanksgiving dinner.

"Mmm, something smells good," her father declared as he rolled his wheelchair into the kitchen. "How long before dinner is ready?"

"I'm just waiting on the turkey and the sweet potatoes." Mara slid the shelf into the oven and closed the door. "Another half hour or so, and they'll be done."

"When are you going to set the table?" Adam asked.

"I have." She absently motioned to the one in the kitchen while she searched for the right size lid to fit the pan holding the peas.

"Since it's Thanksgiving, don't you think we should eat in the dining room?" he suggested. "It's a special day and a special dinner, turkey and all the trimmings."

"I suppose we could." Finding the lid, she covered the pan and turned off the heat to let the peas steam cook. "I want to put the dinner rolls in the oven first, then I'll set the table in the other room."

"You don't need to. I'll do it," Adam volunteered, and wheeled his chair to the kitchen table. "We'll need another place setting, though."

"What?" Mara frowned.

"There are only two settings here." Adam stacked the two plates on his lap and set the silverware on top of them. "We need another."

"For who?" She stiffened, already guessing the answer.

"For whom?" he said, correcting her grammar.

"You didn't invite Sin Buchanan for dinner?" She hadn't seen Sin since Monday and she wanted to keep it that way.

"Yes, I did," said Adam as if it was the most reasonable thing in the world to do.

"Well, you can just uninvite him!" She slammed the cupboard door after taking out the sheet pan for the dinner rolls.

"Mara!" He tsked at her in teasing remonstration. "Where is my charitable daughter with the halo circling her head? It's a holiday, a time to sit down with your fellow man and give thanks for the bountiful goodness we've been granted."

"I am not sitting at any table with him." Her refusal lacked its usual conviction. She wondered where her vehemence had gone.

"It's Thanksgiving. Here Sin is in Pennsylvania, without any family or close friends. He shouldn't have to eat his holiday dinner alone, should he?" It wasn't really a question. "There's so much turkey and whatnot, the two of us couldn't possibly eat it all. We'll be having leftovers for a week. It isn't as if we can't spare the food."

"I never said it was," she protested.

"The Pilgrims sat down to dinner with the Indians. Surely you can sit at a table with Sin?" His light-hearted mood made it difficult for Mara to take offense.

"And if I can't?"

"It seems to me you have two choices," her father answered. "Either you can eat in the kitchen while Sin and I have dinner in the dining room. Or else you can tell him he isn't welcome here for dinner. You'd better make up your mind, because here he is now."

His last statement was followed immediately by a knock on the door. Adam had seen Sin approach through the door's window. Mara pivoted sharply toward the sound.

"Why did you wait until the last minute to tell me you'd invited him?" she hissed at her father. He'd done it deliberately so she wouldn't have time to think of an adequate escape. "You knew I wouldn't like it."

He merely smiled. "You'd better answer the door."

Mara flashed him an angry look as she walked to answer the second knock. In a fleeting moment of vanity, she was glad she had changed into the cranberry wool dress she was wearing. It was a fitting choice for the holiday dinner and it looked great with her dark hair and pale skin. The minute she realized what she was thinking, Mara pushed the thought aside. Why should she suddenly care that she looked particularly attractive?

Her heart was beating a crazy tattoo against her ribs

when she opened the back door. Which was nothing compared to the sudden acceleration of her pulse when she faced Sin and met his steel-blue eyes. He, too, had dressed for the occasion in a charcoal gray suit, a shade that enhanced the burnished silver mane of his hair.

"I was invited to dinner today." Sin gave faint emphasis to the verb to let her know he remembered her order not to come to the house unless he had been invited.

"Yes, I know," she admitted. "But Adam neglected to let me know until a few minutes ago that he'd asked you to join us for Thanksgiving dinner." Indecision warred within her as she continued to stand in the doorway, the cold November air chilling her to the bone.

"I see." Sin took a step backward as if he thought the invitation was about to be canceled.

His apparent willingness to accept her decision forced Mara to second her father's invitation. "It doesn't matter. There's more than enough food for three of us. Come on in."

He gave her a considering look as he inclined his head in polite acceptance. "Thank you." After Mara had stepped out of the way, he entered the kitchen to greet her father. "Hello, Adam. How are you feeling?"

"I'm glad you could come, Sin," her father replied with a twinkle in his eyes. "I'm fully recovered from my cold. My only problem now is imminent starvation."

"A problem not helped by the appetizing aroma in the air," Sin sympathized.

It was a compliment to Mara's cooking, but she pretended not to hear it. She pretended to concentrate on arranging the dinner rolls on the sheet pan, her back turned to Sin.

"I'll need that third place setting for the table, Mara," her father reminded her. "Would you hand it to me?"

Wiping her hands on a towel, Mara took a plate from the cupboard and silverware from the drawer and handed them to her father.

"Never mind the glasses," Adam instructed. "We'll use the crystal goblets from the china cabinet in the dining room." Turning his chair, he was careful not to let the plates slip from his lap. "We have time for a glass of sherry before dinner, Sin. Or something stronger, if you like."

"Sherry is fine." Sin glanced at Mara. "Will you join us?"

"No." Her refusal was quick, self-consciously so. "Thank you, but I'd better stay here in the kitchen where I can watch the turkey."

Neither man argued the necessity of it with her and Mara was left alone. Listening to their voices in the dining room, she put the dinner rolls in the oven to brown and checked the turkey once more. Not as if it's going to run away, she told herself. Even though she wanted to do just that.

She pottered around, finding excuses not to join them in the other room until it was time to start carrying the dishes of food in to set on the table. Even then Mara tried to be as unobtrusive as possible, not wanting to call Sin's attention to her. When she carried the turkey in on its platter, the men were seated at the table. She started to set the turkey in front of her father to carve.

"Let Sin do it," he told her. "Guest of honor and all that."

A protest hovered on the tip of her tongue, but she knew his suggestion was only polite. Reluctantly she walked over to Sin's chair. Her shoulder brushed against his as she reached in front of him to set the platter down. But Sin didn't seem to notice.

For Mara, the accidental contact heightened an awareness that was already too intense. She found herself unable to take part in the small talk. Any attempt by either her father or Sin to include her in the conversation was met by a stilted response.

The food, for all that it was tasty, invariably seemed to become lodged in her throat, and she was glad she had kept her portions small. Her discomfort was increased by the way her gaze kept straying to Sin's strong hands. She kept remembering how they had caressed her flesh, skillfully arousing her desire. Just thinking about it sparked a similar response.

It was a relief when she could claim she'd had enough to eat. In truth, she'd lost her appetite the second Sin had entered the house.

"Excuse me." She rose from her chair. "While you finish, I'll dish up the dessert."

"Pumpkin pie?" Adam darted her a hopeful look.

"Of course," she nodded.

"With some whipped cream?" he tacked on.

"Yes, I still have to whip it, but it won't take long," Mara promised, and retreated to the relative security of the kitchen.

Dragging out Old Faithful, the electric mixer that never quit, she whipped the cream into stiff peaks. She added a scant quarter-cup of superfine sugar and a dash of vanilla, and whipped it again. The swinging of the kitchen door drew her gaze. Sin walked in, carrying the dinner plates.

"Clearing the table seemed the least I could do to show my appreciation for an excellent meal," he said.

She riveted her attention on the bowl of whipping cream and the beaters whirring in it.

"Thank you." Her response was routine. "I'll bring the dessert in shortly."

"I'll help you carry it in," Sin volunteered, walking to the counter where she was working.

The pie was already sliced, individual pieces on the dessert plates. All that was left to do was add a generous dollop of whipped cream to each piece. As Sin paused beside Mara to watch her finish beating it, her sensitive radar sounded the alarm at his closeness.

"It really isn't necessary." She tried to refuse his assistance and deny his continued presence.

"I don't mind." He dismissed her protest as nothing more than a polite gesture not to be taken seriously. "Besides, I wanted to thank you privately for asking me to have dinner with you in spite of Adam's oversight."

"It wasn't my idea to invite you." She wanted to make that clear. Normally she would have whipped the cream another couple of minutes, but Sin's nearness prompted her to turn off the mixer. Under the circumstances, it was fine.

"I know who issued the invitation," he replied dryly. "At the time, I wondered—well, you could have vetoed it and you didn't. So, thank you."

"You're welcome." It was a polite phrase. End of discussion.

Trying desperately to ignore him, Mara removed the beaters from the mixer. Foamy peaks of whipped cream clung to the mixer blades. She wiped the excess from them with her forefinger, the bulk of it dropping into the bowl. Some remained on her finger.

When she started to wipe it on a towel, a hand closed around her wrist, strong fingers overlapping her slender bones. The fingertip with the whipped cream was lifted to Sin's mouth. Her heart raced as he slowly and erotically licked the whipped cream from her finger.

All the while, his gaze held hers. Mara felt herself drowning in the unfathomable depths of his blue eyes. She was being pulled down, down, with no hope of being rescued and no will to care.

"Stop it, Sin," she whispered.

Satisfaction glowed briefly in his expression, but he didn't let go of her wrist. "I don't want to. Can I have a kiss instead?"

"Oh, Sin," Mara breathed in surrender.

She was already swaying toward him when his mouth began its descent to her lips. His iron arms encircled her waist and pulled her against his chest. The hungry dominance of his kiss whetted her own appetite, and her arms curved around his broad shoulders to the hard muscles of his back.

Sin tasted the completeness of her response and demanded more, stimulating her to a passion that left her weak at the knees. When she was utterly his to command, Sin lifted his mouth from her clinging, eager lips.

Bewildered by his withdrawal, she looked up at him in confusion. Her silent appeal drew a light, totally unsatisfying kiss.

"Adam will be wondering what's happened to the dessert," Sin offered in explanation. "We'd better take it in to him."

Dessert? Adam? Could he possibly care about either of them? She didn't. Only the realization of how openly she had revealed her emotions to Sinclair Buchanan made her withdraw from his arms.

Her hands trembled as she tried to spoon the whipped cream onto the pumpkin pie. She felt slightly intoxicated, a warm, heady glow that temporarily kept her from thinking straight.

When all three slices of pie had their allotted dabs of whipped cream, Sin picked up two of them, leaving Mara to carry her own into the dining room. She accompanied him into the adjoining room as if in a trance, not caring about the dessert in her hand or wanting to eat it. It was what he expected her to do and she did it.

"I was beginning to wonder where you were," Adam commented when they appeared. "What took so long?"

"It was my fault," Sin answered, negating the need for Mara to think of something to say. He set one of the dessert plates in front of Adam, then politely held out Mara's chair for her. His gaze briefly met hers, suggestively and intimately. "I was sampling some of the cook's wares." He glanced briefly at her mouth before he turned to smile at her father.

Mara kept her eyes downcast to avoid the inquisitive look Adam directed her way. She knew what wares Sin had sampled, and she hadn't yet recovered from the sampling. It was a relief that the pie didn't require much effort to eat. She poked it with a fork, taking tiny nibbles rather than bites.

With the dessert finished, her father leaned back in his wheelchair. His hand patted his stomach in appreciation. "Ah, that was a delicious meal, Mara," he declared.

"There's more pie," she offered.

"I can't eat another bite. What about you, Sin?" Adam asked.

"I'm done. And it was very good, Mara, all of it." Sin, too, extended his compliments, but in her sensitive state Mara wondered if his remark held a double meaning. It was difficult to tell. Trite phrases escaped her, so she simply nodded an acceptance.

"There is one more thing I'd like," her father stated. "Coffee."

"I've made a fresh pot. Why don't the two of you have your coffee in the living room?" Mara suggested, adding hurriedly, "That way I can clear the table without stumbling over you."

"Have coffee with us first," Sin invited. "The dishes will wait, I'll help you with them later."

"No." She refused his assistance in a rush, but her

hasty rejection bordered on rudeness and she tried to lessen her bluntness. "Thank you, but I don't care for any coffee right now." Rising from her chair, she began stacking the dessert plates. "Go ahead into the living room. I'll bring your coffee directly."

As Adam rolled his chair away from the table, Mara carried the dishes into the kitchen. The kitchen door made its usual swing behind her as she pushed it open. Mara glanced over he shoulder to see Sin following her with the glasses and silverware she hadn't been able to carry.

"Thanks for bringing that in." Her words were lies. The last thing she wanted was to be alone with him again.

"I told you I would help," Sin reminded her.

Mara wasted no time arranging china cups and saucers on a tray. "Good. You can carry the coffee into the living room and save me a trip." She began filling the coffee server with the freshly brewed liquid.

"You don't need the second cup on the tray. I'm not having my coffee now," he said. "I'll have mine with you after we've cleaned everything up. Would you like me to wash or dry the dishes?"

"Neither." Her reply was abrupt. "I'd rather do it by myself. I know where everything is and where it belongs."

"You cooked the meal. It isn't fair that you have to clean up the mess afterward by yourself," he said pleasantly.

"I'm used to it. Believe me, it doesn't bother me." Not a tenth as much as you do, Mara thought.

"It bothers me," Sin reasoned.

"Adam would like you to have coffee with him. You're his guest," she pointed out tightly. "Please, join him in the living room. He'll enjoy your company."

"Meaning you won't?"

"No." Mara added the sugar bowl and a spoon to the

tray. Picking it up, she turned to face him, her gaze faltering under his disbelieving look. "Will you take this in or shall I?"

"I'll take it in." Before he did, Sin removed the second cup and set it on the counter. "But I'll be back to help."

"No." But Sin had already disappeared through the swinging door. Mara turned toward the sink with a feeling of helplessness, her teeth clenched in exasperation.

Where was her emotional armor? What had happened to the invisible walls that had protected her for so long? They seemed to have crumbled under his onslaught. Her hands gripped the edge of the kitchen counter as she tried to think of some way to keep him at a distance.

At the sound of footsteps approaching the door, Mara grabbed for the apron on a rack and tied it around her waist. She was at the sink filling it with water when Sin walked in.

"If you're going to do the washing, then I'll dry," he said. "Where are the dish towels?"

"It's thoughtful of you to help, but I can't let you." She answered quickly to keep her fragile control from snapping. "This china belonged to my grandmother. I don't want to chip a single piece. That's why I wash it by hand. I mean, we don't have a dishwasher because there's just the two of us but—" She stopped, realizing that she was babbling.

"And I thought you were just compulsive," he grinned. "Don't worry. I'll be extremely careful."

"Really, please don't. What if you get something on your suit and ruin it?" She grasped at a straw of an excuse.

"Give me an apron. I don't care if it's frilly." His calm voice sounded determined to counter her every argument.

"Don't be ridiculous!"

"I'm not. You are," he said.

"Sin, why don't you get it through your head that I don't want you to help me?" she demanded, feeling the frayed edges of her nerves give way.

"Why don't you stop being so damned obstinate?" He crooked a finger under her chin to turn her face to his.

The touch was her undoing. She jerked free of it. "Don't you understand that I don't want to feel the way you're making me feel?"

"Why?" He met the blazing look in her eyes. "Because you suddenly realized you're vulnerable?"

"I don't know. And I don't care." Mara dismissed his suggestion as unimportant. "I just want you to leave me alone."

Sin snorted with amusement. "But will you promise to leave me alone?" he asked. "Sexual attraction is something of a common denominator. No one is completely immune to it."

"Sex has nothing to do with it," she lied.

"Maybe not," Sin agreed, then contradicted himself. "Or should I say not yet?"

Mara felt herself being drawn into the force field of a powerful magnet. "I'll buy back your lease on the cottage," she rushed out. "Whatever amount you say. I don't care. I want you out of it. I want you out of my life!"

Her voice had been rising in volume, in direct proportion to the panic racing through her. She had been so intent on the danger before her she didn't hear the whirring of the wheelchair.

Adam pushed open the door to the kitchen, frowning at the pair of them as he entered. "What's going on? Sounded like you were shouting in here. What's the problem?"

Mara turned to her father, unable to summon up her

usual cold control. "Get him out of here!" she ordered, pointing at Sin. "Get him out of this kitchen! Out of this house!"

Shooting a questioning look at Sin, Adam seemed simultaneously puzzled and concerned. "Sin, I think you'd better—"

"I think your daughter and I ought to thrash this out in private," Sin interrupted.

"No!" The word exploded from Mara. "We have nothing to discuss! I don't want you here! I don't need you here!"

"That's where you're wrong." He was an immovable object, as solid as granite.

She glared at her father, daring him to take sides against her again as he had done in the past. His measured look took in her expression and Sin's impassive face. Adam seemed pleased by some secret thought.

"Sin, it would be best if you come with me. From past experience, I can tell you that Mara's not in a mood to listen to reason." Adam turned his chair and pointed it at the door, confident that Sin would follow him.

Sin hesitated, his flinty gaze seeming to warn Mara that she hadn't seen or heard the last of him. Half turning, he picked up the cup and saucer sitting on the counter, the one that had been on the coffee tray.

"Adam is right." His gaze leveled on her once more before he followed her father. "Sometimes it's wiser to lose one battle in order to win the war."

As he walked out of the room, she realized that victory wasn't always a joyful experience. She turned her back on the door and closed her eyes tightly to shut out the tears. But they trickled down her cheeks anyway, as silent sobs racked her. Her teeth bit into her lower lip to hold back any sound.

She had never indulged in so much emotion before,

not even in the privacy of her room, keeping it locked away. Somehow Sin had acquired the key and she felt as if he had just opened Pandora's box. Now that everything was being released, she wasn't sure she would be able to bring it all under control again.

The feelings Sin aroused whenever he was near her or touched her were new to her. Sexual attraction, he had called it. Mara wanted no part of it under any label. She couldn't handle the havoc it created within.

After she had cried herself out at the kitchen table, head down on her folded arms, Mara looked up and looked around.

Back to work, she told herself. It beat crying. Anything beat crying. Mara was weak and shaky and it took longer than usual to wash the dishes and put the kitchen back in order. Once this was accomplished, a blessed numbness enveloped her.

She folded a dishcloth and soaked it with ice water, patting it over her swollen eyes. Then she abandoned the sanctuary of the kitchen to join her father in the living room. And Sin.

She felt capable of confronting him again, unaware of how pale she looked or the vulnerable sadness in her eyes.

The men ended their conversation the second she entered the room, and Sin's gaze encompassed her. His whole bearing was one of total relaxation, leaning back in his chair, his long legs crossed. Behind his unreadable expression, Mara had the impression of alertness.

"Are you still here?" The numbness kept her voice flat and indifferent despite her rather rude question, which earned her a sharp look from her father. "I would have thought you'd have left by now."

"If you want some coffee, Mara," her father said

crisply, "I'm afraid you'll have to make more. Sin and I drank the whole pot."

"You should have said something," Mara replied, grateful that they'd left her alone.

"I could have made more myself," Sin said. "I know my way around a coffeemaker. But Adam and I got to talking. Really talking." Sin watched her arrange their empty cups on the coffee tray with an air of detachment. "We were discussing a very interesting topic."

She favored him with a wary look. "Uh-huh." Things got a little too interesting when they had to do with Sin.

"Adam and I have been talking about you and your—well, your life."

His statement seemed to hover in the air before its implication sank in. "It's bad manners to talk about people when they aren't around to defend themselves." Mara couldn't exactly claim her manners were all that good at the moment. Having him around made her . . . react. In unexpected ways.

"My apologies." He didn't sound any too sincere. "The next time we'll make it a group therapy discussion."

"I'm not interested in your brand of therapy," she retorted, all too conscious of the forms it might take.

"Adam and I have come to the conclusion that you're something of a coward." Sin didn't even glance at her when he passed on that startling information.

"What?" Mara's astonishment was exceeded by her anger. She stared at her father in wordless accusation.

"It's only a theory," Adam offered in consolation.

"Yes," Sin agreed. "It hasn't been put to a hard test yet."

"Have you two been drinking or something? I didn't walk into a chapter meeting of professional character assassins, did I?" A crazy hurt was beginning to spread through her, though she didn't want to believe that either of the two men in the room had anything to do with it. Neither answered her.

"I'm not interested in your theories or tests either," she said at last.

"Aren't you going to ask us if we'd like some more coffee?" Sin wanted to know.

"After what you just said, no."

"None for me, thank you," her father said.

"Well, I guess I won't bother to make more after all. The kitchen is your domain, Mara. You made that pretty clear." Sin exhaled a contented sigh. "I know I'm repeating what I've said before, but the meal was delicious."

"Thank you." She tried to conceal her surprise that he had allowed her to change the subject.

"You're welcome." There was a hint of arrogant amusement in the slight nod of his head. As Mara picked up the coffee tray to carry it to the kitchen, Sin continued, "As a matter of fact, I'd like to return your hospitality and invite you to have dinner with me at the cottage on Saturday night."

She darted him an even warier look. "Thank you, but Adam has difficulty negotiating some obstacles. We won't be able to accept your invitation."

"I wasn't inviting your father, only you." Before she could voice a definite refusal, Sin went on, "Adam already said it was fine with him. I talked to him about it first and convinced him that I could be trusted not to seduce his daughter."

A heat flamed through her that wasn't sparked by anger. "I don't care whether Adam has given his permission or not. I am not having dinner with you. There would be absolutely no point to it."

As Mara started toward the kitchen with the tray, Sin rose to his feet with a lithe swiftness and blocked her path. He towered in front of her, too broad to sidestep.

"You're forgetting one point. There was something you wanted to discuss with me," he reminded her.

"Oh?" Her knees threatened to buckle. "I don't recall wanting to talk to you about anything." Her air of bravado was quickly deserting her.

"Don't you?" He looked down into her eyes as if he could read her mind. "It was something to do with the cottage and when I would be leaving it."

Her gaze fell under the dominance of his. "Yes, well, that discussion doesn't have to happen at the cottage. You can come here."

Sin appeared to loom closer. "Saturday night at six o'clock, at the cottage, is the only time I'll discuss my terms for leaving."

"Don't try to push me around." Mara breathed out the words. She looked at her father. "Adam, did you put him up to this?"

"I didn't say no, if that's what you mean," her father said affably.

"No, he didn't," Sin agreed.

"This is so manipulative. I can't believe you said what you just said. You two are a couple of—I wouldn't want to say. I don't know which of you to kick first!"

"Kick me," Sin offered. "Just show up at the specified time and place. Unless you're a coward, you'll be there." He ignored her openmouthed look of indignation and addressed her father. "It's time I was leaving, Adam. I enjoyed talking to you. Happy Thanksgiving." He said the last to both of them.

Mara still hadn't found her voice when the front door closed behind Sin. She turned to her father, who was looking at her with something akin to sympathy. His expression didn't endear him to her.

"I don't know what you're up to, but your conniving won't work. I am not going to dinner with him."

"That's your decision." Her father shrugged, indicating he wasn't going to argue or try to persuade her into accepting.

"And what was all that about saying it was all right for me to go out with him?" Mara demanded. "I'm of legal age. I don't require your permission."

"I didn't exactly give my permission," he corrected. "Sin asked me if I had any objections to being alone for a couple of hours on Saturday night because he wanted to have dinner with you. Just you. I merely told him I didn't object and that you were free to go out with him if you wished."

"Well, I don't wish," she snapped. "And what's all this nonsense about convincing you he wouldn't seduce me?"

"I think it was an attempt on his part to assure both of us that, despite first impressions, he's an honorable man," he answered, referring to Sin's female companionship the first couple of weekends in the cottage. "I'd already guessed he was a man of his word. He said he wouldn't seduce you on Saturday night and I believe him."

"He isn't going to get the chance," she retorted, and immediately sought to clarify a point. "Not going doesn't mean I'm a coward, either."

"If you say so." Adam's skeptical tone didn't indicate that he agreed with her.

"I'm not a coward," Mara repeated angrily.

"There's an easy way to prove it." Using one wheel as a pivot point, Adam turned his chair around. "I think I'll watch the football game in my room."

After he had pushed himself out of the room, there was no one left for Mara to argue with except herself.

Chapter Eight

Pulling the collar of her heavy jacket tighter around her neck, Mara paused to stare at the lighted windows of the cottage. It was Saturday night, cold with the threat of snow in the air. She had never admitted to being nervous about anything, but she was now.

Half a dozen times during her walk to the cottage she had been on the verge of running back home. But something kept driving her on. Mara realized that she was playing Sin's game and taking his dare.

Shivering and not only from the cold, she walked the last few feet to the door and knocked twice, taking a deep, calming breath. The door opened and immediately swung wide to admit her. Shakily expelling the breath she had taken in, Mara walked in.

Sin's physical presence intimidated her more than it ever had before. Her gaze moved over him. A white roll-neck sweater showed off his impressive chest. Dark jeans gave added length to his legs.

A fire crackled in the fireplace. Except for one dim lamp, it provided the only light in the living room. The mantel clock chimed the hour.

"Right on time," Sin observed. "You're punctual."

"Yes." Mara couldn't shake off the feeling that she was a lamb being led into the den of a silver-tipped wolf.

His hand reached toward her and she backed away from it instinctively, looking at him with alarm. His mouth slanted in amusement.

"May I take your coat?" he offered.

Mara told herself he had only intended to help her out of it, not rip it off her back along with all the rest of her clothes. Fighting the self-conscious waves of foolishness, she fumbled with the buttons. Her chilled fingers weren't very cooperative. When at last they had completed the task, she started to shrug out of the coat. Sin's hands were there to help her, brushing her shoulders and sending tingles down her spine.

"Thank you," she murmured, hoping he wouldn't guess his assistance had shook her up.

A strong sense of self-preservation made her notice where Sin had put her coat. It was near the door draped over a hook on the hall tree, a new addition of furniture to the cottage.

"How do you like your steak?" Sin inquired.

"Well done," Mara responded automatically.

Again a smile teased the corners of his strong mouth. "Somehow I guessed that."

He surveyed her coatless self. The frankly sensual look prompted Mara to hug her arms across her stomach. She wasn't dressed in any way that could be called suggestive, but Sin made her feel she was.

Her pants and loose jacket were peacock blue, not at all clinging. Her fingers made an unconscious inspection of the buttons of her cream silk blouse to be sure they were all fastened. They were. Ill at ease, she lifted her chin and tried to shake away the uncomfortable sensation.

"How about a drink?" It was the polite inquiry of a host, but it didn't mask the light dancing in his eyes.

"Nothing, thank you," Mara refused, steadfast in her determination to have a working brain this evening.

"Would you excuse me, then?" Sin asked. "I put the steaks in the broiler a few minutes ago and I'd better check them. You can have a seat in the living room if you like, or come along with me to the kitchen."

One glance at the dimly lit living room and the intimate feeling it evoked made up Mara's mind. The kitchen was a lot better lit than the living room. She opted for it.

"I'll come with you if you don't mind," she said.

"Think I can't cook?" he joked, but didn't seem to expect a reply.

Sin entered the kitchen, aware that Mara had followed, but he paid no attention to her as he checked the steaks in the broiler. The small table held two place settings. Wooden bowls of tossed salad sat at each place, along with cut glass goblets.

"Unless you would prefer to wait, we can have our salad now." He straightened from the broiler and noticed her preoccupation with the wineglasses. "I hope you like wine with your meal."

"Champagne?" Mara heard herself question dryly, her thoughts turning to the day he had first arrived when Celene had brought in a bottle of champagne.

His gaze slid over her, remembering, too. "No, you don't strike me as the champagne type," he answered. "Something staid and prosaic like hearty burgundy seems more your line."

He produced a decanter of deep red wine and filled the two glasses. After setting them on the table, he held out a chair for her.

"About the cottage," Mara began, wanting to get to the objective of her visit.

"I never discuss business before or during a meal."

Impatience surged through her, but she was deter-

mined not to give rise to it. She sat down in the chair
Sin offered and tried to ignore the brief contact with
his hand as he pushed her chair to the table. While he
was sitting down at the opposite end of the narrow
table, she shook out her linen napkin and spread it
across her lap.

"I hope you like the dressing on the salad. It's a special concoction of mine," Sin informed her. "Italian
with variations."

She sampled the salad. "It's very good," she admitted, trying to be the courteous guest.

"The secret is fresh oregano," he confided. "Gives it a
touch of piquancy. Easy to grow but not in winter. This
is hydroponic. I get it at a gourmet grocery in Baltimore."

"Oh." Had he gone to that much trouble for her?
Mara was having difficulty adjusting to this kind of conversation. She was accustomed to battling his teasing or
personal comments. This casual small talk was putting
her off stride. She sensed he knew it, too.

After a couple of minutes Sin rose from his chair to
check the steak. The succulent aroma coming from the
broiler was decidedly appetizing. Mara, who had thought
she wouldn't be able to eat a bite, felt the first pangs of
hunger.

"You're an excellent cook," Sin observed when he
was reseated at the table. "Do you like to cook?"

"I've never thought of it in terms of liking it or dislik-
ing it." Her fork rested in the salad bowl as she considered his question, surprised to find she didn't have a
ready answer. "It's always been something that had to be
done. But yes, I think I enjoy it. Do you?"

"I wouldn't if I had to do it every day, but it's a form
of relaxation for me."

"What do you do when you're in Baltimore? Do you
mostly eat at restaurants or—" She didn't want to ask if

anyone else he knew liked cooking. Just because he
hadn't been married to Celene as she had first supposed, it didn't mean he wasn't married, or hadn't
been married, or didn't do the cooking himself.

Mara realized there was a great deal she didn't know
about him—his background, his work, his interests,
anything. She cast a glance at his left hand. Not that she
hadn't seen it before but this time she was looking
more closely, for the telltale white skin where a wedding
band might have been.

He saw the direction of her glance and tried to conceal a knowing smile.

"I'm not married. Did you think I had an understanding wife waiting patiently in Baltimore for me to
return after Thanksgiving?" Sin shook his head. "I can't
imagine any woman being that understanding."

Mara admitted to herself that he was right. "You
could be divorced or separated . . ." She pointed out
the possibilities.

"Neither, I'm a widower. My wife had MD—muscular
dystrophy. She died seven years ago." His voice remained
completely conversational, registering no sorrow.

"I'm sorry." She felt obliged to voice some sympathy.
But she looked at him anew, trying to visualize the circumstances of his marriage and his feelings about a
wife with rapidly deteriorating health. How had he re-
acted, she wondered.

"I was aware of Ann's condition when I married her,"
Sin said, answering her unspoken question.

Startled, Mara blurted, "Then why did you marry
her?"

"Because I cared for her," he answered simply. "I
wanted to look after her and see that she had the best
help possible."

His response made her uncomfortable. She didn't

want to believe his motives. Her fork attacked the last bit of salad in the bowl.

"You could have done that without the noble gesture of marriage." She could have kicked herself for that tactless reply. Where it had come from, she had no idea.

"It wouldn't have fulfilled my sense of obligation and duty. Ann didn't have anyone else. You should know about that, Mara. You could have paid for Adam's care, rather than take him into your home." Sin defused her comment, the calm pitch of his voice unchanging.

"Different situation," she said softly. "Very different."

"Is it?" He gave her an abstracted look and murmured a thought aloud. "I seem to continually collect lost souls." Then he glanced at her empty salad bowl. "Are you finished?"

"Yes, thank you." Mara sat rigidly in her chair as Sin rose to clear the dishes.

The steaks were done. He set a plate before Mara containing a generous cut of charbroiled beef and a baked potato, butter melting inside its split skin. A garnish of sliced apple rings brightened the dish.

"Anyway, getting back to your previous question, I eat out occasionally when I'm in Baltimore." Sin resumed their conversation as he sat down. "I have a housekeeper and cook on staff, so I generally have my meals at home. Part of the appeal of coming here to the cottage each weekend is the fact that there's no one around to wait on me. That and privacy as well as the freedom to work without interruption."

"What kind of work do you do? I know you're the head of a company." Mara remembered Harve Bennett mentioning it before she leased Sin the cottage.

"It's a growing conglomerate. I've acquired a bunch of companies, some tech, some traditional. And I've raised venture capital for a couple of bioengineering startups run by friends of mine from Stanford. Brilliant theoreticians and researchers, both of them, but they know nothing about running a business."

"I assume you graduated from there."

"Yup. You're looking at a former geek. Bioengineering is the next big thing, in terms of pure science and profitable applications. But my work is mainly in administration and organization. Basically, I have a very challenging desk job."

Mara sensed that his reply was an understatement. There was no reference to the tremendous power he commanded or the pressure of high finance. She had no doubt that he handled both with ease. He was noticeably self-assured.

"My father started the company," Sin continued, pausing to sip his wine. "I inherited it from him when he passed away a few years ago."

The information didn't surprise her. Mara had suspected his wealth wasn't newly acquired. His indifference to the cost of things, this cottage for instance, indicated that he was accustomed to having what he wanted, regardless of the price.

"So you took over the company and did wonders for the bottom line?" He had too much drive to be content with things as they were.

Over the rim of his wineglass his blue eyes briefly met hers. "Like I said, we're growing," Sin admitted, but with the attitude that this was an unimportant fact.

The information she was receiving about him was being mentally filed in a haphazard way and whetted her curiosity to know more. She was eating the food on her plate without being all that conscious of its taste or quantity.

"Why did you spend Thanksgiving here? With your father gone, don't you have any other family?" Mara questioned.

"I have some cousins on the West Coast and an aunt and uncle, but no brothers or sisters. My mother died suddenly of a heart attack when I was in college." He seemed not to mind her personal questions. "If I'd stayed in Baltimore, Ginger, my cook, would have insisted on fixing a big dinner with several courses. It would have been a total waste for one person. So instead I gave my staff the week off to spend the holidays with their own families, and came here." He glanced at her across the table, a sexy smile curving his well-defined mouth. "As it turned out, I had an perfectly prepared Thanksgiving dinner anyway and the pleasure of Adam's company and yours."

Her pulse hammered slightly—whether from his smile or his reference to the pleasure he found in her company, she wasn't sure.

"What do you find to do here, besides jogging, I mean? Aren't you bored?" Mara took a sip of her wine, surprised to find more than half of it gone.

"I do a lot of thinking and planning. I usually bring up my laptop so I can get around to e-mails and memos— and reports and spreadsheets. Mostly I relax." Sin refilled her glass and his own. "Tonight, with you, will probably turn out to be one of the livelier evenings I've spent here."

The others must have been spent with Celene, Mara concluded. "Why don't you bring your, uh, friend here anymore?" she wondered aloud.

"You mean Celene?"

Mara nodded.

"Taken in small doses, she can be fun," he explained dryly. "But she gets to be a bit much after a while."

"Too many 'Sin honeys'?" Mara intended it as a taunt, but it sounded more like a teasing exchange between friends.

"Something like that," Sin agreed, his lazy glance not

revealing that he found anything unusual in her new tone. "How was your steak?"

"It was very good." She had eaten it all, not toying with it once from nervousness. "Where did you learn to cook?"

"I picked it up here and there, mostly by trial and error during my starving student days."

"That was a while ago," she said with a smile.

"Yeah, but it still comes in handy when a business meeting drags on until midnight. I don't have to wake anyone up to fix me a meal."

"Does that happen often?" Mara asked.

"Often enough." Sin finished his dinner and straightened from his chair. He took her plate, stacked it on top of his and set it on the sink counter. "Dessert is a plate of assorted fruits and cheeses. I thought we'd have it with the rest of the wine in the living room. I'll clear the table first."

"I'll help you," she volunteered.

"No." He refused her assistance flatly. "You wouldn't let me help you on Thanksgiving, so you can't help me tonight. I'll just put them in the sink and wash them later."

His reminder had the desired effect of keeping Mara in her seat while he smoothly and efficiently cleared the table. In the interim, her self-consciousness returned and she felt stiff and ill at ease again. Rising awkwardly when he'd finished, she carried her wineglass into the living room. Sin followed with the dessert plate and his own wineglass.

The dimness of the living room immediately enveloped Mara in a feeling of intimacy. The fire had died to red embers amid a bed of charcoal-gray ashes. Sin set the dessert plate on the inlaid surface of a small wooden serving table in front of the sofa. Mara stood nervously to one side, the cozy atmosphere too much for her.

"Help yourself." Sin gestured toward the fruit and cheese and walked over to add wood to the fire.

Hesitantly, Mara took a cube of cheese and nibbled at it. The plump sofa cushions were too inviting and the chairs seemed too pointedly isolated. So she remained standing, her shoes sinking into the lush pile of the alpaca rug, while Sin knelt in front of the hearth, poking the embers into flames around the fresh wood. Of all the questions she'd asked him, one came back to her now—the one he hadn't answered.

"About the cottage . . ." she began as she had before. "When will you be leaving?"

Sin didn't turn around. "When my lease runs out next fall."

"But—"

"You signed it." He stood up when the fire flickered and blazed. "You should be familiar with its clauses and conditions."

"Well, I didn't memorize it," Mara said.

"You were the one who insisted on a year's lease," he reminded her.

"But I thought I was here to discuss when you would vacate," Mara said, completing the sentence she had begun earlier.

"Consider it discussed. I've told you what you need to know," he replied calmly.

"I see. You had no intention, ever, of terminating the lease early, did you?" she asked. "You only let me think you would."

"No, there was nothing to discuss as far as I was concerned, but you didn't come here about the cottage. You came because I essentially dared you to come," Sin concluded. "Didn't like being called a coward, did you?"

"Don't you know when to stop, Sin?" Her fingers gripped the stem of her wineglass so tightly that it was in danger of snapping.

"Not one of my strong points. Sorry." He turned his back to the fireplace, the flames crackling and popping over the bark of the new logs. He made no move toward her, although his gaze was on her.

"Anyway, I'm not a coward."

"Adam and I talked a lot about that while you were washing dishes the other day. We talked about many things," he added.

"I can just imagine," Mara said bitterly.

"He explained to me how much his divorce from your mother had hurt you." His features were shadowed by the back light of the fire, but she felt the intensity of his gaze.

"Hurt me?" She was incredulous at the statement. "It crippled my mother emotionally. Did he neglect to mention that?"

"Don't you believe he cared?"

"I believe in the fickleness of men," she retorted, and walked to the fireplace to stare into the yellow flames licking hungrily over the wood.

"You know, I first thought you'd built those invisible walls around you so people couldn't get close to you. I was half-right," he observed. "You want to keep everybody away so they'll never be able to hurt you. You're determined not to care about people because they might leave you the way your father did."

"Don't you think that's wise?" Mara took a sip of wine to show her indifference to his remarks.

"It may be wise, but it's just about impossible." After sending her a sideways glance, Sin moved to stand behind her. "You can't roll all your emotions and feelings, passions and desires into a neat little bundle and stuff them into a pocket."

Mara slid her forearm across the small of her back, trying to ward off her awareness of how close he was to her. She was conscious of his physicality and felt the warmth of his body, although no part of him was touching her.

"Even if you could," he continued, "your body is designed to perform certain biological functions that respond to outside stimuli." His hands curved around her slender waist.

"How interesting, Professor Buchanan. Will that be on the midterm?" When Mara tried to step away, his hold tightened.

"It doesn't matter whether you want to feel the way I make you feel. Chalk it up to chemistry. There's nothing you or I can do about it."

"You mean sexual attraction." She referred to the term he had used before, a breathlessness to her voice.

"Yes. It doesn't do any good to fight it." He reached around her to take the wineglass from her unresisting fingers and set it on the mantelpiece.

He drew her to him until her shoulders were against his chest and her buttocks pressed against his solidly muscled thighs. The outline of his hard male frame seemed to burn its impression into her. It started a heavy, sweet fire that flamed through her body. His hands moved over her middle, his fingers spreading open just below her breasts. An aching tension twisted her stomach in knots.

Her hands crossed each other to seek his wrists. When they found them, she could only hold them in the same position. The thought of removing them had fled the minute her fingers felt the pleasantly prickly masculine hair on his arms. Her sensitive nerve ends vibrated with the sensual contact.

His head was bent toward hers, his jaw and chin brushing near her ear, his warm breath stirring the silken shortness of her dark hair. His scent was a mixture of wine and woodsmoke and the heady fragrance of an elusive cologne. Her heart tripped wildly against her ribs. She closed her eyes against the reaction of her senses to Sin, but the darkness only increased his potency.

"It's natural for my touch to excite you." His voice was pitched low, soothing in its warmth and disturbing in its huskiness. "It's a physical response that has nothing to do with what your mind wants. You have to learn to separate the two."

But the thought of him was dominating her mind, too. There wasn't room for anything else. She could only shake her head in dazed protest.

"When will it stop?" she wanted to know.

"The only cure I know for sexual attraction is prolonged exposure." His mouth explored the side of her neck, sending delicious shivers over her sensitive skin. "Tonight can be the beginning of a series of experiments."

"Yes," Mara agreed, her voice hardly above a whisper.

Sin nuzzled her ear, his teeth gently nipping at the lobe. The caress unleashed a torrent of reactions. She melted against him, his outline more sharply defined against her curves. He removed one arm from around her as his mouth lingered near her ear, then moved away.

"Here's your wine," he said.

Mara blinked at the glass he held. She had no desire for wine, but he seemed to want her to take it. She took it from his hand and held it unsteadily in her own. A second later Sin was bending and lifting her off her feet. Her arm automatically curved around his neck as he carried her effortlessly to the couch. There he sat down, cradling her on his lap.

"Drink up." His hand closed around her fingers holding the glass and moved it toward her lips. At her apprehensive look, a slight smile softened the firmness of his mouth. "Don't worry, I'm not trying to get you drunk. But the wine will help you relax."

His reasoning made sense. Mara knew that tension was making her hold herself stiffly in his lap. She kept wondering if she was too heavy or if he was comfortable in this position.

Sin watched her sip the wine. His fingers slid down her hand, his thumb rubbing the inside of her wrist and making exciting forays to her sensitive palm. When she lowered the glass from her mouth, his gaze studied her lips, faintly moist from the wine.

"We need to get you used to being touched and held first before we can graduate to other things," Sin told her huskily. The mantel clock chimed the quarter hour and Mara started guiltily, only to be restrained by his arm. "Do you see what I mean?"

Leaning slightly forward, he reached for the dessert plate on the serving table and set it on the seat cushion beside them. Mara watched him separate a pale green grape from its cluster and offer it to her.

"Have a grape," he suggested. "It's the seedless variety, so you don't have to be concerned about how you're going to dispose of the seeds." He carried it to her lips and hesitantly she let him slide it into her mouth. The brush of his fingers evoked provocative thoughts. "Good?"

"Yes." But Mara was struggling with a whole new set of erotic sensations.

"Have another." This time Sin offered her the cluster so she could pluck her own grape.

At his insistence, Mara ate two more. When she took the fourth he set the cluster on the plate and captured her hand before she placed the grape in her mouth. Instead, he carried it to his own. Her fingers trembled as they touched his mouth to slide the grape inside. Her pulse raced madly through her veins from the sensuous implication of her actions.

After that the grapes were divided between them and Sin took sips from her wine. He kissed her now and then, the taste of grapes and wine mingling together with their lips. Her position on his lap became more natural; in spite of its intimacy, she became more relaxed.

When the wine was gone, Sin put the glass and the dessert plate on the table. The emptiness of her hands made them feel useless until Sin found a purpose for them. He cupped one to his face, kissing the palm, then letting it slide along his jaw.

Her breath caught, trapped by the sudden tightening of her throat as his head slowly bent to hers. The kiss that followed was leisurely and sensual. Instead of Mara having to feel her way through her relative lack of experience, Sin was showing her the way.

The lesson was deliberately, deliciously slow and Sin was teaching her to enjoy every minute of it. Meanwhile his hands were caressing her, wandering over her hips and thighs and gliding over her spine. Their touch aroused her at an unhurried tempo.

The intoxicating pleasure of his possessing kisses was a heady thing. Gradually they sent raw desire spreading through her veins, heating her flesh to a fever warmth. Sin molded her according to his will. Nothing registered in her mind but the aching needs and wants he was instilling in her.

Unerring fingers found the buttons of her blouse, and she shifted on his lap in faint protest. Not forcing the issue, Sin bent his head to kiss her throat. His hand covered a breast, the rounded flesh swelling firm under his touch. The silk of her blouse was no barrier, she realized.

Sensing her acquiescence, Sin efficiently but unhurriedly unfastened the buttons. Seconds later, the lacy engineering of her bra was disposed of and her soft flesh was spilling into his hand. His lips made a breathtaking investigation of the new territory. Dizzying excitement thundered through her veins as she shuddered from sheer rapture.

It was a new world for her, with fresh discoveries to be made at every turn. His power over her grew stronger instead of weaker during the prolonged exposure. When his mouth returned to take passionate command of her lips, she submitted, surrendered and returned his fire.

The passionate foreplay showed her the glorious promise of the real thing, made her eager to know the wonder of it, but her teacher was repeating the same lessons, wisely not rushing her. And Mara didn't object. The chimes from the clock sounded again. She had grown used to their softly ringing tones, having mixed them up several times with the sound of bells ringing in her head. But they distracted Sin's attention.

His mouth lingered on her lips an instant longer. Then his hand was stroking her cheek as he drew away. His eyes were darkly blue as they met the passionate light in hers. He took a deep breath, seemingly in an attempt to control himself and hold back just a little longer.

"I promised Adam I'd have you home by ten," he told her, and glanced briefly at his watch. "That gives us only half an hour."

Ten o'clock. Adam. Promise. The words echoed through her mind, its thought processes slowed. While Mara tried to surface from the irresistible tide of desire, Sin began fixing her clothes, fastening clasps and buttons.

Restless and unsatisfied, she moved off his lap.

"So what's next? Are you going to tell me this seduction scene is officially over because of that other promise you gave Adam? What if I don't want it to be over?" Her voice was remarkably steady, considering her frustration.

Sin got to his feet, taking her by the shoulders and turning her to face him. He caught her downcast chin between his fingers and tilted her face up. Her eyes glimmered with mingled mutiny and regret.

"I have no intention of ever seducing you, Mara," he told her. Pain stabbed through her with the sharp breath she took. The firm line of his sensual mouth softened. "I will never persuade you to let me make love to you against your will."

Realizing how much of her innermost feelings she had betrayed, Mara turned away from him, mumbling, "I'll get my coat." She walked swiftly to the hall.

He followed but made no attempt to help her on with her coat as he took his own from a hook. "Instead of taking the car, I'll walk you home," he said. "The cold air will do us both good."

Mara didn't argue. She readily admitted to herself that she needed something to cool her flesh and her senses. She couldn't find any consolation in the fact that Sin apparently felt the same way.

Once they were both outside the cottage, Sin produced a flashlight from his pocket. The brilliant beam picked out the track through the woods and led the way. They followed it in silence, the frosty air nipping at their faces and turning their breath into vaporous clouds.

When the lights of the house came in sight, Sin spoke. "I'll be leaving for Baltimore tomorrow. I won't be back until next weekend, probably very late Friday night."

Mara continued walking toward the back door, staring straight ahead. "Don't forget to leave a list of what you need."

The flashlight went off as his hand stopped her and turned her to face him. "Don't forget what you've learned."

His mouth came down on hers with double the intensity of before. His fierceness stole her breath and heightened all her senses. The walk had chilled none of her desire. Just as quickly as it had begun, the kiss was ended and Sin was striding into the night.

Chapter Nine

The following Saturday Mara had finished leafing through a college catalog and circling courses that interested her. The breakfast dishes were piled in the sink, but for once they didn't seem to be screaming *do me* at her. She rose from the kitchen table to look out of the window above the sink. Sin would have arrived at the cottage sometime last night, she knew. Her anticipation at seeing him again was running high, partly with eagerness and partly with apprehension.

A familiar silver-gray car was stopping in the driveway to park beside the house. Her heart gave a little leap and she turned away from the window. She didn't want to admit that she had been watching for him. And she didn't want to offer an oh-so-domestic excuse for being there. And she didn't want another cup of coffee.

But she took a mug from the cupboard anyway and fussed with the coffeemaker. As the car door slammed, Mara kept her back to the door so she could pretend she didn't know he was coming. The thick walls of the house prevented her from hearing his footsteps. She could only wait for the knock on the door.

Sin entered without knocking. The only advance warning Mara had was the sound of the doorknob turning, and in the next second he was in the kitchen. She turned, giving him a wide-eyed glance that she hoped didn't look too fake.

"Hello, Mara." The warmth of his low greeting did amazing things to her.

Unable to respond naturally, she turned back to the coffeepot. "I was just going to pour a cup of coffee. Would you like some?"

"No, I don't want any coffee." The sound of his voice came closer and Mara knew he was walking toward her. Her silly heart skipped a beat, then rocketed when his hands slid around her waist. "And neither do you."

The breath she took became more of a gasp as Sin nuzzled the side of her neck. "Where's Adam?" He spoke against her skin.

"In the other room." Her voice wavered under the spell of his caress. Sin turned her sideways in his arms, her shoulder against his chest and her hip pressed against the strong column of his thighs. Curving a hand along the side of her neck, he tilted her chin with his thumb. His mouth closed over hers, parting her lips with sweet intensity. When the coolness of uncertainty ended and Mara responded, the kiss lingered for a second longer before Sin raised his head. His thumb made a feather tracing of her warm, trembling lips.

"I told you not to forget," he murmured. He released her from the blissful circle of his arms to take hold of her hand. "Let's find Adam."

"Why?" Mara asked in confusion.

But Sin didn't bother to answer as he led her from the kitchen. Adam was in his study, taking notes from the field diary of a rebel soldier. He glanced up when they entered, his gaze moving to Mara's hand held firmly in Sin's.

"Hello, Sin." He seemed not at all surprised to see them.

"Have you made any plans for today, Adam?" Sin asked, ignoring Mara's attempt to wiggle her hand free.

"No. Should I?" Her father was trying hard not to smile.

"I'm taking Mara away for the day," Sin explained further. "I've never been to the Amish country around Lancaster, so I'm going to make use of her services as a guide again. We'll be gone for the better part of the day and I know she won't want to leave you alone that long."

Mara stared openmouthed at the announcement. She couldn't think of even a halfhearted protest. She was being swept along in the tidal force of Sin's persuasivenss and had no desire to save herself.

"No problem," Adam assured them with a shrug. "Sam Jenkins will come over. Since he's retired, he welcomes any excuse to get out of the house."

"Give him a call while Mara gets ready," Sin suggested, and glanced at her. "How long will it take you? I'll give you ten minutes, no more."

Before Mara could take a breath, she was being turned toward the staircase in the foyer. With the ten-minute limit, she didn't have time to consider whether going with Sin was something she wanted to do. She changed out of her jeans into a fitted wool skirt of winter white and pulled an angora sweater over her head. Cuddly and sexy, a killer combination. Pausing only to fluff her hair with her fingertips, she hurried back downstairs.

"Ready?" Sin had her coat and scarf in hand.

Mara glanced at her father, who answered the unspoken question in her dark eyes. "Sam's on his way over. Don't worry about me, I'll be fine."

"There's vegetable stew in the refrigerator. Have Sam warm it for your lunch," she instructed as Sin helped her on with her coat. "And there's some cold cuts for sandwiches."

"We'll find plenty to eat," Adam replied. "Sam is good at raiding a refrigerator."

The arm around Mara's shoulders firmly guided her to the front door so that no more time was wasted with last-minute instructions. Outside, Sin walked her to the passenger door of his car.

"I'll drive," he explained, helping her inside. "That way I'll have something to concentrate on besides you." Flirty words, but his look was meaningful, throwing her more off balance than she already was.

Trying to hide the exciting confusion she felt, Mara glanced back at the house when Sin slid behind the wheel of the car. "Do you think Adam will be all right?"

"Instead of thinking about Adam, maybe you should be wondering if you'll be all right . . . with me." His glance was teasing.

"Will I?" Mara felt a little foolish when the provocative question seemed to hang in the air.

This time when his gaze met hers, it lingered longer. "It all depends on whether you're better at being a guide than a distraction." He looked away as he turned the car onto the gravel road. "We'll soon find out if you know as much about the Pennsylvania Dutch as you did about Gettysburg."

Mara smiled and settled into the role of guide. "For starters, the term Pennsylvania Dutch has nothing to do with Holland. They're descended from German immigrants. The word Dutch is an American corruption of deutsch, and Deutschland is the German homeland."

"That's a good start." Sin flashed a brief smile in her direction.

Mara looked out the window at the crisp blue day. It was too perfect to be spoiled by anything and she hoped the feeling would stay with her. When they got closer to Lancaster, she guided him onto the side roads, away from the commercialism of the main highway. The information she relayed about the area was never given as a means of defense; it just flowed, and she entertained herself and him with odd details about the area.

They lunched at a local restaurant specializing in Pennsylvania Dutch dishes. Now, when Sin flirted with her, she no longer felt skittish or tense. On tours in the area, they walked hand in hand or he curved an arm around her shoulders. The action seemed part of the natural order of things.

By midafternoon Sin turned the car toward Gettysburg and home. Mara sat close to him, or as close as a bucket seat and a gearshift would allow, filled with contentment.

Sam Jenkins was just leaving when they arrived at the house. Adam insisted he hadn't been aware of Mara's absence; his day had been too full. It was Adam who invited Sin to stay for dinner, an invitation that Mara seconded. Sin didn't need any persuading to accept.

Afterward her father and Sin played chess in the living room while Mara started in on a book she had been meaning to read. Adam had just scored a checkmate when she finished the first chapter. She looked up to see him leaning back in his wheelchair, a knowing smile on his face.

"I don't think your mind was on the game, Sin," her father declared. "That win was almost too easy."

"You could be right," Sin acknowledged, his gaze sliding to Mara as if she was somehow the cause of his loss.

She had been absorbed in her book, not looking at him once, so it was illogical that she was to blame for his lack of attentiveness. Still, the implied compliment made her feel all warm and shaky inside.

"How about some hot chocolate?" she suggested.

"Sounds good," her father was the first to agree. "Only I'll have mine in my room. It's been a long day and I'm beginning to feel the effects."

He didn't look tired. In fact, Mara had the fleeting thought that she had never seen him looking more alert. But she could be wrong or at least willing to think she was wrong if it would give her another chance to be alone with Sin.

"I'll help you, Adam," Sin offered before Mara had a chance to step forward. "Mara can make the hot chocolate."

Mara found herself returning to the kitchen, where she hadn't been all evening, for a change. It didn't take long to mix the unsweetened cocoa with sugar and a little water, then pour hot milk over it and stir. When it came to hot chocolate, Mara was a traditionalist, and she hated the powdered stuff that came in packets. Marshmallows bobbed and melted on top of the steaming liquid as she carried the tray of mugs into the living room. She left two mugs there and carried the third on the tray to her father.

When she entered the bedroom, Sin retreated to let them say good night in private. Her father was in bed. Mara set the tray on the bedside table within his reach.

"Sin mentioned that you had a good time today," Adam commented.

"Yes, it's been a while since I've been in Lancaster. It was interesting. And fun." Her response was deliberately noncommittal. Her emotional reaction toward Sin was too new to be discussed openly, and certainly not with her father. "Good night, Adam."

"Good night."

Soft music was being played on the radio in the living room. Sin turned as she entered and held out a hand to her in silent invitation. Mara hesitated, aware suddenly of the limitation of her experience.

"I don't dance very well," she told him.

"It isn't necessary for you to know," he returned. "The man's supposed to be in charge. All you have to do is let me lead."

"Okay. I might even like that."

With casual purpose, he crossed the distance necessary to reach her hand and draw her into his arms. It seemed she had waited all day to be in his embrace, so naturally did her body fit itself to his.

The hand at the back of her waist guided her to the slow tempo of the music in swaying steps that required little concentration. Mara was capable of little. An avalanche of sensations seemed to tumble on top of her. The lower half of her body was welded to his hard, muscled thighs, his heat burning her. His gaze roamed possessively over her upturned face, its look sending her senses spinning into orbit.

The smell of him, the feel of him was boldly male and sensual. Sin carried her hand to his mouth, his white teeth nibbling at her sensitive fingertips. She lost all awareness of the music playing in the background. When he opened her hand to press a kiss into its palm, her limbs quivered. The sensual probing of his tongue against its hollow released a shuddering sigh of surrender from her throat.

All pretense of dancing ended as Sin's mouth sought her parted lips, taking them with languid passion. Her deep yearning had her trembling in his arms. His caressing hands made a slow, intimate exploration of her shape, their leisurely investigation kindling a hotter fire between them.

At some point they gravitated toward the nearest chair, where Mara ended up on his lap. His deliberate was just what she had wanted to do.

day was spent selecting the perfect tree, carry-
boxes of decorations from the attic, setting the
its stand, trimming it, and arranging the Nativity
on the mantel amid boughs of evergreens and
. In the bottom of one of the boxes of Christmas
rations Sin found a sprig of mistletoe. Tying it with
bbon, he hung it in the living room archway to the
ry hall.

He stood beneath it, his gaze a wicked invitation.
oo conscious of her father's presence, Mara tried to ig-
ore his message, laughing it away as a joke. Sin walked
over, picked her up and ignored her embarrassed protests to stand her beneath the mistletoe, where he kissed
her thoroughly.

But it was the only kiss she received that day, a fact
that bothered her. The previous weekend she'd had the
impression that Sin was keeping her at arm's length
even when he was kissing her. She had tried to ignore it
by blaming it on her imagination, but the feeling of distance between them was becoming too strong to ignore.

The feeling returned on Sunday when she was lying
beside him on the rug in front of the fireplace at the
cottage. They had gone for a walk in the snow-covered
woods and had stopped at the cottage to get warm.
They had all the privacy they could want, but Sin had
done little more than cuddle.

The silence between them was broken only by the
crackling of the flames. Mara wasn't comfortable with
the quiet that enveloped the room. Her head was resting on a pillow from the sofa. She turned onto her side
to study Sin's profile. One arm was crooked beneath his
head to serve as a pillow. His eyes were closed, but she
knew he wasn't sleeping.

and total mastery of her senses had turned her into a
very willing accomplice in her own seduction—that
word again. Maybe it wasn't politically correct but Mara
wanted to be seduced.

There was a raggedness to his breathing as Sin ended
a lingering kiss. Her hand curved along his chiseled jaw
to draw him back, but he resisted her tender touch, for
no reason that her dreamy mind could think of.

"The hot chocolate is getting cold," he murmured.

"I don't care," Mara admitted with a total lack of in-
hibition.

He removed his hand from beneath her sweater and
turned her so that her feet were on the floor. "Neither
do I, but I think you'd better reheat it just the same."
Ignoring her resistance, Sin stood her up and pushed
her toward the kitchen as he rose from the chair.

Reluctantly Mara took their hot chocolate into the
kitchen and warmed it. The marshmallows had melted
into sugary pools and it was even sweeter and thicker
now. Sin joined her within a few minutes. They talked
of trivial things and avoided any reference to the passionate embrace in the living room. Before he left, Sin kissed
her good night and said he'd see her in the morning.

Mara sat down at the table, feeling a little sulky as she
stirred her hot chocolate. The next best thing to sex
was sugar, she thought. And right now, she didn't have a
choice. She drank it down.

That weekend became the pattern for the weekends
that followed. Almost every waking moment was spent
together. They took a few hours away from the farmhouse, either touring a local point of interest or having
dinner. For Mara, Sin's arrival was a thrill every time—
and he made it clear that he felt the same way about
seeing her.

The weekend before Christmas arrived, along with a major snowstorm. On Saturday morning Mara waited anxiously for Sin to appear at the house, wondering if he had even driven up the night before. The roads were still dangerously slippery. She had made a dozen trips to the window above the sink for a glimpse of him.

As she started toward it again, Adam remarked, "A watched pot never boils."

Self-consciously Mara turned away before reaching her destination. "I don't know what you're talking about."

"You don't, huh?" he teased with a half smile. "My mistake. I thought you were looking for Sin."

She glanced at the kitchen wall clock. "That's right. He usually is at the house by this time, isn't he?" she replied as if it was the first time she had realized it.

The ploy didn't fool her father. "Mara, I'm not blind." He shook his head and smiled. "For three consecutive weekends you two have been inseparable. I'm getting used to doing without my daughter. If you're worried about Sin, why don't you walk down to the cottage and see if he's there?"

"Do you think I should?"

"Anything is better than having you pace the floor," Adam replied.

Mara hesitated, torn between acting cool and admitting to her anxiety. Finally she started for the coatrack where her jacket was hung. "I think I will."

"If he's there, don't hurry back on my account," her father told her, watching indulgently as she hurriedly put on her coat.

Half of the buttons were fastened when the back door opened and Sin walked in. Mara turned, her face lighting up at the sight of him. At the slightest invitation from him she would have run into his arms.

But he seemed withdrawn, and his gaze was shut-

tered when he noted her expres[...] tention to her father and smiled a[...]

"Hello, Adam." He spoke to h[...] glanced at her. "Were you going som[...]

His odd aloofness kept Mara from [...] truth. "Just for a walk." Hurt twinged th[...] began unbuttoning her coat. "The c[...] Would you like a cup?"

"Please." Sin walked to the table and s[...] near her father.

While she hung up her coat and poured hi[...] coffee, the two men discussed the weather and[...] dition of the roads. Mara took a chair opposit[...] the table. He smiled at her once, but continue[...] versing with her father.

"One thing is for sure—we're going to have a wh[...] Christmas this year. This snow isn't going to melt in fiv[...] days," Adam stated. "Will you be staying over until after Christmas, Sin?"

"No, I have to drive back to Baltimore tomorrow afternoon, but I'll be back on Christmas Eve. I'll be staying until the following Monday," Sin explained, and joyful relief warmed Mara's heart.

Guessing her reaction to the news, her father sent her a smiling look. "At least Sin will be here long enough to help you hang the decorations and trim the tree."

"Yes," she agreed, trying to contain some of her bubbling pleasure.

"I'm an expert at putting stars on the top of Christmas trees," Sin admitted, half in jest.

"Good, because Mara can't reach it, and I certainly can't." Her father patted the arm of his wheelchair.

"Have you bought the tree?" Sin asked Mara.

"Not yet." There was a breathless ring to her voice. "I was going into town today to pick one out."

"We can do it together," Sin suggested.

"Did you love your wife, Sin?" she asked, tracing the woven pattern of his sweater with her fingertips. She struggled to maintain an attitude of friendly interest and not jealousy.

His eyes opened, though not all the way. "Yes, I loved Ann. There are varying degrees of love, though, Mara. Your father loved your mother, but he loved another woman more."

It wasn't a satisfactory answer, but Mara wasn't sure what she had hoped to learn. She let the subject drop and rolled onto her back to stare once more at the ceiling.

Sin changed the subject. "We should have brought some of your Christmas decorations from the house down here to the cottage. The place doesn't look very festive with Christmas just around the corner."

"We should have thought of that," she agreed, and glanced idly around the room. "I like the improvements you've made. Did you pick out the furniture or did Celene?"

"I did. Celene made a few suggestions, but the decisions and choices were mine." There was a hint of drawling amusement in his voice.

There, that nagging question had been answered at last. Mara felt slightly better about liking the place. Turning her head on the pillow, she looked at him. "Did you get bored with Celene?"

"Yes, I guess you could say that," he admitted with marked indifference for the subject.

She looked away, a frightening tightness in her throat. "Are you bored with me yet?"

Uncurling his arm from under his head, Sin used it to lever himself onto his side. He removed the pillow from beneath her head, a dark light in his gray-blue eyes.

"What do you think?" he countered, an instant before his mouth covered hers.

His response told her nothing. His kiss lacked the persuasive mastery that usually fired a response from Mara. He *was* becoming bored with her: the knowledge burned its pain into her heart. Mara wondered what she would do without him and knew she didn't even want to think about it.

Turning away from his kiss, she twisted out of his arms and hurriedly stood up. She couldn't bear for him to go through the motions of making love to her when he felt no desire. She heard him rise and stiffened when his hands touched her shoulders.

"What's wrong?" His voice sounded puzzled.

She shrugged free of his touch. "Please don't."

"Why?" The one word carried the hint of demand.

Mara couldn't tell him the truth. There was too much chance he would argue and she would tell herself that her intuition was wrong. Her only chance to stay in control of the situation was to brazen it out.

"I think the truth is that I'm becoming bored with you," she lied.

"What?" Sin caught her by the shoulders and spun her around, holding her in front of him.

"You said something once about how it could happen, that physical attraction waned after prolonged exposure." Mara wasn't sure if he'd used those exact words but she stuck to them to back up her story. "I don't feel the same thing when you hold me now as I did at first." Which was true, since her emotions had grown stronger and ran deeper.

He looked at her if he didn't quite believe her.

"Did I say that?" he asked, but his tone discounted the worth of that remark in the same breath.

"I wasn't going to tell you how I felt. I know how fragile the male ego is," Mara went on, noting the way his jaw tightened at that statement. "But I decided it was better to be honest."

"What is it you're trying to say?" Sin demanded.

Staring at the front of his sweater, Mara tried not to betray how much pain it was causing to tell these lies. "I'm trying to say that there isn't any need for you to drive all this way for Christmas. There isn't anything to be gained by seeing each other anymore. If you want to come to the cottage for Christmas, that's your business. And I'm sure Adam will welcome you at the house, but . . ." She let the rest of the sentence trail off, unable to tell the ultimate lie that she wouldn't be glad to see him.

"But you wouldn't," Sin finished the sentence for her. The air of finality rang in his voice, slicing into her like a sword.

"I . . . I don't have any reason to be," she responded in a tightly quiet voice.

"No, I don't suppose you do." His hands fell away from her shoulders as he took a step away. "I guess there isn't any point hanging around now, either."

He took the news in a businesslike way that made Mara think, *That fits. It all fits.*

"Good thing that I'm all packed," he was saying. "If you don't mind waiting a couple of minutes, I'll drop you off at the house on my way back to Baltimore."

Now that the moment had come, Mara would have preferred walking back to the house alone rather than riding with him. But a little voice dictated that she should accept his offer to prove that his company meant nothing to her, that she could get along without it or simply tolerate it.

"I don't mind waiting," she said. "It's cold outside."

"I'll only be a few minutes," he promised curtly, and walked toward the bedroom.

While he was gone, Mara picked up the poker and scattered the burning logs so the fire would die. But she knew it would never be that easy to put out the fire that burned for him in her heart. The consequences of her impulsive decision—and even more impulsive words—were just beginning to sink in.

When Sin reappeared, she was able to turn and face him. Her expression was coolly composed, but she was the only one who knew how thin and brittle the ice was.

"Shall we go?" A black leather carry-on bag was in his hand, and a hint of steel was in his voice.

Mara walked to the door in answer.

During the drive to the house the silence hung between them. Its weight pressed on Mara until she wanted to scream away its presence.

Sin pulled into the driveway and stopped in front of the red brick house. As Mara quickly stepped out of the car, he said, "Say good-bye to Adam for me."

"I will," she agreed stiffly, and shut the door.

Chapter Ten

There was a lump as big as a Pennsylvania apple in Mara's throat as she entered the house. The sound of Sin's car pulling out of the driveway echoed painfully in her ears. Her eyes smarted with large, unshed tears.

The multicolored lights blinking on the Christmas tree seemed garishly bright. The satin balls and silver tinsel looked ludicrously cheerful when her heart felt as if it were splintering in a million pieces.

The draft from the closing door sent the clump of mistletoe swaying above her head. Mara glanced up and an excruciating pain stabbed her heart as she remembered the way Sin had maneuvered her under it only yesterday. Shuddering away the memory, she grabbed the nearest chair and pulled it under the mistletoe. Her eyes were so blurred with tears that she could hardly see as she stepped onto the chair seat and tugged the ribboned mistletoe from its place.

Her father wheeled his chair in from the study. "What are you doing, Mara?"

"I'm taking the mistletoe down. What does it look as if I'm doing?" She spoke harshly to keep her voice from trembling. Carefully, she avoided looking at Adam as she pushed the chair to its former place.

"I can see that. What I wondered was why," he answered, patient yet curious.

"Because we don't need it hanging there. We don't need it hanging anywhere." Mara flung the mistletoe in the living room's wicker wastebasket.

"I think Sin will have a different opinion. He'll want to know what's happened to it when he comes at Christmas," Adam teased.

"He isn't coming at Christmas." A tear slipped out the corner of her eye and Mara hurriedly wiped it away before it trailed too far down her cheek.

But Adam noticed. He tilted his head to one side to peer at her averted face, and a frown creased his forehead.

"What happened? Did you and Sin have an argument?"

"Not exactly." Her voice was tight and she didn't trust it.

"C'mon, tell me." He sat quietly in his wheelchair waiting for her explanation.

An inner war kept her silent for a moment. "I told him it would be best if he didn't come at Christmas," she admitted finally.

"Best for whom?" Adam lifted a dark brow in dry inquiry.

"Best for me—and for him, too, as far as that goes." Mara rushed out the answer in a burst of agitation. "It was hopeless from the beginning, if I'd known or guessed—oh, what does it matter!" She wiped angrily at another tear. "He never cared about me anyway."

"Is that what Sin told you?" her father asked after listening attentively to her declaration.

"Yes," she breathed out, her lungs hurting from the constant constriction of controlled emotion. "All he felt for me was"—she chose his phrase—"a sexual attraction. Sooner or later he would have become bored and dumped me, the same way he did Celene."

"Celene? Who's Celene?" Adam frowned.

"That redhead!" she flashed. "The one he brought along with him when he first came, who was always saying 'Sin, honey.' Celene Taylor." The cattiness of her tone didn't make her feel better.

"So you dumped him first?" Adam guessed.

"Yes, I had to before . . ." Mara swallowed the rest of the sentence. "I told him I was beginning to become bored with him, that whatever I'd felt, it was gone."

"Is it?" His gaze narrowed to pierce any shield she might try to use. "Have you stopped caring for him, Mara?"

She lifted her gaze to him, her eyes suddenly brimming over with tears she couldn't check. The anguish was written in every line of her expression for him to see. She couldn't contain her feelings or her heartbreak anymore. Gasping back a sob, she moved uncertainly toward his chair.

When she reached his side, Adam took hold of one of her shaky hands, and the comfort and understanding he offered turned loose a storm of tears.

"Daddy, I love him," she sobbed, and collapsed to her knees, burying her head on his lap and hugging his lifeless legs.

One hand gripped her quaking shoulder while the other stroked her hair. "Go ahead, baby," he crooned, his own voice slightly choked with deep emotion. "Cry it all out. It's okay, honey. Believe me, it's okay."

Years of stored grief, pain and bitterness were washed away by the violent tears. Mara sobbed herself into oblivion. The soothing touch of her father's hand and the sound of his voice were her only lifeline to sanity. Even after her mind had blanked out the pain, her breath came in hiccupping sobs. Adam took off his sweater and draped it around her shoulders, letting her use his legs for a pillow. A fierce love glistened moistly in his eyes as he gazed down at her tear-streaked face.

"It's all right, Daddy's here." He got the words past the lump in his throat somehow.

It was dark when Mara finally came around. Her muscles were cramped from the unnatural position of rest, but all the pain, physical and emotional, seemed distant. A numbed haze kept it at bay.

"How do you feel?" Adam's quiet voice penetrated the protective mist.

"I . . . I don't know." As she rose awkwardly to her feet, the sweater slipped from around her shoulders. Mara looked at it blankly, half-recognizing that it was his, but the gesture registered only dimly. She did the automatic thing and gave it back to him. "I feel . . . as if I've been drugged."

"Lie down on the sofa for a while," her father suggested.

Drained and without energy, Mara moved to the sofa. She murmured a halfhearted protest when Adam pulled a quilted comforter over her. She stared at the ceiling, empty of thoughts but uneasy all the same.

"You lie there and rest. I'll be back in a moment," Adam promised.

Mara was barely aware of him leaving. She had no conception of how long he was gone; it could have been a minute or an hour. When he returned, he positioned his wheelchair parallel with the sofa.

"You need to eat." He held a spoon to her mouth. "I warmed some soup for you."

Indifferent to the appetizing aroma, she opened her mouth, feeling a lot like a baby bird as the warm liquid trickled inside. She stirred under its reviving taste and sat up for the second spoonful. Her eyes sought his in silent gratitude. The rest of the soup in the bowl in his lap went down little by little.

"How did you make it?" she murmured, briefly curious.

"I'm not such an invalid that I can't manage a can opener and a burner on the stove," he teased gently.

Memory flashed in Mara's mind back to a time when she had cared for her mother like this. She realized that her mother had loved none too wisely, either. Pain twisted through her.

"It hurts," she whispered.

"Yes." Adam didn't deny it. He took the apron away. "Sleep now. Life may not look so bleak in the morning."

Mara doubted it, but she obediently closed her eyes. When she awakened the next morning, Adam was there. She felt like one big, throbbing ache. But the realization that he was there, waiting on her, looking after her, made her throw aside the comforter and sit up.

"I'll make some coffee," she offered.

"Good idea." He followed her into the kitchen, not speaking again until she had started the coffeemaker. "Isn't there a possibility that you're mistaken about Sin?"

Hope sprang, but Mara quickly squashed it. "I only wish I were." She paused to glance at her father. "I know you like Sin, you did from the beginning, but you have to face the truth the same way I did," she said, still somewhat emotionally numb. "I attracted him and provided him with weekend entertainment. He probably even considered me something of a challenge." The first sting of tears since yesterday's torrent burned her eyes, and she turned away, not wanting to start weeping again. "Anyway, it's over. And I don't want to discuss it any more."

* * *

It was a refusal that Mara repeated twice more in the next two days whenever Adam attempted to introduce the subject. The tenuous bond between father and daughter had strengthened in the intervening time. Someday she knew she would talk to him about Sin, but not while the hurt was so fresh.

The holiday spirit was sadly lacking in their household. Staying with family tradition, they exchanged gifts on Christmas Eve. There had been two presents under the tree for Sin, one from Mara and the other from her father. Both had disappeared during the last couple of days—Adam's doing, Mara guessed, so she wouldn't be reminded that Sin had been going to celebrate Christmas with them.

Christmas morning seemed no different from recent mornings. After breakfast, Mara glumly got through a stack of dirty dishes while vowing to buy a dishwasher during the January appliance sales. Her father retired to the living room to watch the televised Christmas services. Christmas hymns filtered joyfully into the kitchen.

An aching loneliness swept over her. Tears welled in her eyes and she began angrily slamming cupboard doors and clattering pots and pans as she put the dishes away, anything to cover the music from the living room. It didn't work very well. She finally had to stop and wipe her eyes. Sniffling a little, she put a ham roast in the oven and filled the colander with some potatoes to peel and slice for scalloped potatoes.

The singing stopped and the muffled sound of the sermon began. Mara sat in a kitchen chair at the table and began peeling the potatoes. Keeping busy, she had discovered, was therapeutic.

"Mara?" Adam called. "Come in here, will you? Santa Claus has finally delivered your present."

Glancing at the swinging door, Mara breathed out a

sigh. There was a temptation to tell him she was busy, but she guessed he had manufactured some kind of surprise to boost her spirits—as if anything could.

Santa Claus. A smile tugged at her mouth. Santa Claus hadn't visited her since she was fifteen, the last Christmas she and her parents had spent together as a family. Santa had never forgotten to leave her a present then, regardless of whether she believed in his existence or not. Perhaps her father had remembered, too.

Either way, his thoughtfulness couldn't be ignored or set aside until she was in the mood to accept it. Setting down a partially peeled potato, Mara wiped her hands on a towel.

"Coming," she answered.

As she pushed open the swinging door, she heard the front door close. Delivered had been the term Adam used. A curious frown drew her brows together as she wondered who would make deliveries on Christmas Day. Her father was practically beaming when she entered the living room. His gaze moved to the entryway and Mara's followed. She stopped short when she saw Sin framed in the opening. Dressed in a suit and tie and navy blue topcoat, he looked stern and unyielding. The hoary chill of winter seemed to sweep around him. Her heart somersaulted with joy—foolish joy—but fear kept her from voicing it.

"Sin!" Mara breathed his name at last. Confusion raced through her. "What are you doing here?"

His jawline tensed. "Adam told me you were lying. That you really want to see me."

"How . . . When . . . ?" She glanced at her father, her pained expression accusing him of betraying her.

"I called him yesterday." Adam volunteered the information.

"How could you?" she demanded tightly.

"What the hell difference does it make how I found out?" Sin demanded. "All I want to know is whether he's telling me the truth. Were you lying?"

Trapped as she was, Mara was forced to admit, "Yes."

Her answer didn't seem to please him. Sin continued to glare at her across the distance of the room.

"Why? Why, Mara, why?" His voice was a low growl, obviously meant to intimidate.

"Because . . . I could tell you were getting tired of me," she replied defensively.

"I—what!" It was an explosive reaction, disbelief and anger ringing together.

"Don't pretend you don't know what I'm talking about," Mara was stung into retorting. "You were beginning to keep a distance between us. Even when we were together, you weren't that into it. Or me."

"So you concluded I was getting tired of you. Brilliant deduction." Sin ground out in a voice that questioned her intelligence. "It didn't ever occur to you that I'm only human or anything, did it?"

"No, it didn't," she admitted.

"Or that I might be putting together a merger worth millions. Much as I like rolling around on a rug in front of a fire with you, I have to pay attention to my business some of the time—sorry, Adam. I didn't mean to be so blunt."

Mara put her hands on her hips and took an assertive stance. "Why are you apologizing to him?"

"Because you're his daughter. I shouldn't say, in front of him, that I was rolling around on a rug with you—"

Adam raised a hand. "Not a problem. Finish the fight, you two."

"We aren't fighting," Mara yelled.

"Yes, we are."

"You know something? I wish you were boring. Then I wouldn't care."

His eyes narrowed on her. "We were just experimenting. But you care, huh?"

Her lips closed together mutinously, but her father supplied the answer. "She's fallen in love with you."

Sin's gaze never wavered from her face. "Is that true?" he demanded without an ounce of softness.

Angered by the feeling of being attacked from both sides, Mara shouted, "Yes!"

Briefly he flicked a glance to her father. "Adam, I want your permission to marry your daughter."

"Granted." Adam's dark eyes twinkled brightly at Mara's stunned expression.

Reaching into the pocket of his topcoat, Sin took something out and tossed it across the room to Mara. Sheer reflex enabled her to catch the ring box. She was dazed by the unexpected chain of events. She wasn't even certain if she knew what was happening. With shaking fingers, she opened the box. A diamond solitaire winked rainbow hues back at her.

"Will you marry me?" Sin demanded. The room still separated them.

Dragging her gaze from the ring, she looked at him. "Yes," she answered, starry-eyed and breathless, adding, "And I don't need his permission."

For the first time since he had arrived, his hard features began to soften, relief mixing with another, stronger emotion. The edges of his mouth turned faintly upward.

"If you take the first step, Mara, I'll meet you halfway," Sin promised.

Mara had the giddy feeling that she floated across her half of the room. Her feet never seemed to touch the ground. They certainly didn't when he took her in his arms to claim her mouth in a possessive kiss. Her father discreetly left the room.

"I don't believe it," she gasped when he finally let her up for air. "Am I dreaming this?"

"It's no dream." His mouth moved roughly over her hair, unsatisfied not to be touching her.

"And you really love me?" She felt the shuddering force of his arms around her, but still needed the reassurance of his words.

"Yes, you lunatic," he muttered against her throat. "Every time I saw you I fell a little bit more in love with you until I was hopelessly lost."

"It was the same for me." Her lips began brushing feather kisses over his face.

"When I first met you, I thought you were cold. Then I began to figure out just how hot you really were." Sin stopped her teasing lips with a demanding kiss. Mara gave it back with vibrant intensity. "Leaving you alone is not a good idea," he said softly. "Your imagination runs away with you. What did you think I was doing in Baltimore? Adding new redheads to my collection?"

"I thought I was losing you," Mara tried to explain. "I decided I'd rather make the break swift and clean than let it drag on until you did it. I knew I'd be that much more in love with you and the hurt would be that much greater."

"And I was determined not to rush you into anything. You were just coming back to life after going through . . . how many years of emotional hell? I wanted you to trust me, and I scared you instead. Oh, Mara. We have to work on that next." He held her even closer.

"What if Adam hadn't called you?" She suddenly realized she wouldn't be in Sin's arms or have his ring on her finger.

"I hadn't given up. I was just trying to come up with a new battle plan," he assured her. "Now I don't have to worry. You're going to be my wife . . . and soon."

"Yes," Mara agreed readily. "I would like a church

wedding, though, so my . . . father can give me away to you."

Sin lifted his head long enough to smile at her. "I'm glad to hear you say that." Then he made sure she didn't say any more for quite a while.

Here's a sizzling excerpt from
Janet Dailey's
BRING THE RING,
available now from Zebra . . .

"I don't mean to shock you, Red"—he smiled without amusement—"but I don't wear pajamas in bed. Those were a gift from someone who didn't know that. Now, go and take your shower."

She colored furiously. "I don't want to take a shower. I don't want your clothes. And I don't intend to go to bed!"

Roarke stopped and turned back to her, his jaw set in an uncompromising line. "Let's get something straight. You're going to take a shower if I have to strip you and shove you in there myself. And unless you want to walk around in a skimpy bath towel, you're going to wear those pajamas. Lastly, you're going to go to bed. No more arguments."

With his decree ringing in the air, he walked over to a smaller chest and took out a pillow and some blankets.

"What are you doing?" she demanded.

"Since I'm going to be sleeping on the couch, I thought I might like some covers," he answered shortly before a wicked glint appeared in his eyes. "Or were you going to offer to share the bed with me?"

"Absolutely not!" Tisha declared vehemently.

"Selfish," Roarke taunted. "I could make you sleep on the couch, you know."

"You're not going to make me do anything."

"Guess not." He waved her away. "Go and take your shower before you catch cold."

"I hope you get pneumonia and die!" she called after him as his long strides carried him up the steps to the hallway door.

"Thanks. You sleep well, too. G'night." The door closed with a finality that left Tisha with the impression that Roarke was glad to get her out of his sight. For a moment she stood there, the silence of the room closing in around her, muffling the growls of thunder outside the window. A shuddering chill quivered over her as the dampness of her clothes began to seep into her bones. However reluctantly, she had to admit that the tingling spray of a hot shower would feel good.

With the pajamas still clutched in her hand, Tisha walked into the bathroom, locking the door behind her. For several minutes she stood motionless under the pounding spray as it beat out the emotions that had strained her nerves to the breaking point. When she finally stepped out of the shower stall and toweled herself dry, she was feeling a little more human.

And a little more vulnerable to a certain very sexy man.

Going through the motions of hanging up her wet clothes, she told herself she was glad he had essentially rejected her. If anyone had tried to tell her that she could feel such lust for a man she didn't like, she would have called them a liar, but her own actions had proved her wrong. No matter how hard she tried, she couldn't wholly blame Roarke for the emotional storm that had broken open in the middle of the actual one.

She wrapped her long hair in a towel and piled it on top of her head as she reached for the pajama top. The silk felt cool and slippery against her skin, but the sleeves hung far below her fingertips. It took some time to roll them up to a point where her hands were free. With the buttons buttoned, the ends of the pajama shirt stopped a few inches above her knees. One glance at the pants and Tisha knew they were miles too long and too big around the waist, so she simply folded them back up and laid them on the counter.

Unlocking the door, she reentered the bedroom and walked to the bed, giving the lustrous Thai silk of the spread that covered it an absent-minded pat. Roarke did have incredibly good taste.

She felt a little guilty for liking his things, liking his house. She picked a spot near the edge of the bed and sat in a cross-legged position with her back to the door. Unwrapping the towel from her head, she began vigorously rubbing her long hair dry.

A knock on the door was followed immediately by Roarke calling out, "Are you decent?"

"What do you want?"

But the door opened without an answer, and Roarke walked in. He still wore only a pair of jeans, but they were older than the pair he'd had on before. The light, faded color accented the deep tan on his chest. Tisha watched him from over her shoulder as he walked in.

"I brought you some cocoa to help you relax and get some sleep." His face wore an inscrutable expression as his dark eyes flicked over Tisha.

"Thoughtful of you," she said, turning away from him to continue rubbing her hair with the towel.

"There'll be a crew out in the morning to clear the

road, and the phone line's already back up. I called Blanche to let her know I was putting you up for the night," he continued.

"I could have done that myself."

"I think the operative phrase is 'thank you.'"

"Thank you." Reluctant gratitude edged her voice.

"Do you want this cocoa or not?"

She could tell that he was still standing right where he'd stopped. It would have been quite simple to walk over and take the cup from him, but she didn't care to meet the indifference of his gaze.

"You can put it on the bedside table. I'll drink it later," she replied, keeping her head averted as she heard his footsteps moving down the stairs toward the bed. Through her long hair, she saw him walk by her without a glance. When he turned to retrace his steps, she asked, "Is there a comb I can use to get these tangles out of my hair?"

"There's probably one in the medicine cabinet."

"Thanks," she said shortly, uncurling a long leg from beneath her to slip off the bed.

She was halfway to the bathroom when his voice barked out at her. "Where's the bottoms of those pajamas?"

Tisha stopped and glanced back at him, surprised at the restrained fury on his face. "They were too big." She shrugged.

"Put them on," Roarke ordered.

"I told you they were too big!" she repeated, bristling at his bossy tone.

"And I told you to put them on. What are you trying to do—look like a sex kitten?" he jeered.

"Meow, meow," she said, adding a descriptive word for him that would've scorched his ears if she'd said it loud enough for him to hear. She glared at the tall figure standing at the steps. "The last thing I would try to do is entice you," she snapped. "I told you they were too big for me, but don't take my word for it."

Spinning around, she stalked into the bathroom and slammed the door, grabbing the bottom half of the pajamas from the counter. Fighting the long legs, she finally managed to draw the waist around her chest while her feet wiggled through the material to touch the furry carpet. She shuffled over to the door and swung it open.

"See what I mean?" she demanded, looking from Roarke to the baggy pajama pants crumpled around her feet.

"Roll up the cuffs," he growled.

"Fine." A sweetly mocking smile curved her mouth. "What do I do about the waistline? You're not exactly a size ten!"

"Improvise."

"How? And what's wrong with wearing only the top? It nearly comes to my knees. What's so indecent about that?"

Tisha took two angry strides in his direction. On the third the material tangled about her feet and catapulted her forward. Her arms reached out ahead of her to break the fall, but her hands encountered Roarke's arms and chest as he tried to catch her. Off-balance, they both tumbled to the floor, Roarke's body acting as a cushion as Tisha fell on top of him.

"Are you hurt?" he asked, gently rolling her off him onto the carpeted floor.

"No," she gasped, momentarily winded by the shock of the fall. "No thanks to you."

"Was I supposed to let you dive headfirst onto the floor?" he muttered.

"You shouldn't have made me put on these stupid

pajama bottoms," she retorted, suddenly conscious of the heat of his body against hers. "I told you they were too big, but you wouldn't listen to me."

"Guilty, guilty, guilty," Roarke declared angrily, reaching over her to place his hand on the floor and lever himself upright.

His arm accidentally brushed her breast. Tisha drew in her breath at the intimate contact. That jellylike weakness spread through her bones as he turned his enigmatic gaze on her. He was propped inches above her, his bared chest with its curling dark hairs close enough to caress. The desire to touch him came dangerously near the surface, and Tisha turned her head away, a solitary tear trickling out of the corner of her eye.

"Tisha—"

"Oh, go away and leave me alone!" Her voice crackled slightly on the last word.

His fingers closed over her chin and forced her head around to where he could see the angry fire blazing in her eyes.

"I can't stand this," she said hoarsely.

"Tish, Tish—what are you talking about? I still don't understand what happened this afternoon."

"Neither do I."

His gaze was focused on her parted, trembling lips. She brought up her hands to ward him off. The instant her fingers touched the burning hardness of his naked chest, Tisha knew her body was going to betray her again. When his mouth closed over hers, she succumbed to the rapturous fire that swept through her veins. The hands that had moved to resist him twined themselves around his neck while his hands trailed down to her waist, deftly arching her toward him.

Her nerves were attuned to every rippling muscle of his body as they responded to his searching caress. It was a seduction of the senses, in which she knew nothing but the ecstasy of his touch. An almost silent sound of feminine bliss came from her throat as he pushed the pajama top away from her shoulder and treated her skin to erotic little nips. Then his mouth sought out the hollow of her throat.

"You're a witch," he murmured against her lips, then moved to nibble her earlobe. "A beautiful rainy-day witch."

And here's
RANCH DRESSING,
available now from Zebra . . .

His voice was low and it was difficult to see his face in the shadowy dimness of the room. There weren't any lights on downstairs. What light there was came from the stairwell and outside. Yet Charley could feel the disturbing intensity of his gaze.

"Then what are you doing here?" Forced anger was her defense against him.

"After I had my steak dinner, I went to a bar. There was this drunk there ..." His voice took on a different quality, gentle, almost caressing. "He kept singing 'Charley Is My Darling.' And I started wondering what I was doing in that bar when my Charley was here."

Her heart cried out for him, loving him all the more for saying such beautiful words, but it hurt, too. Charley turned her head away, closing her eyes tightly.

"You can skip the sweet talk, Shad." She fought for self-control.

"I'm telling you what I feel," he countered.

She tried to take the potency from his words with an accusation. "You've been drinking."

"Yes, I've been drinking," he admitted. As she started

to walk away from him, he caught her wrist and pulled her around. She was in his arms before she had a chance to resist. "But I'm not drunk."

"Let me go, Shad." She tried to twist out of his arms but they tightened around her, holding her fast. The warmth of his hands seemed to burn through the thin material of her robe.

"Wow!" He spoke under his breath as he became suddenly motionless. An exploring hand moved over her hip. "You don't have anything on under this."

Aware of the imprint his body was making on hers, her own senses echoed the aroused note in his voice. Yet she tried to resist it.

"Shad, don't," she protested.

But he merely groaned and rubbed his shaven cheek against hers, brushing her ear with his mouth. "It's no use, Charley. I've tried to stay away from you, but I can't."

His mouth rocked over her lips, persuading and cajoling, sensually nipping her lower lip until she was reeling. Restless male hands wandered over her back, caressing her. She was helpless against this loving attack.

"Do we have to deny ourselves?" Shad muttered thickly as her lips grazed along his jaw. "I don't see any reason to pretend I don't want you. Do you know what I mean?"

"Yes." The aching admission was torn from her throat, the ability to think lost. "I want you too . . . just as much."

It was the answer he had been waiting for as he swept her off her feet and into his arms. Her hands circled his neck while her mouth investigated the strong column of his throat, savoring the taste of him. He carried her to the couch and lowered her to the cushions while he sat on the edge facing her.

He leaned down to cover her parted lips with his mouth, his hard tongue taking total possession. Raw desire licked through her veins, a spreading fire that left none of her body untouched. His hands deftly loosened the buttons of her robe and pushed the material aside to expose her beautiful breasts.

Just as eagerly, her fingers tugged at his buttons. When the last one was unfastened, Shad yanked his shirt free out of his jeans. She moaned softly as she felt the heat of his flesh beneath her hands. Her fingers moved over his flexed and rippling muscles, excited and stimulated by this freedom to touch and caress.

Forsaking her lips, his mouth began a downward path. Delighted quivers ran over her skin as he explored the sensitive cord in her neck and left a kiss in the hollow of her throat. Her fingernails dug into his flesh when his mouth grazed her breast, its point hardening with desire, luring his attention to it. Charley shuddered with uninhibited longing under the arousing touch of his tongue.

When she was weak with need, he returned to soften her lips with his kisses. "Tell me you want me, Charley," he begged. "I want to hear you say it again."

"I want you, Shad," she whispered against his skin. "More than that, I love you."

"I want you more than I've ever wanted any other woman in my life," he told her roughly.

"Stay with me tonight, Shad," she murmured. "Tonight and tomorrow night and every night of my life. I don't want you to leave me."

"You know I can't promise that, Charley," he muttered, brushing his lips over her cheek.

She knew. Her arms curved more tightly around him, fusing the warmth of his bare flesh with her own. "Hold me," she whispered. "Don't ever let me go." Her eyes were tightly closed, but a tear squeezed its way through her lashes. It was followed by more until Shad tasted the salty moisture on her skin.

"Don't cry, Charley." She felt the roughness of his

callused hand on her cheek, wiping them away. "For God's sake, don't cry." His voice held no anger, only a kind of anguished regret.

"I can't help it." She honestly tried to check the flow of tears but it was unstoppable.

With a heavy sigh he eased his weight from her and sat up. She blinked and felt his hands closing her robe. Then he was leaning his elbows on his knees and raking his fingers through his hair to rub the back of his neck. Charley sat up, a hand unconsciously holding the front of her robe. She touched his shoulder, tentative, uncertain.

"Oh, Charley," he said, then turned to look at her. A dark, troubled light was in his eyes. "I swear to God I never meant to hurt you."

"I know," she murmured gently and a little sadly. "It isn't your fault. You didn't ask me to fall in love with you. Maybe if you had, I'd be able to hate you, but I don't."

She swung her feet to the floor and slowly walked to the stairs, leaving Shad sitting there alone on the couch. It was almost an hour later before she heard him come upstairs. He paused at the top of the stairs and Charley held her breath. Finally the door to his bedroom opened and closed. The tears started again.

Sleep eluded her. The hours that Charley didn't spend staring at the ceiling, she tossed and turned fitfully. By Wednesday morning the lack of rest began to paint faint shadows below her eyes. They didn't go unnoticed by her brother.

"You feeling okay, Charley?" he asked at the breakfast table that morning, studying her.

"I'm fine," she insisted.

"Well, you don't look so good," he concluded bluntly.

"Thanks," she snapped and paled under his scrutiny.

Gary's eyes narrowed suspiciously, but he made no comment. Charley knew that her brother probably guessed the cause of her sleeplessness, but there was nothing he could do about it.

When she crawled into bed that night, she expected it to be a repeat of the previous nights. She listened for the longest time, waiting for the sound of Shad's footsteps on the stairs. She dozed off without hearing, then awakened later and strained to hear sounds of him in the other bedroom—boots dropping on the floor, jeans flung across a chair. But there was nothing. Finally fatigue overtook her and she fell into a heavy sleep.

The buzz of the alarm clock was insistent, making her open her eyes despite her attempt to ignore it. She climbed wearily from the bed, irritated that the one time she'd managed to sleep, she had been forced to wake up. She dressed in her usual blue jeans and blouse and left the bedroom in a daze.

Charley barely glanced at the closed door of Shad's bedroom. She didn't know whether he was still sleeping or already downstairs. Not that it mattered, she told herself and entered the bathroom. With her face washed and her teeth brushed, she lost some of that drugged feeling.

At the bottom of the stairs, Charley was shocked to find Shad sleeping on the couch in the living room. Too tall for it, he was sprawled over the length of the cushions with his feet poking over the end of the armrest. From somewhere, he'd gotten a blanket, which was loosely draped over him. She couldn't imagine what he was doing sleeping on the couch. She walked over to waken him.

Her hand touched his shoulder and he stirred, frowning in his sleep. The second time Charley gripped his shoulder more firmly and called his name. "Shad. Shad, it's time to get up."

He shrugged off her hand but he opened his eyes. They focused slowly on Charley's face as she leaned over him. He gave her a slow smile.

"Good morning." His voice was husky with sleep, its drawl thicker.

"Good morning." She wanted to ask him what he was doing on the couch, but his hand reached out to capture one of hers and pull her onto the cushion beside him.

"Don't I get more of a greeting than that?" Shad mocked and put his hand behind her neck to bring her head down.

Charley stopped needing direction when she neared his mouth. Her lips settled into it naturally and moved in response to his sampling kiss. She was breathing fast when she finally straightened. He started to shift his position and winced from a cramped muscle. The discomfort made him take note of his improvised place to sleep. He seemed to register vague surprise when he figured out that he was on the couch.

"Why are you sleeping here?" Charley finally asked her question.

"The mood I was in last night, if I had gone upstairs, I would have ended up sleeping in your bed." There was impatience in his expression as his hands settled onto the toned muscles of her upper arms and began rubbing them absently.

"Oh, Shad." She trembled with the quick onrush of desire.

"Yeah, you should say, 'Oh, Shad.' I don't think you know what you're doing to me," he muttered. "At this rate, I'm going to be sleeping in the barn next, just to keep my hands off you."

Don't miss Janet Dailey's
compelling new hardcover,
CALDER STORM,
available now from Kensington . . .

Trey hesitated, then headed in the opposite direction. Away from the dance area, people tended to gather in clusters or travel in twos and threes, making it easy for him to spot a solitary figure. There were few of those, and all male.

Then he spotted her coming his way, the neon light of a bar sign flashing over the sheen of her hair, and everything lifted inside him, his blood coursing hot and fast through his veins. His long striding walk lengthened even more, carrying him to her.

A smile broke across her lips. "You forgot to say which stage. There happens to be three of them."

The glistening curve of her lips and the sparkle of pleasure in her eyes acted like the pull of a magnet. When mixed with the pressures of waiting, wondering, and wanting, the combination pushed Trey into action.

His hands caught her by the waist and drew her to him even as he bent his head and covered her lips with a long, hard kiss, staking his claim to her. There was an instant of startled surprise that held her stiff and unre-

sponsive, but it didn't last. It was the taste of her giving
warmth that lingered when Trey lifted his head.

Through eyes half-lidded to conceal the blatant desire he felt, he studied her upturned face and the
heightened interest in her returning gaze. He allowed a
wedge of space between them, but didn't let go of her
waist, his thumb registering the rapid beat of the pulse
in her stomach. Its swiftness signaled that she had been
equally unnerved by the kiss.

"I was just about convinced that I'd have to turn the
town upsidedown to find you," he told her in a voice
that had gone husky.

"It wouldn't have been a difficult task," Sloan murmured. "After all, you know where I'm staying."

"I forgot," Trey admitted with a crooked smile.
"Which shows how thoroughly you've gotten to me."

She laughed softly, paused, then reached up, fingertips lightly brushing along a corner of his mouth.
"You're all smeared with gloss."

He pressed his lips together and felt the slick coat-
ing, but it had no taste to it. "You use the unflavored
kind, too." Automatically he wiped it off on the back of
his hand. "My sister claims that a man should taste her
and not some fruit."

"You have a sister?" Sloan asked, absorbing this personal bit of information about him. "Younger or older?"

"Younger." By less than two minutes, but Trey didn't
bother to divulge that and have the conversation di-
verted into a discussion of the twin thing. Instead, he
took note of the change in her attire—the bulky, multi-
pocketed vest and tan pants replaced by a femininely
cut tweed jacket and navy slacks. "You ditched the
camera and changed clothes."

"The others were a bit grimy from all the arena
dust." Her matter-of-fact answer made Trey wish that he
had taken the extra time to swing by the motel, shower

and change his own clothes, but he'd been too anxious to get here. A quick smile curved her lips, rife with self-mockery. "This is my first street dance," she said. "So I had to ask the desk clerk what to wear. He assured me it would be very casual."

"Your first street dance, is it? In that case it's time I showed you what it's all about." Grinning, Trey shifted to the side and hooked an arm behind her waist, drawing her with him as he set out for the dance area.

"I should warn you," she said, slanting him a sideways glance, "I'm not much of a dancer."

His gaze skimmed her in frank appraisal. "I'm surprised. You have the grace of one." He guided her through a gap in the row of onlookers, then turned her into his arms, easily catching up her hand. The band was playing a slow song, which suited Trey just fine. "Don't worry about the steps," he told her with a lazy smile. "Dancing was invented solely to provide a man a good excuse to hold a woman in his arms."

A laugh came from low in her throat, all soft and rich with amusement. "Something tells me it was a woman who came up with the original idea. How else would she ever coax a man onto the dance floor?" she teased.

"And something tells me, you're probably right."

By Best-selling Author
Fern Michaels

Weekend Warriors	0-8217-7589-8	$6.99US/$9.99CAN
Listen to Your Heart	0-8217-7463-8	$6.99US/$9.99CAN
The Future Scrolls	0-8217-7586-3	$6.99US/$9.99CAN
About Face	0-8217-7020-9	$7.99US/$10.99CAN
Kentucky Sunrise	0-8217-7462-X	$7.99US/$10.99CAN
Kentucky Rich	0-8217-7234-1	$7.99US/$10.99CAN
Kentucky Heat	0-8217-7368-2	$7.99US/$10.99CAN
Plain Jane	0-8217-6927-8	$7.99US/$10.99CAN
Wish List	0-8217-7363-1	$7.50US/$10.50CAN
Yesterday	0-8217-6785-2	$7.50US/$10.50CAN
The Guest List	0-8217-6657-0	$7.50US/$10.50CAN
Finders Keepers	0-8217-7364-X	$7.50US/$10.50CAN
Annie's Rainbow	0-8217-7366-6	$7.50US/$10.50CAN
Dear Emily	0-8217-7316-X	$7.50US/$10.50CAN
Sara's Song	0-8217-7480-8	$7.50US/$10.50CAN
Celebration	0-8217-7434-4	$7.50US/$10.50CAN
Vegas Heat	0-8217-7207-4	$7.50US/$10.50CAN
Vegas Rich	0-8217-7206-6	$7.50US/$10.50CAN
Vegas Sunrise	0-8217-7208-2	$7.50US/$10.50CAN
What You Wish For	0-8217-6828-X	$7.99US/$10.99CAN
Charming Lily	0-8217-7019-5	$7.99US/$10.99CAN

Available Wherever Books Are Sold!